THOSE WHO WISH ME DEAD

Also by Michael Koryta

Standalone novels
The Prophet
The Ridge
The Cypress House
So Cold the River
Envy the Night

Lincoln Perry series
Tonight I Said Goodbye
Sorrow's Anthem
A Welcome Grave
The Silent Hour

MICHAEL KORYTA

THOSE WHO WISH ME DEAD

HODDER &
STOUGHTON

First published in Great Britain in 2014 by Hodder & Stoughton
An Hachette UK company

1

Copyright © Michael Koryta 2014

The right of Michael Koryta to be identified as the Author of the Work has been
asserted by him in accordance with the Copyright, Designs and Patents Act 1988.

A CIP catalogue record for this title is available from the British Library.

Hardback ISBN 978 1 444 74257 2
Trade Paperback ISBN 978 1 444 74256 5

Printed and bound by CPI Group (UK) Ltd, Croydon, CR0 4YY

Hodder & Stoughton policy is to use papers that are natural, renewable
and recyclable products and made from wood grown in sustainable forests.
The logging and manufacturing processes are expected to conform
to the environmental regulations of the country of origin.

Hodder & Stoughton Ltd
338 Euston Road
London NW1 3BH

www.hodder.co.uk

This one is for Ryan Easton—from Stout Creek to Republic Peak, with a couple decades and a lot of good miles in between.

Part One

HIDDEN WITNESS

I

ON THE LAST DAY of Jace Wilson's life, the fourteen-year-old stood on a quarry ledge staring at cool, still water and finally understood something his mother had told him years before: Trouble might come for you when you showed fear, but trouble doubled-down when you lied about being afraid. At the time, Jace hadn't known exactly what she was talking about. Today he did.

It was a sixty-five-foot drop from Rooftop to the water, and Jace had a hundred dollars riding on it—a hundred dollars that he didn't have, of course—all because he'd shown a trace of fear. It was a stupid bet, sure, and he wouldn't have made it if the girls hadn't been there, listening to the whole thing and laughing. But they had been, and so now it wasn't just a hundred bucks, it was a hell of a lot more than that, and he had two days to figure out how to pull it off.

Not everyone who tried Rooftop succeeded. They'd pulled bodies out of the quarry before, and those were older kids, college kids, maybe even divers, he didn't know. He was certain none of them had been terrified of heights, though.

"What did you get yourself into," he whispered, looking behind him at the cut in the wire fence that led out of the old Easton Brothers quarry and into his yard. His house backed up to the abandoned quarry property, and Jace spent hours there, exploring and swimming—and staying far from the ledges. The one thing he did *not* do in the quarry was dive. He didn't even like to get too close to the drop-offs; if he edged out just for a quick glance down, his head would spin and his legs would go weak and he'd have to shuffle backward as fast as possible. Earlier in the day, though, all of his hours alone in the quarry had provided the lie he needed. When Wayne Potter started giving him shit about being scared of heights because Jace hadn't wanted to climb the ladder that some maintenance worker had left leaning against the side of the school, allowing access to the roof, Jace had blown it off by saying that he didn't need to climb a ladder to prove he wasn't scared of heights because he did quarry dives all the time, and he was sure Wayne had never done that.

Of course Wayne called him on the bluff. Of course Wayne mentioned Rooftop. Of course Wayne had an older brother who would take them out there over the weekend.

"You're an idiot," Jace told himself aloud, walking down a gravel path littered with old cigarette butts and beer cans, out toward one of the wide slabs in the old quarry that overlooked a pool he was *certain* was deep enough for a dive. Start small, that was his plan. He'd get this jump down, which was probably fifteen feet, and then move on to the next pool, where the jump was a good bit higher, thirty feet at least. He looked across the water and felt dizzy already. Rooftop was more than *twice* that high?

"Just try it," he said. Talking to himself felt good, out here alone, it gave him a little added confidence. "Just try it. You can't kill yourself falling into the water. Not from here."

Still, he was simply pacing the ledges, giving himself a good three feet of buffer, as if his legs might just buckle and send him sliding down the stone on his face, leave him floating in the water with a broken neck.

"Pussy," he said, because that was what they'd called him earlier in the day, in front of the girls, and it had made him angry enough—*almost*—to start up the ladder. Instead, he'd used the lonely quarry to defend himself. In retrospect, he probably should have climbed the ladder.

Thunder cracked and echoed back off the high stone walls and the water, sounding deeper and more dangerous down in the quarry than it would have up on the road. The wind had been blowing hard ever since he got out of school, and it was really gusting now, swirling stone dust, and out of the western sky advanced a pair of pure black clouds, trapped lightning flashing within them.

Bad time to be in the water, Jace thought, and then he latched on to that idea because it gave him an excuse not to jump. "Wayne Potter is not worth getting electrocuted over."

And so he started back, was almost all the way to the hole in the fence before he stopped.

Wayne Potter wasn't going away. Come Saturday he'd be there with his brother, and they'd take Jace out to Rooftop and watch him piss down his leg and they'd laugh their butts off. Then Wayne would go back to school Monday and tell the story, assuming he hadn't called everyone first. Or, worse yet, brought them to watch. What if he brought the girls?

It was that idea that finally gave him some resolve. Jumping was frightening, but *not* jumping in front of the girls? That was scarier still, and the price was higher.

"You'd better jump it," he said. "Come on, coward. Just go jump it."

He walked back fast, because dawdling only allowed the fear to build, so he wanted to go quick, get it over and done so that he knew he *could* do it. Once that start had been achieved, the rest would be easy. Just a matter of adding height, that was all. He kicked his shoes off, then pulled his T-shirt and jeans off and left them in a pile on the rocks.

As thunder boomed again, he squeezed his nose closed with his thumb and index finger—a baby thing, yes, but he was alone and didn't care—and then spoke again.

"I'm no pussy."

Since he was holding his nose, his voice came out high and girlish. He took one last look at the water below, shut his eyes, bent at the knees, and sprang off the ledge.

It wasn't much of a drop. For all of his worrying, it ended fast, and it ended pain-free, except of course for the jarring shock of cold water. He let himself sink to the bottom—water didn't bother him in the least, he loved to swim, just didn't like to dive—and waited for the feel of smooth, cool stone.

It didn't come. Instead, his foot touched something strange, an object that was somehow soft and hard at the same time, and he jerked back in fright, because whatever it was, it didn't belong. He opened his eyes, blinking against the sting of the water, and saw the dead man.

He was sitting almost upright, his back against the stone, his legs stretched out in front of him. Head tilted sideways, like he was tired. Blond hair floating in the current Jace had created, strands rising off the top of the dead man's head to dance in the dark water. His upper lip was curled like he was laughing at someone, a mean laugh, mocking, and Jace could see his teeth. There was a rope around his ankles and it was attached to an old dumbbell.

For a few seconds, Jace floated there above him, suspended not five feet away. Maybe it was because he was seeing it through the dim water, but he felt separated from the scene, felt as if the corpse down here had to be something imagined. It was only when he realized why the man's head was leaning to the side that the terror he should have felt initially overcame him. The man's throat was cut, leaving a gap so wide that water flowed through it like an open channel. At the sight, Jace began a frantic, clumsy churn back up. He was no more than fifteen feet down but still he was certain he wouldn't make the top, would drown down there, his body lying forever beside the other corpse.

When he broke the surface he was already trying to shout for help, and the result was awful; he inhaled water and choked on it and felt as if he'd drown, was unable to get air into his lungs. He finally got a gasping breath in and spit out the water that was in his mouth.

Water that had touched the dead man.

He felt a surge of sickness and swam hard, only to realize he was angling in the wrong direction, toward the steep walls that offered no way to climb out. He panicked and spun, finally getting his eyes on some low rocks. The world echoed with more thunder as he put his head down and swam. The first time he tried to pull himself out, his arms failed, and he fell back into the water hard enough that his head went under.

Come on, Jace! Get out, get out, you've got to get out...

On the second try he made it, flopped up on his stomach. The quarry water was pouring off him and it was in his mouth again, dripping from his lips, and for the second time he thought of the way it had flowed through that gaping tear in the man's throat. He gagged and vomited onto the rock, throat and nose burning, and then crawled weakly away from the pool as if the water might reach up for him, grab one leg, and pull him back in.

"Holy shit," he whispered. His voice trembled and his entire body shook. When he thought he could trust his legs, he stood up uncertainly. The storm-front winds chilled the cold water on his skin and his soaking boxer shorts and he hugged his arms around himself and thought stupidly, *I forgot to bring a towel.* It was only then that he realized he'd also come out of the water on the wrong side of the quarry. His clothes were piled on the ledge across from him.

You have to be kidding me, he thought, looking around at the steep walls that bordered this side of the pool. It wasn't easy climbing. In fact, he wasn't sure that it was *possible* climbing. Nothing but vertical smooth stone above him. Farther down, below the pool, there was a drop-off that led to an area littered with brush and thorns. Going in that direction would be slow and painful with no shoes or pants. The fastest option was simple: get back in the water and swim across.

He stared at the pile of clothes, close enough he could throw rocks onto them easily. The cell phone was in the pocket of his jeans.

Need to get help, he thought, *need to get someone out here, fast.*

But he didn't move. The idea of going back into that water…he stared into the murky green pool, darker than it had ever looked before, then suddenly lit bright by a flash of lightning, the storm sweeping in fast.

"He's not going to hurt you," he said, edging toward the water. "Not going to come back to life and grab you."

Saying that made him realize something he hadn't processed yet in his desperate attempt to get away—the man wasn't going to come back to life, no, but the man also wasn't far removed from life. His hair, his eyes, the lip curled back against his teeth…even the skin around the wound in the throat hadn't begun to decompose yet. Jace wasn't sure how long something like that took, but it seemed like it would go pretty fast.

Hasn't been there long…

This time the thunder made him jump. He was staring around the quarry, eyeing the top ridges of the stone walls, looking for a watcher.

Empty.

Get the hell out of here, he instructed himself, but he couldn't bring himself to swim for it. Couldn't imagine being immersed in that water again, swimming right above the man with the dumbbell tied to his ankles and the lopsided head and gashed throat. Instead, he walked down toward the drop-off. There a ledge connected one side to the other: the pool he'd just been in, on the right side, and another one to the left. The drop to the left was the thirty-foot monster he'd intended to use as his practice for Rooftop. For some reason, the narrow ledge was home to plants, but only mean ones. Anything that grew in stone seemed to have thorns. He narrowly missed a broken bottle as he entered the weeds. With his first steps, the thorns began to rake his flesh, and he grimaced but pushed ahead slowly, warm blood mingling with cool water on his legs. The first drops of rain started to fall and the thunder boomed overhead and then echoed back through the quarry as if the earth wanted to respond.

"Ouch! Damn it!" He'd managed to step right on a thorn, and the sticker remained in the bottom of his foot, so his next step drove it in farther. He was standing on one leg and had just pulled the thorn out of his foot, blood rushing to fill the hole, when he heard the car motor.

His first thought was that it might be a security guard or something. That would be nice. That would be *wonderful,* because whatever hell he was going to catch for being in the quarry was worth it to get back out. For a long moment he stayed just like he was, balanced up on one leg, holding his bleeding foot in his hand, and listened. The engine came on and on, someone driving up the gravel road that was blocked by a locked gate.

Killer coming back, he thought, and now the frozen indecision turned to wild terror. He was standing in the middle of the ledge in the most visible spot in the entire quarry.

He turned and started to return to the place from which he'd come, then stopped. There was no cover there. The rock face was sheer; there wasn't even anything to duck behind. He spun and headed in the other direction again, trying to plow through the weeds, indifferent to the thorns that raked him and left ribbons of blood along his chest, arms, and legs.

The engine was very close now.

He wasn't going to make the other side. Not fast enough.

Jace Wilson gave one look at the water below, one quick attempt at picking a safe landing zone even though the water was too dark to show what waited beneath, and then he jumped. Talk about doubling-down on your fear—he was scared of heights, but of whoever was coming? That wasn't fear. That was terror.

This time, the drop felt real, felt long, as if he'd started from a truly high place. He was thinking of rocks and pieces of twisted metal, all the junk that was left behind in these quarry pools, all the things his dad had warned him about, when he struck the water and tunneled down. He tried to stop himself early, but his velocity had been high and he sank even as he tried to rise, plunging all the way down. The pool wasn't nearly as deep as he'd expected. The landing jarred him, his feet striking stone and sending a sparkler of pain up his spine. He pushed back off and let himself rise slowly. He didn't want to break the surface with much noise this time.

His head cleared the water just as the sound of the engine cut out. The car had come to a stop. He swam toward a slab of limestone that jutted up at an angle, offering a narrow crevice that he was sure he could slip into. He'd just reached it when he chanced a look up and saw a man walking toward the water. Tall and broad-shouldered, with long, pale blond hair. His head was down, following the path, and he hadn't seen Jace yet. The quarry had grown very dark as the thunderheads moved over, but in the next strobe of lightning, Jace saw the glistening of a badge and realized the man was in uniform.

Police. Someone had already called them, or somehow they already knew. Whatever had happened to get them here didn't matter to Jace. They *were* here. Help had arrived. He let a long breath out and was filling his lungs to shout for help when he saw the others.

There was another police officer, also blond, his hair cut shorter, like he was in the military. He had a gun on his belt, and he was shoving forward a man in handcuffs. There was a black hood over his head.

Jace stifled his shout and went still, clinging to the rock with his feet and one hand. Trying not to move. Not to breathe.

The first cop waited until the other men reached him. He was standing with his arms folded over his chest, impatient, as he watched the man blinded by the hood stumble forward. The man in the hood was trying to talk and couldn't. Just a series of strange, high noises.

Something's over his mouth, Jace realized. He might not have been able to make out the words, but he got the meaning clear enough: The man was begging. He was scared, and he was begging. It came in whines and whimpers, like a puppy. When the first cop swung his foot out and upended the man in the hood, dropping him hard to the ground, blind and unprepared for the fall, Jace almost cried out, had to bite his lip to keep silent. The second cop, the one who'd brought the man down from the car, knelt and put a knee in his spine and jerked his head up by the hood. He leaned down and spoke to him, but it was soft, whispered. Jace could not hear the words. The cop was still talking to the man in the hood when he put out his hand and curled the fingers impatiently, waiting for something, and the first cop offered a knife. Not a pocketknife or a kitchen knife, but something like soldiers used. A fighting knife. A *real* knife.

Jace saw the man's head jerk in response to one fast motion with the blade, and then saw his feet spasm, scraping the earth in a search for traction as he tried to lift his cuffed hands to his throat, tried to put back the blood that was spilling out from under the hood. Both of the cops grabbed him then, fast and efficient, taking hold of his clothes from the back, careful to stay away from the blood. Then they shoved him off the rock and he was tumbling, falling just as Jace had. He outpaced his own blood; a red cloud of it was in the air above his head when he hit the water.

At the sound of the splash, Jace finally moved. Now that it was just the two of them up there, no distractions, they'd be likely to look around. Likely to see him. He pulled himself in under the rock and squirmed into the darkness, trying to push back as far as possible, scrabbling at the stone with his fingers. He couldn't get far. He'd be visible to anyone who was level with him on the other side, but that would require that person's being in the water. Still, if they came down that far, his hiding place was going to turn into a trap. There would be nowhere to run then. His breath was coming in fast, rapid gasps, and he was dizzy and felt like he could throw up again.

Don't get sick, don't make a sound, you cannot make a sound.

For a few seconds all was quiet. They were going to leave. He thought that they were probably going to leave and he would get out of here yet, he'd get home today, despite everything.

That was when he heard one of their voices loud and clear for the first time: "Well, now. It would appear someone has been swimming. And chose to leave his clothing behind."

The voice was so mild that for a moment Jace couldn't

believe it came from one of the men who'd done the killing up there with the knife. It seemed impossible.

There was a pause, and then the second man answered. "Clothes are one thing. But he'd also choose to leave his shoes?"

"Seems like rough country," the first voice agreed, "to walk without shoes."

The strangely serene voices went silent then, but there was another sound, a clear metallic snap. Jace had been around the shooting range with his dad enough to recognize that one: a round being chambered into a gun.

The men circled the quarry rim, and down below them, pinned in the dark rocks, Jace Wilson began to cry.

2

THE WEATHER-ALERT RADIO went off just as they settled into bed, speaking to Ethan and Allison in its
disembodied, robotic voice.

*Potent late-spring storm system will continue to bring heavy
snow to area mountains....Heaviest snowfall above seventy-
five hundred feet....However, several inches of heavy wet snow
are possible as low as forty-five hundred feet before morning.
Heavy wet snow on trees and power lines may result in power
outages. Snow should taper off Sunday morning. One to two
feet of snow expected with locally heavier accumulations on
north- and east-facing slopes. Mountain roadways will become
snow-packed and icy tonight and may become impassable in
spots, including over Beartooth Pass.*

"You know what I love about you?" Allison said. "You're
leaving that thing on, even though we've been watching it
snow for the past four hours. We know what's happening."

"Forecasts can change."

"Hmm. Yes. And people can sleep. Let's do that."

"Could get fun out there," Ethan said. "Surely someone

decided they'd take a quick hike this morning, ahead of the weather. And of course they wouldn't need a map, because it was just going to be a quick hike, right?"

Those were the kinds of decisions that usually drew Ethan into the mountains in the middle of the night. Particularly the late-season storms, when the weather had been temperate enough for long enough to lull people into a false sense of security.

"May every fool stay indoors," Allison said, and kissed his arm, shifting for a more comfortable position, her voice already sleepy.

"Optimistic wish," he said, pulling her close to his chest, relishing her warmth. The cabin had cooled quickly once they let the fire in the woodstove burn down. Beside them, the window rattled with a steady drilling of sleet. On the shelf above the bed, next to the weather-alert radio, the CB was silent. It had been a good winter—only one call-out. Winters were usually better than other seasons, though; most tourists stayed away from Montana in those months. Ethan didn't like the feel of this storm. Last day of May, summer looming, a week of sunshine and fifty-degree weather just past? Yes, some of the fools Allison mentioned might have taken to the mountains. And once they got stuck, that radio above Ethan Serbin's head would crackle to life, and his search-and-rescue team would assemble.

"Got a good feeling," Allison said into the pillow, fading fast the way she always did; the woman could probably sleep on the tarmac of an active airport without trouble.

"Yeah?"

"Yeah. But just in case I'm wrong, turn off your radio. At least the fool frequency."

He smiled at her in the dark, squeezed her one more

time, and then closed his eyes. She was asleep within minutes, her breathing shifting to long, slow inhalations he
could feel against his chest. He listened as the sleet changed
back to snow; the rattle against the glass faded to silence,
and eventually he started to fade too.

When the radio went off, Allison awoke with a groan.

"No," she said. "Not tonight."

Ethan got out of bed, fumbled the handheld unit from
its base, and walked out of the bedroom and across the cold
floorboards to the front window. It was fully dark inside
the cabin. They'd lost power just after sunset, and he hadn't
bothered to use the generator; there was no need to burn
fuel just to sleep.

"Serbin? You copy?" The voice belonged to Claude
Kitna, the Park County sheriff.

"Copy," Ethan said, looking out at the white world beyond the dark cabin. "Who's gone missing, and where,
Claude?"

"Nobody missing."

"Then let me sleep."

"Got a slide-off. Somebody trying to get over the pass just
as we were about to shut it down."

The pass was the Beartooth Pass, on Highway 212 between Red Lodge and Cooke City. The Beartooth Highway, as 212 was also known, was one of the most beautiful—and dangerous—highways in the country, a series of
steep switchbacks that wound between Montana and Wyoming and peaked at over ten thousand feet. It was closed
for months in the winter, the entire highway simply shut
down, and did not reopen until late May at the earliest. The
drive required vigilance in the best weather, and in a snowstorm in the dark? Good luck.

"Okay," Ethan said into the radio. "Why do you need me?" He would roll with his team when someone was missing. A slide-off on the highway, or, as Claude liked to call the really nasty drops, a bounce-off, might require paramedics—or a coroner—but not search-and-rescue.

"Driver who thought it was a wise idea to push through says she was on her way to see you. Park service bumped her to me. Got her sitting in a plow truck right now. You want her?"

"Coming to see me?" Ethan frowned. "Who is it?"

"A Jamie Bennett," Claude said. "And for a woman who just drove her rental car off a mountain, I have to say, she's not all that apologetic."

"Jamie Bennett?"

"Correct. You know her?"

"Yeah," Ethan said, confused. "Yeah, I know her."

Jamie Bennett was a professional bodyguard. Since leaving the Air Force, Ethan had taught survival instruction as a private contractor, working with civilians and government groups. Jamie had been in a session he'd taught a year ago. He'd liked her, and she was good, competent if a bit cocky, but he could not imagine what had her driving over the Beartooth Pass in a snowstorm in search of him.

"What's her story?" Claude Kitna asked.

Ethan couldn't begin to answer that.

"I'll head your way," Ethan said. "And I guess I'll find out."

"Copy that. Be careful, now. It's rough out here tonight."

"I'll be careful. See you soon, Claude."

In the bedroom, Allison propped herself up on one arm and looked at him in the shadows as he pulled his clothes on.

"Where are you headed?"

"Up to the pass."

"Somebody try to walk away from a car wreck?"

That had happened before. Scared of staying in one place, people would panic and set off down the highway, and, in the blowing snow, they'd lose the highway. It seemed like an impossible thing to lose, until you experienced a Rocky Mountain blizzard at night.

"No. Jamie Bennett was trying to get through."

"The marshal? The one from last spring?"

"Yes."

"What is she doing in Montana?"

"Coming to find me, is what I was told."

"In the middle of the night?"

"That's what I was told," he repeated.

"This can't be good," Allison said.

"I'm sure it's fine."

But as he left the cabin and walked to his snowmobile in the howling white winds, he knew that it wasn't.

The night landscape refused full dark in that magical way that only snow could provide, soaking in the starlight and moonlight and offering it back as a trapped blue iridescence. Claude Kitna hadn't been lying—the wind was working hard, shifting north to northeast in savage gusts, flinging thick, wet snow. Ethan rode alone and he rode slow, even though he knew 212 as well as anyone up here, and he'd logged more hours on it in bad weather than most. That was exactly why he kept his speed down even when it felt as if the big sled could handle more. Of the rescues-turned-to-corpse discoveries he'd participated in, far too many involved snowmobiles and ATVs, people getting cocky about driving vehicles built to handle the elements.

One thing he'd learned while training all over the world—and the lesson had been hammered home here in Montana—was that believing a tool could handle the elements was a recipe for disaster. You adapted to the elements with respect; you did not control them.

It took him an hour to make what was usually a twenty-minute ride, and he was greeted at Beartooth Pass by orange flares, which threw the surrounding peaks into silhouette against the night sky, one plow, and one police vehicle parked in the road. A black Chevy Tahoe was crushed against the guardrail. Ethan looked at its position, leaned up on one side, and shook his head. She'd come awfully damn close. Pull that same maneuver on one of the switchbacks and that Tahoe would have fallen a long way before it hit rock.

He parked the snowmobile, watching the snow swirl into the dark canyons below, lit orange by the flares as it fell, and he wondered if there was anyone out there in the wilderness whom they didn't know about, anyone who hadn't been as lucky as Jamie Bennett. There were tall, thin poles spaced out along the winding highway, markers to help the plows maneuver when the snow turned the road into a blind man's guessing game, and on the downwind side of the road, the snow was already two feet high against them, three feet in areas where the drifts caught.

The passenger-side door of the plow truck banged open, and Jamie Bennett stepped out of the cab and into the snow before Ethan had cut his engine. Her feet slipped out from under her and she nearly ended up on her ass before she caught herself on the door handle.

"What frigging country do you live in that has a blizzard the last day of *May,* Serbin?"

She was almost as tall as him; her blond hair streamed

out from under a ski cap, and her blue eyes watered in the stinging wind.

"They have these things," he said, "called weather forecasts? They're new, I guess, experimental, but it's still worth checking them, time to time. Like, oh, before driving over a mountain range at night."

She smiled and offered a gloved hand, and they shook.

"I heard the forecast, but I figured I could beat the storm. Don't worry," she said. "I'm keeping my positive mental attitude."

That was one of the seven priorities for survival Ethan had taught in the course Jamie had taken. The first priority, in fact.

"Glad you've retained your lessons. What are you doing here, anyhow?"

Claude Kitna was watching them with interest, staying at a courteous distance but not so far away that he couldn't overhear the conversation. Farther up the road, the headlights of another plow truck showed, this one returning from the pass gate, which would now be shut and locked, the Beartooth Highway closed to all traffic. They'd opened the pass for the first time that season just four days earlier. Last year, it had been closed until June 20. The wilderness was more accessible now than it had once been, but that didn't mean it wasn't still the wilderness.

"I've got a proposition for you," Jamie said. "A request. You may not like it, but I want you to hear me out, at least."

"It's a promising start," Ethan said. "Any job that arrives with a blizzard has to bring good things."

It was a joke then. There in the wind and the snow and the orange signal flares, it was only a joke. Weeks later, though, in the sun and the smoke, he would remember that line, and it would turn him cold.

3

By the time they got back to the cabin, Allison had a fire going in the woodstove.

"You want me to start the generator?" she said. "Get the lights back on?"

"It's fine," Jamie said.

"Get you some coffee, at least?" Allison said. "Warm you up a little?"

"I'd take a bourbon or something, actually. If you have any."

"Like I said—coffee," Allison told her with a smile, and then she poured Maker's Mark into a steaming mug of coffee and offered it to Jamie, who was still trying to get her jacket and gloves off, shedding snow that melted into pooled water on the floorboards in front of the stove.

"Now you're talking. Thank you. It is *frigid* out there. You really stay here year-round?"

Ethan smiled. "That's right."

Allison offered Ethan a cup of coffee as well, and he accepted the warm mug gratefully, rotated it in his hands.

Even through top-of-the-line gloves, the wind could find your joints. Allison's eyes were searching his, looking for a reason this woman had blown in with the storm. He gave the smallest of headshakes. She understood that he still had no idea.

"Gorgeous place," Jamie said, sipping the whiskey-laced coffee. "You said you guys built it yourselves?"

"Yes. With some help."

"You give it a name? Isn't that what you're supposed to do with a ranch?"

He smiled. "It's not a ranch. But we call it the Ritz."

"Seems a little rustic for that."

"That's the idea," Allison said. "That's the joke."

Jamie glanced at her and nodded. "Sorry about this, by the way. Crashing in during the night, during the storm. Invading the Ritz."

"Must be important," Allison said. She was wearing loose sweatpants and a tighter, long-sleeved top. She was barefoot, and Jamie Bennett had at least six inches on her. The storm didn't concern Allison—she was old Montana, third generation, a rancher's daughter—but Ethan had the sense that Jamie did, somehow. And not because she'd arrived in the middle of the night. Allison was used to those kinds of calls.

"It is," Jamie said, and turned back to Ethan. "You still run the same summer programs?"

"Summers I work with kids," he said. "I don't do any training for anybody else until September. Summer is the kids."

"That's what I'm talking about."

He raised an eyebrow. Ethan worked with probation and parole officers from around the country, took in kids who were facing lockup somewhere and brought them into the mountains instead. It was a survival course, yes, but it was a lot more than that. The idea had hardly originated with him; there were plenty of similar programs in the country.

"I've got a kid for you," she said. "I think. I'm hoping you're willing to do it."

Inside the woodstove, a log split in the heat with a popping noise, and the fire flared higher behind the glass door.

"You've got a kid," he echoed. "That means...you've got a witness."

She nodded. "Nice call."

He took a seat in front of the stove and she followed suit. Allison stayed where she was, leaning against the kitchen counter, watching.

"Why do you want him with me?"

"Because his parents are refusing traditional witness protection."

"Nontraditional witness protection is what you do now, I thought." Ethan remembered Jamie saying that she'd been with the U.S. Marshals but had left to go into executive protection. High-dollar private-bodyguard work.

She took a deep breath. "I've got to be very limited in what I tell you. Understand that? I'll try to give you the best sense of it that I can, but it won't be as detailed as you'd like."

"Okay."

"This boy is...he's beyond a critical witness. I can't overstate his value. But what I'm dealing with is a situation in which he and his parents have a pretty healthy distrust of law enforcement. With good reason, based on what they've seen. The boy is at risk. *High* risk. And the parents want to stay with the son, avoid the WITSEC program, and just generally control everything. Enter me, as you said. But..."

She stopped talking. Ethan gave her a minute, and when she didn't pick back up, he said, "Jamie?"

"But I'm not doing too well," she said softly. "I could lie to you, and I was about to. I was about to tell you that the family can't afford me. That's true enough. But Ethan, I would protect this boy for free if I could. I really mean that. I'd make it my only job, I'd…"

Another pause, a deep breath, and then, "They're too good."

"Who is?"

"The men looking for him."

Allison turned away just as Ethan searched for her eyes.

"Then why me?" he said. "You're better at it than me."

"You can take him off the grid. Completely. And that's where their weakness will be. If he's around a cell phone, a security camera, a computer, a damned video game, I feel like they'll get him. But here…here he's just a tiny thing in a big wilderness."

"We all are," Ethan said.

"Right. It's going to be your call, of course. But I was desperate, and it struck me. At first, a wild idea, this implausible thing. But then I looked into it a little bit more—"

"Looked into Ethan a little more?" Allison said. They both turned to her.

"That was part of it," Jamie Bennett said evenly. "But it was more looking into the feasibility of the whole thing. We make him vanish for a summer. But he's not in the situation the parents are so worried about, he's not in some safe house in a new city, scared to death. I have a very good sense of the kid. What he likes, what he'd respond to, what would make him relax. He is not relaxed right now, I assure you. He's very into adventure things. Survival stories. And that,

25

of course, made me think of you. So I pitched it, told them about your background, and I think I've got them sold on it. So I came here to sell you too."

"Shouldn't it have run the other way, maybe?" Allison said. "Clearing the plan with us before selling the child and his parents on it?"

Jamie studied her for a moment and then gave a small nod. "I understand why you feel that way. But the reality is, I'm trying to minimize the number of people who know that this boy exists. If I'd told you and then the parents wouldn't agree to it, there'd be people in Montana who'd been informed of the situation for no gain. That's a risky approach."

"Fair enough," Ethan said. "But Allison raises a good point. It's not just a matter of selling *me* on it, or the two of us. There are going to be other kids up here. Other kids who may be at risk if we do this. That's my primary responsibility."

"I will tell you, will assure you, that I would not consider doing this if I felt it put other children at risk. First of all, the boy is going to seem to disappear from the outside world before he arrives here. That much I've worked out carefully. I know how to make him vanish. I'd enter him in the program with a false identity. Even you couldn't know who he was. And you wouldn't try to find out."

Ethan nodded.

"The second thing," she said, "is that we know who we're watching. We know who is threatened by him. If they move from…from their home base, I'm going to be aware of it. They aren't sneaking up to Montana without me noticing. And the minute they move, you'll have total protection for your entire group. For *everyone*."

Ethan was silent. Jamie leaned toward him.

"And, if I may offer an opinion: This boy needs what you teach. It isn't just about hiding him here, Ethan. The kid is damaged, and he's trying to hold it together. He's scared. You can make him stronger. I *know* that, because I've been through it with you."

Ethan looked away from Jamie and over to Allison, but her flat stare revealed no opinion either way. His decision to make. He looked back at Jamie.

"Listen," Jamie Bennett said, "I didn't come out here on a whim. But I'm not going to pressure you on it either. I'm telling you the truth about the scenario and asking for your help."

Ethan turned from her and looked out the window. The snow was still falling fast, and dawn's light was far from arriving. In the reflection in the glass he could see Allison and Jamie Bennett waiting on him to speak. Jamie seemed more frustrated than Allison, because Allison understood that Ethan was not a man given to rapid decision-making, that he felt rushed decisions were often exactly what got you into serious trouble. He sat and drank his coffee and watched them in the reflection, trapped there in the lantern light with the snow swirling outside, part of that beautiful mystery of glass, of how, seen at the right angle, it could show you what lay both behind it and beyond it.

"You believe he will be killed if the situation is allowed to continue in its current fashion," he said.

"I do."

"What is your alternative plan? If I say no."

"I'm hoping you say—"

"I understand what you're hoping. I'm asking what you'll do if I say no."

"I'll try to find him a program similar to yours. With someone who'll take the child off the grid, someone who is qualified to protect him. But I won't find one I trust as much, I won't find one I can vouch for personally. That matters to me."

Ethan looked away from the window and back into Jamie Bennett's eyes.

"You truly will not let the boy be pursued here? You believe you can guarantee that?"

"One hundred percent."

"Nothing is one hundred percent." Ethan got to his feet and gestured to the darkened room behind them. "There's a guest bedroom in there. Take the flashlight on the table, and make yourself at home. We'll talk in the morning."

Jamie Bennett stared at him. "You're not going to give me an answer?"

"I'm going to get some sleep," Ethan said. "And then I'll give you an answer."

Alone in the dark bedroom, they spoke in whispers beneath the wailing wind and considered the best-case scenarios and the worst-case. There seemed to be many more options in the latter category.

"Tell me what you think, Allison. What *you* think."

She was quiet for a time. They were facing each other in the bed and he had one arm wrapped around her back, her lean muscles rising and falling under his hand as she breathed. Her dark hair spilled across the pillow and touched his cheek.

"You can't say no," she said at last.

"You think we have to do it, then?"

"That's not what I said."

"Clarify."

She took a deep breath. "You won't be able to say no. You'll be watching every news story, searching for some kid who was killed or who disappeared. You'll be calling Jamie asking for updates she won't be able to give you. Your entire summer will be lost to wondering if you put him in harm's way when you could have taken him out of it. Am I wrong?"

He didn't answer.

"You also believe it," she said. "And that's a good thing."

"Believe her story? Of course I do."

"No," Allison said, "you believe that this can help him. That when he goes back to the world to face it all down, he'll be more ready than he was before he got here. Before he got to you."

"I think it works," Ethan said. "Some of the time, I think it works."

"I know it does," she said softly.

Allison had understood from the beginning. Or understood how it mattered to him, at least, and believed that *he* believed it worked. That was a critical starting point. Many people he spoke to about it got the theory of the program without the soul. Maybe that was on him. Maybe he'd not been able to explain it properly, or maybe it wasn't something you could explain but, rather, something that had to be felt. Maybe you needed to be sixteen years old with a hard-ass, impossible-to-please father and facing a long stretch in juvie and knowing that longer stretches in worse places waited and then arrive in a beautiful but terrifying mountain range, clueless and clumsy, and find something out there to hold inside yourself when you got sent back. When the mountains were gone and the air blew exhaust smoke instead of glacier chill and the pressures that were on you couldn't be solved with a length of parachute cord and an ability to tie the right knot with your eyes closed. If you could find that and hold it there within yourself, a candle of self-confidence against the darkness, you could accomplish great things. He knew this. He'd been through it.

So you learned to build a fire, his old man had said when Ethan explained the experience, unable to transfer the feeling to him. Yes, he'd learned to build a fire. What it had done for him, though, the sense of confidence the skills gave and the sense of awe that the mountains gave…those were impacts he could not describe. All he could do was show everyone: No trouble with the law since he was sixteen, a distinguished Air Force career, a collection of ribbons and medals and commendations. All of those things had been within the flame of that first fire he'd started, but how could you explain that?

"So you'll do it," Allison said. "You'll agree to it in the morning."

He offered a question instead of confirmation. "What don't you like about her?"

"I never said I didn't like her."

"I'll repeat the question. Hopeful for an answer this time."

Allison sighed and leaned her head on his chest. "She drove her car off the road in a snowstorm."

"You're bothered by the fact that she's a bad driver?"

"No," Allison said. "I'm bothered by the fact that she rushes, and she makes mistakes."

He was silent. Intrigued by the observation. It seemed unfair on the surface, critical and harsh, but she was only commenting on the very things he'd taught for so many years. Good decision-making was a pattern. So was bad decision-making.

"Just keep that in mind," Allison said, "when you tell her that you're going to do it."

"So now I'm going to do it?"

"You were always going to do it, Ethan. You just needed to go through the rituals. That way you can convince yourself it's the right choice."

"You're saying it's not?"

"No, E. I'm saying that I truly don't know what will come of it. But I know you're going to say yes."

They slept then, finally, and in the morning he told Jamie Bennett that he would take the job, and then they set about finding a tow truck to deal with the damaged rental. A simple mistake, he told himself, representative of nothing.

But he couldn't help thinking, after Allison's warning, that the first thing Jamie had admitted to him upon her disastrous midnight arrival was that she had heard the forecast and ignored it, convinced she could beat the storm.

Up at the Beartooth Pass, chains rattled and winches growled as they pulled that mistake free from the snowdrifts.

4

I AN WAS OFF DUTY when they came for him, but he was still in uniform and still armed, and usually that meant something to people. Badge on the chest, gun on the belt? He felt awfully strong in those situations. Had since the academy, could still remember the first time he'd put on the uniform, feeling like a damned gladiator.

Bring it the fuck on, he'd thought then, and the years hadn't eroded much of that swagger. He knew better than to believe he was untouchable—he'd attended too many police funerals for that, and he'd shaken a few too many of the wrong hands and passed cash to too many people he shouldn't have—but day by day, hour by hour, he still felt strong in the uniform. People took notice. Some respected you, some feared you, some flat-out hated you, even, but they sure as hell took notice.

The single most unnerving thing about the Blackwell brothers was that they didn't seem to. The badge meant nothing, and the gun even less. Their pale blue eyes would just roll over you, taking inventory, showing nothing. In-different. Bored, even.

He saw their truck when he pulled in. That black F-150 with blacked-out windows, an illegal level of tint. Even the grille was black. He expected they were still inside, and he got out of the cruiser and took a deep breath and hitched up his belt, knowing they were watching and wanting to re-mind them of the gun, even though they never seemed to care. He went up on the porch and flipped the lid on the beer cooler. Ice had melted but there were still a couple cans floating around in relatively cold water, and he took out a Miller Lite and drank it there on the porch, leaning against the rail and staring at the blacked-out truck and waiting for them to appear.

They never did.

"To hell with it," he said when the beer was done. Let 'em sit, if that's what they wanted. He wasn't going to walk down there and knock on the damn door like he was ready to do their bidding. That wasn't how it worked. They'd come to him, like it or not.

He crumpled the can and tossed it in the recycling bin on the porch, which was so full the can just bounced off and fell to the floor. He ignored that as he went to the door and unlocked it, hating the uneasy feeling that came with hav-ing his back to their black truck. Then he opened the door and stepped inside and saw them in his living room.

"What in the hell do you think you're doing? You broke into my *house*?"

They didn't answer, and he felt the first real chill. Shook it off and slammed the door behind him, trying to hold the anger. They worked for him. He needed to remember that in order to ensure that they would remember it as well.

"You boys," he said, shaking his head, "are going to get your asses in trouble someday, you know that?"

Jack Blackwell was sitting on Ian's recliner. Had it leaned back so he could stretch his legs out. He was the older of the two, a little taller, a little thinner. Neither of them had much in the way of visible muscle, but Ian had seen the strength in those rangy frames at work, had seen the vise-tight grips of their unusually large hands, the way those long fingers could turn into steel bands. Jack had hair like a damned Beach Boy, hanging down to his collar, so light that it looked bleached. Dressed in faded, rumpled clothes, most of the time in black. His younger brother kept a different look, as if it were important to him to be separate from Jack, even if he never moved far from his side. Patrick could have passed for a Marine, had hair that was cut with a razor and not scissors, wore shirts with crisp creases, boots that shined. He was standing between the living room and the kitchen, arms folded. He never seemed to sit.

Ian said, "Stupid damn thing to do, you know that? Risky. I get one neighbor who watches you dumb bastards letting yourself in here, one neighbor who calls out a patrolman, and we've got major issues then. Fucking stupid, that's what this is."

Jack Blackwell said, "He lectures a lot."

Patrick Blackwell said, "I've noticed. Most times, it's about intelligence. Lack thereof, rather. You noticed that?"

"I have indeed."

This was their routine. Talking to each other as if they were alone in the room. Creepy fuckers. Ian had heard it before, and he never did like it.

"Listen," he said, "it's been a long day, boys. I don't have time to serve as the straight man for your act. Tell me what in the hell you're doing here, and then get the hell out."

"Hospitality is lacking too," Jack Blackwell said.

"Noticeably so," Patrick agreed. "Man stood out there on his porch and enjoyed a cold beer without so much as offering us one."

"Didn't appear to be his last beverage either. So the opportunity for the offer is there, certainly. And still it hasn't been made." Jack shook his head, looking at his brother. "You think this goes back a while? The lack of manners?"

"You're suggesting his parents are to blame? That it was learned behavior?" Patrick pursed his lips, giving the matter due consideration. "We can't say that with any level of certainty. But it's possible. It's possible."

"Hey, dickheads?" Ian said, and he let his hand drift down to his gun. "I'm not fucking around here. If you've got something to say, now's the time. Otherwise, get out."

Jack was still looking at Patrick, but Patrick was watching Ian. Patrick said, "If I didn't know better, I could interpret his attitude as threatening. Got his hand on his gun, even. You see that?"

Jack turned and fixed his pale blue eyes on Ian. "I had not. But you're correct. It's a threatening posture."

Ian decided he was done with them, and the feel of the gun in his hand helped build his confidence. He reached for the door, twisted the knob, and pulled it open.

"Get out."

Jack Blackwell let out a deep sigh, then lowered the recliner's footrest and sat leaning forward, head down, arms braced on his knees.

"The boy is still gone. You were supposed to have intel by now. A location."

Ian closed the door. "I'm working on it."

Jack nodded slowly, the gesture of a man both understanding and disappointed. A father hearing his troubled son's excuses; a priest listening to the confession of a repeated sin.

"Your sources with the marshals, Ian, are not what they were promised to be."

"A great deal of hype," Patrick agreed, "but very little result."

"The kid isn't in WITSEC," Ian said. "Trust me."

"Well, he's also not at home. Trust *us*."

"I understand that. But I'm telling you, he didn't enter the program. My sources aren't overhyped. They're every bit as good as promised."

"That would seem hard to believe at this point, based upon the evidence."

"Give it time."

"Time. Sure. Do you understand how this situation troubles us?" Jack said.

Ian felt a dull throb building behind his temples, a pulse of frustration that usually led to someone bleeding. He was not a man who handled frustration well. He'd understood for a while now that he might have made a mistake with this alliance, but for all their strange quirks and bizarre behavior, the Blackwell brothers were good. They did professional work and they did not make mistakes and they kept a low profile. They were cold and they were cruel but he understood men who were cold and cruel and in the end all he cared about was whether they were good at their jobs. The Blackwell brothers were that, if nothing else. His patience for their attitudes, though, was fading fast.

"That kid," he said, "is a problem for me too. All of this

comes back to me in the end, you better remember that. Better remember who pays you for your work."

"The lectures again," Patrick said, and shook his head. "You hearing this?"

"I am," Jack said. "Appears to be questioning our level of understanding. Yet again."

"Shut the fuck up," Ian said. "That shit, the talking-like-I'm-not-here shit? End it. I'll lay this out for you once, okay? The kid is not with WITSEC. If he ever is, I'll know about it. He's not right now. So your job is to figure out *where* he is. And do it fast."

"There were rumors afloat," Jack said. "You recall those, Patrick?"

"Negotiations with prosecutors. Are those the rumors you're thinking of?"

"Well, it wasn't the Cubs' possibilities before the trade deadline. So it must have been that, yes."

Ian was listening to them and wondering why in the hell he hadn't driven away as soon as he saw the truck. He'd always been in control of these two, in theory at least, but he'd never *felt* that control. Now he was seeing the mistake in this association. A wise man didn't rent attack dogs; he raised them himself. Why? Because he'd never be able to fully trust them otherwise.

"Listen," he said, "I don't know what in the hell you're talking about, with the rumors and bullshit. Nobody wants this done more than me. The parents know where the boy is, you can count on that."

"Does the mother talk to us, Patrick? What do you think?" This from Jack.

"Anyone will talk to us with proper encouragement. Or so we've found over the years."

"True. But do the parents say what we need them to say in the course of our conversation?"

"A far more difficult question. They have, after all, nothing but the boy. In such circumstances, even the most persuasive approach may not be effective. It would depend upon the depth of their affection."

"My point exactly. The parents also have watchers now. Law enforcement support, a prosecutor who is determined to use that boy as a critical witness and who probably has conned them into believing the boy can be kept safe, and all the boy has to do is simply appear in court. You might remember that we were told by Ian here to leave the scene without the boy, that we couldn't waste time on a kid who, quote, 'might not even have seen a thing.' And that allowed the parents time to seek help. I would say, and you may correct me if you feel it's necessary, that the parents are a very poor opening option."

"I would concur," Patrick said. He hadn't taken his eyes off Ian. Lord, they were pale eyes. Ian hated their eyes, their stupid verbal games, their general demeanor. Even when you tried to piss them off, you couldn't. He hadn't succeeded in rattling those flat monotones yet.

"Then find another option," Ian said. "That was your job. Go do it. Get the hell out of my house and do it."

"For how much?" Jack said.

Ian stared at him. "For *how much?*"

"Yes. What pay rate, Ian?"

"You expect me to pay you to kill a witness *you* left alive? Pay you to clean up your own damned mess?"

"The mess," Jack said, still looking at the floor, "occurred while we were already in your employ. This mess is part of a previously existing mess. One that you paid us to clean up. For you."

"I expected it done better."

Jack glanced to his right, at Patrick, who was some ten feet away. He had drifted farther from his brother by a few steps.

"We've disappointed him, Patrick."

"It seems that way."

Jack turned to face Ian. Now both brothers were staring at him, two sets of those glacial gazes. Ian suddenly wished he hadn't closed the door.

"The new mess is part of the old one, Detective O'Neil," Jack said. "You own one, you own the other. Can you follow that? Consider us…" He waved a hand between himself and his brother. "There was one payment. There were two Blackwells. You got the one, you got the other. Are you with me here? Do you see the correlation?"

"I've got no money for you," Ian said. His mouth was dry, and his hand was all the way over the pistol grip now. Neither of them had so much as blinked at that. He knew that they had seen it, and he wanted them to care. Why didn't they care?

"If there's no money in it," Jack said, "then why on earth would we kill this boy?"

"You're serious?"

Jack gave a patient nod.

"Because he can put you in fucking prison. Both of you. Get one, get the other, you tell me? Well, bud, he's going to get you both. Get all of us. Me? At least I got a chance. But you two? He *saw* you two."

"Your thesis, then, would be as follows: We kill for money, or we kill to protect ourselves. There are those who pay, and those who threaten. Correct?"

"Correct," Ian said.

Jack looked at him for a long time and didn't say anything. It was Patrick who finally broke the silence by saying, "And you, Ian, are no longer one who pays."

The problem was that there were two of them. You tried to watch them both but they never stood together. There was always the distance. So one spoke and you looked at him and the other you could see only out of the corner of your eye. Then that one spoke and you'd look at him and now the other could be seen only out of the corner of your eye. Ian had been speaking with Jack, had been focused on Jack, had been looking at Jack with his hand on his gun, ready to pull it and fire. Then Patrick spoke, and Ian did what instinct told you to do—he looked in that direction.

He was facing the wrong way when the rush of motion came from Jack then, and by the time he spun back and drew the Glock, there was already a suppressed pistol in Jack Blackwell's hand and it bucked twice and Ian was down on his knees in his living room with blood spilling rich and red onto the hardwood floors. He wasn't going to die like that, without even getting a shot off, but now he was looking at Jack and there was Patrick on the other side, Ian saw him out of the corner of his eye, and when the shots came from that direction, Ian was facing the wrong way yet again.

You got one, you got the other.

Detective Sergeant Ian O'Neil was dead on his living-room floor when the Blackwell brothers left his house, making sure to lock the door behind them, and returned to their truck.

"He made some sense," Patrick said as he slid behind the wheel. "That bit about reasons for killing? Money or threat? He was a convincing man."

"He had his moments," Jack said, putting the pistol into the center console and leaving the lid up until Patrick added his.

"All the same," Patrick said, "I'd like to have been paid to find the boy."

"Young Jace offers us no reward, that's true. The risk, though…"

"Yes," Patrick said, gunning the big V-8 to life. "The risk is substantial. And so I suppose we'll have to find him."

"I suppose we will."

5

D<small>ON'T TRY TO GUESS.</small>
That had been Allison's rule for the day. She had
seen all of their files, she knew the boys by heart in some
ways, and she hadn't even met them yet.

"It doesn't matter," she said aloud when she fed the
horse, Tango, her baby, a rehab horse. He'd been kicked
and sustained a fracture that went almost the full length
of his leg. The bone was broken but not shattered. If it
had been, he would have had to be put down. Instead,
there was hope, though he'd never be able to perform at
the level he once had. He was now on the third month of
his rehab—which meant that he hadn't lain down in three
months. Tango had been standing up for ninety-four con-
secutive days. He wore a bit connected to two tension bands
that kept him from lying down. If he did get down, the
chances that he'd destroy the leg were high, because he'd
have to put a huge amount of force on the foreleg in order
to push himself up again.

And so he remained standing. He betrayed no trace of

pain or frustration or fatigue. Allison had been around horses her entire life, and she knew they didn't have to lie down for sleep or to rest in the way that humans and many other animals did, but still it astounded her to see him there, day after day, so patient, so steadfast. So trusting.

She spoke to him while she groomed him, and he gave a series of low snorts and, in trademark Tango fashion, shot a streamer of snot onto her arm. This was a compliment. This was true affection.

"Two more weeks, big guy," she said. That was all he had left wearing the bit. The foreleg should be fully healed by now, he'd taken walks and shown no trace of pain, but he hadn't held a rider. She couldn't wait to return to this horse. It was something to look forward to in a summer of unease.

Once she'd ridden horses for show. Fairs, competitions, bizarre Montana beauty pageants. Her mother had loved that world. Allison, not so much. The horse was always an afterthought to her mother—Allison's wardrobe, her hair, her stance: that mattered most. After a while, you began to wonder which creature was really being trotted out for show.

She was still talking to the horse when the van pulled in, and there they were: six boys of the sort she'd met every summer and one who was on the run from a killer. They unloaded in front of the bunkhouse, a simple cabin with no electricity or running water. Allison was already scrutinizing them during introductions, couldn't help it, *don't try to guess* a laughable command now.

There was Drew, sixteen, from Vermont. Tall and sullen and wanting to be someplace else. Raymond, fifteen, from Houston. Dark eyes that darted around as if he were taking an inventory of all possible threats. Connor, fourteen, from

Ohio, who stared at Allison's breasts instead of her eyes when he was introduced and then blushed when he realized he'd been caught. Ty, fourteen, from Indiana, a smaller kid but knotted with muscle and puffed up to show it as much as possible. Jeff, fifteen, from Kansas, who stood behind the others and didn't make eye contact with anyone when he introduced himself. Marco, fifteen, from Las Cruces, already stepping into the role of class clown, making a series of soft jokes about the "compound" that earned smiles from Bryce, fifteen, of Chicago, but they were nervous smiles.

Already she was handicapping them. Bryce looked uneasy and was trying hard to find a friend. Possible. Jeff and Drew both looked like they wanted to be on the first flight out, but Drew's expression carried more attitude problems. Jeff just looked scared.

Probably Jeff, she thought, and then she realized Ethan was watching her and she smiled at him and turned away, chastising herself.

It doesn't matter.

But it felt like it did. She was frustrated that they couldn't know, even if the logic for the decision was clear.

"Remember those cows we saw in the road?" Ethan said. "The feared mountain cows? They belong to my wife here."

"How do you just let them wander around in the highway?" the one named Raymond asked. "We had to honk to get them to move."

"Lease on public lands is cheap," Allison said with a smile. "What can I say? I like to save my dollars."

"How in the hell—"

"Language," Ethan said.

"Sorry. How do you get them *back*?"

"Cowboys do it," Allison said.

"*No shit?* Actual cow—"

"*Language,*" Ethan repeated. "Raymond, are we going to have a problem with this?"

Raymond shrugged. A faint smile played on his face. Allison looked at him and thought, *No, too confident, he's not scared, and the right one will be scared.* They were all white except for Marco, who was Hispanic. *A big drug case, maybe, or some kind of border killings, one of those smuggling rings you read about,* Allison thought, and then, right on the heels of that thought, *You racist bitch, did you actually just think that? What are you turning into over this?*

"Cowboys," Raymond said, and he shook his head and laughed. "You gotta be kidding me."

"Go on and get settled in the bunkhouse," Ethan told the boys. "There are sixteen bunks in there and only seven of you, so there shouldn't be much trouble finding a bed. We'll meet at four by the campfire over there. Get some rest, relax. Enjoy those mattresses. Soon you're going to be sleeping up there."

He pointed to where Pilot Peak and Index Peak loomed against the gray sky, and the boys looked up. Judging by their faces, you'd think they were staring at menacing stone monuments to the memory of those who had perished in the mountains before.

"We climb them?" Connor said.

"No, dude, we take the escalator." This from Marco, drawing laughs.

"We'll do some climbing," Ethan said. "But not on those bad boys. Not just yet. All right, get settled in, and then be at the fire at four sharp. We're going to review all of the gear you need for the trail. Anything you don't pack, you won't be able to use, so I'd suggest you listen good."

They hauled their luggage into the bunkroom. Most of them had suitcases or duffel bags; a few were already outfitted with backpacks. It was a small group, but that was intentional. Ethan's permits and insurance allowed him to be the sole instructor only with groups of eight or fewer. Get above eight, as he sometimes did, and he had to have an extra instructor.

When the boys were in the bunkhouse and it was just the two of them, Ethan turned to Allison and said, "I think it's Drew. Doesn't talk like he's from New England, which is supposedly his home, and definitely doesn't want to be here, but he's kind of curious about what we do."

She stared at him in astonishment, and he smiled and said, "Baby? It's human to wonder. We won't *try* to find out, but be honest with yourself. It's human to wonder."

She shook her head and sighed. "I'd like to know."

"No gain to knowing."

"Maybe there is."

"I don't see it."

She nodded.

"They have an hour," Ethan said. "And I'd like them to get some space. They need to start feeling each other out."

"You think you've got an hour till the first fight?"

"Let's hope so," he said, and then he took her hand and guided her inside the cabin.

They were in bed in the cabin, a stolen hour while the kids settled into the bunkhouse, and Allison lay there and traced the muscles in his chest with her fingernail and said, "Have you thought any more about it?"

"About what?" Ethan asked, and she took her hand away, rolled onto her back, and sighed, staring at the shadowed ceiling. Ethan missed the warmth of her immediately. A minute passed and then maybe five and finally she broke the silence.

"If someone comes for him," she said.

"They won't."

"But have you thought about it?"

He paused. He didn't know what she wanted to hear, but he decided to tell her the truth whether she wanted to hear it or not.

"Yes. And I think I'm ready if they come. But they won't."

"You could lose a lot, betting on that," she said. "Could lose it all."

"I won't lose it all."

"No? Something happens up there in the mountains, Ethan? Somebody takes a shot at one of those boys? You're done, then. Everything you've built is done."

"It won't happen, Allison."

She sighed again, and when he reached for her, she stayed motionless, unreceptive. The outline of her was visible in the dim room with the shades pulled and he could smell her hair and skin and he wanted to stop talking about this; their hours together in the summer were few and couldn't be wasted on argument.

"I can help him," he said, tracing the side of her breast and squeezing her hip. "Whichever one he is, I can help him."

Long ago, when Ethan left the Air Force after years working as a survival instructor in every climate known to man and made his home in the Montana mountains, he'd had an idea of what he wanted to do with his skills. The Air Force trained survival instructors in every elite branch of the military; if an Army Ranger told you he was a survival instructor, it meant he'd been through the Air Force program; same for the SEALs, same for everybody, no matter what unit or how elite. Ethan had done well with those types because he understood something that needed to be understood. They were bad sons of bitches, they could kill you with any weapon known to man or with no weapon at all if necessary, and his job was not to impress them or try to match them; his job was to make them proficient in yet a few more areas of combat, known as SERE: survival, evasion, resistance, and escape. And in those areas? Ethan was as good as anyone got.

One of the things he learned, teaching those warriors, was that a survivor had specific skills, and almost all of them were between the ears, a convergence of cognitive prowess and emotional control. Some of the muscled-up types had trouble with that. Others didn't. But in the attempt to instill those ideas, he became fascinated with the concept of whether someone could *build* a survivor mentality. Did you have to be born with it, carry it in some twisted strand of DNA, or could you learn it?

These were the things you had time to consider when you spent weeks in the desert, alone under a night sky so laden with stars it was hard to comprehend; or in the jungle, sleeping in a homemade hammock that kept you elevated from the insects that would otherwise devour your flesh; or in the Arctic, building a fortress out of ice blocks. What Ethan had decided, what he'd determined from years invested in the study and craft of survival, was that the gain could extend far beyond what he taught in the military. By now he'd helped teens from all around the country, in every circumstance imaginable, and he knew that he'd done good work, that he'd made a difference. You did the best you could, and you didn't hold your-self responsible for the ones you couldn't reach, because you couldn't reach them all. You had to acknowledge that early, had to let yourself accept that some would falter de-spite your best efforts. He could not get his head around that with this summer's special case, though. Whoever the boy was, Ethan wanted to make an impact. He believed that he could.

Beside him in their bed, his wife was still silent.

"Allison? Please."

She turned back to him then, rolling onto her side. Ran one hand up his arm and then held the side of his face, propping herself up on an elbow. Looking into his eyes.

"I'd feel better if there was more help," she said. "If you'd gotten a few people in here, just for these weeks. Reggie, maybe. He'd be good."

"Reggie's in Virginia. He's got his own thing."

"*Someone,* then. So it's not just you out there, alone."

"You know the agreement I made on this. I *have* to be alone."

"You're taking them into the mountains tomorrow. The first morning, and you're taking them up?"

"It's how it will need to go this summer. Not bad, just dif-ferent. I want my usual patterns disrupted. Just in case."

"You should have demanded someone else come along."

"I love you," Ethan said.

"That's sweeter than saying *end of discussion.* Even if it means the same thing."

"I love you," he repeated.

She leaned down and kissed him, then rested her forehead against his, and her lips grazed him when she spoke.

"I'll let it go. I won't speak of it again. You don't need it, and Lord knows, I don't need to beat my head on the chunk of granite that you like to call your *opinion*."

"Nasty tone, Miss Montana."

"Don't call me that."

"Sorry. I know you were only the runner-up."

Usually he could get a rise out of her with this, could turn anger to laughter. This afternoon, though, she was silent. He took her in his arms, pulled her on top of him, and still something was wrong. Tensed muscles where loose ones belonged. He put his hands on her sides and pushed her back, and now it was his turn to search for eye contact in the darkness.

"What's wrong?"

She shook her head. "I don't know. I just have a bad feeling. I can't put my finger on it. Maybe that's why it's so easy to worry about him. Whichever one *he* is. But it's more than that. I just…something doesn't feel right. I've been restless. Uneasy. Like something's on the way."

He laughed at her then, something that he would recall over and over in the days to come, the serious weight of her warning and how melodramatic it had sounded to him there in the darkened bedroom with her body pressed to his and the cabin full of warmth and wood smoke.

"You've been back to the folklore books?" he said. They were a favorite of hers, and she'd spoken countless times of her envy of those with the gift of premonitions, which was always a source of amusement to him, both that she believed in it and that she desired it. "What do you see, baby? Shade of the moon, shadow of a spider, the way the cat holds his tail?"

"No," she said. Her voice soft. "Nothing like that. But I feel it, all the same."

"I haven't gotten killed in these mountains yet," he said. "And it won't happen this year."

She was silent.

"Baby?" he said. "It…won't…happen."

"All right," she said. "All right." But her tone was still heavy and somber. He touched the side of her face gently and she kissed his palm and said it a third time. "All right, Ethan."

He meant to ask her more then, because she was so serious. Not that she would have had answers for a feeling that rose from someplace inexplicable or primal or, hell, maybe mystical, for all he knew. She slid her hands down his chest and over his stomach and found him, though, and then any questions that were on his lips faded, first within her cool palm and then within her warmth, and later she was asleep on his chest and he didn't want to disturb her, but he had to be out at the fire to meet the boys, so he slipped out quietly.

They did not speak of her unease again before he entered the mountains.

6

Jace Wilson was dead.

He'd perished in a quarry, and Connor Reynolds needed to keep that in mind. The hardest part of the new name wasn't remembering to identify himself by it; it was reacting when other people called him by it.

"Connor? Yo? Connor? You, like, coherent, dude?"

They were on the first trail day when the loud kid, Marco, started talking to him, and Jace was focused on the countryside around them, in awe of the sheer size of it. The distances were staggering. He'd hiked a lot in Indiana and thought he was familiar enough with the idea. There, though, you'd come up over a ridge and look ahead to the next point in the trail and then it would be maybe five, ten minutes until you were there. Up here it would be an hour, an exhausting, sweating-and-gasping hour, and you'd stop for a water break, turn around, and realize you could still see the place you'd started from. It looked like you weren't gaining any ground at all.

They were walking in a shallow gulch with mountains

looming high on each side, and he didn't mind looking at the peaks from down here. He'd been unnerved at the start, fearing they were going out on some sort of mountain-goat trail where a fall would be your death—even the highway had felt like that; he'd had to pretend he was asleep to keep from watching the switchbacks, with all the other kids awake and talking and laughing about it—but so far the trail hadn't been bad. Had been, honestly, pretty cool. And he felt safer out here, which was strange. Up in the mountains, he had the sense that nobody was going to sneak up on them. Certainly not on Ethan Serbin, who seemed to notice every out-of-place pine needle. So he was feeling pretty good, pretty secure, and then the loud kid started calling him by his new name, and he didn't respond.

By the fourth time Marco yelled the name, they were all watching him. Even Ethan seemed interested. Jace felt a panicking sensation that he'd blown it already, they were onto him, and he'd been reminded time and again that this was the only way it could go bad up here in the mountains. If he let anyone know the truth, let anyone know he wasn't who he was pretending to be, that was when the men from the quarry would arrive. He thought of them now and heard their voices in place of Marco's and as the panic rose, it brought with it the realization that he had to explain this somehow, come up with a reason he was ignoring this kid. He couldn't just say he was distracted or hadn't heard him. It wasn't enough. He had to play his role.

"If I wanted to talk to you," Jace said, staring right at Marco, "I would."

Marco pulled his head back, eyes wide. "The *fuck?* Hey, man, I—"

"Stop it!" Ethan Serbin thundered. "Both of you, stop

talking. Now. And you're going to owe me for the language, Marco. You'll enjoy that once we get back to camp. Hope you like gathering firewood. You can call the logs whatever you'd like."

"Man, this kid—"

Ethan held a hand up, silencing him. Everyone was still staring at Jace, and he felt exposed but tried to keep a tough expression, tried to look like what he was supposed to be: a problem kid with a bad attitude, worse than the rest of them. If he was the worst, they'd leave him alone.

"Connor? What's your problem today? Is there a reason you feel the need to disrespect your friends?"

Got to stick with it, Jace told himself, even though he hated acting the part in front of Ethan Serbin, who had this powerful way of showing disappointment through silence that reminded Jace of his dad. And Jace had to please his dad, because his father worked long hours and he worked in pain and he took pills to help but they never did. Jace had learned early that the more he did on his own, the more problems he fixed by himself, the better. It wasn't that his dad was mean, or angry all the time. It was that life hadn't been kind to him, so Jace tried to be.

So while the Jace half of him said, *Please, Ethan,* the Connor half of him said, *Give him what he thinks you are,* and Jace was smart enough to listen to that half.

"He's not my friend. We're not up here because we're friends. Or because we want to be. Everybody knows that."

It sounded good to him, sounded right. *Fit the part, fit the part.* That had been his dad's advice. Of course, a key element of fitting the part was remembering your own name.

"All right," Ethan Serbin said. "It's not your choice. I remember being deployed in more than a few places that weren't my choice either. And in a survival scenario, Connor? You think it'll be your *choice* if a plane goes down? Will that be anybody's *choice*?"

Jace shook his head.

"So we work with what we have," Ethan continued. "That's true with the elements, the weather, supplies, all of it. Certainly, it's true with your companions. You work with *who* you have. Not friends yet? Fine. Maybe you will be. Maybe not. But one thing we can't tolerate—because in a different situation it could get us killed—is disrespect. You keep disrespecting Marco, then how's he going to look at you when you *need* him? When you've got a broken leg and need him to haul your butt out of here? You think you're going to wish you'd shown him a little more respect then, a little more courtesy?"

Jace shrugged, trying to look sullen and unimpressed.

"I think you will," Ethan said. "And when the two of you work together to get all of our firewood tonight, him for his language, you for disrespect, maybe you'll consider that."

"Maybe," Jace said, still trying to show just enough attitude to get by. Ethan looked at him for a long time, and then he turned away.

The rest of them were all watching Jace, and Jace knew the look in their eyes and knew what it meant. He had seen it on Wayne Potter's face enough times. He was a target now, not just of the men from the quarry, but of the boys he was supposed to spend the summer with. All because he couldn't remember his own fake name.

"All right," Ethan Serbin said, "time for somebody to tell me where we are."

Ethan would do this often enough, stop abruptly and challenge their awareness of the land around them, but this

time Jace had the sense that he was doing it to draw the attention of the others away from him, as if Ethan, too, knew
that trouble was brewing.

"No maps, no compasses," Ethan said. "Tell me which
way we're facing."

They were facing a mountain. Behind them was a mountain. To their left and right, more mountains. Which direction? This should be easy enough. Jace looked for the
sun—was it rising or descending? That would tell him east
or west.

"What are you doing, Connor?" Ethan asked.

"Nothing."

"What were you looking at?" Ethan said patiently.

"The sun."

"Why?"

Jace shrugged again, still not willing to give up the attitude, and Ethan looked disappointed but didn't press him.

"Connor's instinct is the right one," he said.

"Good little Boy Scout," Marco whispered.

Yes, it would get bad from here.

"The sky will reorient us when we're lost," Ethan was
saying. "At night, you'll use the stars, and during the day,
the sun. But right now, I suspect Connor is a little confused.
Because where is the sun, guys?"

"Straight up," Drew said.

"Exactly. We know that it rises in the east and sets in the
west, so those times of day are easy. But right now? High
noon? How do we know which way we're facing?"

Nobody had an answer.

"The shadows will tell us," Ethan said. He lifted his hiking stick, a thin pole with telescoping sections to change the
length, and drove the tip into the dirt so that it was stick-

ing straight up out of the ground. "Drew, grab a stone and mark the shadow. The very end of it, the tip."

Drew dropped a flat stone where the shadow faded into dust.

"Two things we know are always true," Ethan said. "The sun will rise in the east, and it will set in the west. You could be having the worst day of your life, everything about the world might have just imploded on you, but, boys, the sun will still rise in the east and set in the west. And an object placed in the sun is going to make a shadow. You each have a shadow right now."

Jace felt an uneasy chill. No, they didn't each have just one shadow right now. Jace had his own, and he also had two others. They were out there somewhere in the world, and they intended to catch him.

"In the Northern Hemisphere, that means that shadows move clockwise," Ethan said. "So give the sun just a little time. We're going to wait on that shadow to move."

They stood around and sipped some water and waited on the shadow to move. Eventually it crept away from the stone and found the dusty earth beside it. Ethan ate some trail mix and stared at the ground patiently while everyone else fidgeted or gave up and sat down. Jace stayed on his feet, watching the shadow.

"Okay," Ethan said at last. "Drew, mark it again, with another stone."

Drew laid a second stone beside the first. They were nearly touching. Ethan pulled his hiking pole from the dirt and laid it across the stones, then knelt and withdrew a long-bladed knife from its sheath on his belt. He laid the knife across the hiking stick so that the tip of its blade was at right angles to the hiking stick.

"Take a look now," he said. "What does this setup look like to you?"

"A compass," Ty said. "Four points, four different directions."

Ethan nodded in approval. "And we know what about the sun? It will never lie to us about what?"

"How it's moving," Ty said. "East to west."

"Exactly. We watched it move just a little bit, not enough to tell us much if we'd just stared up at it, but by using the shadows, we have one stone marking the general east, and another marking the general west. Those directions give us the others, of course. So somebody tell us which way we are facing."

"North," Jace said. The knife blade pointed north.

"You got it. Now, this is hardly as precise as a compass, but it will give you the cardinal directions. And if you ever put your stick in the ground and don't see a shadow at all, that means the sun is due south. You might not see the shadow, but it is still telling you the directions."

They began hiking again, and the incident with Marco was gone from Jace's mind; he was hiking along and thinking of the men from the quarry and comparing what he remembered of them with what he knew of Ethan Serbin. He thought that if anyone had a good chance against those two, it was probably Ethan. The problem, as Jace saw it, was simply a matter of numbers: two against one. The odds would be in his hunters' favor if they came. But maybe out here in his element, Ethan Serbin was good enough that it evened the odds. Maybe he'd see them coming, be aware of them before they were aware of him, and that would turn things in Ethan's favor. If it came to that—and Jace had been promised that it wouldn't—he felt that he should probably tell Ethan who he was. His only instruction was to be Connor, but if the men from the quarry arrived, instructions wouldn't matter. He'd need to be part of the team then, he'd need to help Ethan work with—

When Jace's feet went out from under him, he had his head up and his hands gripping the pack straps. He wasn't prepared, and he fell forward onto the rocks, a little cry coming out, not from pain but from surprise. By the time Ethan and the others looked back, he was already down, and nobody up front had seen what had happened: Marco had tripped him.

"You all right?" Ethan said.

"Yes." Jace was back on his feet, brushing the dirt off and trying to show no pain. It hadn't been a bad fall, and ordinarily he would have been able to catch himself without really going down, but the weight of the pack was new and threw off his balance, so he'd landed hard. There was a warm wet pulse below his knee that had to be blood. His ripstop pants hadn't torn, though, so the bleeding was hidden from Ethan's eyes.

"What happened?"

Ethan was already looking past him, back to those kids in the rear of the line, Marco and Raymond and Drew.

"Just tripped," Jace said, and now Ethan's eyes returned and focused on him.

"Just tripped?"

Jace nodded. Marco was standing right behind him; he had made a big show of helping him up and then hadn't stepped back, was so close Jace could smell his sweat.

"All right," Ethan said, turning away and starting to walk again. "We have our first man down. Let's talk a little about how we walk, and how we land when we fall. That second part is the most important. Remember that the pack doesn't affect just your balance, it affects how hard you go down, so if you can, try to—"

Marco whispered, "Stay on your feet, faggot," into Jace's ear as they marched along, and Raymond and Drew laughed. Jace didn't say a word. His right calf was warm with blood, and drops of it showed now on his boot.

Your own fault, he told himself. *You can't even remember your name.*

He kept his head down and counted the drops of blood as they appeared on his boot, and with each fresh drop, he reminded himself of his new name.

Connor. Connor. Connor. I am Connor, and I am bleeding, I am Connor, and I am alone, I am Connor, and two men want me dead, I am Connor, and Jace is gone, Jace is gone for good.

I am Connor.

7

THEY WATCHED THROUGH A MODIFIED gun sight as the boys hiked, watched them in silence and marked their course on the map, then took their bearing and heading.

"That's the basics," the bearded twenty-something-year-old named Kyle said. "Of course, if it's smoke, you've got a lot more to report. Not just the bearing."

Hannah Faber straightened and stepped away from the Osborne fire-finder and nodded, wetting her lips and looking at the door of the fire-tower cab and wishing that Kyle would walk out through it and leave her here alone, wishing he could grasp that if there was anything she did not need coaching on, it was Wildland Fire 101. His words washed over her: he had worked for the forest service for two years and was tired of the grunt labor they offered him and had thought this would be relaxing, a chance to maybe do some writing, he knew he had a novel in him or maybe a screenplay but sometimes poems seemed best...

All of this poured out of him as asides as he took her on a tour of the place, which certainly didn't need much commentary. Bed here, table there, woodstove. Check, check, check. The closer he got to her and the more he talked, it seemed as if she could actually feel the nerves fraying inside her, peeling in overstretched threads, not much left. Fire season. It was back and it was close. She wanted to be alone.

He'll be gone soon, she told herself. *Just make it through a few more minutes.*

Kyle had stopped talking and was eyeing her pack, and that annoyed her. Sure, it was only a backpack, but it held the contents of her life, and Hannah had grown awfully private about her life in the past ten months.

"Some damn serious boots you brought to sit up here," Kyle said.

Tied to the back of her pack was a pair of White's fireline boots. To those who laid trench lines and swung Pulaskis, they were the stuff of legend. She'd tried to save some money the first year by buying cheap boots, only to have them blow out within two months, and then she followed the lead of the experienced crew members and bought the White's. The pair on her pack was brand-new, waiting for action they would never see. She knew it was stupid to have brought them, but she couldn't leave them behind.

"I like nice boots," she said.

"I've heard women say that. Usually talking about a little different look, though."

She managed a faint smile. "I'm a little different woman."

"You spend a lot of time in this area?"

"Been up a few times," she said. "Let's get to it, shall we? You were going to talk me through the radio protocol."

Then it was on to the radio, his eyes away from her pack and from the fire boots. Finally they moved to the topographic maps on a chart table.

"When you see smoke, you call it in. So your first job is to see it, obviously, and then you have to give them the right position. That's where this little thing comes in." He indicated the Osborne again, which was essentially a round glass table with a topographic map underneath it. On the outside of it were two rings, one fixed and one that rotated. The rotating ring carried a brass sighting device, just like a gun sight.

"Harder to demonstrate with no active fire," Kyle said. "That's why we used that camping group or those Boy Scouts or whoever they are. Think you can find the mountain they were hiking beneath on your own?"

She found it again. Immediately.

"Good work," Kyle said. "Now comes the harder part. Try to guess, without using the map, what distance they are from us."

Hannah stared out the window and off to the south, locating the peak above the group, and while she didn't look at the map, the map was in her mind. She studied the mountain, let her eyes trace a creek running down from it, and said, "Seven miles."

"Seven?" Kyle smiled. "You like to be precise, right? Well, you'll like Ozzy, then."

"Ozzy?"

He shrugged. "You get bored up here, you start nick-naming shit, I don't know. Point is, it will let you be a lot more precise. Here." He rotated the bezel of the table and lined the brass sight up with the group of hiking boys again. She knelt and peered through, taking the boys in as a whole, not wanting to focus on any particular one—she couldn't have the memories that might shake loose, absolutely could *not* revisit those memories here, in front of him.

"Okay. Got them."

"Great. That was fast. Now pretend they're not a group of kids but a fire. Something in there could burn you. You're flustered, you're scared, something out there is *dangerous*. You're pointing at a hundred and sixty-one degrees, see that? So now you know it's at a hundred and sixty-one degrees from your tower. Now look at the map and show me where you think it's burning."

She studied the topographic map, its gradients showing elevation changes, and found the most visible peak near the blaze, then worked down and pointed with her index finger.

"Around there?"

"Pretty close. Actually…wow, that's real close. An inch is two miles on that map. Use the ruler there and tell me how many inches it is from us."

It was just a shade under three and a half inches. Seven miles.

"Damn," Kyle said softly. "Good guess."

She allowed a smile. "I've watched some smoke in the past."

"In towers?"

"No."

"Where, then?"

"Hotshot crew."

He tilted his head. "And now you want a tower?"

She'd said too much. Her pride had reared up, but it had been a mistake to mention the crew, because now Kyle understood. He'd listened to enough radio traffic to understand the food chain. When the regular-hand crews got into a blaze they couldn't handle, the hotshots would roll, and the only ones higher up on the food chain than them were the smokejumpers. Bunch of guys parachuting in behind walls of flame. *Cheaters,* Hannah had said to Nick once, watching them descend. *We had to walk our asses in here.*

Nick had laughed hard at that. He'd had a beautiful laugh. At night, she went to sleep hoping that his laugh would come to her in her dreams instead of the screams.

It never did.

She kept her eyes away from Kyle's when she said, "Yeah, the fire line is more than I can handle these days. So, listen, when I see the fire, I call it in, and what else?"

"Hang on," he said. "Hang on. You're Hannah Faber, aren't you? Were you at Shepherd Mountain last year?"

"There were a lot of fires last summer," she said. "I was part of some of them."

He must have sensed her desire to short-circuit the conversation, because he ducked his head and spoke briskly. "You'd report the distance and heading. That way, when they send a plane out for a look, they can pinpoint it easily. Then you use this breakdown to clarify for them."

He showed her a clipboard that contained checklists of information for each sighting—the distance, the bearing, nearby landmarks, and then three categories of information about the smoke:

Volume: small, medium, large

Type or character: thin, heavy, building, drifting, blanket

Color: white, gray, black, blue, yellow, coppery

"You report all that," he said, "and then you sit back and listen to them sort it out."

"No bad ones yet?"

"None. Late-season snow helped. But it melted fast, and it's dried out since then. Temperatures started climbing, and the wind started blowing. No rain. If that holds, they think it'll be a busy season. Lately the winds have been up. Trust me, you'll feel that. This thing seems solid until the wind starts to blow. Then it'll sway on you pretty good. So if the weather keeps on like this? Yeah, it'll be busy. Supposed to be a run of storms early next week. If those develop, it could be trouble."

He was right. You would think rain would help, but thunderstorms were trouble. They were sitting on top of the world here. Lightning didn't have to travel all that far to make contact. And when it made contact with dry timber...

"Could be a busy summer," Hannah said. Her heart was beginning to hammer now. He was standing too close to her, making the small room feel smaller. She wet her lips and took a step back. "Listen, I don't want to be rude, but I've had a long walk out here and—"

"You want me out?"

"No, I'm just saying...I'm good here. I understand it, you know? And I'm tired."

"Okay," he said. "Guess I'll get on the trail, then. You're sure I didn't rush you too much? I was supposed to show you all of the—"

"I'll figure it out. And I love it up here already."

He gave a wry smile. "Get through a night before you say that, okay?"

She ignored that and returned to the Osborne, peered through the gun sight and, because there was no smoke on the peaks, located the group of hikers once again. She watched them plod along and she pretended that they were fire.

8

Connor Reynolds was a different kid than Jace Wilson, and as the days passed, that began to take on a certain appeal.

The kid he had to pretend to be now was the kind of kid he'd always wanted to be. Tough, for one. Fearless, for another. Jace had spent his life trying to be good and fearing the trouble that would follow if he slipped up. His parents had split when he was so young, he hardly remembered it. Two years later came the accident, a chain on a forklift letting go, a pallet falling, his dad earning a life of eternal pain in a few quick seconds because of somebody else's mistake. He still had a job at the same warehouse, a foreman now, but the pain followed him and so did the mistake. His obsessiveness with procedure had seeped into Jace, who knew he came across to people as a nervous kid — double-checking locks, insisting on using seat belts in the third row of a friend's parent's SUV, reading the instructions on a model-plane kit five times before he even opened the bag of parts.

He knew how he seemed to people. The kind word was *cautious*. The mean one (real one?) was *scared*.

But Connor Reynolds was not scared. Connor was *supposed to be* a bad kid. There was a kind of freedom in that. You could say what you wanted, act how you wanted. Jace tried to embrace it without pushing it. He didn't want to draw attention, and, truth be told, he didn't want to get his ass kicked. After the initial flare-up with Marco, Jace had kept his distance and given him enough respect to appease him, evidently. He tried to do it without showing any fear, though. Kept his sullen stares and silence. The longer he wore them, the better he felt.

He was glad to be out of the camp and on the trail too. He always felt better on the trail, felt like he was vanishing, every trace of Jace Wilson disappearing, nothing left but Connor Reynolds. Today, Ethan was telling them about bears, and everyone was listening, even the loudmouths like Marco, because all of them were scared of bears. It almost made Jace laugh. If the other boys had had any idea who might be following them, they wouldn't have given a crap about any bears.

"When we come into a blind curve or a dark area, one of these thick stands of trees, or when we break out of them and into a meadow, we want to advertise our arrival," Ethan was saying. "Talk a little louder, give a few claps, make your presence known by sound. They're more eager to avoid us than we are to avoid them, believe it or not. They'll have no problem with us hiking through their territory, assuming we understand them. That's our job. In this situation, understanding them is largely limited to one word: *surprise*. We do not want to surprise the bear, because then he will not have the chance to react with his true personality. He'll turn aggressive even though he'd prefer to be passive, because he will feel that's what we're forcing him to do. So we make a little noise to advertise our presence in the right areas, and we pay attention to our surroundings so we don't go into areas that we should avoid."

"All our surroundings look the same to me," Ty said.

"They won't in time. And it requires all of your senses. All of them. You watch, of course, you keep scanning the landscape. Drew, back there, he's key, because he's guarding the rear for us. He's got to turn around and double-check for us now and then."

Drew seemed to puff up at that, and Jace wondered if he realized that being the guy in the back also meant you were the first guy the bear ate.

"We have to listen," Ethan said, "because the last thing we want to run into is a tangle between bears, and if that's happening, we should be able to hear it. We have to use our sense of smell—"

"You can probably smell bears at, what, two miles? Three miles?" This was from Ty, another of the jokers, contending with Marco, and he said it seriously but while winking at Connor, who gave him dead eyes in response. Jace Wilson would have laughed, but Connor Reynolds wasn't a laugher.

"I cannot smell bears," Ethan said, "but I can smell crap. That helps. Sometimes, you see, a bear takes a crap in the woods. I'll let you check it out as soon as we find one, Ty. I'll give you plenty of inspection time."

Now Jace really wanted to laugh, and the rest of them did laugh, but he stayed silent. He'd decided that was Connor Reynolds—strong and silent. And fearless.

"I'm also interested in the smell of something rotten,"

Ethan continued. "A carcass gone bad. If I can smell it, you better believe a bear can—they actually *can* detect odors from over a mile away—and we need to stay far from that, because what smells nasty to us smells like a free meal to them. No hunting required. Bears are lazy; they appreciate free meals. We'll be talking *a lot* about this once we set up camp and store the food."

"That's three senses," Jeff said. He was one of the few who'd dared to express any real interest so far; the rest were maintaining their wilderness-camp-is-bullshit attitudes, for the most part. "And if I have to taste one or touch one to know it's a bear, I'm a pretty huge dumb-ass."

The rest of them burst into laughter, and even Ethan Serbin smiled with them.

"I won't argue that point, language aside," he said. "But you might taste a few berries along the trail. Might see a thicket of berries and try one and think, *Dang, these taste pretty good.* Remember—if it tastes good to you, it does to the bear as well. Be more alert, because you are in a feeding ground."

"What about touch, then?" Jeff asked.

"Feel the wind. Always, always, always be aware of that wind. Because bears rely mostly on their sense of smell, and if you are downwind of them, you're going to be able to get pretty close before they can smell you. What else is wind taking away from them?"

"The sound of us," Jace said, and regretted it immediately. He wanted to avoid all attention, but sometimes out here he got caught up in things despite himself. This was the sort of thing he loved, which was where the whole idea had come from. All the survival books, the adventure stories, the way he'd taught himself how to tie more than thirty knots with his eyes closed—his parents thought that they could hide him up here and have him be happy. And, he had to admit, there were moments when they were almost right.

Then the voices of the men in the quarry would return.

"Exactly," Ethan said. "We always need to be aware of which way the wind is blowing. That's a help with bears, but it's critical to everything we do. We set up camp based on the way the wind is blowing, we anticipate weather changes based on what the wind does, we build our fires with the utmost respect for the wind. If you do not respect the wind in the backcountry, you will not last long."

It was interesting, hearing all of the things that Ethan Serbin held in his mind. Jace was paying attention all the time, because if the killers came for him, he wanted to be ready. They'd come expecting Jace Wilson, the scared kid, and they'd run into somebody new: Connor Reynolds, who could make it on his own in the woods, who could outlast them. Connor Reynolds, a survivor. That's who he was now.

Montana was better than the safe houses, better than being surrounded by people who *knew* you were in danger. That just fed the fear. They'd thrown every distraction they could at him, from movies to music to video games, and none of them worked, because none of them could pull his mind away from those memories, a dead man's hair fanning out in the dim quarry waters, a knife tugging through the muscles of a throat, and, above all, a pair of oddly musical voices discussing where Jace might be and whether they had time to find him and kill him.

This was better. He hadn't believed that it would be, because he'd be out here without anyone he knew, but he'd been wrong. Montana was better because it forced distraction. Video games and movies hadn't been able to claim his mind. Out here, the land *demanded* his mind leave the memories. He had to concentrate on the tasks of the moment. There were too many hard things to do for any other option.

Connor Reynolds marched along the trail, and Jace Wilson rode secretly inside of him, and both of them were safe.

There were times, in the first week, when it felt like any other summer to Ethan. Or better, even. A good group of kids, by and large. He watched them and enjoyed them and tried not to think too much about the one who was there to hide. He'd heard nothing from Jamie Bennett, and that was good. Things were going smooth on her end, and he expected them to remain smooth on his.

They spent the first five nights at camps in five different meadows within a mile of their base. This was not the way it usually went. In a standard summer, the boys always slept in the bunkhouse, not on the trail, during the first week, allowing them some time to adjust and, hopefully, form bonds—sometimes they did, often they did not. Every day they went into the mountains, but every night they returned.

Not this summer. This summer they returned briefly by day and were back into the dark mountains by night because Ethan refused to be lulled into complacence by any promise of security he had been given. He believed Jamie Bennett, and he believed the summer would pass without incident. But he'd been tasked with being prepared and he did not take that lightly.

In an ordinary summer, he'd have more boys and a second counselor out here, and his route and campsites would be known to the county sheriff and shared with Allison on a GPS tracking device. This summer, he'd instructed the sheriff to speak to Allison if he needed to reach Ethan, and he'd turned off the computer tracking on his GPS. It still had a messaging function, allowing him to reach her through short text messages, but even his wife would be unaware of his precise location.

During those first days, they discussed first aid, studied with topographic maps and compasses, did all of the classroom work that Ethan knew they'd forget the instant they were in trouble on the trail. You couldn't replicate the wilderness, though Ethan did try. His favorite exercise was a game he called the Wilder—a mispronunciation of an archaic word that was supposed to be pronounced "will-der." Over the years he'd given up on saying it correctly, because the altered version felt right.

He explained the origin of *bewildered*. The word that described that sense of confusion and disorientation did not come from a term meaning "incomprehension" or "surprise" but from the same root word as *wilderness*. Those who were lost in a frightening and foreign land were the bewildered. Or they had been, back when wilderness was so common as to demand its own words for the experience of being lost in it. The word had been hijacked by civilization, of course, as everything had been. You could now say you'd been *bewildered* during a text-message exchange. But the term could be traced back to the verb *wilder*. That was the act of intentionally leading people astray, of causing them to become lost and disoriented.

When he started the game, Ethan would pick one of the boys and say, "All right, you're the wilder for the day. See what you can do."

The boy's job was simple: Lead the group off trail in whatever direction he chose, for whatever reason he chose. Keep on going until Ethan brought it to a stop. Then Ethan would turn to the others, who were generally pissed off and irritated by the route that had been chosen—it was *far* more fun to be the wilder than to follow him—and he'd ask them to lead the way back.

This would begin with bungled efforts involving the maps and compasses. It rarely led anywhere good. They'd progress day by day, learning to read the terrain as they went, learning to create a mental archive of key landmarks, points of change. Learn little tricks, such as the rule that almost everyone, when faced with the choice between climbing and going downhill, went downhill. This was unwise, because hiking through a drainage was a hell of a lot more difficult than walking a ridgeline, but it was the standard choice of inexperienced woodsmen.

The game was useful prep for Ethan as well, useful for the real search-and-rescue calls, because he had the chance to watch how the boys reacted to the unfamiliar, to watch the mistakes in live action, and to understand the reasons for them. In the course of a game he demonstrated all the critical mistakes he had seen over the years, showed them how simple slips could become deadly, and taught them how to recover from the mistakes they made. Anticipate and recover, anticipate and recover. If you could do the first well, you were ahead of most people. If you could do both well? You were a survivor.

Some of the boys loved it. Some rolled their eyes. Some bitched and moaned the entire way. That was fine. The lessons were being ingrained, slowly but surely. Today they'd been at it for four hours straight, stumbling through the brush and learning fast just how difficult this country was to traverse when you got off trail, and they were thoroughly worn out when they got to the campsite he'd selected.

"Burning daylight," he said. "We have to get shelters up."

Groans in response; the kids were stretched out on the ground, sucking air.

"We're all tired," he said. "But we don't rest right now. Because, of the priorities of survival, shelter is number three. Positive mental attitude is number one. We understand that. But without shelter, gentlemen? Without shelter, you're going to be corpses. Proper shelter will keep you alive. Anyone remember the chain? The order of our priorities?"

The wind was beginning to push a little harder as the sun went down, putting a nice chill in the air, and he could see that the last thing any of them wanted was a lecture. That was fine, though. They had to remember these things.

"Jeff?" Ethan said, going right at one of the quiet boys, forcing him to engage.

"Food," Jeff said.

"No." Ethan shook his head. "Food is *last,* in fact. Ask most people to rank things you need in a survival situation, and they'll say water first, and food second. But the reality is, your body can go a hell of a long time without food, and it can go awhile without water. Certainly, it can go long enough for you to die by other means."

He unfolded one of the small sheets of ten-mil plastic they had all been given. A painter's drop cloth, essentially. The best portable emergency shelter that ever existed.

"Positive mental attitude, wilderness first aid, shelter, fire, signal, water, food," he said. "Obviously, you need to deal with medical problems immediately. But then we need shelter. With shelter, we can stay warm and dry, or cool and dry, while we prepare to deal with the rest of our needs. With shelter, the environment is no longer in control."

They began the shelter-building lesson then, and he watched them regard their thin sheets of plastic with skepticism. But when he used the parachute cord to create a center-pole line and then stretched the plastic over it, they began to see the classic tent shape and started to understand. He used the button technique to make an anchoring device; this involved placing a small rock or even a squeezed handful of soil at a corner of the plastic, looping the plastic around it with a slipknot, and tying it off to a stake, which would hold that corner of the sheeting in place.

"Anyone have an idea why we'd do that instead of simply cutting a hole in the plastic and tying it off that way?" he asked.

Connor got it. Connor was one of the few in the group who was paying attention wholeheartedly. Good with his hands too, mechanically inclined; his shelter actually demonstrated proper angles, while some of the others looked like downed parachutes that had been stuck in the trees.

"If this was really all we had," Connor said, "we wouldn't want to risk cutting it up. It's harder to put it back together. This keeps us from needing to."

"Exactly. I learned this one from an Air Force instructor named Reggie. Stole it and claimed it as my own. All of the good stuff I stole from somebody else."

A few of them smiled. They were getting a little energy back. It was hard work just walking up here, far harder than they'd anticipated. The backpacking was arduous, and in addition, they were camping at nine thousand feet; for many, it was their first experience with thin air. You'd take a deep breath, intending to fill your lungs, and realize with confusion that you seemed to have filled only about a quarter of your lungs.

He watched as they built their shelters, offering advice when it was needed and lifting his head and scanning the forested hills when it wasn't. They gathered more firewood, and then Ethan took them down to collect water from one of the creek runoffs. Once they'd filled all of their water containers, he passed out chlorine dioxide tablets, a single-stage purifier, and they measured out the water and dropped in the appropriate number of tablets and recorded the time.

"Safe to drink in four hours," he said.

Raymond regarded the dissolving tablet in the container, unscrewed the top of his own water bottle, and sniffed.

"Smells like chlorine, dude."

"It's a form of chlorine, dude."

"I'm supposed to drink pool water? No, thanks."

"You want to drink the stream water instead?"

Raymond eyed the stream skeptically, the water running over green algae and carrying mud and silt down to the creek.

"Don't really like my options, man. But I don't want to drink any chlorine."

"Fair enough. Now, there's always a chance you'll find some cryptosporidia in these creeks. Unlikely, up here so high, but you never know."

"Crypto-what?"

"It'll give you mud butt," Ethan said affably. "But if you don't mind that, I'm sure the rest of the group won't."

THOSE WHO WISH ME DEAD

"Mud butt?"

"You'll crap your pants," Ethan said. "But again, it's up to you."

"I'll take the chlorine," Raymond said.

Ethan smiled. "Not a bad choice."

They dined on MREs, the military-developed "meals ready to eat." The combat component of the food intrigued some of them, at least, and they were impressed by the way you could pour just a few ounces of water in the plastic pouch, fold it over, and then, after the chemical reaction did its magic, you had a hot meal. Most of them gave unkind reviews to the cuisine, but all of them ate. It had been a hard walk and they were hungry.

"Good day?" Ethan asked.

"Long day," Drew answered. He had flopped on the ground and was lying there, exhausted, and most of them had matched his posture, staring at the fire through fatigued eyes. They'd hiked just over ten miles to get here, crossing out of Montana and into Wyoming. It didn't seem so much, ten miles in a day, until you added in the elevation changes and the terrain and the pack.

"We climbing again tomorrow?" Marco asked.

"For a bit. Then we get to go down. But in the morning, we have some *up* yet to handle."

They all groaned in unison. The groaning faded to conversation of aching legs and blistered feet, and Ethan leaned back against a rock and stared at the night sky as the boys talked and the fire crackled. A nearly full moon left the tops of the surrounding peaks and pines clearly silhouetted and then melted into shadow at the creek basin below. Behind them, the moon picked up the slope clearly, and so the climb away from the place they were now and the places they had been seemed less foreboding, because it was il-luminated. But that was merely a tease of the moonlight, because they still didn't know what was ahead.

For a moment, though, as the boys began to fall asleep, Ethan felt as if he could see it all.

9

A CHAIN SAW WAS A BEAUTIFUL TOOL.
When it worked. And in Claude Kitna's experience, the damned things didn't work too often.

A mechanically inclined man, Claude took personal umbrage at his chain-saw failures. Probably because he knew the reason for them damn well and just didn't want to admit it. He'd never purchased a new model; he'd always bought them used, to save some dollars, and he should have acknowledged to himself along the way that a man rarely sells something that works problem-free, and if he does, he surely doesn't sell it at a discount.

Now Claude was working with a battered five-year-old Husqvarna that he'd snagged over the winter for just a hundred bucks, which was such a good deal that he'd talked himself out of breaking down and buying a new one. First cut of the summer, and he was already turning the air blue over the thing.

There was good firewood in the ridge above his cabin,

where a few hardwoods had died the previous summer, some sort of blight. He'd waited until there was a good dry week and he had a day off and then he loaded the chain saw into the back of his ATV and went on up to get to work, figuring he'd have at least four cords, his winter taken care of before summer even ended.

On the third cut, the blade had pinched and nearly stuck, and he'd checked the bar oil and everything looked fine, so he went back at it, the harsh whine of the chain saw the only sound on the mountain, everything still and baked by the sun, a beautiful afternoon for some outdoor work.

The next time the blade caught, he shut the engine down fast, but not fast enough—the chain pulled right off the bar. That set him to swearing, and by the time he had the carburetor cover off and realized the chain-tensioning screw was gone entirely, he was truly in foul spirits. He was hunched over the chain saw, still wearing his ear protection, and he had no idea that he wasn't alone until he saw the shadows.

Two of them, man-shaped but not man-size, because the slope faced west and so at this time of day, the sun spread the shadows out large, turning them into a pair of giants. When he pivoted to find the source, he saw two strangers of nearly equal size standing about ten feet apart. Similar-looking too, both men blond-haired and blue-eyed and square-jawed. They were on his land, and he was doing nothing wrong, but there was something about the way they stood and studied him that brought a sense of authority to them, and as he took off his ear protection, he found himself asking, "Everything all right, fellas?" instead of saying, *Who in the hell are you?*

"Seems to be struggling with the chain saw," the one with longer hair said, and Claude was just about to acknowledge the obvious truth of it when the other one spoke.

"He surely seems to be, yes. Not much progress made yet either."

Claude blinked at them. That was a hell of a strange way of talking.

"Can I help you?" he said.

"With any luck," the long-haired one said. "Would you be Claude Kitna?"

"That's my name and this is my property. Now who are you?"

The man looked over the mountainside as if the answer were hidden in the rocks.

"I see no need to hide a name," he said. "Do you?"

Again, Claude was about to answer when the second man spoke.

"There's no harm in it."

They were some sort of strange, no doubt about that. Claude wiped a greasy palm dry on his jeans, wishing he'd brought his weapon and his badge, though he wasn't exactly sure why.

"I'm Jack," the first man said, "and this is my brother, Patrick. Now we're all acquainted."

"Terrific," Claude said. "And I'm the sheriff here. Maybe you weren't aware of that."

"We certainly are."

"All right. What are you doing on my land?"

He couldn't see his house from this spot on the ridge. Surely they'd driven up, but he didn't recall hearing an engine. With the ear protection in and the chain saw whining, though, it was possible he'd missed it. That was the only reason they'd been able to just appear out of the woods like that, two huge and silent shadows.

"You're police, as you mentioned," the one named Patrick said. "Have many accident calls down along that highway, Two-Twelve? A nasty stretch of road."

"Imposing," his brother agreed with a nod. Claude didn't like either of them, but he felt like he needed to pick one to focus on, because they stood an odd distance apart and circled around a little as they talked. He chose the young guy, the military-looking one.

"You put your car off the road?"

"No, sir. We remain firmly planted on the asphalt, thank you."

"You got a funny way with words," Claude said.

"I apologize."

"Don't need an apology. Also don't need my time wasted. Now, tell me what in the hell you're doing here." Claude straightened up, the chain-saw blade in his hands. It made for a piss-poor weapon, just a long, oily string of teeth that weren't even particularly sharp and didn't do much damage unless they were buzzing. As blades went, this one wasn't much use once you had it removed from the motor. Couldn't stab with it, couldn't slash with it. All the same, he wanted something in his hands.

"We have an interest in a car that ran into some trouble on Two-Twelve during the last snow," the longhair, Jack, said. "A rental. Hertz, I believe."

Claude could see her then, the tall woman with the lead foot, and he had a sudden, sure sense that this had turned into a dangerous day.

"Lot of accidents on Two-Twelve in the snow," he said.

"And I don't discuss the details with anyone who hasn't got a badge."

"Should we show him a badge?" Patrick said.

"We certainly could. I'm not sure which variety would impress him most, though."

"That's the problem with our collection. I've told you this before."

"I've heard the argument. All the same, I like to hold on to them."

The men were far enough apart now that Claude had to turn his head to see one or the other; he couldn't keep them both in sight. His palms were sweating, and the sweat mixed with the grease on the chain-saw blade and made it slippery. He wiped one palm on his jeans and tightened his grip.

"Gentlemen, I'm going to ask you to leave my property. If you have a question about a car accident, I don't give a shit if you're Hertz adjusters or FBI agents, you'll direct it through headquarters. Am I understood?"

"Her car was on the road overnight," the long-haired one said. "And she didn't spend those hours in the snowdrifts. You know where she went, Claude?"

Somehow, Claude knew that repeating his instruction wasn't going to be worth anything. So instead he answered the question.

"I have no idea. Might check the hotels."

"I think you do have an idea. The tow-truck driver remembers you calling someone to come get her. A man on a snowmobile? The tow-truck operator was quite certain you'd know who that was." The long-haired one took a breath and lifted his right index finger, tilting his head as if he'd just recollected some forgotten detail. "By the way—he's dead."

"Oh, yes," the other one said. "He is indeed. Excellent thought, Jack. It was incumbent upon us to notify the authorities of his passing."

"Consider it done, Patrick."

Claude felt himself begin to tremble then. Like a damn dog. Something gone so wrong in the world that he'd literally begun to shake? What in the hell was the matter with him? He took a shifting step sideways to stop the tremors. He'd seen plenty of hard men, never once had to keep himself from shaking in their presence, not even when he was young and green. These two, though...

They aren't joking, he thought. *Roger is dead, and they've done it, and they aren't scared of telling you this. The idea of consequence isn't a notion with which they are familiar.*

When the one called Jack removed a semiautomatic handgun from a holster at his spine, Claude let the chainsaw blade fall free and lifted his hands. What else was there to do?

"Come on, now," he said. "Come on."

"Pick that blade back up and pass it to my brother."

Claude looked toward his house, not so far away but screened by all those pines. And empty too. There was no help coming, but still, to be so close to home and yet so helpless felt wrong.

"Nobody's going to save you today," the one with the gun said, reading Claude's thoughts. "Now, pick up that blade and pass it to my brother."

When Claude bent to retrieve it, he knew what he had to do. Go down swinging, by God. He'd be damned if he'd simply stand here with his hands in the air and let a pair of boys like these do what they wanted to him. Claude Kitna had lived too many proud years to end them like that. The chain-saw blade wasn't much but it was what he had, and if he moved fast enough…

In his mind, it played out better. He was going to lunge upward and whip the blade at the son of a bitch's face, and it was likely the trigger would be pulled then, but at least he'd have the man on his heels. If he missed with the shot, and Claude got the gun, things could change mighty fast. It was going to be a matter of speed, and though he was no longer a young man, he wasn't an old one either, not a man without a burst left in him. Claude bent slow and gathered the blade from one end and then moved, sudden as a panther, whipping it backward and then lashing it forward.

Only the blade didn't lash with him. It stayed back, the free end caught in the other man's fist. Claude didn't want to let go, it was the only weapon he had, and so he hung on and stumbled after it, right into the man's foot, and tripped and fell on his ass, and this time he lost the blade. Claude was down then, unarmed, staring up at them, the two giant shadows turned to two average-size men but now twice as menacing.

"The man on the snowmobile? What was his name?" The long-haired man with the gun was speaking, and his brother looked disinterested, studying the chain-saw blade and blowing on it to clear bits of dust. There was blood pooling in his palm but he didn't seem to care.

"I ain't saying it," Claude told him. He made sure he looked right into the son of a bitch's face, right into his arrogant blue eyes. "Not ever. Not to the likes of you."

"'Not to the likes of you.' Very good, Claude. Very tough. Do you prefer to be called Sheriff? I can respect your authority if you wish. Is that the reason this isn't going well? Is it a perceived lack of respect?"

"Leave now," Claude said. "Just go on down the road and whatever this is, take it with you. It'll be trouble otherwise."

"Trouble has arrived, you are correct. Trouble will leave with us, you are also correct. But Sheriff? Claude? We won't be leaving until we have what we've come for. So put any notion of our leaving without it far, far from your mind. Focus on reality here. Reality is standing before you and reality has a gun. So you focus on that, and then we'll try again. Tell us the man's name."

"Go to hell."

The long-haired man smiled and said, "Ethan Serbin. That's his name."

Claude was puzzled. All of this, the threats and the violence against an officer of the law, for what? A name they already knew?

"There you go," he said. "You're smart boys. Don't need any help from me."

"Ethan Serbin," the long-haired one said, "usually has a group of boys on his property. Troubled boys, delinquents. The kind that the local sheriff would have to be aware of. The boys are gone, they are in the mountains, it seems, and considering that these boys have had struggles with the law…"

He paused and his brother picked up seamlessly. "It would seem the law would want to keep track of them. Our understanding, Claude, is that you're aware of the routes they take."

Ordinarily, he was. Ordinarily, their understanding of the world would have been accurate. But the world was different this summer, for reasons Claude didn't understand. Ethan Serbin had refused to give him a detailed itinerary, had simply told him that any questions should be directed to Allison. It was unusual, but Claude trusted Ethan as much as any man he'd ever known, and so he'd let it ride. If he needed to reach him, he'd go through Allison. It wasn't so difficult.

Now, though…

"Where are they?" the long-haired one said.

"I honestly do not know."

"We've been told otherwise, Claude. And, contrary to your perception of me, I prefer to be an honest man. I suspect you're of the same breed, so we're compatriots, you and me. We're honest men. Maybe guided by different stars, but I believe it is safe to say we share an appreciation for the truth. So let me share some truth. I could wait for Mr. Serbin to reappear. I could go into the woods and search for him. I could do any number of things, but, Claude? Sheriff? I am short on time and patience. You know the routes he takes. I'm going to need that information." He paused and gave Claude a long, measured stare before saying, "There's my truth. What's yours?"

"I don't know where he is."

The long-haired man let out a sigh and exchanged a look with his brother, and then they advanced on Claude like wolves on a downed elk, prey so easy it hardly piqued their interest. Claude thought he got himself upright before the blackness came. He was pretty sure he'd cleared the ground at least.

10

THE SUN WAS STILL VISIBLE above the mountains when Ethan Serbin handed Jace a knife called a Nighthawk. It was all black except for a thread of silver along the razor-sharp edge of its eight-inch-long blade. Ethan wore it on his belt at all times, but now it was in Jace's hand. It looked like a twin of the one he'd seen pulled through a man's throat not that long ago. He was afraid his hand was shaking, tried hard to steady it.

"You hold the knife by the blade when you're passing it to someone," Ethan said.

"*By* the blade?"

"That's right. Using the underside, just like this, keeping the dull portion in your palm. You don't ever want to point the blade at the person you're giving the knife to. That's how an accident happens. You keep control of it until you're sure he has control, right? So take it by the bottom, like this, so your palm and fingers aren't near the sharp edge. Then you pass it over, and say, 'Get it?' Wait for the other person to say, 'Got it.' Then you let your hand fall away and say, 'Good.' You wait on all three—*get it, got it, good.* Because if anyone pulls too fast or gets sloppy, people get cut. We don't want people getting cut."

Jace glanced at the rest of the group and saw all the boys watching with interest.

"All right," Ethan said. "Let's do this." He passed the knife over. "Get it?"

"Got it."

"Good."

Ethan let his hand fall away from the knife and then the Buck Nighthawk was in Jace's control. The feel of the knife gave him a strange sense of power. *Let's see Marco try something now.* He wanted one of his own, on his belt just like Ethan's.

Ethan said, "Do you remember what you're doing with the fire?"

"Yeah."

"Then get to it."

Jace sat on his knees in the dirt and cut strips of tinder from a piece of something that Ethan called pitch wood, carefully selected because the waxy substance inside the timber acted almost as a burning fuel, helped your flame catch and hold. He cut a series of long, thin curls of tinder and then, at Ethan's instruction, he turned the knife sideways and scraped, creating a shower of small shavings. The rest of his fire materials were gathered and ready; all he needed to do was spark the flint and get his tinder to start burning.

He knew it wasn't going to start, though. He'd watched Ethan do it, the whole thing looking effortless and easy, but he knew it really wasn't. He would spark the stupid firesteel tool for an hour and nothing would happen and then

Marco would make some wiseass comment and everyone would laugh and Ethan would take his tools back.

"Get that bundle a little tighter," Ethan said. "Think of it like a bird's nest."

Jace formed the tinder into a cluster with his hands, and then Ethan said, "Give it a shot."

"Want somebody else to do it?"

"What?"

That had sounded too much like Jace Wilson, too nervous, and so he tried to find Connor again and said, "Why do I have to do all the work? I made the kindling, let somebody else do the rest."

"No," Ethan said, "I'd like you to do it, thanks. If you're ever alone in the woods, Connor, you're not going to be able to share the workload."

Jace wet his lips and picked up the Swedish fire steel, a tool with a thin tube of magnesium and a metal striker. He braced the striker with his thumb and pushed down and sparks showered as soon as he began, but nothing caught. The sparks died in the air, just as he'd known they would.

"You've got to hold it lower," Ethan said. "All the way down against the tinder. Brace it on that platform piece, that's why we have one. And don't flick at it. However fast you want to go, make yourself do it at half that speed. Think of yourself in slow motion. The tool will do the work for you; it's not a muscle move, it's a control move. Yes, just like that. Again. Again."

Jace was aware of all the eyes fixed on his failure and he was starting to hate Ethan for it, was looking for something Connor Reynolds could come up with to stop it, a bit of bad attitude, maybe even some real anger...

He jerked his hand back in surprise as the tinder caught and a wisp of smoke began to curl.

"Okay," Ethan said. "Now, when you give it air, be real gentle. Real light."

Jace lowered his face to the tinder and blew gently and the flame grew and spread, and now the larger pieces were burning, and Ethan told him to add his sticks. He had a brace piece at one end and a series of pencil-lead-size pieces to be added first, leaning against the brace at a forty-five-degree angle. Once those caught, on to the pencil-size, and then the finger-size. He jumped to the second stage too fast, and the smoke began to come thicker and darker, the sign of a fire fighting death, and Ethan said, "This is where you use your brace."

Jace took a free end of the brace piece and lifted it gently. Ethan's design wasn't the tepee style Jace had seen before but more of a ramp, everything angled over the flame and toward the brace. When Jace lifted the brace, the fire that he'd been threatening to smother from above received immediate oxygen from below and the flame caught and grew and crackled.

The sound of it got attention. Everyone in the group murmured a little, impressed.

"We all get to try it?" Drew said.

"Yes. Nice work, Connor. It's a fine fire. May I have that knife back?"

Jace took it by the bottom of the blade, offered Ethan the handle, and said, "Get it?"

"Got it."

"Good."

The Nighthawk was gone from him then, and Ethan was moving on, but Jace didn't care. He was staring at the flames. He lifted the brace piece again, gave it another gust of air, and couldn't keep from smiling.

I can make fire, he thought.

When Claude woke, the sun was hot on his face and his arm ached worse than his head, though that pain was powerful too. He blinked and saw nothing but a harsh golden sun and a cobalt sky and for a moment the pain was forgotten, because he believed they were gone, that they'd moved on and left him there.

He tried to sit up and discovered that his arms were bound back over his head, and then he was concerned but still not scared because at least the two strangers were gone. This situation he could deal with somehow; with the two of them, he'd have had no chance.

"Seems to be among the living again," a gentle voice said from behind him, and that was when the fear returned, icy prickles bubbling along his flesh.

"The waking dead," a second voice said, and then they rose and again Claude saw only shadows as they returned to him. He was aware for the first time of the smell of wood smoke and the soft poppings of a small campfire.

They circled around in front of him. The one called Jack had the gun back in its holster, but the one called Patrick was still holding on to the chain-saw blade. Steam rose from the oil and grease trapped in the links, wisps of black smoke. It had been in the fire.

"We'll take that location now," Jack said. "Where Serbin has the boys. We'll take it from you."

Claude tried to move, scrabbling his boots in the dirt. They'd bound his hands back against one of the trees he had felled, and there was no chance of moving its weight.

"I'll give it to you," he said. His voice was a high fast rasp. "I'll tell you."

The man looked down at him and shook his head.

"No, Claude," he said. "You misunderstood me. I said that we were going to *take* the name from you now. Your chance to just give it away is gone."

The one with the smoking chain-saw blade approached from the right and Claude tried to kick him but missed, and then the long-haired one grabbed his boots and held his feet down as the other wrapped the hot string of saw teeth around Claude's arm. His skin sizzled on the metal and the smell of burned hair and flesh rose to him as he screamed. The one holding his feet had steady, unblinking blue eyes. They never changed expression. Not even when his brother began to tug the blade ends back and forth, back and forth.

They'd gone through all of the muscle and arteries and half the bone in his left forearm before Claude screamed Allison Serbin's name loud enough to satisfy them.

The blackness came again and this time it would not leave, he could not clear himself from it, he just faded in and out, and the fade-out was better, because the pain was numbed some then. Not enough, but some. He knew that he was going to die here on the hill above his own home, on a sunlit, blue-sky day, and he was less troubled by that than by what he'd just done, how he had given them what they wanted. He could feel his own blood warm and wet on his back, pooling beneath his arm and then running down the slope, and he hoped that it would pump faster, empty his body swifter.

Bring it to an end.

Their voices came and went in the blackness.

"I'm in favor of it. Would take a fine crime-scene team to determine he died anything but a fool's death, and I suspect they do not have such a team in this area."

"Does it matter how he died?"

"Time might matter. What this man Serbin hears and when he hears it might matter."

"True enough. Of course, if you do that, the whole hill-side goes up. Awfully dry. Good breeze blowing and taking it up the mountain, into all that timber."

"Might provide quite a distraction, then."

"Another fine point. You've won me over, brother. But you're assuming we'll have no need for him again."

"I've seen lying men and I've seen honest men. In that last moment, when he said the wife was the only one who knew? He had the characteristics of an honest man. In my assessment."

"I concluded similarly."

What they were discussing, Claude had no idea. He was distracted by wondering what had happened to his arm. The pain suggested it was still part of him, but he had trouble believing that it was. If he was strong enough, he could move it, and that might tell him whether the arm remained, but moving seemed a terrible idea; he wanted to hold on to the blackness longer, where the pain was less. He tried to find it again and could not, because the sun was too hot. The sun was keeping him conscious, and he hated it, oh, how he hated it. What he'd give for a single cloud, something to block out that heat.

But the sun came on stronger, relentless, and with it came the smell of smoke, and he realized then that the sun had somehow set the mountain on fire, and he thought that was one hell of a thing, because in all of his years in this country, he'd never encountered a day so hot as to set the earth to smoking. Someone should do something about that. Someone should make a cloud.

The mountain crackled around him as the sun strengthened, and Claude Kitna squeezed his eyes shut tight and moaned low and long and prayed for a cloud as the world turned to fire.

I I

HANNAH DIDN'T TRUST HER EYES. She'd sighted the smoke late in the afternoon and promptly went to the binoculars, certain it was a trick of the light or maybe some backpacker's campfire, nothing more. She'd already sighted one campfire and found the same boys who had been in various spots around the mountains for nearly a week. Scouts or something. When she saw the second fire, all she was expecting to find with the binoculars was the same group, but when she glassed the hillside above the tree line, she saw a steady column of smoke, growing and thickening, too much for a campfire.

Still, she didn't call it in immediately. She lowered the binoculars and blinked and shook her head. For days she had watched the empty mountains for fresh smoke and had seen none, and there had been no storms and no lightning, nothing to give her cause for suspicion.

But there it was.

She lifted the glasses again as if the second viewing might

prove her wrong; she felt like someone on a ship in ancient times who, sighting land after many months at sea, was afraid that it was an illusion.

It was not. The smoke was there, and it was spreading, and Hannah Faber had her first chance to help.

She was nervous going to the radio; the simple protocol suddenly felt infinitely complex.

Get it together, Hannah. Get it together. This is your damn job, they'll do the rest, all you have to do is tell them where the hell it is.

That was when she realized she didn't *know* where it was, that she was rushing to the radio without first identifying the location. She went to the Osborne, rotated the bezel, put her eye to the gun sight, and centered it up with the smoke. Looked at the map and got her bearing. This one wasn't far off at all. Five miles from her tower.

Too close, too close, get the hell out of here.

She shook her head again, chastising herself. It was the first flare-up, and they'd get it under control fast. Nothing was coming this way.

Easy to say, hard to believe. She was supposed to be removed from it up here. She was supposed to be far from the flames, supposed to—

"Supposed to do your damn job," she said aloud, and then she went to the radio and keyed the mike.

"This is Lynx Lookout. Do you copy?"

"We copy, Lynx."

"I've got smoke."

She felt as if it were a stunning proclamation, a real showstopper, but the response was flat and uninterested.

"Copy that. Location?"

She recited the location and bearing, told them the volume was small, the character was thin but building, the color gray.

"Copy that. Thanks, Lynx. We're on it."

"Good luck. I'll keep watching."

Keep watching. What an impotent thing to say, and do. Once she'd have been putting on the Nomex gear and the White's fire boots; once she'd have been strong and tanned and ready to take it on—the whole world afire couldn't scare her. Now...

I'll keep watching.

"Hurry up, guys," she whispered, watching the gray plumes grow, seeing the first tongues of orange in the mix now, and she wondered how it had started. There on a ridge so close to the road; how had it started?

Nick would say a campfire. There'd been no lightning, she'd watched for it every night and had not seen any, and so the source was likely humans. It was an odd place for a campfire, and a dangerous one. She looked at the map and traced the contour lines and saw what it might do. It could burn up off that ridge and find open grasses and scorch through them and then hit the high forest, pushed by the wind. If it did, it would run into the rock, and in its quest for fuel, it would climb sidehill and find the gulch that waited, lined with dry timber. And then they'd be fighting it low. Down in a basin rimmed by steep slopes.

Some of the best friends she'd ever had died trying to outrun a burning wind in a basin like that.

She didn't like the way those contour lines looked. There was plenty of fuel in the gulch below the place where the fire had begun to burn, and, dry as it was with this early drought, the flames would be moving fast.

The first crew got there within thirty minutes, and they

encountered more than they'd bargained for. The wind was pushing the fire upslope, toward a stretch of dry jack pine, and the reports over the radio were grim and surprised.

"We can get a pump truck to the bottom, but no higher. It's climbing pretty well."

"So trench it and bladder-bag it," Hannah said. She wasn't on the air, they couldn't hear her, but she hoped they'd somehow sense her advice and take it. If they got up high enough, they should be able to contain it. With the truck soaking the bottom of the hill and a proper trench cutting it off from climbing toward any more fuel, they'd be fine. It would be hot, hard work, though, and the sun would be setting soon, and then it would be just the crew and the firelight and the wind. The wind was the great enemy, the most menacing and most mysterious. This she knew as well as she knew her own name.

They didn't hear her advice but they followed it anyway, and she listened as they sent a trenching team a half a mile farther up the mountain, where they could cut the blaze off from the next stretch of forest and hopefully leave it to burn out in the rocks.

"It will go sidehill, guys. It will have no choice, and the wind will help it, and then you'll have to fight it at the bottom."

That was what they probably wanted. The fire would be bordered by creeks and road and rock there, and they would believe they had it sequestered. Unless the wind had different plans.

Her first fire with Nick hadn't been all that different from this one. A wooded windblown hillside. She was on her second summer then and had a sophomore's cockiness—been there, done that, seen it all, though of course she hadn't. Rookie bravado, sophomore cockiness, and veteran's wisdom. The three stages she'd come to know. She suspected that some sort of law required wisdom and loss to be partners. At least, they always seemed to ride together.

She'd loved Nick from the start. In the way it wasn't supposed to happen, the way you weren't supposed to trust. Love at first sight was a fairy tale. Tough girls rolled their eyes at it. And she'd meant to, she had absolutely meant to, but the really special thing about love was that it scorned your attempts to control it. That was a great thing. Sometimes.

Rule number one for a woman on the fire line: you had to outwork everyone.

Rule number two: when you did, you'd be considered less of a woman because of it.

That had been infuriating in the first summer. Fighting fires was a male-dominated world—weren't they all, though?—but she hadn't been the lone woman. There were three on the crew, but she was the only rookie. The jokes came early and often, but she was cool with that, because, frankly, that seemed to be the way it went. Boys being boys. Giving each other shit over any perceived weakness, circling wolves settling pack order, and her weakness, as they saw it, was readily apparent: the extra X chromosome. So you took the jokes and you gave them back and then you went to work, and here's where it mattered—would you live up to the identity that the jokes created, or would you forge a new one? You couldn't be the joke, there was no respect to be found there, no room for softness among crew members for whom fatigue was often the starting point and not the finish line. When you erased the jokes, though, when you matched the guys' work or exceeded it, a fascinating thing happened—apparently, you lost your femininity. Now the jokes came out of respect, and the tone was altogether different. Once your nickname was Princess; now it was Rambo.

All of this wasn't to say she had had bad relationships with the boys of summer. On the contrary, they were some of the best friends she'd ever had, or would ever have—if there were no atheists in foxholes, then there were no enemies on the fire lines. But dating someone on the crew was different. It was like giving something back that you'd worked hard to earn. She'd made a rule before the second summer, a sophomore's rule, the unyielding kind that broke the minute you applied it: The fire line was work. End of story.

And so of course there had been Nick. And of course he hadn't been just on the crew; he'd been the boss.

That was the summer she wore makeup to a trench line, the summer of the cosmetology-school jokes, the summer of the happiest days and nights of her life. She'd become certain of the invalidity of her own rule—it didn't have to be all work. You could work with someone you loved, even on the most dangerous of tasks.

She no longer believed that. On the witness stand, pointing at the topographic map and the photos and explaining how it had all happened, she knew that her rule had not been invalid. You fought fires as a crew. Lived and died as a crew. And if you were in love with one person on that crew, just one? All your best intentions didn't mean a damn thing. Love always scorned your attempts to control it.

She sat in her tower now with her feet up and her eyes on the wispy smoke over the mountains and she spoke to the radio without keying the mike, spoke as if she were out there with them. A constant stream of chatter. She was warning them to watch out for widow makers—burning limbs that dropped from above without warning—when the pump truck reported a victim.

Hannah lifted her hands to her face and covered her eyes. Not already. Not on the first fire of the season, the first *she* had called in. She felt as if the death had come with her, somehow, as if the death had followed her back. A certain wind chased Hannah, and it was a killing wind.

Fifteen minutes after they announced the victim, they came back with more:

"I think we've got a campfire source. Appears to be a fire ring here, stones, and the fire must have jumped it and gotten into the trees that were brought down. Look like fresh cuts too. Only seeing one DOA. Can't tell if it's male or female. Burned up pretty good. We've secured the body and what's left of an ATV and, I believe, probably a chain saw."

There was your source. Someone had been felling timber and decided to keep a fire going while he did it, then left it untended, in the wind. Oblivious to the risk.

"Stupid bastard," Hannah whispered, thinking of those who were walking into the flames right now for some foolish mistake, thinking of all that might be lost just because someone wanted to roast a hot dog.

It felt strange, though. Somehow, it felt off. She'd spotted the smoke around four and the sun had been high and hot, hotter than it had been all summer. Nobody would have needed or wanted a campfire for warmth. And it was late for lunch and early for dinner, and it didn't sound as if the victim had been camping, anyhow, not with an ATV and a chain saw. He'd been working, probably. And what person doing sweaty work on a hot afternoon wanted a campfire?

There was something off with the fire source, no question. But the first task was putting the blaze out fast enough so they could figure out what the real story was. Until those flames were gone, nobody was concerned about determining their source.

The tower swayed more as the sun descended, the wind freshening at dusk.

12

As the boys sipped water and stretched aching legs beside the campfire, Ethan sent Allison a short text on his GPS messenger:

ALL FINE. WE ARE ALONE IN THE WOODS.

He put the GPS away then and let his eyes drift as he scanned the rocks and forested hills and the high mountains beyond. Empty. He had told the truth: they were alone. They had hiked all day beneath a high hot sun and a cloudless sky, and if you'd told people that only a few weeks ago, the Beartooth Pass had been closed with two feet of snow, they'd have laughed in your face.

No one was out there.

Not yet, at least.

And what if they come?

He'd asked himself that question the night Jamie Bennett had arrived and every waking hour since. What if they came, these men who were trained killers?

I'll handle it. I've had my share of training too.

But he hadn't. Not that kind. He didn't end up in the Air Force by mistake. The son of a Marine who didn't leave the combat overseas quite as well as he should have, Ethan had grown up pointed toward the military, and enlisting was the same sort of free-will decision that the sun made when it chose to set in the west. All his father had wanted was another Marine—a fighter, not a teacher. His old man hadn't been impressed when Ethan tried to explain that he was teaching military personnel how to have what he called a survivor mentality.

"There are two kinds of men in war," his father had said. "The killing kind, and the dying kind. If you're the dying kind, you won't survive shit. If you're the killing kind, you will. It's already in there. You're teaching woodcraft, and that's fine. But if they're the dying kind, all your tricks won't save 'em."

Ethan shook himself back into the moment, back into watching, which was his job; killing wasn't. The smoke from their campfire wasn't heavy, the wood had been properly selected, but only a few miles out, someone else had one as well, the smoke visible above the ridgeline. It seemed like a lot of smoke. Ethan watched it for a while and wondered if a campfire had gotten away from someone. With this wind, it was certainly possible.

"You guys see that?" he said. "That smoke?"

They were tired and uninterested, but they looked.

"We're going to keep an eye on it," he said. "That one could turn into something."

"Turn into something? You mean, like, a forest fire?" Drew said.

"That's exactly what I mean. These mountains have burned before. They'll burn again someday. Now, all of you look at the smoke and then look at your maps and tell me where it's burning and what it means to us. First one to do that, I'll build his shelter myself."

Jace cared, and maybe that was a problem. The caring had started with the fire, when he struck two pieces of metal together and made a spark that made a flame that made a campfire. His vision of Connor Reynolds as a boy who did not care began to vanish. His bad attitude was disappearing even when Jace tried to keep it in place, because this stuff was pretty cool. It was *real,* it mattered in a way most things you were taught didn't—this stuff could save your life.

He didn't know what Connor Reynolds was running from up here, but back behind Jace were men who intended to take his life, and he began to think that maybe Connor should pay a little more attention. For the both of them.

Now Ethan had laid down a challenge, and while Jace really didn't care about winning the shelter—he enjoyed building them, and they were improving with each night's effort—he did want to be the first to place that column of smoke accurately. This was the sort of thing that most people couldn't do. The sort of thing that could save your life.

He looked up at the mountains and down at the map and then back up again. To his right was Pilot Peak, one of the most striking landmarks in the Beartooths, easy to find. Move along from that and there was Index, and the fire wasn't in front of either of them. Keep rolling and there was Mount Republic and beyond that Republic Peak, and now he began to get it. They were supposed to hike to Republic Peak, then claim the summit—that was what Ethan called it, at least—and hike back down the way they'd come. On every trip, though, Ethan gave them an escape route. Jace enjoyed those, even if the rest of the boys thought the idea was corny. The other kids didn't know about the need for escape routes yet.

The smoke wasn't between their camp and Republic Peak, but it seemed to be coming from the back side of Republic Peak. Connor traced the contour lines that lay to the west of the peak—they fell off in a tight cluster, indicating a steep and fast decline, toward Yellowstone National Park, and then those to the north were more gradual, spaced apart. A creek wound down from near the glacier that lay between Republic Peak and its nearest cousin, Amphitheater.

"It's burning by our escape route," he said.

Everybody looked up with interest, and Jace was proud to see it on Ethan Serbin's face as well.

"You think?" Ethan said.

Jace felt a pang of uncertainty. He looked up at the mountains, wondering if he'd gotten it wrong.

"That's what it looks like," Jace said. "Like if we had to use the escape route and come down the back side of Republic, going backcountry, the way you were talking about, we'd run right into it. Or pretty close."

Ethan watched him in silence.

"Maybe not," Jace said, and now he was searching for the Connor Reynolds attitude again, shrugging and trying to act as if he didn't care one way or the other. "Whatever. I don't mind building my shelter, I don't need you to do it."

"You don't? Well, that's too bad because I was about to start on it."

"I got it right?"

"Yes, you did. If that fire actually is spreading, which is how it looks right now, it's going to be spreading pretty close to our escape route."

13

T HE HORSES WOKE HER.
A whinny in the night, answered by another, and Allison was awake quickly. She was a deep sleeper usually, but not since Ethan had gone into the mountains. She had no fear of being left alone on the property; most of her life, she'd been alone on the property. Some days she wanted to *send* him into the mountains just to be alone again.

This summer, though, the ill winds had blown through her mind daily. She tried to adopt Ethan's amused disregard for such things, but she couldn't. You could offer the heart all the instruction you wanted. The heart was often hard of hearing.

She was a different woman this summer, and not one she cared to be. She was a fearful woman. In the corner of the room, leaning against the wall near her side of the bed, was a loaded shotgun. On the nightstand where usually a glass of water and a book sat, she had her GPS, the one Ethan would text her on if something went wrong. Only a single message received today: they were alone in the woods. That was all he would say, and she knew that, but still, she'd taken to looking at the GPS far too often, and though she knew well that the horses had woken her and not the GPS, she checked it anyhow. Blank and silent.

Bastard, she thought, and hated herself for it. How could she think that? Her own husband, the love of her life, and that was no joke, better believe he was the only love she'd encounter in this life, at least the only one that would run so deep. Deeper than she'd believed was possible.

And still she cursed him now. Because he'd made a choice, and he hadn't chosen her. The resentment had plagued her ever since Jamie Bennett left Montana, the deal made. How could you resent a man who'd agreed to protect a child?

Jamie was reckless, and he knew it. She appealed to his ego, and he let her. I warned him, and he laughed…

Stop it. Stop those thoughts.

She rose, considered picking up the shotgun for a moment, then dismissed the idea. There was no need for a weapon, or for her resentments. Ethan had made the right choice; the only danger was with him, and she should be thinking of him instead of herself. She would go as far as the porch and see what there was to see. If there appeared to be real trouble in the stable, then she'd return for the shotgun. Occasionally you heard of problems with mountain lions and livestock, the sort of thing that happened when you offered up perfectly good prey in the homeland of a perfectly good predator, but in all her years there, the horses had never been bothered by one.

They also rarely woke her in the night.

She crossed the living room in the dark. A dull orange glow came from behind the glass door of the woodstove, remnants of a nearly extinguished fire. She hadn't been asleep long. Just past midnight now. Between the living room and the porch was a narrow storage room, the washer and dryer crammed inside, rows of shelves surrounding them. She found a battery-powered spotlight by touch and then pulled a heavy jacket off the hook beside the door. Summer, sure, but the night air wouldn't admit to such a thing, not yet. In the pocket of the jacket she put a can of bear spray. You never knew. One year they'd had a grizzly on the bunkhouse porch; another time one had inspected the bed of Ethan's pickup after a garbage run. If a grizz was out there now, the pepper spray would be far more useful than the shotgun.

She went out into the night, and the breeze found her immediately and pushed its chill down the collar of her jacket. She walked to the far edge of the porch, leaving the door open behind her. Fifty yards away, in the stable, the horses were silent again.

She knew the shadows that lay between the cabin and the barn from years of night checks. In what should have been a stretch of open ground, every tree cleared from it long ago, something stood, black on black.

Allison lifted the spotlight and hit the switch.

A man appeared, halfway between her and the stable, and though he blinked against the harshness of the light, he seemed otherwise untroubled by it. He was young and lean and had bristle-short hair and eyes that looked black in the spotlight. The glare had to be blinding, but he did not so much as lift a hand to block it.

"Good evening, Mrs. Serbin."

This was why she had the shotgun. This was why it was kept loaded and propped near the bed and now she had walked away from it because for too long she had lived in a world where a shotgun was unnecessary.

You knew, she thought, even as she stared at him in silence. *You knew, Allison, somehow you knew he was coming, and you ignored it and now you will pay.*

The man was advancing toward her through the narrow beam of light, and his motion induced her own, a slow backward shuffle on the porch. He did not change his pace.

"I'd like you to stop there," she said. Her voice was strong and clear and she was grateful for that. "Stop there and identify yourself. You know my name; I should know yours."

Still he came on with that carefree stride, his face a white glow and his eyes squinted nearly shut. Something was wrong with that. His willingness to accept the glare, to walk directly into it without taking so much as a side step, that wasn't right. She'd caught him in the beam and for some reason he was embracing it. Why?

"Stop there," she said again, but now she knew that he would not. Her options rolled through her mind fast because they were few. She could wait here and he'd come on until he'd joined her on the porch and whatever had brought him here in the night would be revealed. Or she could turn and run for the door, close and lock it, and get the shotgun in her hands. She knew that she could make it before he caught her.

He knows I can too. He can see that.

But still he walked without hurry, squinting against the spotlight.

She knew then. Understood in an instant. He was not alone. That was why he was not hurried and it was why he did not wish her to move the light away from him.

She pivoted and headed for the door only to stop immediately. The second man was already almost to the porch.
Far closer to the door than she was. He'd come from
around the other side of the cabin. Long blond hair that
glowed near white in the beam. Boots and jeans and a black
shirt unbuttoned almost to midchest. Pistol in his hand.

"Be still," he said. He had a doctor's bedside tone. A professional soother.

She stood where she was as he walked toward her from
the front and the other one reached the porch at her back.
No way to face them both. At once, she was relieved that
she had not taken the shotgun. She could shoot only one of
them at a time, the way they were positioned, but that was
still more shooting than they likely wanted, and if they'd
thought she was a threat, they might have fired first. Right
now, they did not think that, and in their perception of
her as harmless, she was being given one last valuable tool:
time. How much of it, she did not know. But there was
some, and she needed to use it now, and use it right.

She thought of the bear spray, and then she lifted her
hands into the air. To reach for it was to admit it was there.
The bear spray was of little comfort in the face of a gun but
it was what she had and she intended to keep it. Keep it and
earn more of what these men could grant: time. Whether it
was hours or minutes, whether it was seconds, her hope lay
in buying more.

"What do you want?" she said. Voice no longer so strong.
"There's no need for a gun. You can tell me what you'd
like."

"Hospitable," the long-haired man said. "That is a pleasant change from others we've encountered."

"It certainly is."

"A calm woman, all things considered. Middle of the night, you know. Strangers."

"Strangers with guns. Very calm, I'd say. Unusually so."

They were talking around her as they advanced, conversational as two men on a road trip making observations about the scenery. It chilled her more than the sight of the gun had.

"What do you want?" she repeated. They were almost upon her, one at the front and one at the back, and it was harder now to keep her hands in the air; she wanted to bring them down and throw a punch, wanted to run, wanted to drop to the porch floor and curl up and protect herself from their impending touches.

But none of those options would buy her time. She kept her hands in the air, though they were shaking now.

"May we step inside, Mrs. Serbin?"

The one facing her, just inches away, asked the question, but he wasn't looking her in the eye. His gaze was covering her body, and she had the sense that he was inventorying her in every way. There was violation in his stare and also threat assessment. She wore black leggings, nothing over them, her boots loose along the calf, and when she'd lifted her arms, the jacket had pulled back to reveal the long-sleeved T-shirt she'd been sleeping in. There was no place on her body, under the jacket, to hide a weapon, and that was evident. The oversize jacket hid the bear spray well. She had a feeling that they would take the jacket, though. That, too, was only a matter of time.

Out in the stable, one of the horses whinnied again. A high keening sound. The moon was visible now, clean white light. Would things have been different if it had been out when she opened the door? Would she have seen enough to step back inside? Could a cloud change your life?

"Yes, I think we'll go inside," the man behind her said. He reached out and pushed her hair back over her shoulder, one fingertip on her skin, and that was when she dropped her hands and screamed and then his arm was around her, drawing her body hard against his, pinning her arms to her sides. The spotlight fell to the porch floor and bounced. He'd wrapped her up in such a way that her hands were pressed up near her face, useless.

The man in front of her had watched the brief flurry of resistance without reaction. Heard her scream and did not blink. He stood still while the other one held her, and for a time there was no sound but the horses stirring, unsettled by Allison's scream. The spotlight beam shot crookedly into the night sky, illuminating half of his face.

"Still hospitable?" he said at last.

The grip around her felt like a steel band and there were tears threatening, pain and fear mixing. She blinked the tears back and forced herself to look directly at him when she nodded. She didn't say a word.

"Marvelous," he said. He drew the word out slow and looked away from her, taking stock of the grounds a final time, the stable and the pasture and the empty bunkhouse and the garage beyond. She had a feeling they'd inspected the property thoroughly before approaching the house. She didn't like that measured surveyor's stare. He saw too much, missed too little. It was the way Ethan took in a place. It wasn't a quality she wanted to see in a man like this.

When he was satisfied with his assessment, he made the smallest of nods and the other one shoved her forward, through the door and into the living room, without loosening his hold.

"I believe I'll give myself a tour," the long-haired one said.

"One of us probably should," the other answered. Allison could feel his breath on her ear. Could smell his sweat and a heavy odor of stale, trapped smoke. Not cigarettes. Wood smoke.

He held her in the center of the room and did not speak while the other one took a patient stroll through her home. He unplugged phones and lowered window blinds and talked while he moved, and the one holding her answered.

"Quite an empire they have here."

"Beautiful place."

"They like mountain landscapes, did you notice?"

"Seems to be the favored artwork, yes."

"Strange, living in a place like this. Why do you need the paintings, the photographs? Just look out the window."

"Gifts, I suspect. What do you give someone who lives in the mountains? A photograph of the same mountain that person sees every day. It doesn't make sense, but people do it all the same. Like that man who raised the dogs. Remember him? The bloodhounds."

"Pictures of bloodhounds all over the place. Even though the real deal was right there."

"Exactly. I'm telling you, they are gifts. No one has any imagination these days."

The grip on Allison hadn't loosened a fraction, though the man who held her spoke easily. Another smell mingled with the wood smoke, but it took her a minute to confirm what it was. Or accept it.

He smelled of blood.

The long-haired one faded from sight but she could hear his boots as he moved through the rooms behind them. Then he reappeared and crossed the living room. He had a hat in his hand. A black Stetson, wide-brimmed. Ethan's hat, one that he'd never worn. He hated the cowboy look, but people had their assumptions.

"I like this," the long-haired man said. "Very Wild West." He put the hat on and inspected himself in the reflection from the glass door. He smiled. "Not a bad touch."

"Not bad at all," the short-haired one said.

"Is it your husband's hat?" He turned to face Allison.

"It was a gift," she said. "He doesn't like it."

They laughed at her then. "Excellent," the long-haired one said. "That's excellent, Mrs. Serbin." He wandered away again, still wearing the hat, and entered her bedroom. He'd picked up the spotlight when they came inside and was using it rather than the overhead lights. She watched the beam paint the walls and then come to a stop on the shotgun. He went over to it and lifted it with one hand and opened the breech. When he saw the shells inside he snapped the breech shut and returned to the living room, carrying the spotlight in one hand, now turned off, and the shotgun in the other, held down against his leg. The pistol was in a holster at his back.

"Oh my," he said, easing onto the couch, stretching his legs out in front of him, and leaning the shotgun against the cushion. "It's been a long day, hasn't it?"

"Productive, though."

"True." The longhair gave a heavy sigh, chest rising and falling, staring at the woodstove. He looked at it for a long time before glancing back at them. "You good?"

"Just fine."

"Do you think she needs to be held?"

"I suppose we could give her a chance now that you've completed the tour."

The long-haired one fixed his eyes on Allison's. Cold empty blue. "What do you say, beautiful? Can we take that chance?"

"Yes."

"Well, then. We get our first test of your honesty."

The iron grip was gone, as if it had never existed. She was free again. The one who'd held her stepped back after releasing her. She hadn't seen his face since he'd walked toward her in the spotlight. The two men never stood together.

The long-haired man said, "Do you know why we're here?"

She shook her head. Immediately, he sighed again and turned from her and ran a hand over his face as if he were exhausted.

"Mrs. Serbin." The words were heavy with disappointment.

"What?"

"You know. You do know, and you just lied, and that, at this point in the night…" He shook his head and rubbed his eyes. "It's not what we need. It simply will not do."

"My brother's had a long day," the one behind her said. "I'd warn you that he's a less patient man when he's tired. You're not expected to know him as well as I do, so I'll give you some insider perspective. He's worn down right now. It's been a trying day. For us, and for others."

She wanted to turn and see him, but looking away from the one on the couch seemed risky. He had the only pistol she'd seen but surely the other one was armed too. *My brother,* he'd said. She wondered where they were from. They spoke without accent. Flat affect. Someplace in the Midwest. Someplace near the center of hell. They had not taken her jacket from her and so she still had the bear spray, but what use it might be she couldn't imagine now. Cause them some pain, but that would only anger them more. Blinding them in a cloud of poison and running through it for the shotgun? It would never work.

"Tell me, then," Allison said.

That brought a tilt of the head and an almost amused stare from the man on the couch. "Tell you?"

"Yes. Why are you here?"

For a long time he looked at her and did not speak. Then he said, "I believe your husband is in the mountains. Leading a group of boys. Troubled boys. Very honorable thing to do. Because if you don't stop the trouble in a boy early? Well, then. Well."

"It simply won't stop," his brother said. "Once trouble takes hold, Mrs. Serbin? It won't stop."

The man on the coach leaned forward and braced his arms on his knees. "Do you know which boy it is?"

Allison shook her head. "I don't."

"This time I believe you. But it's irrelevant. Because *we* know which one he is. So we don't require that information from you. What we require is his location."

She knew what was coming now as if a map had been drawn for her. They wanted the boy and they wanted to move with speed. The thing she had wanted to take from them, time, was the very thing they could not afford to grant. There were other ways to find Ethan, but not faster ways, not for them. So they intended to travel via shortcuts. She was one of those.

He commenced rubbing his face again with a gloved hand. Somewhere behind Allison, his brother shifted, but still she did not turn. Let him move. She couldn't watch them both, so there was no point in trying. They would ask her for Ethan's location now, and when she did not tell them, it would go bad fast. She saw that on the map but she also saw that the destination was the same no matter which route she took. There were detours available to her but no exits.

So it would go this way, then. They would ask and she would answer and they would be done with her. Or they would ask and she would not answer and they would not be done with her.

"We're going to need to catch up with your husband," the man on the couch said. "I assume you realize that by now."

"Yes."

"Will you tell us where we might find him? Remember that he, personally, is of no interest to us."

He was willing to try one tactic, at least, before resorting to more direct means. Willing to pretend. She would now hear that no harm would come to Ethan if she told them where he was, and no harm would come to her. His heart wasn't in it, though. At some point he had looked at her and an understanding had transpired between them. He would not waste his efforts on a lost cause, and convincing her that she had any hope of safety was a lost cause. She knew that they were here to kill a boy because that boy had seen them, and now she had seen them. All of this lay unspoken between them. And what it meant.

"He will be," she said.

That earned a raised eyebrow. "You think?"

She nodded. "You won't just take the boy. Not from Ethan."

"But we're going to have to."

"It won't go easy for you."

He seemed pleased by that prediction. "Sometimes it doesn't."

He left the couch and leaned down on one knee and reached for the woodstove. Opened the door and let smoke out into the room. A few embers clung to life. There was a basket of kindling beside the stove and he took a handful and began to build a fire.

"The technique has been good to us today," he said.

"It has," his brother answered. "Cold in here too. A cold night."

The flames caught the fresh fuel and grew and he added a log then and sat back and watched the fire take hold. There was an iron rack of tools on the wall—ash broom and dustpan, poker, tongs. He ran his fingertips over all of them as if undecided on the best option and then let his hand float back to the tongs. Removed them from the rack and dipped the business end into the flame and allowed the iron to soak in the scorching heat.

"Please," Allison said, and he looked up at her as if with genuine surprise.

"Pardon?"

"Please don't."

"Well, you've had your opportunity to cooperate. Surely you can't blame me for the consequences of your own decisions, your own actions?"

"You'll spend your life in prison for this," she said. "I hope the days are long for you there. I hope they are endless."

He removed the tongs from the fire and smiled at her. "I don't see anyone here to arrest me, Mrs. Serbin. In fact, it is my understanding that your sheriff is dead. The law has changed with our arrival, do you see? You are now in the jurisdiction of a new judge."

"This is the truth," his brother acknowledged, and then the deep red glow of the iron tongs was approaching Allison and she spoke again.

"There's a GPS."

He seemed almost disappointed. As if he'd expected her continued resistance and had not thought she would be so easy to break.

"Cooperation," he said. "Marvelous." That word again, said slow, as if he liked the flavor. "Where is this GPS?"

"Nightstand. By the bed."

His brother moved without a word and quickly returned with the GPS in his hand. He was studying it.

"Does it track them or does it just have the planned route?"

"Tracks them."

The one by the fire rose and hung the tongs back on the wall. Allison prayed that he would come closer, join his brother in looking at the GPS, finally be close enough that she would have a chance to get them both with one shot of the bear spray.

He didn't. He walked to the end of the couch, the two men still well separated, and said, "Show us where they are."

She reached for the device. Her hand was trembling. The man who smelled of smoke and blood handed her the GPS and she tried to make it look as if she fumbled it on the transition, tried to hide the way her thumb came down on the red emergency button, the one that issued the distress signal. You couldn't just tap it, though; the emergency responders didn't want to be inundated with accidental SOS calls. You had to hit it three times in succession.

She'd hit it twice before the first punch came, and as she fell she hit it the third time and then dropped it as a kick caught her high in the stomach and hammered the air from her lungs and left her curled in a ball of agony, trying to choke in a breath as blood flowed from her shattered nose and torn lips.

"Emergency signal," the man who'd struck her said, not even looking at her, his attention back on the GPS. "She just called for a rescue."

"Can you stop it?"

"I don't know. I'll see."

Allison writhed on the floor and tried to suck in air, but all that came was the taste of hot copper. She wanted to reach for the bear spray but first she needed to breathe, and her hand went to her stomach instead of her pocket, a reflex action—touch where it hurts. The long-haired man bent and grabbed her by her hair and dragged her backward, fresh pain flooding in even as she drowned in what was already there.

"She should hope," he said, "that the rescue team is very fast."

He dragged her close to the fire and dropped her on the floor and then knelt to take the tongs from the rack. His brother was still looking at the GPS, trying to abort the signal. Allison rolled onto her shoulder and found the bear spray and withdrew it. There was a plastic guard on the trigger. She snapped that off with her thumb, and at the sound of the breaking plastic, the long-haired one turned back. When he spotted the pepper-spray canister, she saw something unsteady in his eyes for the first time. Saw all of the anger he kept wrapped behind the cloak of cold calm. It was there for a flicker and then gone. The cloak returned, and with it a menacing amusement. A smile spreading beneath that frosted stare.

"Very good," he said. "Pepper spray. Very good. But Mrs. Serbin? As proud as I am of you for the effort, you're pointing it the wrong way."

The muzzle of the spray canister was facing away from him, back toward Allison herself.

She spoke to him through a mouthful of blood. "No, I'm not."

She closed her eyes then and depressed the trigger, aimed not at his face but at the open door of the woodstove just behind her head, and the living room seemed to explode. A cloud of fire rolled out of the stove and over her and the flames caught her jacket and hair and then found her flesh.

She willed herself to keep holding the trigger down. Keep spraying. Keep feeding it. Knowing even in the agony the thing that she had known from the start: the pepper spray was not weapon enough to fight these men.

Fire might be.

The flames rolled across the living room and drove them away from her, pushed them back toward the front door. The canister exploded in her hand then, and new needles pressed into her nerves. The shotgun was just to her left, still leaning against the couch, still loaded. She rolled to it and when she grabbed the metal barrel, it seared her palm, but she was hardly aware of the pain. Her right hand didn't respond the way she wanted it to, didn't seem to respond at all, so she braced the butt of the gun against her stomach and dropped her left hand to the trigger. The flames rose in a wall before her but she could see twin shadows on the other side of it. The cabin was bathed in scarlet light. She pulled the heavy trigger back with two fingers of her left hand.

The shotgun bucked wildly and she dropped it, which was bad because she had wanted both shots, but she was on fire now and that thing that she had treasured—time—was no more.

Roll, she thought. *Roll, roll, roll.*

Common sense. A child's knowledge. If your clothes were on fire, you rolled to put them out.

But what did you do when everywhere around you was more fire?

She had no answer for that, and so she continued to roll, out of the scarlet and into the black.

They stood in the yard and watched the cabin burn.

"You're bleeding pretty well."

Jack looked at his side. Against the black shirt, the blood was hard to see; it was just added shine. He removed the shirt. A scattering of birdshot. Small-gauge shotgun, smaller load.

"It'll stop."

"I'll go back for her." Patrick lifted his pistol and gestured at the cabin. "Don't know if I hit her or not. I was walking backward, she was rolling. I'll go finish it."

"I think she finished it herself. And if she didn't? Well, we'll come for her again. Not now. Time to ride."

"I'd like to know it's done."

"I'd like to be gone when they answer that distress call.

Somebody will. And you know how I feel about this highway."

"I do." Patrick was staring into the burning house.

"You're displeased, brother. I understand. But I'm shot. Let's head out."

They walked together into the darkness and away from the orange light. The truck was a half a mile away and they covered the ground swiftly, not speaking. Jack's breath came heavy and uneven but he did not slow his pace. When they reached the truck, he handed the keys to his brother.

"Right or left?" Patrick asked.

"We go right, we have to go through the gates into Yellowstone. It's the only way."

"Yes."

"I'd expect there are more police in the park. More places to close the highway too."

"Left is longer. All those switchbacks. Even driving fast, we're on the road for a good while."

Jack nodded. "As I said, I don't care for this highway. We've found ourselves in the only part of the country that has just one damned road."

"Call it, and call it fast."

"Left."

Patrick gunned the motor to life and turned on the lights and swung out of the gravel and back onto the asphalt. On the hill above them, the firelight flickered through the pines.

"Havoc," Jack said. "We are leaving havoc in our wake. Could be trouble."

"We've never left one standing before. Not like this."

"I doubt she's standing."

"We don't know. We need to be sure."

"She set herself on fire, and the fire is still burning."

"Regardless, they may know we're coming now. Serbin and the boy."

"They may."

"We could leave. Call it off," Patrick said.

"You'd consider that?"

Silence filled the cab and rode with them for a time.

"Yes," Jack said at length. "That was my feeling on it as well."

"We came a long way for him."

"We did. And we came in good health. Now I'm burned and bleeding. That leaves me even less inclined to call it off. Leaves me, in fact, completely unwilling to do so."

"Understood."

"This will bring him down, you know. Out of the mountains. He'll have to come back for her, and he will have to bring the boy with him."

"Yes. And the boy will vanish again quickly. They'll move him fast."

"It would seem we should be there, then."

"It certainly would."

Part Two

POINT LAST SEEN

14

THE MESSAGE CAME FOR HIM in the dead hours. Predawn, when the night sounds had dulled but the gray light of day hadn't yet broken.

He knew the GPS chime was bad before he opened his eyes. Middle-of-the-night phone calls scared you with possibilities. Middle-of-the-night distress calls didn't even tease you with possibilities; they promised you the truth.

He sat up, bumping against the plastic and showering himself with drops of the condensation that had gathered on it overnight, and fumbled in his pack for the GPS.

It told him no details. Just that Allison had issued a distress call. When the SOS went out, it was shared with Ethan's device as well as with the emergency responders. There were two ways to call for help on the GPS—send a message with some details, or send one with none. The whole point of the advanced unit was that it let you add those details.

Allison hadn't.

He sat there looking at the GPS and tried not to imagine

the scenarios in which this could happen. His breathing was slow and steady and he was on the ground, still half wrapped in his sleeping bag, and yet it felt as if he were no longer connected to the earth, as if he were drifting away from it fast, as he stared at the glowing screen that told him his wife was calling for help.

From their home.

"No," he told the device reasonably. "No."

The device didn't change its mind. The screen went black in his hand and he was alone in the darkness. Through the milky-white plastic, the night woods looked like something from another world. He pushed the plastic back and rose from his shelter and stood in the cold air and tried to think of what could be done. If he ran all out and left the boys behind, he could reach town in perhaps four hours. Perhaps.

He clicked the GPS messenger back on. Sent a one-word text.

ALLISON?

There was no response.

Her message would have gone to the International Emergency Response Coordination Center. An underground bunker in Texas, just north of Houston. Staffed every minute of every day, operating on an independent and backed-up electrical grid. Painstakingly designed never to fail a call.

He sent the next message to them.

RECEIVED DISTRESS SIGNAL. WHAT IS RESPONSE STATUS?

Above him in a beautiful night sky an unseen satellite inhaled his Montana message and exhaled it toward Texas. The satellite would check for a response in sixty seconds.

It felt like a very long time.

Scattered around him on the hillside were the other shelters. He could hear one boy rolling over and another snoring. If anyone was awake and aware of him, he was silent. Ethan stared at their shelters as if he did not recognize them or even understand their purpose. Everything in the world was foreign right now.

The chime again. He looked back down at the GPS unit.

LOCAL AUTHORITIES ADVISED AND EN ROUTE.

The closest local authority was going to come from Yellowstone. They'd pass through Silver Gate and Cooke City and reach his driveway. Fifteen minutes, at least. Maybe twenty. By the standards of those in the Texas bunker, that was swift. No ship would be lost at sea, no climber would be stranded on an icy peak. A fast response.

So very fast.

He could measure the seconds in heartbeats.

The wind rose and the plastic shelters rustled all around him and he began to stare at them again. He did not like the way he was looking at them. Did not like anything of this night or of this world. The messenger unit in his hand was silent. Heartbeat, heartbeat. Local authorities en route. Allison not answering. Heartbeat, heartbeat.

He turned his face to the wind and then he stood motionless and waited. Above him the clouds had pulled away to the northeast and the moon was bright and the stars glittered and a satellite circled amid them, looking down on his world and ready to destroy it. Catch a signal, sling it back. Break him in a single message.

The wind kept blowing and the moon kept shining. Time passed slow enough for him to become well acquainted with it. To make friends with the minutes. He urged them to hurry by, but they winked at him and lingered.

Finally, a chime. The GPS claimed that only nineteen minutes had passed. He could not agree with that assessment. All that impatience, all that desperate need, but when the device finally chimed, he no longer wanted to see the message. The waiting was suddenly not so bad.

He took his eyes off the moon with an effort and looked back at the display.

HOUSE FIRE REPORTED. FIRST RESPONDERS ARE ON SCENE. SEARCHING FOR SURVIVORS. WE WILL ADVISE IMMEDIATELY WHEN NOTIFIED. WHAT IS YOUR CONDITION?

Ethan dropped the GPS into the rocks and then, a few seconds later, fell onto his knees beside it.

Searching for survivors.

He knew already what they did not. He knew in his heart how it had come to pass and why and he knew that it all belonged to him. All belonged to one choice.

I'll keep him safe, he had said. And he had. The boy was safe, but back at Ethan's home they were searching for survivors.

"Which one of you is it?" Ethan said. His voice was as unfamiliar as all the rest of his world had become. The words came slowly but loudly.

There were a few shifting sounds as some boys woke. Others, deep sleepers, remained still. Ethan lifted his flashlight and clicked it on and began to pan over the shelters. He saw reflected eyes diffused through plastic, saw hands raised to block the light.

"Who is it?" he said, and this time it was a shout. "Get out here! Damn you, *get out here! I need to know which one of you it is!*"

Two of them obeyed. Marco and Drew, heads poking out of shelters, fear on their faces. The others stayed inside. As if the plastic could protect them. Ethan stumbled to his feet and grabbed the nearest shelter, took the plastic in his fists and tore it away, and there was Jeff, cowering, hands held up to protect himself. The posture of helpless fear.

The sight of him broke Ethan. He took a drunken man's weaving steps backward, still holding the plastic balled in one hand, the flashlight in the other.

"Guys," he said, his voice strangled. "Guys, I'm going to need you to get up. My wife is...there's been some trouble at my house."

They were all staring at him. Nobody answered. He realized for the first time that Raymond held a piece of wood in his hands like a bat.

"My house is on fire," Ethan said stupidly. "My house is...it was burning. It burned."

He dropped the tent he'd just ripped from over Jeff's head. Breathed and looked at the moon and said, "Stop." Very soft. Talked to himself now as he walked away from the boys to find the satellite messenger where he'd left it in the rocks. Whispered to himself.

"Be what you tell them to be," he said. "You need to do that now."

It felt like a stranger's advice. He was detached from reality and needed to return to it fast. His whole life spent telling people how to deal with disaster, how to survive. What was the first priority? Positive mental attitude? Sure, that was the one. Okay, he could do that. *She might be alive.* There you go. How positive. How fucking positive.

"Get your head together," he whispered, and his mind whispered back, *Anticipation, Ethan. Preparation, Ethan. The first rules, and you ignored them. You are prepared for people to come after the boy, but you did not anticipate how they might do that.*

He spoke louder then, as if he were teaching, and addressed the boys. "We need to…we need to do this right. Okay? We're going to do this right. Bad start. Sorry about that start. But now let's…let's think. First things, guys, what are the first things? Respond. I need to respond."

None of them spoke. He found the GPS and picked it up and wiped the dirt from it. *What is your condition?* they had asked him from the bunker in Texas. He wondered how to share that in 160 characters.

He sensed the boys were gathering behind him. Forming a tight knot. Good for them. That was the idea. They were supposed to learn to come together out here. Now he'd helped them do it. So, good for him too. Look at him go. Still teaching. His house was on fire and his wife was missing, but damn it, just look at him go.

His hand was shaking as he typed a response message.

IN MOUNTAINS ONLY ADULT WITH GROUP OF TEENS. PLEASE ADVISE THAT I AM RETURNING TO PILOT CREEK TRAIL AND SUPPORT IS REQUESTED.

He looked away, back up into the night sky, and then typed a second message.

PLEASE ADVISE ON SURVIVOR.

"Okay," he said. "Okay, now we go." He turned to face them. "I'm sorry. But we have to start hiking. My wife…I need to get back."

Marco finally broke the silence. "It's okay, man. We'll walk fast."

Ethan wanted to cry. He laughed instead. Maybe it was a laugh. Maybe it was a sob.

"Thank you," he said. "I'm going to need to walk fast."

15

CONNOR REYNOLDS WAS DEAD and Jace Wilson had risen from his grave.

The fearless boy, the bad-attitude boy, was gone and all that remained was Jace Wilson, afraid and alone, and he knew that he would not last long.

They had come for him. They had found him.

He knew that he was going to die when he woke to Ethan Serbin's wounded shout, more of a howl than a scream, demanding to know the identity of the boy responsible for unnamed crimes. Everyone was confused except for Jace.

They had come for Jace, and they had burned Ethan's house to the ground. Jace's mind wasn't on himself as they all gathered behind Ethan and began to stumble down the dark trail, headlamps bobbing and weaving. It was on Mrs. Serbin. Allison, that was her first name. Beautiful and kind and strong. A rancher's daughter who still hired cowboys.

She was dead now. Ethan might not know that, but Jace knew. He had seen the two men in the quarry and he had heard more about them in the days following as his parents tried to find the perfect way to hide him, before they'd decided on this place in the mountains. He knew that those men did not leave any survivors. He had been determined to be the first.

Any hope of that was gone now.

The group walked maybe half a mile down the trail in silence before Jace allowed himself to consider what was waiting ahead of them. He pictured their faces and heard their voices, the strange calm they spoke with as they talked of things so violent. They were here. They'd come for him.

I wish they were dead, he thought as the first hot tear leaked from the corner of his eye. *I wish they'd been with the one I saw in the water, I wish they were dead.*

And they wished he was.

The reality of that was still hard for him to process. He understood it, always had—he was a witness and therefore he was a threat—but the idea of someone wanting to kill him was so bizarre that at times it didn't seem real. *They wish me dead. They honestly wish me dead.*

He was beginning to cry harder now and slowed his pace so that the others would not hear him. It was hard walking here even in the daylight, and in the darkness the narrow beam of the headlamp required all of your attention, so nobody saw him fall back.

He reached up and wiped the tears away from his eyes with his right hand and watched the group pull away from him and thought of the men who would be waiting somewhere in the darkness, and then he made his decision: he needed to be alone when they found him.

He'd hated some of the boys at the start. But as he looked at them walking ahead now, he felt sad for them, felt like he needed to apologize, catch up to them and shout that this was his fault and they needed to let him go off on his own because he was the one they wanted, the only one, and once they had him, they would leave the others alone.

Ethan wouldn't accept that, though. Jace knew that, despite the anger he'd heard in the man's voice. He would say a lot of silly things to Jace if he heard the truth, and Ethan would believe them all. Survivor mentality, all of that. He would talk of plans and backup plans and escape routes and fail-safes, and he would think that one of these would work, somehow.

That was because Ethan had never seen them or heard them.

Jace stopped wiping at his tears and lifted his hand to his forehead and clicked off the headlamp. He thought that the vanishing beam of light might stop them, that someone might notice the darkness had grown a little deeper. Instead, they carried on along the trail as if his light had never been a part of theirs at all.

Jace sat down on the trail as the lights pulled away from him and he waited for what would come out of the darkness.

They walked down the mountain in silence except for the sounds of hard breathing as the boys fought to match Ethan's pace. He wanted to break from them and run. Once glaciers had carved the mountain on which he stood, and he understood now how time had felt in that world.

"We good?" he said a few times. "Everybody good?"

They muttered and mumbled and continued to struggle along the trail. He knew he needed to stop and give them a break but the idea of standing still was too terrible.

If they could reach the Pilot Creek trail, there was the chance that ATVs could be brought up to help them. The trail was closed to motorized vehicles but maybe the police would make an exception. Maybe not, though. You had to protect your wilderness. Those who entered it were supposed to be aware of the risks.

They'd gone just over a mile when the GPS chimed again. The boys stopped without being told. Watched him and waited. He saw a few stepping back, probably remembering the outburst that had woken them. Fearing him. He freed the GPS from the carabiner that held it to his pack and read the message.

POLICE EN ROUTE TO PILOT CREEK TRAILHEAD. ONE SURVIVOR FOUND. MEDICAL CARE ADMINISTERED ON SCENE, AMBULANCE EN ROUTE.

Ethan said one word to the boys: "Alive." He meant to explain it in more detail, but he could not. They seemed to understand. He typed a response.

WE ARE ALSO EN ROUTE. SURVIVOR STABLE?

He could have called her his wife. Could have called her by name. There was no need for the formal protocol, but it felt safer, as if it removed him from reality just enough to allow him to walk around the edges, aware of it but never looking it in the eye.

The message disappeared and he had to wait for an answer. He looked up at the boys, blinked at them. Headlamps glaring at him like a circle of interrogators.

"I'm sorry, guys. This is…this is the real deal. What

we're doing here. Middle of the night, walking in the dark, an emergency. A leader who is…who is struggling. You're doing great. You're doing great. Survivors, each and every one of you. None of the dying kind here."

A chime.

SURVIVOR STABLE. TRANSPORTED TO BILLINGS HOSPITAL. UNDERSTAND ADDITIONAL POLICE ARE ALSO ON SCENE.

They were still confused in Houston, but at least they knew a little. Maybe more than he did. Enough to understand it was not an electrical fire or a gas leak. Now they were the ones hinting around the edges of reality. Not sure what they could tell him. It occurred to him then, for the first time, that he was next in line. An obvious thought that had simply not mattered until he knew Allison was alive. All of this violence at his home had its reason. The reason traveled with him.

"We're going to walk down and meet the police," he said. He was looking around at all those white beams. Counting them. Two, four, six. He blinked and counted again. Two, four, six. His own made seven.

"Everyone turn your light on, please."

The beams turned and looked at one another. No additional light went on.

"Names," he said. "Guys? I can't see you all in the dark."

Marco, Raymond, Drew, Jeff, Ty, Bryce.

"Where is Connor?" Ethan said.

Only the night wind answered, whistling through the pines.

"When was the last time anyone saw Connor?"

A beat of silence, and then Bryce said, "He was packing up right next to me, and he was walking in the back. I didn't hear him say a word. He was right there. Right with me."

Well, Ethan thought, *that answers that.*

The killers had come for Connor, and Connor was gone.

16

T HE DREAM THAT NIGHT WAS as it always was, a dance between vivid memory and something spectral and mythic. Around Hannah there was only the smoke at first, and somewhere inside it the hiss of distant hoses, like snakes, and then the smoke parted and there was the canyon that separated her from the children. In reality it hadn't been so deep, maybe fifty feet below the ridge on which she'd been standing, but in the dream, the ridge always took on the feel of a balance beam and the canyon stretched on endlessly beneath it, a bottomless pool of black. As she crossed the ridge, the hissing of the water rose, the snakes becoming creatures that could roar, and then inside the smoke were ripples of red and orange heat, and still she walked, crossing that expanse of blackness.

When she saw the children in the dream, they were silent, and somehow that was worse. In reality they'd been screaming, they had *shrieked* for her help, and it had been terrible; at the time she could not have imagined anything worse. Then came the first dream, their silent eyes on her through the smoke and the flames, and that was a far more powerful pain, always. *Scream for me,* she wanted to tell them, *scream as though you believe I will get there.*

But in the dream they already knew she would not.

The dream children vanished, lost to blackness filled with hundreds of minuscule red dots, tiny embers that floated toward her on a blanket of heat. She woke at the same point she always woke—when the heat seemed to become real. It built in the back of her mind, came on and on, and then suddenly the whisper was a scream and she knew that it was too hot, that she was going to die, that the flesh was actually beginning to melt from her, peel away in long charred strips from her bones.

She gave voice to the screams that the children could not and then she was awake. The heat was gone, those blazing lead blankets whipped away, and she was aware of how cold it was in the cab of the tower. Her breath fogged as she took rapid, hysterical gasps, stumbling to her feet. She always had to move, had to run, that was the first instinct. If you could run, *run.*

The night it happened, she could not run. Or did not. Others had. She'd looked up the side of the mountain, saw the litter of deadfall, massive downed pines the whole way. It was breccia rock up high, loose and prone to sliding. Behind them, the fire caught a southwestern wind and howled; she would remember that sound until the day she died—it *howled.* Inside the flames, spectacular, horrifying things were happening—eddying colors, deep red to pale yellow, as the fire fought itself, adjusting for position, seeking fuel and oxygen, which was all that it needed for life once someone provided the spark. It had been given the spark, and then the wind gave it the oxygen and the dried-out forest gave it the fuel, and the only thing capable of stopping the monster's growth was Hannah's crew.

There was a choice, waiting there in the drainage, in an area they never should have approached: Break protocol and run, or hold protocol and deploy shelters. It was evident to everyone by then that the fire was gaining speed and was not going to be stopped. They all fell silent for a few seconds, recognizing what they had done, the way they'd trapped themselves, and she believed that more than a few of them also remembered the way it had happened, the way Nick had decided they would not descend into the gulch and Hannah had convinced him otherwise. There was a family down there, and they were trapped, and Hannah had believed they could be saved. Nick hadn't. She'd won the debate, and they'd descended into the gulch, and then the wind shifted into their faces.

A quarter mile away, on the other side of a too-shallow creek, the family of campers looked at them and screamed. And Hannah screamed back, telling them to get into the water, get under the water. Knowing all the while that there wasn't enough water to save them.

Her crew scattered then. A unit so tight they usually moved as one, but panic was a devastating thing, and it was upon them now. Nick was shouting at them to deploy fire shelters; some were shouting back that they had to run; one guy was telling them all to dump everything, every bit of gear, and sprint for the creek. Another one, Brandon, simply sat down. That was all. He just sat down and watched the fire burn toward him.

Hannah watched them make their choices and then disappear. Someone grabbed her shoulder and tried to tug her up the mountainside. She'd shaken him off, still staring at the family they'd come down here to help, this foolish family who'd camped in the basin, who'd pitched their tents inside the monster's open fist. The screaming children seemed to be addressing her personally. Why? Because she was a woman? Because they saw something different in her eyes? Or because she was the only one dumb enough to just stand there and stare?

It had been Nick's voice that finally registered with her. *"Hannah, damn you, deploy or die! Deploy or die!"*

The shouted words were nothing but surreal whispers in the midst of the fire's roar. The heat registered next, a staggering wave of it, and she had the sense that the wind had picked up again, and she knew that was bad. She looked up the slope and saw the backs of those who'd elected to run and then Nick shouted at her again and finally he'd deployed his own fire shelter and shoved her into it. The shelter popped up like some tinfoil joke tent. The heat was all around her and oppressive then—a deep breath found nothing; the oxygen had been scalded out of the air. She crawled inside as the first tongues of flame advanced through the drainage like a scout party. The rules were simple: You got inside, you sealed yourself off, and then you waited, waited, waited. When the roar of the fire was past, that did not mean that the fire itself was. You could step out thinking you were safe and still be scorched.

She was facing southwest, into the wind, as she brought the flap of the fire shelter down around her. The last thing she saw, other than the living wall of fire marching toward her, was the boy. He was the only one left. The girl and her parents had ducked into the tent, evidently imitating the procedures of the firefighters on the other side of the creek. There was only one problem—their tent wasn't fireproof. The family had pressed it beneath a ledge of stone, hoping to somehow duck the fire, but the boy fought off his parents and stayed outside, terrified of waiting for the flames. He wanted to run, wanted to get into the water.

She watched him splash into the creek, running just ahead of the fifteen-hundred-degree orange-and-red cascade behind him. That was the last thing she saw before Nick sealed her in. She was grateful for that. Grateful that he'd still been running. He made the creek too. Got under the water.

Boiled in it.

She didn't know that until the board of inquiry's investigation.

Hannah had stayed in the shelter for forty-five minutes. Forty-five minutes of the most intense heat she'd ever felt, surrounded by human screams and fire roars. The blaze tried to kill her, it tried its very best, chewing tiny holes through the fireproof shelter material. She'd watched them develop, a hundred glowing dots, like a sky of bloodred stars.

They'd been trained to wait for release from the shelters by the crew boss. By Nick. She didn't know then that the crew boss was dead.

"My God," she said in her fire tower now, and she started to cry again. How long did a thing like that chase you? How long would memories like that keep their hands tight around your throat? When would they decide it was time to let you go?

She laid her head down on the Osborne, the copper bezel cool against her skin.

The man Jace hated most was Ethan Serbin.

Forget about the two coming after him, and his parents, who'd brought him here and promised he'd be safe, and the police, who'd agreed to the plan. The one Jace absolutely despised once his tears stopped was Ethan.

Because Ethan's voice wouldn't go away.

All those silly rules and mantras and instructions, falling on his ears day and night since he'd arrived in Montana, wouldn't stop even though their source was no longer around. The lessons lingered behind like floodwaters. He wanted them gone. He was tired and he was scared and he was alone. It was quitting time.

There is no such thing as quitting time. Remember that, boys. You rest, you sleep, you pout, you cry. You're allowed to get mad, allowed to get sad. But you're not allowed to quit. When you feel like it, remember that you are allowed to stop, but not to quit. So give yourself that much. Stop. Just stop. And then, remember what STOP is to a survivor—sit, think, observe, plan. Spelled out for you, right there at the moment of your highest frustration, is all you need to do to start saving your life.

Jace didn't want to do any of those things, but the problem was the waiting. He didn't know how far off his killers were, how long he'd have to sit here before they found him.

It might be a long time.

He was doing the things he needed to without even intending to do them—he had sat; and he was of course thinking, he couldn't avoid that, not once the tears were done; and without meaning to, when a light went on in the darkness, he found himself observing.

It grabbed his attention because it didn't belong. There was another human presence on the mountain. Someone with electricity. Distant, but not so far away as to be unreachable. He stared in confusion, trying to comprehend how it had come to exist, and then he remembered the lunch break and the landmarks Ethan had used to help them orient themselves to their position on the map. You had to pick things that were unique, features that didn't blend in with the rest of the scenery, and then you triangulated your position using the map and the compass. Pilot Peak was one unique point, and Amphitheater was another, but for the third, they had not used a mountain. They'd used a fire tower.

Jace observed the light and began to see possibilities he hadn't noticed before, possibilities he hadn't even wanted. There had seemed to be two choices—hike down with the others to the death that was waiting for him, or stay back alone in the mountains and wait for death to come to him.

The light beckoned, though. It told him there were other ways this might end.

You've got to observe the world you're in to understand what parts of it may save you. At first, it may all seem hostile. The whole environment may seem like an enemy. But it isn't. There are things hiding in it waiting to save you, and it's your job to see them.

The fire tower was within reach. What it contained, he didn't know. Maybe somebody with a gun. Maybe a phone or a radio, a way to call a helicopter in and get him off the mountain before anyone even knew he was missing.

Despite himself, Jace was beginning to plan.

But in his mind he saw his pursuers again, heard those detached voices, so empty and so in control, and he knew in his heart that he shouldn't have been allowed to get away even once from men like those. They didn't leave witnesses behind. Even the police had said that, had told it to his mother, to his father, had scared them so badly that they agreed to send their only son into the wilderness to hide. He'd escaped once and no one could escape them twice, certainly not a boy, a child.

But I made fire. I'm different now. They don't know it, but I do.

It was a small thing, a silly thing, and he knew that, but still the memory gave him the faintest touch of strength, and he thought of the hiking he'd done and the fire tower that beckoned and he wanted to surprise them all. Not just the evil pair behind him. Surprise them *all.* The police, his parents, Ethan Serbin, the world.

Nobody got away from those two. But Jace already had once. He'd been lucky that time. They hadn't been certain he was there, and the clock was ticking for them. But he hadn't known they were coming then either. He'd been unprepared. He'd been weak.

He was prepared now, and he was stronger. There was no need to pretend to be Connor Reynolds anymore, but while Jace Wilson had once been the secret within Connor Reynolds, now it was reversed. Connor and the things he had learned in these days in the mountains were the secret within Jace Wilson.

And the two evil men coming for him weren't prepared for that. They were expecting to find the same boy they'd left behind once, the boy who'd hid, and waited, and cried.

A boy who looked just like the one on the trail now.

"We don't have quitting time," Jace said aloud. These were the first words he had spoken since he'd been awakened by Ethan's shout. His voice sounded small in the darkness, but at least it was there. It reminded him of his own existence, in a strange way. He wasn't dead yet. His body still worked. It could speak.

And it could walk.

17

ALLISON COULD FEEL HANDS on her, and the hands hurt, but then they hurt less, and she knew that a drug had been in the mix. At first she was on the ground, and then they moved her with care, guiding her out of the wreckage that had once been her home. She heard them complimenting her on her hiding place. She'd done a good job with that, it seemed. Common sense, she thought. She'd just wanted to get to water. In the end she hadn't even turned it on, hadn't been able to, but the shower floor was a good place to curl up. She was low for the smoke, and the tile in the room was unappetizing to the flames. They had moved on in search of fuels more to their liking and then they had been interrupted before they had a chance to return to her.

That perfect bathroom, the granite-tiled room and its porcelain tub with a mountain view, the finishing touch of their golden home together, had saved her. She hadn't gotten any water, but there was plenty in there now — a hose jetted streams of it through the shattered window, steam rising in angry response.

Out in the yard, the paramedics worked on her some more, and no one was asking questions yet, they were just trying to fix her. The questions were coming, though. She knew that and she knew that she had to give the right answers.

When they brought the backboard out, she was terrified. It was something you didn't belong on unless you were hurt very bad, or dying. She tried to pull away from it and she told them that she could stand and they held her down and told her that she could not.

"Tango's been standing for three months," she told them. The logic seemed sound to her, but it didn't alter their decision. She was lifted and lowered onto the backboard and then they were carrying her out through a dizzying whirl of colored lights and toward an ambulance. One of the paramedics was asking her how the pain was, and she started to tell them that it was bad, but then stopped. No more drugs. Not yet.

"Need to talk to my husband," she said. Speaking allowed long needles of pain to enter her face through her lips and slide all the way up into her brain.

"We'll find your husband. He'll be here soon. Just rest."

Most of her wanted to accept that. It would be good to see Ethan, and she wanted to rest, she wanted to do the things they kept instructing her to do—rest, relax, be still. That all sounded excellent. It was a little too soon for it, though.

"He has a GPS messenger," she said; she was in the back of the ambulance now, though the ambulance wasn't moving, and the paramedics seemed to be working hard to ignore her, but thank God there was a police officer present, one she knew, one Ethan had worked with on rescues before. His name was well known to her but she couldn't think of it. That was embarrassing, but she hoped he would understand. She gave up on finding his name and settled for direct eye contact instead.

"Please," she said. "I need to get him a message. You know how. The GPS can—"

"I'll get him the message, Allison. You just tell me what to say. I'll get it to him."

He kept looking away. She wondered what he saw. What she looked like to his eyes.

"You t-tell him..." Now she stuttered, because it was critical to get the wording right. That was imperative. To find a way to make Ethan understand without allowing the rest of the world to understand. A secret code. Husband-and-wife. Why hadn't they ever developed a code? It seemed like something they should have done. Buy groceries, do laundry, create code.

"You need to get this right," she told the police officer. "Just as I say."

He seemed concerned now, but he nodded. One of the paramedics was asking him to step back, trying to close the door, but he held up a hand and told them to wait.

"You tell him that Allison says she is fine, but that JB's friends are coming to see him."

"We'll tell him you're fine. He'll be here soon. You'll see him very—"

"*No.*" She tried to shout and the pain that brought on was excruciating, but she tunneled through it. "You need to say it right. Tell me how you will say it."

They were all staring at her now, even the paramedics. The officer whose name she could not remember said, "Allison is fine but JB's friends are coming to see him."

"*Two.* Say *two* of JB's friends." It was important to be detailed. She knew that. The more details he had, the more prepared he would be.

The officer said that he would. He was receding from her but she couldn't feel the ambulance moving and the door was still open. That was fascinating. How was that happening? Oh, he was stepping back. Funny how fast the drugs worked. Very disorienting. Very good drugs. She told the paramedics that. She thought they would like to know how good these things were. They were busy, though; they always seemed to be busy.

The door closed and the ambulance shifted beneath her and then they really were moving, bumping down the driveway. She could see the men with the pale blue eyes again and she could see her husband's face and she wished that she'd been able to send the message herself. The officer had better get it right. There were two of them, and they were evil. Maybe she should have used that word in the message. Maybe she should have been clearer. She had said that two friends were coming, but that was so far from the truth.

Evil was coming.

This time the dream was different, gentler in its layers but more evil in its content. This time the boy was coming for Hannah. He was walking right toward her, wearing a headlamp, marching to her tower, and she was terrified of him and whatever message he carried.

You've lost your mind, she thought, staring out the window as the boy with the lamp reached the base of the tower steps and began to come up them, the steel rattling against his feet.

He couldn't be real. A boy just like the one who haunted

her, walking out of the night woods, out of the mountains, all alone and bound for her as if he'd been marching toward her all this time?

The terrible thing stopped after ten steps, though. Held tightly to the rail, looked up at her tower and then back down. Came up another few steps in a rush, moving awkwardly with the weight of an outsize pack on his back, then stopped again and put both hands on the step in front of him. Holding on to it as if for balance.

Hannah was still developing her theory of ghosts and she didn't understand much about them, but one thing she was sure of: they weren't afraid of heights.

She rose from the bunk and walked to the door, and down below the boy began his surreal ascent from the blackness again, the white beam of light guiding him toward her. She opened the door, stepped out into the night, and shouted, *"Stop!"*

He nearly fell off the tower. Stumbled into the rail, gave a little cry, and slipped sideways; the pack caught him and kept him from sliding down the steps.

Ghosts were not scared of the living. Nightmares didn't tremble at the sound of your voice.

"Are you okay?" she called.

He didn't answer, and she started down the steps. He watched her come, the headlamp shining directly into her eyes.

"Please turn that light off."

He reached up and fumbled with it and clicked something and then the light shifted from harsh white to an eerie crimson glow. A setting designed to protect your night vision. She walked down until she could see him.

He bore no resemblance to the boy from her memories.

He was older and taller, with dark hair instead of blond. His face was covered with dirt and scratches and sweat, and he was breathing hard. He'd been walking for a while.

"Where did you come from?"

"I'm...I got lost. Heading back to camp."

"You're camping?"

He nodded. She was close enough now to see that there were streaks on his face where tears had cleared the dirt.

"You're with your parents?"

"No. I mean...not anymore. Not now."

It was a strange answer, and his eyes made it even stranger. Flicking around like there were options all about and he needed to find the right one. For a yes-or-no answer? Hannah looked at him and tried to see what she was missing. There was something. He was dressed for camping, yes, and he had the pack and the headlamp, all the proper equipment, but...

The pack. Why was he still wearing it if he'd gotten lost on his way *back* to camp?

"How long ago did you wander off?"

"I don't know. Couple hours."

That put him strapping a full pack on after midnight. A pretty serious bathroom run.

"What's your name?" she said.

Again the flicker of the eyes. "Connor."

"Your parents are out there somewhere, but you don't know how to find your way back?"

"Yeah. I need to get in touch with them."

"I'd say so."

"You have a phone up there?" he asked.

"A radio. We'll call for help. Come on up. We'll get it straightened out."

He got to his feet slowly. Holding to the railing as if he fully expected the stairs to collapse beneath him and leave him dangling from it. She turned and led the way up to the cab. The moon was descending, and in the eastern sky there were the first perceptible lightening shades of dawn. She'd been awake until well past midnight listening to the reports from the fire line. They'd failed to contain the flames before dark and had called for a second hotshot crew to help. In the morning, she expected there would be discussion of a helitack unit. For a brief time, there had been added excitement when reports of a second flare-up a few miles away came in, but that turned out to be a house fire, quickly extinguished. Now it was just the one blaze out there in the night. The wind that had picked up at dusk had blown steadily all through the night and showed no sign of wanting to lie down in front of the oncoming day.

Poor kid, she thought. Whatever he wasn't telling her—and there was something—he needed to get the hell out of these mountains and back to his family. She wondered if he had run away from them. That would explain the full pack and the hesitant answers. It was none of her business. All she had to do was make sure he got to safety. A more active role than she'd expected to have this summer.

She reached the top of the cab and turned on the overhead lights and waited while he made his way up. She'd been going slow but he still had fallen well behind. Even when the lights went on in the cab, he didn't look up from his boots. Step, step, pause. Step, step, pause. Never glancing up or to the sides.

"Here we are," she said. "My little kingdom. Where did you come from? Do you know the name of the campsite, or a landmark? I'll need to offer instructions to find your family."

Again, that strange expression overtook him. As if he didn't have an answer ready and needed time to consider before offering one. It wasn't a deceptive look, just uncertain.

"Who do you call on the radio?" he said.

"People who can help."

"Right. But…who, exactly? Police?"

"Are you worried about the police?"

"No," the boy said.

"Do you *need* the police?"

"It's just…I'm curious. I need to know, that's all."

"What do you need to know?"

"Who *exactly* answers the radio?"

"Dispatch for firefighters. But from there, they'll call whoever you need."

He frowned. "Firefighters."

"Yes."

"Who can hear what they say?"

"Pardon?"

"Is it just…is it two-way communication?"

"Two-way communication?" she echoed. "I'm not sure that I follow."

"Can other people hear what you say? Like, is it just you and another person, the way it would be on a phone? Or can other people listen? On other radios?"

"Hon," she said, "you need to tell me what the real problem is here. Okay?"

He didn't answer.

"Where did you really come from?" she said.

He let his eyes drift away from hers. They settled on the

Osborne. He wandered over to it and stared at the map, silent, then leaned down, investigating it.

Autistic, maybe, she thought. *Or—what's that other condition? When a kid is really smart but you ask him a normal question and he ignores it? Whatever that condition is, this kid has it.*

"If you don't remember, that's okay. I'll just need to explain what—"

"I'd say we were right…there." He had his index finger on the topographic map. She was too intrigued by him now to just repeat the question, so instead she went to his side and looked at where he was pointing.

"That's nine thousand feet there," he said. "And we were one ridge down, in this area that flattened out, and we had the slope at our back. You can see that? The way the line bends, it shows you that there's a flat area there. It's not as steep as what's around it, you see?"

He looked up at her, curious to know if she understood.

"Yeah," she said. "I can see it."

"Well, that's where we were camped. We're working on orienteering, and I saw the smoke and figured out where we were…and then…then, later, when you put the light on, I saw this place. That was probably an hour ago? You'd be surprised how well the light carries, with this thing being so tall. But once I saw it, I remembered what it was. Or what it probably was. When you turned it off, I got kind of worried that I'd imagined it. I mean, it got so dark so fast, it was like it was never there. But I had the angle right, I mean the bearing, it's called a bearing, and so I just…I just kept walking."

He was beginning to ramble now, and his hands had started to shake. For the first time, he looked troubled. More than troubled. He looked terrified.

"Walking away from what?" Hannah said. "What has you so scared?"

"I don't know. Listen, I need you to do me a favor."

Here we go, she thought. *Here's where it gets interesting.*

"Call for help," she said. "Yeah, I'm on it."

"No. No, please don't do that. If you could just...give me a little while to think."

"To think?"

"I just need to...need to stop. Just for a few minutes, okay? I need to just...figure some things out. But I've got to think."

"We need to get you out of here to someone who can help you. Let's do that, and then you can think. You shouldn't be up here. I can't just let you stay up here."

"Then I'll leave. I'm sorry. I shouldn't have come here. It seemed like the right thing but now...I'm afraid I made a mistake. I'm going to leave."

"Don't."

"I should. Forget about it. Just forget I was here. There's no need to make a big scene out of it, calling the police or whatever. I don't think that would be good."

His voice was shaking.

She said, "Connor? It's my job to let people know what's happening up here. If I don't report this, I could get fired."

"Please," he said. He seemed on the verge of tears, and she didn't understand a bit of it, knew only that she needed to get somebody up here to deal with him. An underage kid wandering the backcountry alone at night? That was something you called in *immediately.*

"Let's all think on it," she said. "I'm just going to let my bosses know you're here. That way, if they have a good idea, they can share it, and if your parents have gotten ahold of people already, if they're looking for you, then everyone can relax." She moved toward the radio. "Think about how scared they're going to be. This could do a lot to make them feel better."

"Please," he said again, but she wasn't going to listen, and she kept her back to him as she reached for the mike.

"I'll just report your position, that's all. You don't need to worry." She keyed the mike but got only as far as "This is Lynx Lookout" before he smashed the hatchet down on the desk, severing the cord between the microphone and the radio.

She screamed and whirled away, tripping on the chair and falling to her hands and knees. Turned back and stared at him as he took more careful smashes with the hatchet she kept near the woodpile for splitting kindling. He was using the back of it now, trying to crush the front of the radio. And having success. He was sobbing while he did it.

"I'm sorry," he said. "Really, I am. But I don't know if we can do that. I don't know if that's a good idea. If they already made it this far, then somebody is listening. Somebody is telling them things that were supposed to be secret."

18

The smoke that Connor had located correctly on the map was still visible above the mountains when Ethan reached the Pilot Creek trailhead with six exhausted boys in tow and one missing in the wilderness behind them. It had been a forest fire, just as he'd feared. It seemed to be growing. He stared at it with detachment, this thing that once would have occupied so much of his attention, and then he turned to look back at those who were waiting for them.

Three police cars—two SUVs and one pickup truck from the park. Six people in uniform milling around. One for every boy Ethan had brought back out of the mountains.

He'd had some time to think about it, several hours of walking down through the darkness while behind him Connor walked in the opposite direction. If he walked at all.

In a different situation, Ethan would have cared deeply about that. He wondered what was more selfish, putting the anonymous boy ahead of Allison, or Allison ahead of the boy. There was the responsibility to a child in need, and then there was the responsibility to your wife. Picking one over the other was never the noble choice, not that he could see. So you tried to care for them all, but in the end you couldn't do that. You made choices.

He had made the wrong choice.

Only you can handle this, Jamie had suggested, and his answer had been *Of course, you are right.*

The boys fell gasping onto the ground, some of them not even unfastening their packs first. He looked at them and felt the weight of failure, a weight he had not known before.

He knew several of the officers on scene. While most tended to the boys, passing out water bottles and asking questions, a police sergeant named Roy Futvoye took Ethan aside. They sat beneath the open tailgate of his Suburban and Roy told him that the house was destroyed and Allison was in the hospital in Billings.

"She said there were two of them. She seemed…a little vague with what they were after."

Yes, she would have. Secrecy, Ethan had said. Trust no one, Ethan had said. I'll keep him safe, Ethan had said.

"What did they do to her?" His voice was low and he couldn't look Roy in the eye.

"Far less than they might have. If she hadn't started that fire, who knows."

Ethan looked up. "Allison started the fire?"

Roy nodded. "Used a can of bear spray on the woodstove. It ran them off, but…but she paid a price too. She's got some burns. And one of those guys"—now it was Roy who didn't meet Ethan's eyes—"one of them busted up her mouth pretty well."

"Did he, though," Ethan said. His own mouth went dry.

"She's okay," Roy said. "She'll be all right. But I need to talk to you. If there's a reason these men are here—"

"There's always a reason," Ethan said. His mind was already gone from the conversation. He was back at the cabin, envisioning a man *busting up her mouth pretty well.*

"Serbin? I'm going to need you to focus for me here. If you've got *any* information on these men, I need it. The sheriff is dead and it might be connected. The action I take is—"

"Claude is dead?"

"You see that smoke?"

"Yeah."

"That fire's still going, and Claude was at the start of it. We found his body up there. He'd been timbering. Now, you know Claude. And I know Claude. You tell me—does he start a fire in the middle of the afternoon while he's felling trees?"

"Unlikely."

Any job that arrives with a blizzard, he'd said to Jamie Bennett that night. And laughed.

He turned and stared at the faces of the fatigued, confused boys who knew nothing. Marco was watching him with concern. Marco, who'd be going back to his shitstorm of a home life now. All of them would be.

"She's safe," Ethan said to Roy. "She's okay. Hurt, but okay."

"That's right. You can see her. She's had better days, to be sure, but you're not going to lose her, Ethan. You didn't, and you won't."

He nodded. Still looking around him. Taking in the faces, the questioning stares, the hard smoking mountains beyond.

"I'll come back to find the boy," he told Roy.

"The boy?"

And so Ethan told him what he'd hoped he'd never have to say in his life: he'd lost a child on the mountain.

"We'll get him, Ethan. Don't worry about that."

"I've made a promise," he said. "Made a lot of them. I'll see to his safety. Whether you find him first or not, you don't do a thing before you check with me, understand? Not a thing."

Roy tilted his head and glanced away. "You got anything I should know about this kid?"

Ethan said, "I need to head to the hospital now. I need to see her. But I'll be back." He repeated it again, louder, and this time he was looking at the boys. "I'll be back, guys."

They all looked at him, and some of them nodded, while others already seemed to accept what he didn't—he would never see them again.

The Blackwell brothers watched through rifle scopes as the group emerged at the trailhead, watched with fingers on triggers. They were in the woods opposite the road, a higher elevation, a fine vantage point. It had not been hard to find the boys. The police activity ensured that.

"If you take the shot," Jack Blackwell said, "you better make sure it's good."

"I'm aware of the stakes."

"I'm reminding us both. One clean shot, and then it's all about speed. We better move fast when it's done."

"We will."

"They don't know who he is yet," Jack said. The left side of his face was badly burned. High red blisters forming.

"You don't think?"

"Not much interest being shown in the boys. More in Serbin. And these are all local police. I don't see a fed of any sort, do you?"

"No."

"So then they do not know the value of young Jace."

Together, lying prone in sniper stances with twenty feet separating them, they watched the boys take shape. Adjusted scopes for clearer looks at faces. Six boys. Six fatigued faces.

"I don't see him."

"Neither do I."

"They're acting as if that's all. Nobody else coming."

"They moved him already, then. Got a step ahead."

"No. Too fast for that."

"Then he was never here to begin with."

"You heard the Serbin woman. She knew why we were here."

They watched for a long time. Two uniformed police and a man in an orange vest and camouflage distributed radios, checked them, and then walked away from the boys and up to the trailhead. Disappeared into the woods.

"What are they going back for?" Patrick said.

"I'm wondering the same thing." Jack looked away from the scope and met his brother's eyes. "Interesting."

"Indeed. One missing, you think? Young Jace is very smart. Very resourceful."

"And maybe very alone in the woods."

"Maybe."

"If they find him first, it's trouble."

"We find him first, it's easy."

"That is what we were promised from the beginning. So far, nothing has been easy."

"So it goes with some quests, brother. We must earn our reward today."

"How I treasure your bits of wisdom. Let me never say otherwise."

"I appreciate that."

"Serbin's leaving."

Jack turned back to the scope. One of the police SUVs was pulling away. Serbin riding out. The six boys and the rest of the police remained behind.

"She's alive," his brother said. "I told you."

"You don't know that."

"I do. You watched him. You think that was the reaction of a man whose wife was dead? Pretty calm. And in a pretty big hurry now. Going to see her."

"We need the kid."

"Need them both now."

Jack sighed and lowered the rifle. "I suppose it's good that there's two of us."

"It always has been. Who do you want?"

"If she's alive, she's in a hospital. Figure I'll blend in pretty well in an ER right now, don't you think?"

"So I'm into the woods, then."

"You're better at that than me."

"Yes."

"And I won't be long."

"We'll see. It's been longer than I wanted already."

"Sometimes that's the way of the world, brother. I prefer speed as much as you do. I just understand patience a bit more."

"The men who went in after the boy know more than we do about his location."

"I'd imagine."

"So I follow. And if I see him, I take the shot."

"If you see him, you *make* the shot. Taking it isn't worth much."

"Have you seen me miss?"

"No."

"There you go, then. How do you intend to get me back out of the mountains?"

Jack Blackwell's only response was a smile.

19

H E WANTED TO CRY AGAIN but didn't have the tears left, or maybe the energy. The woman was scared of him, and he felt bad about that, but he wasn't doing anything scary anymore. He didn't even have the hatchet; it was right there on the floor.

"Pick it up," he said.

"What?"

He waved at the hatchet. "Go ahead and take it. Use it on me if you want."

"I'm not going to use a hatchet on you," the woman said. "And you're not going to use it on me. Are you?"

Jace shook his head.

"Then put it back where it belongs," she said.

He was surprised that she was encouraging him to touch it again. When he looked up, she seemed firm about it, though. Her arms were crossed over her chest in a protective fashion but she wasn't trying to run.

"Put it back, Connor," she said.

That tone of voice sounded so much like his mother's.

His mother wasn't a yelling type. She was used to being in charge—in her job she had to be calm and in charge, she told him that all the time, calm and in charge, calm and in charge. So when she got mad at him, she kept up the same attitude. Just like this woman now. She didn't look very much like his mother, though. She was shorter and younger and thinner. Too thin. Like she had an eating disorder.

"Connor," she said again, and this time he listened. He picked up the hatchet by its handle and returned it to the woodpile. She never moved, never even tensed up. When he'd set it down, she said, "Let's talk. Hon? We need to be honest with each other. It's just the two of us now. You made damn sure of that."

"I had to," he said. "I know you don't believe that, but it's true."

"Tell me why."

He didn't say anything.

"It's the least you can do," she said. "You walked in here and destroyed my radio, and I'm in serious trouble now, do you understand that? There's a fire burning out there, and people are counting on me to help, and I can't."

"It was for you," he said. "Not just me. It's to keep you safe."

"Tell me why," she repeated.

He was exhausted, physically and mentally, but he knew he couldn't tell her. They'd hammered that into his brain long before he arrived in Montana. *No one can know…*

But what was the point of keeping it a secret now? The men from the quarry were already here. Telling someone the truth wasn't going to make it any worse.

"Hon," she said, "this isn't fair to me. I can see that you're scared, and I believe that there's a reason. I *know* there must be a reason. But if somebody is going to hurt you or something, and you're with me, then I deserve to know. Don't you see that?"

"You have no idea," he blurted.

"Go on."

"I *can't*."

"You have to. Damn it, I *deserve* to know what's out there!" She waved her hand at the world around them, which was just beginning to brighten. It probably looked darker down on the ground, but when you were up here in the tower, reaching into the sky, the light came early.

"They're coming to kill me," he said.

She stared at him. Started to say something and then stopped, took a breath, and finally said, "Who?"

"I don't know their names. But there are two of them. They've come a long way."

He could see that she was trying to decide whether to believe him. Wondering if he was some sort of crazy kid who'd imagined a wild story. Why wouldn't she think that? The truth was harder to believe.

"You think I'm making it up."

"No," she said, and maybe she wasn't lying. "Who's coming? And why? Tell me why."

"I can't."

"If I'm in danger because you're here, I at least need to understand it."

She was right, and he felt bad refusing to tell her the truth. If they were close—and he knew they were, they had to be—then she was in danger too. It wasn't just him.

"I think they killed his wife," he whispered. "Or hurt her really bad. Burned his house down, all because of me."

"Hang on," the woman said. "Hang on. A house fire? I heard a house-fire call earlier tonight. You were there?"

For the first time, it was clear that she was absolutely willing to believe him. Or at least to listen. The fire had convinced her. Fire had that kind of power.

"I wasn't there," he said. "But…I'm not supposed to tell anybody anything. I'm not supposed to trust anyone. They made me promise that."

"Connor, you can trust me. And I *need* to know."

He looked away and said, "I saw a murder. They brought me up here to hide me. I guess they didn't do a very good job."

She looked at the door and for a minute he thought she was going to walk out of it, just leave him here and not look back. He wouldn't have blamed her. Instead, she took a deep breath and said, "Where did you see a murder?"

"Indiana. I'm supposed to be a witness. People thought I was safe here, but…but I think they found me."

"Who are they? Not their names, but…"

She didn't know how to phrase the question, but he knew how to answer it.

"They're evil," he said. "That's all they are. They were dressed like police, but the people they killed *were* police. They kill people for money, and it doesn't even…it doesn't even stress them out. I watched them do it. They were re-laxed the whole time. People don't matter to them."

He told her all of it. All the important stuff. The plan his parents had agreed to, the way he was supposed to pre-tend to be a bad kid, the way he was supposed to fit in with the group and hide in the wilderness and there would be no cell phones to trace or cameras to spot him; he would be *off the grid*, that was the whole point. He told her about

Ethan and the way he'd woken them all in the night and how they'd been walking back down the Pilot Creek trail when he turned off his headlamp and let them go on. When he was finished, he added, "I'm sorry it had to be you."

"What?"

"I'm sorry you had to be here. I don't want anyone getting hurt because of me."

"It's okay," she said. "Nobody will get hurt. We'll figure it out."

It seemed like she was trying to convince herself, not him, and that was fine, because Jace didn't believe it.

"We can see them coming," she said. "If they're really out there, and they head up here, we can see them coming for a long ways."

He looked at the windows and nodded. "I guess we'll know when they get here, at least."

"You're sure they're coming?" she said.

"I'm sure."

"How long did it take you to get here?"

"A little more than an hour."

"So they could be here any minute."

"I don't know. They weren't with us. If they were, I'd be dead by now."

"I think we should leave," she said. "If we can get back to the road, then we can—"

"It's a long walk to the road."

"Yes, it is. Seven miles. But we can do it. We'll be fine."

"You can stay here," Jace told her. "I'll run for it. You don't need to try to make it with me. Or I can stay and you can run."

She said, "Let's stick together. Whatever we decide, let's both do the same thing."

177

He nodded. He didn't want to see her get hurt because of him, but he didn't want to be alone either. "What's your name?" he said.

"Hannah. Hannah Faber."

"I'm sorry, Hannah. I really am. But they're very good. They found me even when I was off the grid. If you had said anything on the radio, I know they would have been here. They would have heard it, somehow. They hear it all."

"Well," she said, bending to pick up a broken fragment of the face of the radio, "that doesn't seem to be a problem anymore, does it?"

"No."

"Okay. You've taken care of one problem. But now we need to figure out how to take care of the rest. Any ideas?"

He was silent for a minute, and then he said, "I had an escape route."

"Pardon?"

"We all did. Ethan makes us plot one before we set out. This time it was going into Cooke City. But not using the trail. If we're going to leave, we probably shouldn't use the trail. That's what they'll take to find me."

"Fantastic," Hannah Faber told him. "Just you and me and the wilderness? No, let's wait here. Nobody knows where you are. You've seen to that, thanks to your work on the radio. But eventually, they're going to notice that I'm off the air. And when they do, they'll send help."

"So we just wait?"

"Right. We wait it out where we can see people coming a long time before they get here. That's the best thing about this place." She was pacing and nodding to herself the way you did when you were trying to talk yourself into being brave. Jace recognized the behavior. He'd done it on the quarry ledges.

"We can just wait here, like it's a fortress," she said. "It'll be like the Alamo."

"Everybody died at the Alamo," Jace said.

She stood with her back to the window and looked at him as the world of shadows gave way to daylight behind her.

"Probably because they had no damn radio," she said.

20

ALLISON'S FACE WAS ALL but hidden from him. Bandages covered the skin he'd touched with his lips countless times. Only her closed eyes were visible, and her mouth, dark with swelling and laced with black stitches. Hand and forearm wrapped in heavy gauze. Ethan touched her unbandaged hand and said her name, soft as a prayer. Her eyes opened and found his.

"Baby," she said. The word came clumsily from her broken mouth.

"I'm here."

"I did the best I could," she said. "Maybe not so good. But the best I could."

What was left of her hair had been cut down to jagged clumps by the nurses. The rest had burned away. He used to run his hands through it before she slept, or when she was sick, or anytime a comforting gesture seemed in order. One was in order now but he knew better than to touch.

"You did amazing," he said, and his words came out clumsily too. That was no good. One of them should be able to speak. "I'm so sorry. It's on me. They came because of—"

"No," she said. "They came because of her."

"I made a mistake. Should never have agreed to it."

"She made the mistake. You were just part of it."

He wasn't ready to blame Jamie Bennett just yet. He couldn't say that he was ready to forgive her either. *She rushes, and she makes mistakes,* Allison had said. Not wrong, that assessment. Not wrong at all. The one hundred percent guarantee that the men would not get to her witness, her promise that if they even moved toward Montana, she'd know about it? So much for that. Ethan hadn't heard a word. He wondered for the first time if she was still alive.

"Do the police know about her?" he asked.

"Not yet. I was…struggling. Thoughts not clear. Everything was on fire."

"I know."

"What about Tango? I was thinking…" She started to cry then, tears leaking down only to be absorbed immediately by the bandages. "I was thinking that Tango couldn't even try to run. The way we've got him standing, he couldn't even try to—"

"The horse is fine."

"You're sure?"

He nodded.

"The house?"

He didn't answer. Just held her hand and looked into her eyes. He hadn't seen it yet, but he'd been told. The Ritz was destroyed. Their promised land, built together, their little triumph in the world, reduced to cold ashes and dripping water.

"Why'd she have to pick you?" Allison said.

"Don't blame her. Blame me. She asked; she didn't order. I should have said no. I should have done a lot of things different. But I'll make right what I can, Allison. I'll get the boy and—"

"Wait. Wait. What do you mean, you'll get him? Where is he?"

Smart woman, his wife. Beat her, burn her, sedate her. Then slip up and hope she didn't catch it. Good luck with that.

"He's missing," he said. He made himself continue to look into her eyes when he said that. It wasn't easy.

"What?"

"Ran off in the night. When we were hiking down."

"Which one was he?"

"Connor. I suppose I could be wrong. But I doubt it. The boys knew that…that someone had arrived, and trouble was here, and he was the one who ran."

She looked away from him and down to the heavy wrapping around her wounded hand. *All for nothing,* she was surely thinking. All she'd gone through, and still the boy was gone. Ethan had promised to protect them both and had failed to protect either.

"Where do you think he went?"

To hide, Ethan thought, *to run and hide because he was afraid of not only them, but me. He has no friends left in this world, or at least that is how he feels now.* But he said, "Maybe the escape route. He seemed to pay a lot of attention to those. He was the best one with the maps. With land navigation. Maybe the best with everything. So when he left us on the trail, he might have doubled back and tried to come down the other side of Republic."

And into the fire, he thought. He had no idea how much

of it had burned. Maybe they'd gotten it under control by now. But with the way the wind was blowing…he had his doubts.

"What do they look like?" he said. "The men who came for him?"

"There are two of them." She was speaking with an effort, and her words slurred. Lips pulling on the stitches. "Pale. Light hair. They speak strangely…not accents, just the way they say things. Like they're alone in the world. Like it was built for the two of them and they're lords over it. You'll know what I mean if you ever hear them talking to each other." She started to cry harder. "I hope you don't hear them."

"I won't," Ethan said. He was making himself watch her stitched lips move. *Somebody busted up her mouth pretty well.* Yes, somebody had. The hand he didn't have on hers was opening and closing beside his leg, each fist tighter than the last.

"They don't like to let you see them both at the same time," she said. Her eyes were closed now. "It's hard. They're very dangerous. They smell like blood."

He wondered about the drugs now, wondered if she even knew what she was saying. He wiped a hand over his mouth. Looked back at the closed door. When he spoke again, his voice was soft. He meant to tell her that he would ensure that a good group was handling it. He meant to tell her that he'd never leave her bedside. Not until they left together. Lord, how he meant to tell her those things.

"I'm going back to find him," he said.

"No. *No,* E."

She lifted her head off the pillow and stared at him. Thin plastic tubes dangling from one arm.

"Relax," he said. "Please. Lie back down and—"

"Don't leave me."

"I won't just yet. I'm right here. But he's missing, Allison, and—"

"I don't care!"

He was silent as she cried and then she said, "You know I don't mean that."

"I know. But Allison...we can't let it all be for nothing. Can't let them pass through you and get what they came for. I can't allow that. We can't."

"No. Stay. I'll be selfish now. I'm allowed to be selfish now, don't you think?"

"It's not selfish." There was no choice to be made. She'd asked him to stay. "I'll be right here. I promise."

"Thank you. I love you."

"I love you so much. And I'll be right here."

He held her hand until she slept, and then he shifted and held his own head in his hands. She was right. There was nothing left for him to do. Someone else would find the boy. Someone who could help him. Ethan wasn't needed.

He got to his feet, watching her to be certain that she was asleep and would not hear him go, and then he let himself out of the room and went down the hallway and asked for a phone. He made two calls. The first was to Roy Futvoye. Ethan asked if the police had found the boy yet. They had not. He hung up and called the number Jamie Bennett had given him for just such a situation. Straight to voice mail. That was the design. Messages only.

For a moment he was speechless. How did you go about explaining all of this? Finally he said, "They're here." He thought that would be enough, almost. Let her figure out the rest. But he added, "The boy is gone. He's missing.

I'm in the hospital in Billings with my life...I, I mean my wife. Everything is gone to hell." He stuttered to a stop then, thought about saying more, offering explanations (excuses?), but didn't. Hung up the phone.

He went into the men's room, urinated, and then went to the sink and looked in the mirror. He thought he should look as devastated as he felt. He didn't, though. He looked just like the old Ethan. Steady. Maybe that was impressive. Maybe it was sad.

He washed his hands and then turned the water cold and splashed it over his face. The door opened beside him and he was aware of boots that entered the room but did not go to the urinals or to the stalls or to the sink. Whoever it was just stood there. Ethan looked in the mirror with his face still dripping and saw a man in jeans and a black shirt and a black jacket and Ethan's own Stetson, the gift he'd refused to wear. Pale blond hair beneath it, down to the shirt collar. The man's eyes were a chilled blue and the left side of his face was a scarlet swath of blisters that glistened with some sort of salve.

Ethan didn't move. The water kept dripping off his face and the man kept staring and for a time nobody spoke.

"Shall we ride, Ethan?" the burned man said at last. He reached inside his jacket and Ethan was unsurprised to see the gun. Ethan's own weapons were in his truck in the parking lot.

"She wasn't part of it," he said.

The burned man gave an elaborate sigh. "Of course not. *You* weren't part of it. *I* wasn't part of it. Once the world existed without any of us, and someday soon it will again, but today, Ethan? Today we're all spinning along together. We're all part of it."

Like it was built for the two of them and they're lords over it, Allison had said, and Ethan thought of that and then, for the first time, thought of the second man.

"What are you here to do?" he said.

"I'd like to enlist your aid." The man had read Ethan's thoughts well, and he added, "I assume there are some ways to do that that are more convincing than others. I don't suppose, for example, I'd get far by offering you money today. But your wife on the third floor, room three-seventy-three? Perhaps an offer concerning her would be more compelling. What do you say?"

"I'll kill you for what you did to her. Both of you."

The burned man smiled. "You know all the lines, Ethan. Very good. But I don't have the time or the inclination to hear you say them all. You mention 'both of you,' so you know there are two of us. That's going to be important for you to remember. Now, you and I are going to ride together for a time. It will be just us, understand? So the one you're wondering about, where do you think he will be? This is what you do, to my understanding. An expert in lost-person behavior, I believe. So let's consider the lost person in this scenario. Where do you expect you will find him?"

"Close to my wife." The words were a bloodletting.

The burned man reached up and tipped his hat. Ethan's hat. Then he opened the bathroom door and gestured with his gun. "After you."

They walked out of the bathroom and down the hallway that smelled of disinfectant and then down a stairwell and out a side door into the daylight. It was warm now. Warm and windy.

"Go to the black truck," the man said. They were walking close together, and when Ethan felt cold metal on his hand, he expected it was a jab with the gun. It was a set of car keys. He took them, then unlocked the doors. It was a Ford F-150, just like his. Different color, different trim, but the same motor under the hood.

"You'll drive."

Ethan got behind the wheel and started the engine. Everything in the truck was similar to Ethan's, except the window tint on this one was very dark. And it smelled faintly of smoke and blood. He thought of the things he could do. Driving was control, after all. He could run them right through the glass doors and into the hospital. Could take them up onto the highway and off the side, bounce them down the mountain to their deaths together. The driver had total control.

"She'll be just fine," the burned man said, "for exactly forty-eight hours. After that, I'm afraid it's an altogether different situation. Now, do you think you can find the boy in that amount of time?"

"Yes."

"Then you've nothing to worry about."

"What if they've found him already? Then I've got plenty to worry about."

"I didn't say you had to be the first to find him, Ethan. I just said you need to find him."

And so he drove away, riding with the burned man, and behind him the hospital faded in the rearview mirror, and in it his wife slept secure in Ethan's promise that he'd be there when she woke.

21

It was just past noon when they sighted the first group of searchers. Jace had tried to sleep, but he didn't like having his eyes closed. It was as if he thought they might appear without a sound, and he'd open his eyes to find them standing in the door, Hannah Faber already dead, the rest of it just a matter of time...

Then Hannah said, "Connor, the police are coming," and he stood up from the narrow cot to join her at the window.

There were four men walking up the hill, just as Jace had a few hours earlier. Two of them were in uniform.

"Can I look?" he said. He wasn't going to be convinced they were police until he saw their faces. He'd seen the men dress like police before.

"Sure," Hannah said, passing him the binoculars.

For a moment all he saw was sky and peaks, and when he lowered the glasses he dropped them too far and was looking at the tall grass that lined the slope below the tower. Finally he found the men and held his breath as he took in their faces.

Strangers.

Every one of them.

"Okay," he said to Hannah, still staring through the binoculars. "Okay, I think they're all safe. I don't know them, at least, and that's good. They're not the two I saw."

"Good. Let's go down to meet them, then."

"All right."

He paused for just a few more seconds because he was curious to see if Ethan was with them. They'd tracked him over rough country so easily that he thought Ethan might have been their guide. He lifted the binoculars up so he could see over their heads and beyond, and he saw that they were not alone.

There was another man behind them, and it wasn't Ethan, and he wasn't moving with the group. He was trailing them.

Jace's mouth went dry and he reached up with his index finger and fumbled with the knob that changed the focus. Hannah was still talking when the zoom clarified.

It was one of them. The one who looked like a soldier. The one who'd cut the throat of the man with the bag over his head. He wore jeans and a jacket and a baseball cap and he carried a rifle. He was a good distance behind the group of searchers. They had no idea he was there.

"Come on," Hannah said, her hand light on his arm. "Let's go down and—"

"He's watching them." His voice trembled, but he didn't lower the glasses.

"What? Who is?"

"I can see only one of them. Maybe they didn't come together. I thought they'd both be here. But it's him. It's definitely him."

He lowered the binoculars because his hands had begun to shake. "He's not far from us."

He could tell that she didn't believe him. Or didn't want to. But she said, "Let me look."

He handed over the binoculars. "Look behind them."

Her silence told him that she saw the fifth man too. She stayed where she was for a long time and watched him and then she said, "You're sure it's him."

"I'm sure."

"Connor, they're going to come up here. Those men are going to come up here." Now her voice was showing the first signs of panic. Beginning to sound more like his own.

"I know it. I told you this was how it would happen. You can't get away from them. Nobody can." He took three steps back from the window, the farthest he could retreat in the last place he had to run, and then he sat down on the floor.

Hannah said, "Connor? We're going to figure this out. He won't get to you."

He didn't even look up when he answered. "They'll get to me. They won't stop, and there's two of them. They'll get to me in the end."

"Let's get moving," Hannah said. "Let's go, kid, we've got to go."

He watched her blankly as she moved around him and grabbed the hatchet. She looked at his pack, went to it, and opened it and began to rifle through. "Do you have anything in there? Any kind of…weapon? A knife, at least?"

"I wasn't allowed to. I was supposed to be a bad kid, remember?"

"Listen, we know the men are not on the trail to Cooke

City. So we can make it back down to Cooke City and we can—"

He shook his head. "It's better for everyone else to just let them get me. You can leave. I'd like you to tell my mom and dad what happened. Please find a way to tell them that I didn't—"

"*Shut up!*" she screamed. "And damn it, *get up!*"

She tried to tug him to his feet. He fought free of her and scrambled back until he was sitting beside her cot.

"You can go. I'm not going to."

They were interrupted by a voice then. Faint and echoing. The trace of a shout. Hannah turned from him and grabbed the binoculars again.

"They're close, aren't they?" Jace said.

"Yes." She was silent for a moment, then said, "I'm going to go down and talk to them."

"And say what? He'll kill them too. Then you, and then me. He'll kill us all."

"No, he won't. He's just following them, Connor. He's following them because he hopes they will find you. And that's not going to happen. Because I'm going to tell them you're already on the trail to Cooke City."

"What?"

"They're going to believe me," she said. "I've got no reason to lie. I think they've probably followed a few trails before. I think they know that you came this way. So what I tell them is going to matter. If I pretend I didn't see you, they might be suspicious. But if I tell them that I did, I can get them moving fast. I'll say, *You know, I did see him, and I thought it was strange that he was alone.*"

She was trying to convince herself that this was a good plan, but Jace was picturing the rifle in the man's hands.

Picturing the way it would happen, wondering if you heard the shot or just felt it. Or did you feel anything at all? He supposed that depended on where you were shot.

"You think it hurts much?" he said.

"What?"

"Getting shot. Or will I even feel it?"

She turned back to him. "You won't feel it."

"I hope you're right."

"You won't feel it, because it's not happening."

He lowered his head again. She didn't know. She hadn't seen them, she hadn't run from them, hadn't changed her name and gone to hide in the mountains only to look through binoculars and see one of them after all this time and over all these miles. She was like his mother—she believed there was a way to fix it all. But the only way to fix it all was to go back in time.

"I'm going to go down and get them," she said. "When I do, you get under the cot, all right? Hang the blankets down a bit. Enough so nobody can see you."

"They'll see the radio," he said. "That will get their attention pretty fast."

"Right. Damn it." She looked at the radio, took a breath, and said, "I'll go to them, then, and I will keep them from coming up here. Connor, you stay right where you are. I'm going out there and you better not let me down. When I come back, I'll be alone, and they'll be gone."

Then she walked outside and closed the door behind her.

Ethan drove out of the hospital and then out of Billings, took 90 and went west through the flat farm country where the railroads ran parallel to the highway. Neither of them spoke. He left 90 and got on 212 and headed southwest, away from the train tracks that had brought civilization to this place and toward the mountains that had fought it. Ethan was thinking of the way Allison's lips had looked with those stitches. Torn so badly the doctors had to literally sew her flesh back together, all because of a man's fist. Likely the man beside him. Ethan could smell him and he could see him and he could reach out and touch him, but he still could not stop him. It was the most impotent feeling of his life. He was willing to pay the price for killing this man. Willing to die in the truck beside him if it meant he had protected the right people.

Only the second man prevented this. Allison had said that she hoped Ethan wouldn't ever hear the two of them talking to each other. Now he wished desperately that he might.

They passed two police cars as they entered Red Lodge, but neither stopped. The burned man regarded them with casual interest. On the other side of Red Lodge, the road began to climb; the big truck's engine growled louder now. Onto 212 again, headed into Wyoming, over the Beartooth Pass, and then curling back into Montana. The mountain-sides fell off beside them on the left, long, stunning falls, and climbed just as steeply on the right.

"I am curious about one point," the burned man said. "It's of no consequence, so you may lie about it if you wish, but I hope that you won't."

Ethan drove and waited. On the switchbacks above them, a motor home was lumbering down. He drifted as far right as the road allowed, hugging the corner, tight against the mountain.

"Did you leave the boy behind because you knew who he was?"

"No. I wasn't told which one he was."

"Which one. So you were told that he would be present, but you were not given his identity? Not even the false identity?"

"That's right."

"So you were operating without concern over his identity until last night, when you received word of the events at your home."

The events at his home. Ethan gripped the steering wheel harder and nodded.

"This was from your wife? The signal she issued?"

"Initially."

"She is brave and she is smart. Better than I'd expected, certainly. I mean, look at my face." He lifted a fingertip to his blistered flesh and grimaced. "She ruined it. And you haven't even seen my side. There's still birdshot inside of me. No, your wife is not so bad."

"Fuck you," Ethan said.

The burned man nodded. "Of course. Now, if you'll continue to indulge me, I'm curious about the situation that awaits us. You now know which boy it is, but you did not last night. This means that you discovered the reality of him when he ran away. Am I correct?"

Ethan squeezed the steering wheel and imagined it was the son of a bitch's throat. He was glad the mountain road was so demanding. It forced his eyes to stay ahead, forced his hands to remain on the wheel.

"You're correct," he said.

"And when did you notice his absence?" Every question so formal, like they were in a courtroom.

"Middle of the night. When we were hiking down."

"So you can't show me exactly where you lost him?"

"I can get you to the point last seen."

"The point last seen?"

"It's how you start," Ethan said. "When someone is lost. You go to the point last seen, and then you think. You try to think as that person would have when he was there."

"Marvelous. I'm glad we have an expert along. It's a tremendous bit of good luck. To the point last seen, then. There we'll see how good you really are."

On up the mountain they went.

22

HANNAH STOOD ALONE ON the deck of the tower as the searchers came toward it. About twenty-four hours had passed since the first smoke sighting. There was much more of it now, and she stood on the balcony and stared through her binoculars at it. Tried to act like she was doing her job. She looked through the glasses one last time as the searchers reached the plateau. The shadow man followed, as was the way with shadows. Already Hannah was developing a fear of him. Maybe not one that matched Connor's, but it was there, and it was growing. She had four men on the way, two of them armed, and there was only the one behind. Common sense said to tell them about him. Common sense said tell the truth, give up the boy, trust the system that was in place here. Follow your protocol. The last time she'd broken protocol, people had died.

You get another chance.

Maybe she couldn't look at it like that. Maybe that was the worst thing, the most dangerous thing for the boy. She should just play her role, turn him over to them. What was his pursuer going to do then? If she took all of these men up to the tower and told them the truth and gave them the boy? One man wasn't going to risk taking on four. Even an assassin wasn't going to risk taking a shot in these circumstances. He'd never make it back out of the mountains.

You think it hurts much? the boy had asked. *Getting shot?* He had truly wanted to know. It was probably the most important question he'd ever asked.

"Hello! Hello up there!"

The searchers were shouting for her now. It was time. Two choices, two options, right hand or left, heads or tails. Ask them for help and trust that nobody was going to shoot. Or send them on and trust that she could get the boy to a safer situation. Send them on and let the shadow man trail behind and fade out of sight. All she had to do to make that happen was go down and answer some questions. Hang in there for five minutes.

She held the railing as she went down, leg muscles liquid, like after the dreams, her heart hammering so hard, it seemed dangerous. Maybe she'd die before she reached them. Could your heart burst from fear? She thought it had to be possible. She'd read once that some doctors theorized that people who died from heart attacks in the night had literally fallen victims to their nightmares. It was something she'd been unable to purge from her mind once her dreams started.

No dream here, though. The boy in the tower behind her was very real.

Second chance. The kind almost nobody gets. You came back here for a reason, didn't you? Stay on your damn feet, then. Stand your ground. You don't get to run.

She knew she was going to lie by the time she was at the bottom of the stairs. She was going to lie to someone, that much was required now, and it was either these men or the boy hiding under her cot. She had promised him she would send them away. She could imagine lying to these men, but not to him.

The searchers covered the ground to meet her fast. They were on an open plateau rimmed by tall trees and rocks, and somewhere in them the shadow man with the rifle hid. They were certainly within range. A finger squeeze away from death.

"Don't see many visitors," she said. "And you guys look like business. Everything okay?"

"Oh, we've had better days."

"I heard," she said.

"Oh yeah?"

"I was the one who called it in."

They exchanged puzzled glances. "Pardon?" a second officer said. He was a younger guy, complexion and cheekbones that hinted at Native American blood. "What did you call in?"

"The fire." She waved her hand to the smoke. "I understand there was a victim."

This was unplanned, but she was proud of it. She was demonstrating her knowledge and eagerness to help.

"We're not here for the fire," the one who looked like an Indian said. "We're looking for a missing boy."

"Haven't heard about that."

"They were supposed to put out a call to you."

Shit. Of course they were. How could she have failed to anticipate that?

"Really? Must have hit my bathroom run. Toilet's down

here, not up in the tower. That would have been, what, midmorning?"

The bigger one nodded. "Kid ran off from a group that was camping out here. They're, you know, problem kids."

"Yeah?" She turned from them, stared to the west so the wind blew hard in her face. "Would he have been carrying a pack?"

"That's right. You speak with him?"

"No. But I watched him go by, and I thought it was strange. Kid that age hiking alone."

"You could tell how old he was from up in the tower?" This came from the Native American with the skeptical stare.

"My eyes aren't that good. But these?" She tapped the binoculars that dangled around her neck. "These are pretty good. He was wearing a big green pack, an army-surplus-looking thing?"

"That'd be our boy," the big one said. "He came right through here?"

She nodded. "Looked up at the tower, and I thought he might try to climb it. Some people do, you know. But he just hung a right, caught the trail, and went on along."

"When you say he caught the trail, you mean—"

"Right there." She pointed to the place where the trail led away from the plateau. "It goes on toward Cooke City. Been a few hours, at least," she said, thinking that she wanted them to hurry. Thinking that if her heart beat any harder, it would blow apart.

"Yeah?"

"At least," she repeated. She was watching the skeptical man. He had moved to the point where the trail met the plateau and was on his knees, studying the ground. This was not good. A man who believed the ground could tell him more than an eyewitness was not good for her plan at all.

"What do you see, Luke?" the bigger man called.

"I got three clear prints, and none of them are his."

"You sure? Dry as it is?"

"Not so dry that he walks on air. The dust here holds a clear track, and his isn't one of them."

"That's because he didn't walk there," Hannah said.

"Thought you said he caught the trail?" the one named Luke said, still kneeling.

"He did. Climbed up right there"—pointing was a small salvation, because it forced them all to turn their eyes away from her—"and then started back down the way he'd come. Not far, just a few steps. Kind of looking around. Then he walked across the side of the hill there, cut through those trees—you see those pines? Cut through those and he was on the trail. I think the trail surprised him. It wasn't like he knew it would be there. But once he found it, he was gone."

Not a bad liar, Hannah, you are not bad at this at all, a damn fine dishonest woman when you need to be. Put that on the Match.com profile that all your friends want you to cre- ate—Hannah Faber, single white female, killed last boyfriend, excels at lying, please call!

"Hell, it has to be the right kid." These were the first words from a guy who looked tired and impatient and thus was Hannah's favorite of the men.

"Good luck," Hannah said. "I'll have to get going."

"Places to be?" This was from the skeptical man, Luke, who was returning to the group. A fine question too—she stayed in the tower day and night, and she was rushing them along? "You seem in a bigger hurry than we are."

"Remember when I said my toilet was down here?" she asked, and then gave him a nasty smile. "Ah, you've got it now! Good work! So, yes, I have places to be too."

"Go ahead," the bigger cop said. "Sorry about that."

"No problem. Good luck with the search."

"Pretty good view from that tower. Might be worth going up and having a look around, see if we can get a visual on him," Luke said, and Hannah wanted to kill him.

"You can't see him," she said. "I watched him for as long as I could. He took the trail and booked on out toward Cooke City."

"You watched him that long?"

"That tower might look really exciting to you, but it can get a bit boring, believe it or not. I watch *everybody*." She began moving away from them as she said it. "I'm sorry, but I've really got to go to the bathroom. You want to hang here, I'll be back in just a minute."

"We need to get moving," the big cop said. "Appreciate the help, though."

"You bet," she said over her shoulder. "Good luck, guys."

She reached the outhouse and fumbled with the door; the latch was uncooperative and she was panicking and so when she finally got it open, she nearly fell in her hurry to get inside. It should look real enough to them — somebody who had to *go*. They were probably laughing at her, but that was fine. So long as they believed it, and they left.

She sat on the closed seat of the toilet and held her head in her hands until her breathing steadied and the dizziness was past. She could hear their voices but not as loud. They were moving on. She hadn't been impressive, but she'd been functional.

And now she was alone with a boy who was pursued by killers.

When she opened the door she was ready to see the man with the rifle, but the plateau was empty again. She crossed to the tower and went up the steps and opened the door of the cab.

"Connor? It's just me."

The words carried more weight than they should have. *I did not lie to you. I made you a promise and I have kept it and you are still safe and I am part of that.*

"They're gone? Really?" He poked his head out from under the cot.

"Really. Stay down while I wait to see that the other one passes by too." She turned from him and added, "Once we know he's gone, that he's still following them, we need to head out, in the opposite direction. We need to get out of here."

"Why?"

"Because I lied to them, and they bought it, but it won't take long for them to figure it out. Somebody will come back. When they do, you need to be gone. Now, give me a minute."

She opened the door and walked out onto the balcony again. Leaned her forearms on the rail. If she was being watched now, it was important for her to look relaxed. To look as if she had all the time in the world. She forced herself to stay there for a while so it wouldn't seem like she was checking on anything in particular. She counted the seconds as a child would: one Mississippi, two Mississippi, three. When she got to three hundred, she straightened, stretched, and lifted the binoculars. Started by facing the smoke. She'd meant that as a ruse for the shadow with the rifle, but the smoke caught her attention and held it; it had grown substantially in the time she'd been occupied with the search party. They needed a break from the wind down there. *The blow-dryer,* Nick had called this sort of wind. You added a blow-dryer to a red-flag day, and you had serious trouble.

At length she turned from the smoke and found the men soon enough, maybe a half mile away. They were trusting her tip, following the trail out. The tracker, Luke, was going to be screwed now, because there were enough hikers here that following boot prints was not an easy task. In the backcountry, he'd have had better luck.

It took her much longer to find their shadow. He'd moved off the trail and climbed up to where an overgrown ridgeline ran parallel to it but elevated, some eighty feet above. Following that would slow him down but it would also allow him to see everything a little faster. While she watched him, he turned back toward the tower, and he swung the rifle with him. For an instant her stomach tightened and her bowels knotted and she was certain he was going to shoot.

He didn't. He was using the scope in the same way she was using the binoculars. Checking his surroundings, nothing more. He pivoted in a full circle and then continued on. The search party would hike down the trail and he would follow, and so she and Connor could not walk that way. Eventually, it would become apparent that a mistake had been made, and the shadow would return, and when that happened, she and Connor could not be here either. She needed to get him to help, but she'd just blocked her one path to safety by sending his pursuer on the only trail back to town. She had studied the map and stared through the binoculars for hours each day, and she knew well what waited for them off the trail. Treacherous climbs, impassable canyons, swift rivers, remnants of the glaciers. It would be slow going for Hannah and the boy, and they would leave a trail, and they would be caught.

To the west, the smoke met the angled sun and she thought of what was happening down there. Dozens of men and women at work in the woods, radios at their belts, helicopters awaiting a call. The model of emergency response was in action down there, in a place where no one would think to search, because no one would ever walk toward a forest fire.

Unless they understood a forest fire.

A panic run was a fatal run, that much she understood far too well, had learned from far too many aspects of her life, and so she stared at the wilderness through her binoculars and she tried to think of a way out other than the one she saw.

Still, her eyes returned time and again to the smoke.

They could reach the fire by dawn and they would not encounter the man with the rifle, who was walking in the opposite direction, and once at the fire, help would be easy to find. Radios would abound, trucks would be brought in, helicopters might settle down and drop a sling for them if they required it.

Can you make it there? she asked herself, and the ghost of the girl she had been answered, *Of course, it's not so bad a hike at all.* Then the voice of the woman she was now said, *It's not about the miles. It's about returning. Can you make it there?*

Neither voice had an answer to that one.

23

BETWEEN RED LODGE AND Cooke City, Ethan began to count. It had started as a simple exercise, a fight against the adrenaline and rage and fear. It had started as simple numbers. One to a hundred, then in reverse. When that grew old, he counted the cars they passed, and then, because there weren't enough of them, he counted the switchbacks. Later, higher up the mountain, he chose something else.

He began to count the men and women he had trained in the art of survival. Started with the ones from the most recent days, the private work, and went back in time. Back to the Air Force, to the jungles and the deserts and the tundras where they'd dropped him off for a week or ten days or a month. There were about thirty in each group, and he trained four groups a year, and he'd trained for fifteen years. That was eighteen hundred for the military alone. Add in the civilians, and he believed it was close to twenty-five hundred. Perhaps, all told, it knocked on the door of three thousand.

Three thousand people he had taught how to be survivors. For some of them, it had worked. He knew that. A pilot downed in the Pacific; a soldier separated from his unit in Afghanistan; a hunting guide who'd broken his leg in a fall. Ethan had received letters and phone calls. Not to mention commendations and awards.

Three thousand sets of instructions.

Not one test for himself.

Not a real one, at least. He'd trained, and trained, and trained. With the best in the world, for a lifetime, he had trained, but he had never been tested. The finest fighter never to see the ring.

Only he was no fighter. It was the old conversation with his father again: a Marine's son who'd joined the Air Force, that had been the first offense, but his dad had been able to shake it off, reckoning that the world had entered a new age of combat and in the future all scores would be settled with missiles and drones, sad as that seemed to make him. Then Ethan had become a survival instructor, and that was even more of a personal affront to his father somehow, more disappointing in some perverse way that came from his father having measured his own worth based on his ability to kill.

You just teach them what to do if they're out there alone? he'd asked. *From over here? How will you know if it works?*

How it had pained him, the idea that his son would always be *over here.* There was no war at the time, but that didn't matter to Rod Serbin—there might be, there would be, and when it came, his son would be on the sidelines, by choice. Whether or not he saved any lives didn't seem to matter. He wouldn't take any lives, and that was the measure. It bothered him, but not Ethan. Not until today. Now he drove, and he planned, and he wondered.

Could he do it? Would he?

When they returned to town, the smoke from the fire was high and clear and Ethan was surprised to see how much it had grown since the morning. Then again, there wasn't much of the world the same since the morning.

"Where do you believe the boy is now?" the burned man asked into the quiet.

"I have no idea. It's been more than twelve hours. If he kept moving, he could have covered some ground. Or he could have been located already."

"We're going to need to know that. The problem is simple: if they already have him, then we're going into the woods for nothing, and I'm wasting hours that I can't afford to waste. Rather, I'm wasting hours *you* can't afford to waste. I'm sorry, Ethan, to have forgotten the joint nature of our venture. So you have to check. Your job is to find him, regardless of whether he's hiding under a rock or in a hotel room with three marshals outside the door. It could have gone either way by now."

"Then I'll need to make a call."

"That's fine."

"We'll have to stop," Ethan said. "This isn't cell-phone country. You lose signal in Red Lodge and don't get it back up here."

"So we'll stop. You'll check. It should take no more than a phone call. I'll be right here with you. Say the wrong word and you've chosen the outcome more surely than I have. Something you need to remember—she'll go first. I'll see to it."

"You've made that clear. We'll stop at my house. We'll also start from there."

"Allison set that on fire, so it's probably not ideal."

"Don't say her name again, you son of a bitch. Don't say it."

"You prefer 'Mrs. Serbin'? I thought we were past needless formalities."

Ethan focused on peaks, still snowcapped, in the distance. Formidable rock faces that were friends. If he could remain calm, he would soon be surrounded by them.

"I'll stop in town and make a call," he said. "You want to walk in with me and shoot me down if I say the wrong thing, you can. You want to stay in the truck, keep that burned face of yours away from questions, you can do that too."

"You're very gracious, Ethan. But I'm well aware of my options. I trust you to go in alone. You'll have your chances to cause trouble for me, but you'll remember the way your wife looked in the hospital today. You'll remember that, and remember who's at her bedside." He paused, shrugged, and said, "Or you'll let her die. I've been wrong about a man's character before. Perhaps I will be again."

Ethan parked in front of the Cooke City General Store. It had stood there since 1886 and Ethan imagined that over that many years many an evil man had surely passed by it but doubted any like the one who rode at his side.

"I'll walk down to the right," he said. "To Miner's Saloon. I can use a phone there and nobody will be listening. There's a phone on the far end of the bar. The right-hand side. I'm going to walk to it and make a call. You'll probably be able to watch me through the window. Nobody will see you, not with this tint."

"You have my trust, Ethan."

"Am I on a clock?"

"By all means, take your time."

His tone was light, mocking. That was fine. Stay cocky, stay fearless, and Ethan would piss on his corpse.

Ethan walked down the sidewalk to Miner's and pulled open the door without so much as glancing back at the truck.

"Ethan, man, didn't expect to see you in here! I heard about...the fire." This was from the bartender. Ethan figured the man had stopped himself from saying Allison's name because he didn't know what might have happened. Ethan looked up and nodded and said, "She's fine. I've just got to make a call. Sorry."

"Of course."

He called Roy Futvoye. Said that he was back in town and wanted to know if the searchers had had any success.

"I'm afraid not. They spoke to someone who thought she'd seen him, one of the fire lookouts, but they haven't found him yet."

"Where are they?"

"Coming down toward the Soda Butte now."

The Soda Butte was the stream that ran on the south side of town, parallel to the Montana-Wyoming line. That meant they'd made a loop of it, expecting that Connor had broken free and then tried to get back to civilization. It would have made sense to them, because they probably figured he wanted help or at least wanted to get back to familiar terrain. They did not understand his fears yet, and that was good. Another advantage. Ethan did not expect to find Connor on a highway, or even a trail. Not so soon. He had food, he had water, and he had terror. He would have searched for a good place to hide.

"No sign of him beyond that tip?"

"None. But that one sounded valid. She gave a good description, and the timeline was right. Maybe he dropped his pack and picked up the pace, got out to the road faster than we thought he would."

"Maybe," Ethan said. "So your team is going to come out for the night?"

"They're out. We'll send a fresh group. Luke Bowden stayed back."

"What?"

"You know Luke, he doesn't like it when he loses a trail. Damned bloodhound. I guess he wasn't happy with the way they lost the kid's prints at the fire lookout. He decided to backtrack and see what he could find."

"Get him out of there," Ethan said. His tone changed enough that the bartender glanced his way.

"Why?"

Because Luke might actually find the kid, Ethan was thinking, but he said, "Because people shouldn't run searches solo, Roy. You know that."

"He's just back-trailing. Nothing's going to happen to Luke—"

"Things can happen to anybody," Ethan said, and it came out too close to a snarl. He swallowed and said, "There's something wrong with this kid, you realize that. Don't let anybody go wandering around alone."

Especially somebody who may beat me to him. Especially somebody with a radio.

"I'll advise him," Roy said, but his voice had changed now as well. "Ethan, you okay? You know something more than you're telling me?"

"I know I'm shaken up, Roy. It's been that kind of day. Listen, I've got to go. I'll check back in soon. Thanks."

Ethan hung up. He looked at a man sitting at the bar eating a steak and considered the knife he was using. It would be nice to have a knife. But the burned man wouldn't miss that. Ethan thanked the bartender and walked outside into that warm wind. Knowing he had to hurry now. His own clock was speeding up, and the burned man didn't even know it yet.

When Ethan opened the door, the burned man looked at him casually, the pistol in his hand.

"Send for the National Guard?"

"You'll know soon enough."

"I have the patience for my own wit. Not yours." His voice was dark and he tilted his head so that some of the burns fell into shadow and said, "What's the word?"

"No luck yet. If we're lucky, we'll catch him coming up to the road. If we aren't, then we'll have to go back to the place where I lost him, and I'll have to start tracking."

"You don't think we'll be lucky, though."

"No."

"Why not?"

"Because he's too afraid of you to stay on a trail."

"Thinking like the lost person. Good for you. And an accurate assessment, I believe. His approach in the past has been to hide and then run."

"And you couldn't get him yourself. You should have called me then."

The burned man looked at him and smiled.

"Starting to appreciate my wit?" Ethan said.

"No. I was just thinking of how your wife looked with her hair on fire."

24

THE WOMAN NAMED HANNAH had saved him, at least temporarily, and that was great, but it didn't mean he could let her rush him. And she was rushing him now. Telling Jace to get up and get moving, telling him to leave the pack behind because they'd move faster without the extra weight, telling him that if they went fast enough, they'd both be riding out of the mountains on a helicopter by the end of the night.

"Slow down," he said. "We need to slow down."

"Hon, that is exactly what we cannot do. It is time to hurry. I know you're tired, but—"

"We have a goal," Jace said, "but we do not have a plan."

It was funny; if an adult had said this to Hannah, it would have made perfect sense to her, but those same words coming from a kid apparently meant there was something wrong with the kid. Hannah stared at him as if he'd just told her that he wanted to ride out of the mountains on a unicorn.

"It's what Ethan says."

"Ethan, your survival instructor?"

"Yes. The one I was with until last night."

"That's terrific, Connor. That's great. But I'm pretty sure if Ethan were here right now, he'd tell you that we need to hurry."

"That's the exact opposite of what he would say. Panic kills. You rush and you make mistakes. You're trying to rush me."

She laughed. The exasperated, I-am-done-listening-to-you sound his mother made during arguments. "I'm trying to rush you, yes. You arrived at my door with a *killer* behind you, and now I would like to hurry the hell out of here."

"Two killers," Jace said. "We haven't seen the other one."

That had been bothering him for some time. He knew very little of these men, but somehow he was surprised to discover that they were willing to separate. It had felt to him as if they came together, a matched set.

"Connor," Hannah said, "we can talk and walk. Please. The only mistake right now would be staying here any longer."

"Ask my dad—he takes pain pills every day because of somebody who rushed. You're already making one mistake." He tapped on the glass of the Osborne and said, "Aren't we going to want a map?"

This time, the look she gave him was more considered. She even made an odd little smile, as if someone had told a joke, and she stopped arguing with him.

"All right," she said. "We'll take a map. That's a pretty good idea. I will admit not thinking about that was a mistake. Do you see any others?"

She seemed to be asking him seriously, and that gave him

a sense of strength he hadn't felt in a while. Not quite the same as when he'd built the fire, but close. A reminder that he was capable of more than he imagined.

He looked around the tower and tried to see it the way Ethan Serbin would. It was hard; he was sure he was missing things. The map had been obvious, but although he wanted to bring his entire pack, he had to admit she had a point about the walking speed.

"Map, water, some protein bars," he said, speaking slowly, thinking of what they must have and what they could leave behind. "I'll bring the plastic and the parachute cord for shelters. And the fire steel."

"We're going to need to be on the move, not building shelters."

"That's what everyone says a few hours before they realize they need a shelter."

She gave the little smile again, nodded, and said, "All right. I've got water, and some lightweight food. I've got a knife and a multi-tool. You've got the map, the compass, and the rest of what you want?"

He nodded.

"Then are you ready? Or is there something else?" Her eyes were drifting to the windows that faced east, the direction she'd sent them. She was worried that they would return soon, and he wondered how convincing she had been in the conversation.

"Just let me think a minute."

"That's your favorite approach, isn't it, Connor? You are one patient guy. A thinking man, and a patient one." The frustration was clear in her voice, but he ignored it. She had helped him and now he had to help her. Think like Ethan. Think like a survivor. Just *think*.

"Okay," Hannah said after he'd been silent for maybe thirty seconds. "Looks like you're all thought out. Let's move."

"Leave the light on."

"What?" She turned back to him with a confused look because it was a brilliantly bright afternoon, and you wanted, if anything, more shade in the glass-walled room right now. Unless you were thinking like a survivor.

"The light's very bright at night," Jace said. "Trust me, you can see it from a long way off."

"We're going to be very far away by the time it—"

"They may not be," he interrupted, and she fell silent. "If anyone thinks you lied, they'll be even more sure of it if the tower goes dark, right? You're already off the radio, but at least people believe you're still here. If it's dark tonight, they might wonder."

She nodded slowly and said, "Okay, kid. Keep going. You're earning it."

He knelt beside his pack and unzipped it, removed the map, the compass, and the parachute cord, and then stopped and said, "Shit."

"What?"

"I don't have the plastic. We walked away with the shelters still up." He looked at her and said, "Do you have anything that would work? Some ponchos, maybe? Something that could be used as an emergency shelter?"

Her expression changed then for reasons he didn't understand. Her eyes went sad.

"What's the problem?" he asked.

"Nothing. Nothing at all. And, yes, I've got a shelter. That's exactly what it is. An emergency fire shelter. It would probably be a good idea to bring it along, I suppose.

But I want you to promise me something. You need to listen and not argue, all right?"

Jace nodded.

"I will not get in that thing," Hannah said. "I will let you get in it if you need to, but I will not, and you had better not try to make me. You promise?"

"Okay."

She rubbed a hand over her face and said, "What else?"

He thought they had it all. He emptied his pack of the nonessentials and put them under the cot and then added the fire shelter. It didn't weigh much. Looked like tinfoil.

"This is supposed to keep you from *burning*?"

"Yes, it is," she said, and then added, "and yes, it does."

He looked up at her and she turned away immediately.

"Were you ever in one?"

"Connor—just pack the damn thing."

He did as instructed, then stood and put the pack on. It was much lighter than it had been since it held a lot less stuff, but he was still glad to have it. He felt better, more prepared, and how someone felt had a direct impact on what he did. His survivor mentality was coming back. It would be good to be moving again and even better to know that the man who had come to kill him was moving in the opposite direction.

"I think I'm ready," he said.

"Good. Let's get to it, then."

He stepped out and hesitated—the height of the thing surprised him even though he'd been looking out the windows a lot of the time. Then he got moving, one foot in front of the other, keeping his eyes on his boots.

When he stopped short, Hannah Faber almost ran into him.

"What's wrong?" she said.

"What's your shoe size?"

"Pardon?"

"What is it?"

"A ten, Connor. Yes, I have big feet. And I'd like to get them moving."

"Do you have any other shoes?"

"Connor, that's useless weight. We are not going to need two pairs of shoes."

He turned around, holding the rail with one hand, and looked at her feet. They were big for a woman. He put his own foot beside it. Almost the same.

"Do you have any other shoes?" he repeated.

"Connor! We're not going to—"

"The search party tracked me here fast," he said. "I'm pretty sure they know my boot prints by now. It would be nice if they didn't see them leading away from your tower."

She was giving him the stare that he was beginning to regard as normal. Then she turned around and walked back up the steps and into the cabin without a word. He followed her in. She went to the foot of the cot and came back with a pair of boots.

"Perfect," he said. "Let me see if they fit."

She was looking at them funny, as if she didn't want them to be used. When she spoke again, she was still staring at the boots and not him.

"I'll wear these," she said, setting them down by the bed. "You try the ones I have on."

"Why?"

"Don't worry about it." She began to unlace her boots. They were more like hiking shoes, really. The boots by the bed, though, were serious work boots. He ran his index finger over the glossy black leather. Sturdy stuff. The laces went all the way from the tongue of the boot to the toe.

"What are those laces made of?"

"Kevlar."

"You're serious? Like, the bulletproof stuff?"

"Yes."

"Those look pretty tough," he said.

"They sure as hell are, kid. Now, try these on."

He got his own boots off and slipped his feet into hers. A little snug, but not bad at all.

"They work. You really do have big feet."

"It gives me certain advantages, Connor. I won't blow over even in a strong wind." She put on the new boots slowly, as if there were something wrong with them. By the time she had the laces tied, her eyes were closed.

"You okay?"

"I'm fine. Just haven't laced up in a while." She opened her eyes and said, "Now that we've gone to this extreme, make sure to hide your old boots. None of this will be much help if they walk in and find your boots right there on the floor."

Good point. He was disappointed in himself; that was an obvious problem, and he had missed it. He picked up the boots and looked around the room and saw no great option. Looked again, taking slower inventory, and then crossed to the woodstove and opened the door. Cold ashes inside. He put the boots down in them and closed the door.

"Very good," Hannah said. "Very smart."

They left the tower for real then, making sure the light was still on to greet the darkness when it came, and at the bottom of the tower, they turned west and crossed the plateau, and Jace's feet left no trace of the boy who had come this way in the morning.

25

ALLISON WOKE IN THE AFTERNOON to a sea of mud-
dled regrets. Should have brought the shotgun onto
the porch, should have been firmer with her concerns over
Jamie Bennett, should have allowed Ethan to go after the
boy, should have gone with him into the mountains, should
have...

And then awake, fully awake.

And alone.

The hospital room was dim but not dark. Ethan's chair
empty. That was fine. He'd left for some reason, and he
would return. She had been asleep for a long time.

The minutes passed and he did not return and at length
she grew uneasy alone there in the room and pressed the
call button above the bed. A nurse arrived within seconds,
asking if she was in pain.

"A little, sure, but I'm...I'm fine. I was wondering
where my husband is?"

"No idea, Mrs. Serbin. He left some time ago."

"What do you mean, left?"

"I'm not sure. How's the pain? On a one-to-ten scale, if you could estimate what the—"

"He's not been here?"

The nurse gave her an uncomfortable look. "I really couldn't say. He didn't consult with me when he left. But I haven't seen him. Would you like to call him?"

"Yes. But I won't get him. Could you get me the phone? I want to call the police."

Allison looked at Ethan's chair. *You promised. You held my hand and looked me in the eye and you* promised. Then the nurse was back, a phone in hand. She dialed for Allison, then handed the phone over and left the room. Very polite lady, this nurse.

Allison asked for Roy Futvoye. The person who answered the phone was disinclined to connect her, so she said, "You tell him this is Allison Serbin calling from the hospital and that I'd like to talk to him about the fire and the men who attacked me."

Funny how effective a few buzzwords could be. It didn't take them long to patch her through to Futvoye after that.

"Allison, how are you?"

"Been better." Wrong thing to say—the *b*'s pulled at her wounded lips in a painful way. She hated the sound of her voice. So damaged.

"I know. Listen, we'll get them. I promise you we will."

If she heard the word *promise* again, she was going to scream. She said, "Roy, where is my husband?"

Pause. "He didn't tell you?"

"What didn't he tell me?"

"Um…well, I'm not sure what all has been going on with him, you know, but my last understanding—"

"Where is he?" These words came firmer, crisper.

"In the mountains. I just spoke with him. He's gone to find the boy who ran away."

"You *just* spoke with him?"

"Within the past hour. Is there a message you want me to get to him?"

"No," she said. "No, that's fine."

"Are you feeling up to a little more talk, Allison? I'd sure love to ask a few questions about what happened last night. About those two. You know that your memory is going to be a big help to us. Really critical."

"I know," she said. "I'm a little off right now. Let me think about that."

She hung up without giving him time to respond. Sat and looked at Ethan's chair.

You gave your word, Ethan. Why did you pick the boy again?

She closed her eyes and breathed and after a few minutes she realized she'd begun to cry. She opened her eyes and wiped at them with her good hand and when they were dry and she was steady, she pressed the call button again. Same nurse, same swift appearance.

"Yes? Everything all right?"

"I'd like to see a mirror."

The hesitation on the nurse's face told her as much as the mirror would, but Allison held her eyes and eventually the woman nodded and left and came back with a round makeup mirror.

"They'll get it fixed so well, so fast," she said. "You have no idea what they can do these days with burns."

Allison took the mirror and looked into it and closed her eyes almost immediately. After a few seconds she looked again and this time she didn't look away.

Most of the worst was hidden, anyhow. Bandages covered that. Her hair was the real shock — not much left of it, and what was there had been hacked away, probably by the paramedics. Her lips were lined with stitches and there was some sort of film over a split in her chin, like dried superglue. Her eyebrows were gone but a line of blisters showed where each one had been. She studied herself for a long time, and then she said, "You know I was almost Miss Montana?"

"You'll look better than that when they're done," the nurse said.

Allison nodded. "Sure. My husband used to joke about that, though. Call me that, sometimes." She tilted the mirror, saw the nearly bald area on the left side of her head. "He probably won't make that joke again. And now I'll miss him saying it, isn't that funny?"

The nurse looked at her and said, "Are you feeling okay, Mrs. Serbin? Maybe less painkiller? Or maybe more? On a scale of one to ten, could you tell me—"

"Nine," she said. "I was a nine."

The nurse nodded, pleased to be back on track. "You were. And now?"

"Well, there are steps," Allison said. "At twenty, I was a nine. And then at thirty, probably still an eight. I mean, time ain't your friend. Then I hit forty, and then I hit last night, or rather last night hit me, and now...well, we are going to have to wait for those bandages to come off. But for the moment, let's call it a two."

The nurse said, "Mrs. Serbin, you need to stop worrying about this. Surgeons you haven't even met yet are going to do amazing things."

She looked in the mirror and smiled and watched the

glue tighten and the stitches tug. The bandages that hid the rest of her were white as glaciers under a winter sun. She thought they could be called beautiful; at least, they could if you'd ever appreciated a glacier under a winter sun.

"You pretend it's not there when you've got it," she said, "but I wonder if you're allowed to miss it when it's gone. *I was beautiful once.*"

The nurse was silent. Just looked at Allison and waited. Allison handed over the mirror and the nurse took it and left, but the images it had offered remained. Allison tried to push them away and then she looked at Ethan's empty chair and she knew why Ethan had gone. Maybe it wasn't about the boy at all. Maybe it was about her.

He thought he could get them.

He didn't understand who they were, though. What they were. She could see them again and, worse, hear them, those calm voices in a beautiful, still night. Could smell the old smoke and the old blood. Then the fresh versions that had followed.

She prayed for her husband then, prayed that he would not meet them, would not hear them, would not smell them. It felt too late, though. She'd slept too long, and he'd made his choice too early.

26

A S HE PULLED THE TRUCK UP to the Pilot Creek trail-head, Ethan felt relief. They were coming home. Out of the burned man's terrible truck and into Ethan's lovely mountains, which could also be very terrible, especially to those who failed to respect them.

"We'll start here," Ethan said. "And we'll need to walk fast."

The burned man gazed out the window without interest. They were surrounded by high peaks and steep slopes but Ethan was sure the man saw no threat there because he had no intention of getting into a situation where he might fall off a peak. But he would, Ethan believed, allow himself to get into a situation where he climbed toward one.

What Ethan needed was a slope that rose on them abruptly, and for a short length. One that they could walk along until suddenly they needed to make a short scramble to the top. Enough to force the holstering of the gun and demand the total attention of the hands.

Republic Peak offered that opportunity. It was a long,

leg-burning hike, but a hike all the same; you could keep your hands free. Until you reached ten thousand feet. There it leveled out to a wide plateau that overlooked a glacier to the west and the drainage of Republic Creek to the north. The country to the south was blocked by the peak itself, but it wasn't a terrible climb to the top, and for that reason Ethan often used it as a summit for the amateurs he brought into the mountains. No ropes required, no technical experience or gear. Anyone in decent physical condition could make it to the top of Republic Peak—but you couldn't just walk to it. It required a little hands-and-knees work; you had to pick your way among the rocks. At the summit, there was an extraordinary view of the surrounding countryside. There was also, as was common in these mountains, a stack of stones marking the summit, a small pyramid of rocks left by triumphant hikers who wanted to acknowledge their journey to the top of the world, or as close to it as they'd yet been. Ethan's boys had added to it over the years. Heavy, rounded stones and flat, jagged chunks. Killing rocks, in the right hands.

But can I beat Luke? How fast is my clock ticking now?

He was sweating even though they hadn't yet started up the trail. It was all out there waiting for him, he could take care of the man easily if he was left alone, but he might not be left alone. He hadn't counted on the wild card, Luke. He hoped Roy had actually radioed Luke and told him to get the hell out of the mountains.

Then you'll meet him coming back down. And then...

"Ethan? What's our plan? You seem distracted. What's on your mind? Is it Allison? Ah, such a sweet thing, true love. But let's not let it disrupt our focus."

"We're going to have to get high, and do it fast," he told

the burned man as they left the truck. "He'll have a light going as soon as it gets dark. If he's on the move, it will be his headlamp or a flashlight. If he's in one place, it will be a fire."

"If he's hiding, as you believe, why would he have a light?"

"Because I spent the past several days scaring him. In order to get the kids to take things seriously, I share some war stories. Trust me, none of them are comfortable up here at night. Not at first. And if he's moving, which he may be, then a light is simply required. He'll have to see where he's going. I watched this boy start a fire. He's good at it, and he likes it. I'm sure he'll want one going. The fire will give him a sense of strength, of security. You'd be surprised at the feeling that comes with starting a fire."

"Oh, I'm rather familiar with it, Ethan."

Ethan didn't look at him, didn't react. Told himself not to think of Claude Kitna. Not to think of the source of the smoke they'd passed. Instead, he thought of the fire that Allison had started. That was a survivor's fire. That was the heart that he had to match.

"So we hike fast, and we get high," he said. "I'm telling you this so you won't question where we're going or what we're doing."

"I'll question everything, actually. But carry on."

The wind freshened and blew at them warm and dusty from its journey over dry terrain. There was a thickness to it, a humidity that felt misplaced in the high mountains, and Ethan knew there was a storm behind it. The days had been too hot and too dry for too long this early in the summer. It had fed the fires, and now rain would come in and maybe help, maybe hurt. A good drenching downpour

would be a blessing to the firefighters; a lightning storm
might be a disaster. This wind did not feel as if it came from
a savior. "Feel that?" Ethan asked.

"The breeze. Yes, Ethan. I feel it."

"Not a breeze. That's a warning."

"Is it, now?" The burned man managed to keep his voice
drawling and uninterested even when he should have been
out of breath. He was hurt and they were moving fast and
it had likely been some time since he'd slept, but he did not
show any of that. Ethan was concerned by this. Ethan had
the feeling that the burned man was a survivor himself, and
that was trouble.

"It's coming ahead of a storm," Ethan said. "And we're
two miles up in the air. It doesn't take long for lightning to
connect with the earth when you climb this high to meet it."

"I've come through a fire already today, Ethan. I'll welcome the storm."

They continued to work their way along the trail, flash-
lights on now because darkness had settled, and when the
burned man moved, he was loud, too loud, and Ethan
smiled. No, this was not his world. Ethan had made the
right choice. They would reach Republic Peak and there
the burned man would die. It was a matter of hours, that
was all. Two hours, maybe three. That was all the burned
man had left, and he did not know it. Ethan had made the
right choice, and he would prove it in blood.

"You say the searchers have not sighted him, but the fire
lookout did," the burned man said. "Yet we aren't going to
the lookout. You're ignoring that. Seems unwise."

"I'm not ignoring it. One person has seen him. How? By
having the elevation advantage. If we get to Republic Peak,
we'll be higher than him, no question. I don't know how

you're feeling, how much you've got in you. If you want to sit it out and let me make the climb, then we'll do it that way. Running away from you won't help me, so you know I'll come back down for you."

"Your concern is touching," the burned man said, "but I have plenty in me, Ethan. Don't you worry about my resources. You just set the pace, and I'll keep up."

This was the answer Ethan had been expecting, and it was good. He'd wanted to goad him a little bit. Ethan would attempt to discourage him from the summit again when they were closer, and the burned man would hear that and commit to reaching the top because he would not want Ethan to think he was weakening.

"You believe he hid from the searchers, don't you, Ethan?"

"Yes. Because he thinks you'll be with them, or near them. An ordinary boy would try to get out of the mountains as fast as possible. He'd seek help. Connor—that's the name I know him by, at least—is not interested in finding help, because he doesn't trust help. From anyone. As long as he knows you're here—and he does—then he will not willingly give himself up. He made that clear when he ran off last night."

"You can find him?"

"I will find him."

"And what do you think will happen to him then?"

Ethan hesitated. "I'm not sure."

"Yes, you are, Ethan. Yes, you are. So admit it. If you find him, what will happen to him?"

Ethan was silent, and the burned man said, "You're wasting time. Answer the question."

"You'll likely kill him."

"I certainly will kill him. It's not a matter of likelihood. It's a matter of certainty. And you know this, but still you'll find him for me. So you are willing for him to die."

Ethan turned back and looked at him. The burned man was smiling, his face pale in the glow from the flashlight.

"I don't desire it," Ethan said. "But I also don't know him. I don't love him. I love my wife. If sacrificing him allows me to save my wife…"

"A noble husband."

Ethan turned from him, away from that smile. He looked again at the shadow of Republic Peak and thought that they could not get there fast enough.

"Let's get to it," he said. "We need to cover ground."

The voice that floated out of the blackness then was so calm, it didn't even startle Ethan, though surely it should have. It just entered the conversation as if it belonged there.

"Would you prefer I join your party at this juncture, or should I stay with the others?"

Ethan looked in the direction of the sound but the burned man did not. His eyes remained on Ethan.

"If they haven't found him yet," the burned man said, "I suspect it's unlikely that they will. And I have the utmost confidence in my friend Ethan here. So why don't you join us."

"My pleasure."

The way they say things. Like they're alone in the world. Like it was built for the two of them and they're lords over it, Allison had said. And then she had begun to cry.

The second man emerged from the woods soundlessly. He was armed with a rifle. Ethan watched him walk and realized that he had heard nothing from him until the man had wanted to be heard and he understood then with immediate, terrible clarity that these men were the same in awful ways and also different in awful ways. The burned man was not familiar with the wilderness. His partner was. As bad as it was that there were two of them, it was far worse to know the nature of the second man. All of the advantages Ethan had believed he held were gone now.

The second man walked to within ten feet of them and then stopped. He was shorter and more muscular and had close-cropped hair but he looked a great deal like the burned man. Brothers, Ethan thought, they were brothers.

"Good to meet you, Mr. Serbin," he said. "Had the pleasure of making your wife's acquaintance last night. You weren't at home."

Ethan didn't speak. Far ahead, Republic Peak stood against the night sky. The perfect place to kill one man.

Not two.

27

IT WAS NEVER FULL DARK in a hospital room. There was always the glow of some monitor, a night-light in the bathroom, a bright band under the door. Allison eyed the shadows and hoped for sleep and had no luck, and then the old shadows vanished and new ones emerged as the door eased open a few inches.

For a moment, it held there, just cracked, and whoever was on the other side was silent. Allison knew then that it was them, knew that they'd finished with Ethan and had returned for her, and she wondered how it was that this was a surprise to her, because of course they were not men who let you walk away; it was not enough for you to be burned and beaten. They meant to put you in the ground, and she wasn't there yet.

There was a scream in her throat when the door opened wider, and then it stopped again and there was something so tentative in its motion that she was certain it didn't belong to either Jack or Patrick, her last nocturnal visitors. They moved in unusual ways, but never tentatively.

The door opened farther, letting a broad beam of light fall into the room, and Allison blinked against it as a tall blond woman entered.

Allison said, "You bitch."

"I know," Jamie Bennett said, and closed the door behind her.

The room was silent for a few seconds, and dark again, and Allison thought, *Do not say that you're sorry, I don't want to hear that, don't you dare say it.*

Jamie Bennett said, "May I turn on the light?" A click of a switch, and there she was. Tall and blond and beautiful. Unbeaten and unburned.

"Do you know where my husband is?" Allison said.

"I was hoping you might."

"I don't."

Jamie nodded. Allison looked at her face, saw the red eyes and the deep fatigue, and was pleased by them. At least it was costing her something. Not enough, but something.

"They came because of you," Allison said. "Because you screwed up."

"I know it."

"Do you?"

"Yes, Mrs. Serbin. I know more than you do about how much blame there is for me."

"No," Allison said. "You don't know more than I do about it. Have you heard them speak to each other?"

Jamie Bennett stayed silent.

"I didn't think so. Until you've heard them, you don't know."

She was both surprised and disappointed that the other woman had begun to cry.

"He was your problem," Allison said, though her heart

was no longer in the attack, and she hated that, because, damn it, she was entitled to her anger. "It was *your* job to keep him safe. Not anyone else's. You were supposed to do your job like a pro. Look at what's come of your game."

"I couldn't do it like a pro," Jamie Bennett said.

"Obviously."

"I wanted to. You don't believe that, but I wanted to. There was nothing I wanted more in the world than to keep it professional. But it is absolutely impossible to do that with your own son."

Allison opened her mouth, felt the sting along the lines of stitches, closed it, and tried again. Speaking softer now. "Your son?"

Jamie Bennett nodded. One tear traced her cheekbone.

"That boy who is missing, the one they came for, that's your child?"

"That's my child."

Allison didn't say anything for a long time. Outside, a cart squeaked by and someone let out a too-loud laugh and the patient in the room beside them hacked a wet cough and the two women sat there and stared at each other in silence.

"Why?" Allison said finally.

"Why to which part? Why am I here? I'm trying to find him. That's the only thing that I—"

"Why do they want him?"

Jamie Bennett crossed the room and sat in the chair where Ethan had been earlier.

"He saw them kill a man. He found a body, and then he saw these men appear with another man, and they killed him, and Jace saw it all."

"Jace."

"That's his name, yes. He was Connor Reynolds when you met him."

"Yes. Ethan's gone after him. He left me here and went back to find him."

"I've been trying to reach Ethan. I haven't gotten through."

"You don't get a cell signal in the wilderness, Jamie."

"And they haven't found the men who... who did this to you."

"No. They have not." She lifted a finger to her face and touched the bandages and said, "Who are they?"

"I have no idea. I have their physical descriptions, and I have the names they call themselves, and beyond that... nothing."

"They're brothers," Allison said.

"I understand that they look alike."

"More than looks. They're brothers. The names might be lies, but that part is not. They go together. It's a shared blood."

"I'd like to promise you that we will find them," Jamie Bennett said. "But I'm done making promises."

"Who did they kill? Who did... Jace see them kill?"

"Witnesses. My witnesses. For a federal trial, one that was supposed to put seven people in prison, including three police officers. I was hired to do part of the protection assignment. I failed." She took a long breath, brushed hair out of her face, and said, "My witnesses—they weren't just killed. They were taken to Indiana, to the place where my son lives with my ex-husband, and murdered there. They'd sent me a note indicating the location. I was supposed to discover the bodies, or have them discovered. Instead, my son saw it. And now... now they have to address that."

"Why would they have done that? Killed the men and dumped the bodies by your family?"

"To prove that they can't be touched, and I can be," Jamie Bennett said. "I'm sure the message was a threat, and one that entertained them. It's their pattern, or what we understand of it. They're very good at what they do, but they're of...more creative minds than your typical hired killers. More like sociopaths than professionals, frankly. They like to entertain themselves while they work. Killing the witnesses I had promised to protect and then leaving them so close to my son...I think that pleased them."

"They know that he saw them."

"Yes."

"But they didn't kill him. Why not?"

"They didn't find him. He hid well that day, and they ran out of time. I got him away then. To a safe house. The sort of thing I told you his mother wouldn't trust. Remember that, the night I met you, that night in the snow? It wasn't a lie. His mother didn't trust the safe house. His mother had just lost two witnesses from one. Do you remember when I said I would protect the boy for free if I thought I could?"

Her voice broke and she turned from Allison. That was the only motion she made, but somehow she seemed to continue retreating.

"His mother was never a very good mother," she said. "That's why he lived with his father. But his mother still loves him. She loves him more than..." She stopped talking and gave a sob of a laugh and then said, "You like that? How I still have to talk about myself as if I'm not the mother?"

"I understand it, at least."

She turned back to Allison and said, "I'm sorry, Mrs.

Serbin. I'm so sorry. I should never have involved your husband. Or you. It was just an idea that came to me in a desperate time, and I remembered your husband, remembered that training and how good he was and how remote this place was, and I thought…I thought it might work. For long enough, anyhow. Just enough time for them to be caught. I'm so sorry you've paid for my mistake."

Allison stared past her and out the window to where the lights of the town glowed. On the other side of the lights, the mountains lived in blackness, and somewhere on them were Jamie Bennett's son and Allison's husband and the two men who smelled of smoke and blood.

"You might have made a lot of mistakes," Allison said. "But coming to Ethan wasn't one of them. I can promise you that. I can't promise you that he'll get your son back to you safely. But I can promise you that nobody has a better chance."

"I'm going after him."

"No, you're not."

"It's why I'm here. That's my *son*. You heard me say it; you're the only one who knows. I'm going to help find him."

"No, you're not," Allison repeated. "You don't know how. If you were with Ethan, maybe. Without him…you'll just get stopped."

"Then help me. Tell me where Ethan would have gone."

"I *don't know!* If I knew, I'd be there myself! To tell him to quit."

"How would Ethan have started? So far, all I know is that he's gone to search. You *have* to know more than that. This is what he does. What has he told you about the way he does it?"

He would have gone to the last place he'd seen the boy. He would have hiked back up the Pilot Creek trail and found their camp, and there he would have begun to track him.

"Would he have listened?" Allison said.

"What?"

"Your son. Was he the type of kid who would have paid attention to what Ethan said? Would he have listened and retained, or would he have been too scared? Would he have been concentrating only on staying with his false identity and hoping that nobody came for him?"

"He would have listened. It's one of the reasons we . . . one of the reasons *I* picked this approach. I wanted him off the grid, yes. But I also thought that your husband would help him. Mentally, emotionally. That he wouldn't be alone in the way he would have been in other situations."

Allison looked at the dark mountains again and said, "It will probably be too late."

"I've got to try. Mrs. Serbin, if you have an idea, then you've got to let me try. Just tell me where to go or who to talk to and I will leave you alone, I will—"

"We'll go together."

Jamie Bennett didn't say anything, just looked Allison up and down. Taking inventory of the damage.

"I'm burned, and I'm sore. I'm not broken. I can move."

"You don't need to—"

"Bullshit. Your son is out there, and my husband. And I hate hospitals."

"You're in one for a reason."

Allison pushed herself upright. It wasn't pleasant— there were throbs of pain from places she hadn't known were hurt—but she could do it. She swung around and got her feet down on the floor. All that was required now was standing. That was all. Tango had been standing for three months. How many people did she need to explain that to? Only one. Herself.

"Stop," Jamie Bennett said, but there wasn't much heart in it.

"Ethan gave them escape routes this summer," she said. "Every night, at every campsite. He said Connor—sorry, *Jace*—fell back when they were hiking last night. If he hasn't been found yet, then he's not on a trail. They would have found him. If he went into the backcountry, and if he was the type of kid who listened, then he might have tried to get out using the escape route. It would have been the only option he knew."

"So where would he be?"

"Trying to hike into Silver Gate down the back of a mountain."

"Silver Gate," Jamie Bennett said. "That's…that's where the fire is."

"Yes."

"Would it be close to him?"

"I have no idea what's happening in those mountains. Now, I know you can drive fast. You've demonstrated that. So drive fast again, but this time stay on the damn road, all right?"

Part Three

THE DYING KIND

28

THE FIRE CAME INTO VIEW for the first time at the plateau that ran below Republic Peak, which Hannah and Connor reached gasping and sweating. It had not been an easy climb. They could see Amphitheater, the next peak, in the distance, and below them, a long way down, were glimmers of orange and crimson. It looked like the dying embers of the world's largest campfire, but Hannah knew it was hardly ready to die. What looked like small flares from up here were probably flames climbing forty- or fifty-foot pines. The crews down there had lost the blaze to the wind and had likely retreated for the night. She'd heard no helicopters, which was unsurprising considering that it was dark and storms were on the way. There'd been no choppers during the day either, so she surmised that they'd thought they could contain it without the helitack units. Now they were backing off, giving themselves some rest and counting on rain, waiting to see what the storm front would do to the fire.

"That's it?" Connor said, staring down at the colored glows. There was awe in his voice.

"That's it."

"I didn't know we'd be able to see the actual flames. I thought it would just be smoke. I know it's not right to say, but from way up here, it looks kind of pretty."

"Yes," she said, and she was agreeing with both sentiments—it wasn't right to say, and it was pretty. It was absolutely gorgeous, in fact. "You should see it from the ground," she said. "When the flames turn to clouds. When the fire runs up on you like something prehistoric, and you can see it and feel it and hear it. The sounds it can make…it's a hungry sound. That's the best word I can give you. Hungry."

"How do you know so much about fires?"

"Spent some time with them, Connor. Fighting them."

"Really?" He turned to her. "They let girls do that?"

"They do."

"And you were down there?" He pointed. "I mean, you would have been *right down there*?"

"Yes. Usually, we would have trenched and watched the wind and pulled back by now. Waited for sunrise. Not always, though. It depends on the weather, depends on the circumstances, what your time window looks like. Sometimes we worked all day and all night. With this weather blowing in, though, we'd be waiting. We'd keep a safe distance and wait to see what it would do to the fire."

"Was it fun?"

She loved him for the genuine quality of the question. It was something adults would never ask; they'd search for a different word, wonder if it had been *rewarding* or *a rush* or something of that nature, but they'd want to know the same thing this kid did: Was it fun? She was silent for a long time, looking down into the shifting lights in the blackness, shapes that moved like scarlet shadows, a role reversal of light and dark.

"I worked with some wonderful people," she said. "And I got to see some things that were...special. Majestic. There were days when, yes, it was fun. There were days when it was inspiring. Made you think of who you were in the world."

"Why did you quit?"

"Because," she said, "I got a taste of the other kinds of days."

"What does that mean?"

"Sometimes you lose to it."

"To the fire?"

"Yeah."

"Did somebody get hurt?"

"A lot of people got hurt."

Lightning flashed regularly and closer now than before. The warm wind wavered between calm and howling. Stars disappeared in the west as the clouds thickened and crept along. Moisture was heavy in the air. Every warning was being offered, the mountains whispering one imperative instruction: *Get low, get low, get low.* She glanced back at the fire. Miles away still. Not a chance in this world that it would climb toward them fast enough. Not a chance. And if these lightning storms blew in, and they were exposed on top...

"We're going to go another quarter of a mile," she said. "Maybe half, no more. And then we're going to shut it down for the night. It'll be windy, and it might be rainy. But we're going to stay up top, where we can see what's happening. In the morning, we'll figure out how to call for help."

"Ethan said people should always be off the peaks when it storms. He said at this altitude, you're already sitting on an aluminum roof, and the last thing you should do is start climbing an aluminum ladder."

"Ethan sounds like a very smart guy," she said, reaching for her pack. "But I don't know if Ethan's been burned yet, Connor. I have. We're going to stay on top."

He didn't argue, just walked on with her, but she knew he wasn't altogether wrong. Storms were coming, there was no question of that. The wind was gusting just as hard as it had been but now it was sticky-hot; it had swung around to the southwest, and when the gusts came, they howled. Looking back toward the tower, you could see a sky littered with stars, the Milky Way never more stunning than it was in Montana at night, but to the west, the stars vanished, and that was trouble. The front that had pushed all this warm air ahead of it and caused havoc with the fires was about to reveal itself for the monster it was, and Hannah expected it to be a hell of a storm. It had been building too long to go any other way.

The question was, How long before it arrived? She didn't want to be on the peaks when it came, but hiking down the steep, rock-scree slopes at night was begging to break an ankle. If one of them got hurt, both of them were likely to die come morning.

She also didn't want to go down into the tree-lined drainages. The fire was still far away, but not far enough for her comfort. And with a wind like that behind the blaze? No. She wouldn't chance it. They'd stay high as long as they could, and they'd camp if they had to, and if the rain came, maybe it would slow the spread of the flames.

Or maybe you'll get killed by lightning.

It was a greater risk than the fire, she knew. But still...

Deploy or die, Hannah! Deploy or die!

She wouldn't take them down into those gulches yet. Not until she knew what the wind was going to do. Up here on the high rocks there was nothing for the fire to eat. Below them lay the land of the burnout, where scorched trees glittered like a field of candles, tributes to the dead, and that led all the way to where the main blaze raged, several thousand feet down. The wind and the terrain would hold the fire there.

"How long are your legs?"

Hannah stopped walking and looked at Connor. He'd been in front since they left—after informing her of the importance of rotating pace setters so that they didn't wear each other out—and he hadn't talked much as the first mile fell behind them and darkness came on.

"Pardon?"

"Are they the same length?"

"I don't follow, Connor."

"Some people have one leg that's a little longer than the other. I don't know about mine. They look the same, but it's probably not an obvious difference. Do you know about yours?"

"I'm pretty sure they're the same."

"Well, if they're not, we should know."

"Yeah?"

"We'll be veering in that direction. If your legs aren't even. You veer without even thinking about it. That's one way you get lost."

"Connor, we can still see what we're walking toward. We aren't going to get lost."

"It's just something to keep in mind," he said. There was a touch of defensiveness in his voice. He was full of these random facts, and while many of them—like the length of people's legs—were useless, she had to concede that the boots had been a decent idea, and leaving the light on a very good one, and bringing the map so obvious as to embarrass her. She also realized that he took comfort in the odd collection of wilderness trivia. It was where he'd gone to convince himself that it was worth getting up off the floor and trying to run. Where he went to keep the fear away.

"What else?" she said.

"Nothing." He was disgruntled now, and she couldn't have that.

"No," she said, "I'm serious. What else should we be thinking about?"

He was silent for a moment and then said, "We're going uphill."

"Yes."

"Well, that's a good thing, I think, except for the storm."

"Why is that?"

"Most people go downhill when they're lost. I forget exactly what the percentage is, but it's high. We're not lost, but we're trying to get out, so it's about the same thing, and most of the time, people who want out of the woods head downhill."

"Makes sense."

"Not necessarily. If people are looking for you, it's a lot easier for them to see you if you're up high than if you're down in a valley. You can signal better from up high. And you can always see a lot better. Like in your tower, right? It was easier to figure out the route from your tower than it would have been on the ground, just looking at the map."

"Good point." She liked this, wanted to keep him talking. The closer they got to that fire, the sharper the teeth of her memories became. Distraction was valuable.

"Lost skiers always want to go downhill," he said. "Percentage-wise, that is. And lost mountain climbers want to go up. That's pretty obvious when you think about it. It's, like, their habit, you know? So even though things have gotten bad for them, their habits aren't gone. Those stay."

"Right."

"It's a profile. Like the way they try to figure out who a serial killer is. If someone is lost, they'll make a profile of that person. So that's what they'll be doing to find us. They'll be trying to think like us. I wonder what they'll come up with. I mean, who are we, right? We don't have a profile. Maybe I do, and maybe you do, but when they put us together? I think we'd be pretty confusing."

"I certainly hope so." Their pace was unbearably slow, but it had to be. It was hard walking, and unlike Connor, Hannah didn't have a headlamp, so she was using a flashlight. The footwork was treacherous and if you dared to look more than a few steps ahead, the sudden shift in light was disorienting. So they marched on slowly, heads down, twin lights in a dark, windy world. She hadn't hiked the mountains at night—without a fire crew, at least—in exactly thirteen months. At the start of the last season, she and Nick had taken an overnight trip to a lake fed by glacier melt and had camped alone there beside its frigid waters.

That night was the only time she'd ever heard a cougar scream. They'd been setting up the tent, and the lake had a sunset glow that seemed to come from within the water and everything had been still and beautiful and silent until that ungodly shriek.

Nick found the cat—it was sitting on a ledge across the lake from them, up on the rimrock, a shadow against the stone. It looked like it was black in the fading sunlight, but black mountain lions didn't exist. A trick of the light. When Nick spotted the cougar, Hannah wondered if they should leave. Nick said no but that they shouldn't go any closer either. If it was a female and she had cubs, she'd protect them.

"She didn't have to let us know she was there," he'd said.

The cat watched them for a long time and never moved and eventually its shadow blurred with the others, and night claimed the ledge and then the mountain. Hannah hadn't slept well, knowing that it was out there in the dark, but that was all right. They didn't spend much time sleeping anyhow.

"You need me to slow down?"

Hannah jerked her head up, moving her eyes out of the past and into the glare of Connor's headlamp. He'd pulled well ahead of her.

"I'm fine."

"We can rest. You're breathing pretty hard."

Actually, she'd been close to crying.

"Okay," she said. "We'll take a rest." She unclipped the canteen from her belt and sipped some water and said, "I used to be in a lot better shape."

"You don't look too old," Connor said.

She had to laugh at that. "Thanks."

"No, I just mean…you said it the way an old person would. How old are you?"

"Twenty-eight, Connor. I am twenty-eight."

"See, that's still young."

It certainly was. She had her whole life ahead of her, she'd been told.

On her twenty-seventh birthday, Nick had given her a watch, along with a card on which he'd written a line from an old John Hiatt song. *Time is our friend, because for us there is no end.*

He'd been dead nine days later.

Because for us there is no end.

It had been a beautiful sentiment that day. She'd kissed him and told him that it was true. It had proven to be, in a terrible way. There was no escape from him—time for them did not and would not end.

"I didn't mean to upset you," Connor said.

"You didn't."

"Then why are you crying?"

She hadn't known she was. She wiped her face and said, "Sorry. It's been a long day."

"Yeah."

She remembered then that Connor had come her way in the dark, with that one headlight bobbing through the blackness to her. He had been on the move for many hours to get to her, and he hadn't slept since he'd arrived. She was standing here crying over the dead, but right in front of her, the living needed help.

"We're going to go just a bit farther," she said. "I want to get a little more distance between us and the tower. Then we'll rest for a while."

"You think that's safe?"

She pointed ahead, into the blackness. "We've got to do some serious climbing at some point. Up or down, it doesn't matter, it's going to be hard. Going down is more dangerous, probably, especially in the dark. So we'll push on just a little more. Then get some rest."

"Okay. You sure you're all right?"

She clipped her canteen back on her belt. "Just fine, Connor. I'm just fine. Let's keep walking."

29

T HEY SPOKE JUST AS ALLISON had promised they
would: Ethan was the focus but he was not part of the
conversation; it swirled around him. One thing he learned
from listening was their names, or at least the names by
which they called themselves. The other thing he learned
was that they were the most chilling men he'd ever encountered. At first, he believed it was because they were empty
of fear. Later, he decided it was because they were just
empty, period.

"Ethan tells me the searchers found no sign of the boy.
Now, so far Ethan has had a propensity to tell the truth.
Would you say I received it this time, Patrick?"

"I would, Jack. I would. I've been with them most of
the day. There was no sighting. They spent some time at
a fire tower, where they spoke with a lookout, and then
they moved on with renewed purpose. As if she'd told them
something that encouraged them."

"A perfect match to Ethan's account. As I said, I believe
he's an honest man."

"An honorable quality."

"Isn't it, though? And noble. He chose to join us simply to protect his wife. The man has had ample opportunities to cause trouble for me, perhaps even to escape, and yet here he is, walking beside us, guiding us even. Why would a man do that for the likes of us?"

"To keep the wife alive, I'd say."

"Correct again. And Ethan, I tell you, he is one loyal husband. He's working hard, and working against the clock. All for her."

"Protecting her."

"Exactly. The man appears to be nothing short of a local legend, and you know what? I believe he's earned his reputation. That rarest of breeds."

"He seems noble, as you say. Loyal, certainly. But here's my question, Jack, and bear in mind that I hardly wish to impugn a good man's character."

"Of course not."

"We agree that Ethan is a noble, brave man, a smart man, and a loyal one. Do I believe he'd do anything in his power to save his wife? Certainly. But I have to confess, Jack, that I have my doubts that he's willing to give up the boy so easily."

"Interesting."

"He's earned his reputation for protection, has he not? For salvation. Yet we are to believe that he's guiding us to a boy, knowing all the while that we intend to kill that boy?"

"You're dismissing the power of his marriage vows?"

"I'd also say that he looks at me with hate in his eyes. Disgust. Loathing. Why? Because I've killed. And yet, as I said, he's guiding us to the boy. He's playing a role in a child's death now, and he can rationalize it away, because he believes that he's protecting his wife. Perhaps I can accept that. Perhaps."

"What troubles you, then?"

"He knows why we've come for the boy. He knows that the boy poses a threat. And, being the very bright man that he is, Ethan should understand something else by now. Can you guess what that is, Jack?"

"It would seem, using fairly basic reasoning, that both Ethan and his wife represent threats to us as well."

"So you see the flaw here?"

"I do."

Ethan could hear thunder. A prolonged rumble in the west. Somewhere ahead of them, a limb cracked loose from a tree and fell, thrashing down through the branches. The wind had been blowing steadily since they arrived on the trail but now it was gusting. The smell of the smoke rode along with it, stronger than it had been before. He had one flashlight, taken from the burned man's truck, and it was not bright. Behind him, the brothers walked in darkness.

His plan was gone, Republic Peak no longer offering him the opportunity he'd envisioned, and he was trying to adapt, but it was hard. With the weapons and the numbers in their favor, it was very hard.

Where is Luke Bowden? he wondered. Earlier, he'd demanded that Roy bring Luke out of the mountains. He hadn't wanted any help, because he'd had a plan. Now he had nothing, and he wanted the help.

Maybe Luke didn't listen, he told himself. *It's possible. Probable, even. He doesn't like to lose a trail any more than you do. He'll have gone back to find it, and he will hear you coming, and he will know that you should be alone.*

Luke would be armed. Luke would be armed and he would move like the night breeze. He might be watching them now. It no longer mattered whether he'd found the boy or not. All that mattered was that he saw the boy's pursuers in time.

He will have to come this way. Either he's still trailing, in which case we will catch up to him eventually, or he will pass this way when he heads back out of the mountains. He will see us, and he will know what to do.

Even better, Ethan could *tell* him what to do. Ethan realized he was thinking like a passive man, which was both deadly and unnecessary. He wasn't helpless. He knew an ally existed out here, and the Blackwell brothers did not. He could signal Luke; he could do things that only someone who knew Ethan and knew the mountains would notice. Noise would be good, for one thing. Light signals, for another. He had only one light, but its beam could tell a story.

When the burned man spoke again, there was a trace of amused pleasure in his voice.

"He must have determined that there is no difference between himself and his wife and the boy from our perspective, so he has surely wondered what the endgame is. I believe he's been wondering about it for many hours now. Virtually since we met. He's had, as I mentioned, opportunities to change our path. Instead he chose to carry on, knowing that each hour brings his wife closer to death, and yet each step toward the boy does the same. It's fascinating to watch. Fascinating to consider. Because he's seen it all clearly, weighed his options, and made his decision. He will pursue the boy because if he doesn't, it simply speeds us toward the inevitable. We will kill him for lying and wasting our time, and what good would that do his wife?"

"What do you make of this, then? Knowing these things, what would you say Ethan is thinking right now?"

"Well, he has no intention of finding the boy or allowing his wife to die."

Ethan ignored them, let them talk while he continued to hike. As he walked, he passed his palm over the beam of the flashlight. Quick, flickering motions, his hand moving like a Las Vegas blackjack dealer's. He did it in sets of three. Sets of three meant one thing to a trained searcher: distress. Luke Bowden was a trained searcher.

"That's my conclusion as well," Patrick Blackwell said. "Which means…"

"He intended to kill me."

"I believe so. He wasn't counting on me, then. I've hindered him. This is the reason for his apparent antipathy toward me."

"He doesn't seem to have taken to you, no."

"Third wheel. It's often been my curse."

"But I don't sense he's a beaten man just yet. An unhappy one, yes, quite disgruntled about your joining our quest, but not beaten. And so he may still try, Patrick. I'm telling you, I wouldn't be a bit surprised if he tried to kill us both."

Ethan stopped and looked back at him. The burned man was smiling, and when he saw Ethan's face, his smile turned into a laugh. Loud and genuine and delighted.

"You're going to try," he said. "Good for you, Ethan. You are going to try."

Ethan shook his head. "No," he said. "I'm going to succeed." It was important to keep their attention on him. Let them not even consider the idea that there might be a watcher in the woods.

The burned man turned to the other and said, "You hear that? He's going to succeed."

"It will be fun to see, won't it?"

"It certainly will. Let's walk along and see how his confidence holds up."

Ethan didn't understand the full weight of that remark for another quarter mile. That was when they found Luke Bowden's body in the rocks.

30

H E WAS ON THE SIDE of the trail, stretched out on his back, blood pooled around him, eyes to the stars. Ethan stopped walking when the shape of the body came into view, and though he recognized him immediately, his mind tried to reject it. Not Luke, no, it couldn't be Luke, because Luke was too good and Luke was also the wild card that was supposed to tilt this back in Ethan's favor. The last best hope.

His first reaction was a foolish one—try to help. He went to the body and dropped onto his knees beside it and reached for Luke's hand, thinking he might find a pulse, and if he did, it wasn't too late. He had Luke's cold hand in his own when he finally focused on the source of the blood. A diagonal line was laced through Luke's throat, and in the flashlight glow, Ethan could see the cartilage of the larynx exposed, the blood around it already drying and collecting dust from that endless western wind.

"A bit late for medical attention," Patrick Blackwell said.

"Let's not linger too long, because I can assure you, it is a pointless exercise. You'll not breathe any life back into him."

"Damn you," Ethan said. The words were soft and choked. "This wasn't needed. All you came for was—"

"I'm aware of my own goals, thank you. And on the matter of what was needed, I'd differ strongly. He was a curious man, and he had a radio, and I'm afraid that was not a pleasing combination for me."

Ethan didn't speak. There was no point to it. Words from him would do nothing but bring more from them, and he believed their words would drive him mad soon. He looked at his old friend's body. Luke had been done; he could have called it quits along with the rest of them, but he didn't, because he was a rescuer. The search had not been successful and so he had doubled back after a long, hard day and continued on in the darkness, looking for the lost boy.

Ethan's lost boy.

"You didn't need to," he said again. He couldn't help himself, looking at that throat wound, thinking of the waste of it all. Thinking of Luke's wife, who'd danced with her husband at Miner's Saloon just a few weeks ago, full of laughter. She was always laughing, seemed as if she'd never stop.

This would stop her.

"Did you extract anything of use from him?" Jack Blackwell said. He'd joined Ethan in the dusty rocks and was looking at the body as if it were a discarded cigarette butt. "Or were the circumstances not favorable for talk?"

"He wanted to do most of the talking, I'm afraid. I gathered only that he was looking for the boy. He was, as I said, curious about me. Particularly my rifle. I was hoping to ease his concerns, as you can imagine—"

"Of course."

"—and so I offered him the rifle so that he might be reassured. At this point it became clear that he desired to speak with some people on his radio, and I thought that was less than ideal."

"Understandable."

"From there, we had little chance for conversation. But since he returned this way, I can only imagine he did so because he believed the search party had taken a wrong turn earlier."

"Ethan's theory as well."

"I had some time to think about that. I have to ask: How would a boy fourteen years of age, with limited knowledge of the mountains, manage to elude a quality search party that was familiar with the terrain?"

"Your suggestion seems to be that Ethan knows more than he says?"

"I've wondered, at least. It would seem that the boy had a contingency plan, would it not? And if such a plan was in place, well, it would most likely require Ethan's expertise."

"Ethan, your thoughts?"

This came from the burned man, the one called Jack, and Ethan was so numb to them now, he almost didn't respond. It took him a moment to realize the question had been directed at him. He was still holding Luke's hand.

"You'd like my thoughts?" he said.

"Indeed."

"I think that you should die slowly. With every hurt in the world."

The burned man smiled sadly and sighed. "Ethan. There's no time for this."

"Agreed," Patrick said. "I think we should get moving again."

Jack got to his feet and put one hand on Ethan's shoulder and used the other one to press the gun to the back of his head. He lifted Ethan by his shirt, and Ethan didn't fight him, just released Luke Bowden's hand and stepped away. He wished that Luke's eyes were closed. The dead always seemed to prefer to watch, though. He'd noticed that with corpses over the years. They were looking for something in the end, almost always.

"I don't know where the boy is," he said. "Neither did Luke. He could have found him for you as well as I could have, don't you see that? You should have just used him, killed me; it would have been the same. Neither of us knows where he is."

"You'll forgive me, I'm sure, if I say I have difficulty believing that," Patrick Blackwell said. "I've been all day in these mountains, Ethan. I've covered some ground, and I've spent plenty of time with my eye to the scope. Either the boy is possessed of remarkable speed and endurance, or he managed to hide without a trace after leaving a clear trail for the first several hours of his journey."

Eye to the scope. Ethan looked at his rifle then, that bit of machinery that gave the other man dominion. Ethan wasn't much of a gun guy. He'd used them, of course, had trained with them in the Air Force, and he owned a few now, but he wasn't even an armchair expert. It was a heavy rifle, that much was clear, bolt-action, maybe a .300 magnum. It would shoot long and it would shoot accurately, and with that scope, even an amateur would stand a killing chance. This man was not an amateur.

They began to move again, and Ethan walked numbly ahead. All his plans were gone; his ability *to* plan seemed gone. They walked away and left Luke in his own drying blood.

They were walking in a well-spaced formation, with Jack directly behind Ethan, and Patrick floating some twenty feet in the rear. The men hadn't discussed this arrangement, just assumed it, and it was a good one. Ethan could tell, based on the volume of Patrick's voice, that the man changed his pace now and then, sometimes stopping entirely, and Ethan imagined that was because he was scouting the darkness and responding to what he heard or felt or saw. Patrick knew something about tracking, there was no question.

And yet he'd been unable to find the boy. It wasn't an irrelevant point, Ethan thought. Not at all. Ethan had spent time with Connor. The kid was fit, and he would have been running hard on adrenaline, but he was not adept at woodcraft. So how had he vanished?

"One bit of information I was able to glean before things took an untidy turn," Patrick said, "was that the gentleman had decided to return to the fire lookout."

"And why was that?"

"He didn't have a chance to clarify, unfortunately. But I can tell you from my own experience that the boy's trail was clear enough until the searchers were redirected by the lookout."

"Then I'd say maybe the lookout lied."

"I'd suggest we stop at the lookout, then. See what the situation there is and see if perhaps we can get a different version of events than the searchers received today."

"I think that sounds fine," Jack said. "Ethan? Your opinion?"

For a moment he wasn't going to speak, had decided he was done responding to them, but then he thought of the woman from the fire tower and the possibility that the men were right, that she'd lied. There would have been one reason only for her to lie, and that was if Connor had convinced her to. If she'd lied to help him, it made sense.

"We don't need to stop at the tower," he said. "That would be foolish. We only need to consider that she lied."

"And how better to know if she lied than to ask her?" Patrick said. "All due respect to your considerable skills, of course, but I doubt that you're going to sniff the bark of a hemlock tree at just the right angle and know more about the lie than she does, Ethan."

"It's foolish," he repeated. "A needless risk. She lied for a reason, just as you say. That means she's prepared on some level. Nobody lies to a group of searchers about a missing child without cause. What do you *think* the cause is?"

Jack spoke in a mock whisper. "I suspect Ethan is suggesting that the boy has warned the lady of our imminent arrival, Patrick."

"A damned clever man, he is. His talents are wasted in his current profession, I might say. Should have been a detective. Think of the lives that might have been saved."

"Well, he's trying to save one tonight. Give the lad a chance."

"I'd love to. All the same, though…I simply feel we should speak with her directly. You understand?"

"I do. Allow me to convey it to our guide." Jack cleared his throat and then spoke in a mournful voice. "I suppose we are going to meet with dissent here, Ethan. While your perspective is certainly appreciated, you have to grant my brother and me a little leeway. We are given to somewhat different methods of tracking than those to which you are accustomed. Surely, in time, we'll all figure out how to work together. But for now, there must be a give-and-take, don't you see? A bit of patience."

"There's no need," Ethan said again.

"Patience," Jack whispered, and nudged him with the gun.

31

IT TOOK ONLY ALLISON's signature to get them out of the hospital. She heard the words *risk* and *liability* on a loop as she nodded her head and said that she understood and signed her name again and again, an awkward, unfamiliar signature, crafted with her left hand.

They had given her pain pills but she didn't take any yet. Not at the start. She wasn't sure how bad the pain would get, and she'd always been taught that it was wise to save your bullets.

"Why didn't he leave a way for you to contact him?" Jamie Bennett asked as they left the hospital. "It doesn't seem like Ethan."

Allison didn't like how she said that—she didn't know the first damn thing about Ethan—but she couldn't argue either. It *wasn't* like Ethan.

"I think he expected it to be fast," she said.

"But it hasn't been."

"No."

Jamie had rented a Toyota 4Runner instead of a Chevy

Tahoe this time, but if she was less inclined to run a foreign car off the highway than a domestic one, it wasn't obvious. Allison endured three stomach-clenching, tire-testing whips through the switchbacks before she said, "Imagine how Jace is going to feel when they rescue him and he comes home to find a dead mother."

"What?"

"Slow down, Jamie. Slow the hell down."

"Sorry." In the pale light from the instrument panel, Allison saw the blond woman's jaw clench. "It's just that I don't know what's happening," Jamie said. "He's out there, and he's alone, and...or maybe he's not alone. Maybe not anymore."

The way she said it, she obviously wasn't thinking of her son's having been rescued.

"Ethan will find him," Allison said, but her words rang hollow. She knew as much about her husband's situation right now as this woman did about her son's.

"Right."

"We'll get you back to him."

"He won't be happy to see me."

"What?"

She took another switchback, but gentler this time, actually aware of the brake pedal, and her eyes were hard to read in the darkness.

"Trust me," she said. "He won't be happy. Wherever he is right now, whatever is happening, he's blaming me. And he's right. It was my idea. Such a stupid one. Thinking he'd be safe from them up here? I sent him away, and I left him alone, and I told him he'd be safe."

"All that matters is that he does see you. Let's worry about that right now."

"Okay."

Allison had no idea what else to tell her. What did you say to a woman whose son was somewhere in these mountains with killers on his heels, and all thanks to her? Everything that came to Allison's mind sounded like an empty reassurance. She wondered if it might have been different if she'd been a mother herself. Did you know the code, then, did you have the right keys for the right locks? There had been some days, usually when she was saying good-bye to a group of boys at the end of the summer, when she'd wished she'd had the experience. But she also believed in what she and Ethan had decided years ago—they didn't need to have children to have an impact on their lives. She'd seen that play out every year.

Then the boys went home. Then it was just the two of them again, for many months. She didn't know what this woman was feeling, couldn't, never would. And some dark part of her was relieved by that.

"Where's his father?" Allison asked.

Jamie didn't answer immediately. Then she wet her lips, pushed her hair back over her ear, and kept her eyes firmly ahead as she said, "In Indiana, on the phone with his attorneys and the police, trying to make sure that if…that when Jace is found, I won't have any say in what happens next."

"Can he do that?"

"I won't fight it. When I find him, he'll go home. And home isn't with me."

"Why not?"

"Because I didn't want to be a mother, Mrs. Serbin. I have told this story countless times to countless people, and I have never said that. I have hedged and rationalized and made excuses and told lies. I have not told anyone other than my ex-husband that I never wanted to be pregnant in the first place and that I spent the months after I found out I was trying to talk myself into wanting to be a mother, without any luck. I thought it would just happen, maybe. That the body would convince the mind as things went along. It didn't happen. I had a child but never wanted to be a mother. How horrible is that?"

They wound onward and upward and neither of them spoke again until they saw the taillights of another car and Jamie was forced to slow down. The change in speed seemed to disrupt the atmosphere in the car, and Allison said, "Does your ex-husband know that you're here? Does anyone know that you're here?"

"You do."

"That's all?"

"Yes."

"So you're ignoring his calls. Or will he not—"

"I've come to bring Jace home. One way or another, I'm going to bring Jace home."

"Maybe you should call Jace's father. At least to tell him that—"

"Please stop."

"What?"

"I just want to find Jace. Can we just talk about how to do that?"

"Fair enough," Allison said, but she was thinking now about Jace and Ethan, and about the two who were probably already in the mountains, the men who spoke as if time stood still for them while they killed, after which they moved on at their leisure, and she was suddenly certain that she didn't want to be there when Jamie Bennett found her son. *One way or another*, she'd said. Words from a woman trying hard to be brave, but Jamie had not met those men and she did not know what the other way would be like.

The hail started just after they reached ten thousand feet. By then, Jace was gasping without shame, not even trying to hide how winded he was, and Hannah was stopping to rest every fifty or sixty steps. The warm wind had continued to blow in their faces, thunder and occasional lightning behind it, and now came the hail. It was a shower, and the ice pellets were not small. They bombarded the plateau and rattled off the rocks, and the wind picked up to a howl.

"We've got to stop," Jace said.

"Where?" Hannah answered. She had to shout at him even though he was just a few feet away.

He wanted to have an answer for that. He felt like he should have. What had Ethan said about this? Nothing; that was the problem.

"I could build a shelter," he said. But he couldn't. He didn't have the plastic, and there were no trees nearby for a primitive shelter. Even if there had been, what could he build in this wind? The branches would be torn from his hands. Ethan could do something, but Ethan wasn't here.

"We stay high," Hannah told him. "Storms like this blow over fast."

The hail was drilling down on them, stinging, and Hannah had one hand up to shield her face, but Jace could tell there was no confidence in her. She didn't know what to do about the storm either. This was supposed to be his job, but all he knew was that they didn't belong on the peaks in a storm. Great. It wasn't that easy to get *off* the peaks though.

"I'll put up that shelter you gave me. We can get in that—"

"We're *not* getting in that. And it's for fire anyhow. Not lightning. We've got to keep going, Connor."

He turned and tried to look back into the wind then had to lower his head against the stinging ice. He didn't like her choice of staying high. Lightning had been one of the first things Ethan talked about when they got up into the peaks. But down below was the glaring glitter of the mountainside on fire and the smell of smoke so strong that it made his eyes water. He didn't know which choice was worse. He wished he had someone else to ask. He wanted to defer, to avoid making a decision. That was what parents were for. You might not like their decisions, but you had to live with them. Up here, though, with the storms ahead and the men who wanted him dead behind, he wasn't sure if even his parents could make the right decisions.

"I wonder if my dad knows where I am," he said.

That got Hannah's attention. She turned back and said, "I thought they sent you up here to hide you?"

"I mean right now. I wonder what my parents have been told. I wonder if Ethan even made it down to tell them. Because if they were told..." His voice broke and he cleared his throat. "If they were told, why hasn't anyone come for me?"

"People came for you. We chose to send them away."

She was right, of course. But he didn't mean those people. He'd meant his parents themselves, with armed police, the way it had been the night he saw the killings. He'd been scared then, but he'd been in the right place too. With the right people. Everything had happened the way it should have, at first. But then the police couldn't find the men he'd seen, and now...

"Nobody will ever know what it was like," he said.

Lightning flashed and showed Hannah's face in bright white, her eyes dark against her skin, like sockets in a skull.

"I'll know," she said. "Connor, your parents sent you here because they thought it was the right thing, you understand that?"

"Look what it's turned into. This is the right thing?"

He wanted to quit again, the way he had the night before, and the way he had when he saw the man with the rifle through the binoculars. He'd done well for a while. Once they were in the woods and walking, he'd tried to keep his survivor mentality. It was leaving him once more, though, draining away; he was like a battery on empty, and as he squinted against the smoke in the air and let the ice drum away on his skin, he didn't know if he could recharge it again.

"The right choice can go very bad sometimes," Hannah told him. "You have no idea."

He sat down and pulled his water bottle free. He was thirsty, and you weren't supposed to get thirsty. That meant you'd gone too long without water. *Sip, sip, sip,* Ethan said. *Don't chug, don't gulp, just keep sipping.*

Now he gulped, drinking as much as he could. Even the water tasted smoky. The wind was full of it and he was glad for the sting because maybe that meant she wouldn't know that he was trying not to cry. He looked back into the darkness they'd come through, wondering where the men from the quarry were.

"Would you have done it?" he said.

"Sent you here?"

He nodded.

"If I thought it was the safest place."

"You would have sent me alone. Really?"

She didn't answer.

"It was my mom's idea," he said. "And she left when I was three. I see her on holidays and in the summer. That's all. And still my dad let her come up with this."

"Stop bitching," Hannah said.

"What?"

"You're here. You're not happy about how you got here, and neither am I, but that's not going to change reality. Here's your reality: I'm not going to let you sit on your ass on a mountain and wait to die. Now get up."

The next flash of lightning showed her face, and he saw how intense she looked. Angry, almost.

"You don't get to quit," she said. "I will by God get you out of these mountains safely, but you don't get to quit. You'll go home and tell them what you think and I hope they have the faintest idea, the faintest sense, of what you endured. But right now? Stand *up*."

He got to his feet slowly.

"Tell me the mistake you're making," she said. "You're full of observations when it comes to my mistakes. Now pay attention to yourself. What mistake did you just make?"

"Quitting."

"You weren't actually going to quit on me. I know better than that, even if you don't. Tell me the real mistake."

Jace had no idea what she was talking about.

"You're going to run out of water," she said. "And once we get close to the fire, it's going to be awfully hot, and you are going to wish you hadn't wasted all of your water up here. So refill when we get to the creek, and then ration it. Because despite what you might think, we are going to get down to that fire."

32

A LIGHT BECAME VISIBLE in the tower when they were still a mile from it, and Ethan saw the glow and stopped walking, only to be nudged again by the pistol.

"Guess she's home," Jack said. "That's marvelous, don't you think? Would hate to find that we'd missed our chance."

Ethan looked at the light and thought of the woman who waited with it and tried to imagine a scenario in which he could protect her.

Came up empty.

The path was clear to them now, they knew the way even without him, and so he was expendable. They were keeping him on hand in the event that they needed him later, but that need was not so great as to save his life if he did something dangerous. And all of the options left to him were dangerous. Fight or flight, that was what he had, primal as it got, and he'd passed on better opportunities to make both choices before. He'd waited to reach Republic, only to be reminded of that thing that every survivor had to always consider—disaster was never a destination, but always a detour.

"The best thing to do is to let me talk with her," he said. "I'm the one who understands that boy, and she would know about me by now."

"Interesting option, don't you think, Patrick?"

"Fascinating. But I have to say that I don't care for it."

"You feel the need to be involved in the discussion, is that it?"

"Well, I've come all this way."

"True. Would be a shame to endure so much and watch from the shadows while Ethan reaps the rewards."

"Indeed."

"I suppose we'll put it to a vote then. All in favor of staying together?"

Both men said, "Aye."

"All opposed?"

Ethan didn't speak. Just kept walking toward that light.

"Two in favor and one abstains. Not unanimous, perhaps, but as close as you'll get."

When they finally broke out of the woods and headed across the final stretch leading uphill to the lookout tower, Ethan could only hope that she was watching. If the light was on, she was likely awake. If she'd lied about the boy, she knew there was a threat, and maybe...maybe Connor was up there. It was possible she was hiding him now, trying to figure out what to do. Or waiting on help. Something. She might not be alone.

Jack was just behind Ethan, and Patrick floated some fifteen steps back and to the right. They reached the base of the stairs and all of them looked up, studying the cab. No shadows moved inside of it. They went up, turned at the first landing, up again, turn, up again, turn.

Forgive me, Ethan was thinking, a silent whisper to the woman above them. *I had planned it to go another way.*

He came to the top and there the wind blew hard enough that he wanted to grab the handrail. For the first time, he could see clearly through the windows. There was a table, a stove, an empty cot. Nobody moved inside.

"Open the door and then step out of the way," Jack said. The musical good-natured tone was gone from his voice. All bloody business now.

Ethan opened the door. Stepped aside and then glanced behind him, expecting to see that Jack had drawn the pistol and was in a shooter's stance. Instead, Jack stood casually, the black hat cocked low on his head, one hand on the guardrail. It was Patrick, down on the landing below them, who had the rifle to his shoulder.

"Go on in and say hello," Jack said.

Ethan turned and walked through the door and called out hello, and though he had expected the answering silence, he did not expect to see what he did.

The lookout's radio was demolished.

"Something went wrong here," he said, and he was genuinely puzzled. He'd anticipated some possibilities—Connor's presence, for example—but not this. He reached out and picked up a broken plastic fragment and then a severed cord. Why would she have destroyed her own radio? Her only chance to call for help?

"Are you sure you're the only ones looking for the boy?" he said. "Besides the right people, that is?"

Besides Luke Bowden, his blood still hardening in the mountain breeze. Besides Ethan.

"Well, this is interesting," Jack said. "She's gone, brother. And she destroyed her radio before she left. Apparently she didn't want us to be able to report her poor job performance."

Ethan moved away from the radio, studying the room. Saw the Osborne fire-finder and saw the empty glass beneath it. The map was gone.

"They're on the move," he said. "*She* didn't destroy the radio. He did."

He understood it now. The broken radio, the lie to the searchers. Connor did not trust help. Connor did not trust anyone.

"How are you so sure?" Jack said.

"Her life revolves around that radio. It's her job and her lifeline. To him, though? It would have been the scariest thing in the room. He found his way here because it was easy to navigate to. If she turned on the lights, like she did earlier? You can see it for a long ways. So he saw it, and he came here, and once he was here, she went to call it in. That would have been the natural reaction." He pointed at the remains of the radio. "And there we have the unnatural reaction. That would be Connor. He wouldn't want his location broadcasted."

"Why lie to the searchers, though?" This was from Patrick.

"I'm not certain about that." Ethan moved to the window, stared out at the dark expanse of mountains. There were faint red ribbons down below, where the fires coiled and burned. "But she believed him. He told her what he was running from, and she believed him."

"The lights went on less than an hour ago," Jack said. "They've not gone far."

Ethan could see his own face reflected in the glass, seemingly part of the maze of dark mountains and ribbons of fire. He watched his mouth begin to smile as if it were something beyond his control.

"I can find them," he said.

"I'd hope so. You're rather worthless to us otherwise."

"I can find them," he repeated, but again he was whispering in his head to this anonymous woman from the lookout, not an apology this time. *Thank you. I will not fail you now.*

Jack looked up. His burns glistened under the light. Ethan had grown used to seeing him in darkness, had forgotten the power of his hard blue eyes.

"Well, the job is yours if you want it. If not…"

"We can't find them standing here," Ethan said.

"No, I would think not. But before we head off into the night, Ethan, I'd like to hear your ideas. They've left the safety of the tower, which would suggest they feared our arrival. Where do you think they're going?"

"Republic Peak."

Jack looked at him for a long time. He did not speak. When the silence was broken, it was broken by Patrick, standing at the door with his rifle raised.

"They're going to climb?"

Ethan nodded. "It's the highest point they can reach. There, in the morning, they can do two things: see if anyone is pursuing them, and get the clearest possible location to signal for help."

Jack waved a hand at the radio. "Signaling doesn't seem to be a desire."

"She might be able to change his mind. Another night alone in the woods might change it too. But regardless, he'll want to get high, not low. He's already proven that, coming up here. He wants to be able to see where the threat is."

Republic Peak did not hold the appeal it once had, as a kill site. But going there still accomplished a few things. It would surely take him away from the boy. Connor wanted out of the mountains. The woman from this lookout wanted out of the mountains. You didn't get out of them by going higher. So they'd go low, and if Ethan could keep these bastards going high, the odds of intersection were nonexistent. After that, it wasn't a matter of killing anyone, though he'd certainly enjoy it. It was a matter of killing time. The burned man had used Ethan's knowledge of his brother to convince Ethan to bring him to the boy, selling a story that the other man waited inside the hospital, a killer poised for action at Allison's door. Now they were all together, which meant that no one waited outside Allison's door. The ticking clock was a ruse, a con. There were only two brothers, and they were both with Ethan now. He didn't have to kill them, just outlast them. Back in Billings, things had to be happening. New search parties gathering, new information being collected. Jamie Bennett would be involved by now. Facts would be replacing fiction. The ticking clock was for these men, not Ethan.

"How far to Republic?" Jack asked.

"A couple miles. It won't be an easy walk, though."

"It hasn't been so far."

"That's where they'll go," Ethan insisted. "And not just because it makes sense. Because it's what he's been taught. Him coming here today, finding elevation, checking his back trail, and then adjusting to his pursuers? He's listening to my advice. And from Republic? He knows how to get down without using a trail."

"How?"

"The way we planned it. That was our escape route. Getting to Republic one way, and getting down another. He knew what he was supposed to do. Now that you've passed him by once and given him the chance to do it, he'll take that chance."

This was more of the truth than Ethan wanted to tell them, but it would put him exactly where he wanted to be when the sun rose. Lost-Person Behavior 101: Those in need of rescue in the mountains tend to walk down even though they should walk up. Why walk up? Because you were far more visible to searchers.

These two men had been invisible for too long.

Jack Blackwell swiveled to look at his brother. The burned side of his face was exposed to Ethan, who took a strange satisfaction in the deepening color of the blistered flesh.

"Well, Patrick?"

"Two of them walking in the dark will certainly leave a trail. I could find it. But let's see if Ethan can, and faster. If he's right, then he should have no trouble with that. Otherwise…"

"He's of little use."

"Substantially less valuable, yes."

"The crucible looms, then."

"So it does."

Patrick stepped away from the door and motioned to Ethan, who walked back out into the night wind and toward a second chance. It was the old test, his favorite training exercise, and his most familiar role: he was the wilder again.

It was no longer a killer's game. It was a survivor's game.

33

I T TOOK ETHAN NINE MINUTES to find their trail.

He knew, because the Blackwell brothers timed him. Patrick had suggested Ethan should be able to find it in five, Jack had countered with fifteen, and they had settled on ten. All of this covered in one of their standard conversations, washing over Ethan. In truth, he believed he had the trail located within those first five minutes, but he didn't want to look too good, too fast.

It was not a hard trail to find, though it would be tough to follow soon. The plateau was rimmed by tall grasses that fell away to a tree line and then to rock, and each stage would increase the difficulty. Grass was one of Ethan's favorite tracking terrains. You might not be able to find the distinct prints that mud or even dry soil offered, but you could move fast, because grass held the evidence of disturbance longer. It bent, broke, and flattened. The stories it could tell you, it told you quickly. The taller the grass, the quicker the read.

There were two paths into the grass from the lookout,

and Ethan used the flashlight to determine which one was the right one. In so doing, he learned a great deal about Patrick Blackwell. The man had some level of training, certainly; he was better than his brother, but he wasn't elite. Either he'd not received first-rate tracking instruction or he'd forgotten it swiftly, in the way that someone did if not called upon to practice the art.

In the first of the two impressions leading away from the lookout and into the tall grass, the track appeared lighter than the surrounding, undamaged vegetation, a pale beam headed west. The second was reversed: the pale grass on the outside, the beam of the path a shade darker. Subtle shifts, the sort that the untrained eye wouldn't pause at but that a tracker's eye had to pause at.

Patrick Blackwell studied each of them, gave each of them the same scrutiny.

That was all Ethan needed to know. Anyone who gave that darker path any kind of inspection was not capable of understanding a track. Finding it, maybe. Understanding it, no. The dark path had been left by someone walking toward the lookout. This was a fundamental rule and the simplest of tricks, one Ethan had learned from a British SAS member. It was a matter of reflected light, easily understood by anyone who observed the lines left behind a lawn mower from different angles. It was also the sort of fundamental rule that you forgot under pressure unless you practiced under pressure.

"They went this way," Ethan said when the clock was at nine minutes, and he indicated the light path. "I'm sure of it."

"Sure of it," Jack said. "Ah, the confidence. Encouraging, isn't it, Patrick?"

"Immensely," Patrick said. He was looking at the trail

with distaste, though, and Ethan understood why—he wasn't convinced that it was the right one.

"It leads southwest," Ethan said. "It leads toward Republic. Just as I told you. The other is older, probably left by some backpackers a few days ago. You see that, right?"

Patrick nodded.

Excellent, you prick, Ethan thought. *You have no idea what you've missed. You might be able to see that it's an older trail, but you had to examine it far too long to get that, if you even did.*

"Onward, then," Jack said.

They crossed through the grass and on toward lightning that was becoming more frequent. The wind that had been blowing steadily during the day was now only sputtering in uneven gusts, like an engine running out of gas. This was good for tracking, since strong, steady winds could quickly return the grass to its natural position, but bad for their destination. There were storms coming. The fast-and-hard breed. Unlikely to do much to help the early-summer drought conditions and guaranteed to be treacherous up on the peaks. On any other day, Ethan would be taking precautions now, looking to get lower and get a shelter built. Today, he hiked on and up.

Once off the plateau and through the grass, they found a stand of pines perhaps forty feet deep. Here was where an inexperienced tracker would lose himself almost immediately, and Ethan stopped once more and panned his flashlight across the area. Again he watched Patrick Blackwell from his peripheral vision, wanting to see what he did. This time, he did the right thing—ignored the ground entirely and looked at the trees.

This was critical because it was the first thing their

quarry would have done. Reaching a change in terrain, with no trail to guide them, lost people paused to assess the obstacles, and then, nine times out of ten, they chose the path of least resistance. Or anyway, the path that *appeared* to offer the least resistance.

One of the pines had fallen, probably taken down by a lightning strike in a storm similar to the one they were walking into, and it lay horizontal. Nobody climbed over a tree unless he had to, so Ethan looked to the tree's left and right and found the terrain unchanged and the slope no steeper on one side than the other. That determined, he drifted to the right. Most of the world's population was right-handed, and he knew that Connor was too. Turning in the direction of your dominant hand wasn't a lost person's first instinct—taking the easiest path was—but it was common. Combine that with the fact that when you drove a car in America, left turns were far more likely to force you to cross traffic and thus far more dangerous, and Ethan believed that most people would default to the right if given no clear reason to turn to the left.

Off to the right of the fallen pine, then, and there he found the ground covered in lichen and saw the first prints. He moved to the side, careful not to disturb them, knelt, and studied them with his flashlight.

Two hikers, two sets of impressions. He put his own foot beside each one even though he didn't need to—he did it because it was a good time waste, and his job was to waste time and last until sunrise—and demonstrated to the Blackwell brothers that each track was substantially smaller than his own.

"Woman and boy," Jack Blackwell said in a musical, nearly cheerful tone. "That's the idea, I believe."

"I believe it is," his brother said.

They moved on a few feet; the lichen faded to dirt as it led up to the rocks and now the imprints became distinct, and Ethan knelt again, and for the first time since they'd left the tower, he felt true surprise.

These were not Connor Reynolds's prints.

The size was about right, and the depth of the impression indicated someone of about the right weight, but neither imprint matched Connor's boots. Ethan had paid careful attention to boots. They were required gear, but despite that, kids often arrived in sneakers or basketball shoes, and he had to outfit them with boots, because broken ankles were easily acquired on a mountainside. This year, every boy had worn boots, and Connor's had not been a wise choice. They weren't for hiking; they were cheap imitation military-style boots, black and shining and sure to cause problems, because they weren't broken in. Ethan had packed extra moleskin with Connor Reynolds in mind, in fact, expecting the boy to get blisters fast.

Neither of the prints he was looking at matched Connor's. One appeared to be from a hiking boot tread, and the other was more unique. A fine boot, but heavier.

"Perhaps if we give him enough time, he will detect their foot odor," Jack said. "A veritable bloodhound, our Ethan."

"Sadly, we don't have that sort of time," Patrick answered. "We should be moving along, don't you think?"

"I do. Any chance that we are on the wrong track?"

"None. They're proper size, but more important, they're very fresh prints. I rather doubt two people of similar size decided to leave the lookout tower in the night for a mountain hike."

"Agreed. And yet our tracking expert seems perplexed."

"I have a theory on that. I'm beginning to question his pace."

"You think that he'd waste our time? *Ethan?*"

"I'm merely saying I'm curious."

"We certainly couldn't have that. Time is valuable to us. More so than to Ethan."

He let them talk, and then finally he straightened and turned to face them. Patrick was closest to him now, Jack standing well removed. A reversal of position because Patrick was better equipped to judge Ethan's work, or so they thought.

"It's them," Ethan said, though he knew that it was not, and he tried to keep the gratitude at this providential discovery out of his voice. Other hikers had passed this way, rare in the backcountry, and they were headed in the direction he wanted to go. His job had just been made immeasurably easier. He no longer had to convince them that he was following a trail that didn't exist. He simply had to follow the wrong trail.

Hell, he could even pick up the pace.

34

THERE WAS POLICE TAPE stretched across the gravel
drive that led to Allison's home. Everything beyond it
was dark, no sign that it was a home at all. There were fresh
ruts in the grass from the fire trucks and the emergency vehicles that had come to save her less than twenty-four hours
earlier.

For the first time since she'd left the hospital, Allison
thought about the possibility of meeting up with the men
who'd so calmly entered her house in the night and heated
tongs in the stove to burn her flesh. They'd been specters before, plausible but not yet near. Now, seeing the crime-scene
tape, she could see them again, hear them. Smell them.

Jamie Bennett didn't even pause at the tape, just drove
right through it, bowing it inward until it went taut and
snapped and then it was fluttering in the gusting wind behind them, and ahead, the remains of Allison's house took
shape. Charred walls, gaping holes where glass belonged, a
buckled roof.

"Welcome back to the Ritz," she said.

"I'm sorry," Jamie said. Her voice was barely audible and she was looking at the damage out of the corner of her eye, as if she couldn't face it head-on.

Allison didn't answer her. She was staring at the house and remembering passing sheets of shingles to Ethan on the roof as an early-autumn snow flurry fell. They'd slept in a tent that night, as they had every night until the roof was done; they'd made a pact not to sleep in the house till it was finished, but they'd made that pact when it was warm and their bodies didn't ache from the work of it yet. They'd both regretted it in the final weeks, and then the roof was done, and suddenly it made sense again.

"Where do you want me to go?" Jamie said. "I'm not sure why we're here."

Allison put the window down, and the air that filled the car was heavy with smoke. Some of it was stale, traces of the flames that had been hosed out of her home, but more of it was fresh. The mountains were burning, and the wind carried notice of it.

"They'll have the road closed," she said.

"We'll get past them."

"For a quarter of a mile, yes. And then you're going to run out of road, Jamie."

"So what's your plan?"

"Have you ever ridden a horse?"

Jamie Bennett turned to her in the shadowed car and said, "Are you serious?"

"Yes."

"No. I have never ridden a horse."

"You're about to."

Jamie put her foot on the brake but didn't put the 4Runner in park. The headlights were fixed on the burned-out cabin but beyond, in the darkness, the stable stood, and inside it, unless someone had moved him, and Allison couldn't imagine that they had, Tango stood as well.

"That sounds crazy," Jamie said. "We don't need to—"

"They're in the mountains," Allison said. "Not at a campground. It's not a park, do you understand? It's wilderness. You can get us down the road. But nobody is down the road."

Jamie killed the engine. The headlights stayed on.

"We've got to go up," Allison said. "And I can't walk fast enough to do it. I thought about an ATV, but it's the same story—you need a rough trail, at the very least. We could go only so high. We aren't going to get behind the fire, not in a car, and not in an ATV. We can get there on the horse."

Could they, though? Tango hadn't carried a rider in months. Now she was going to ask him to carry two, up a mountain and into the smoke?

"All right," Jamie Bennett said, and then she opened her door and stepped out. Allison followed and they walked through the ashes of her own yard to the stable. When the headlights went off, the yard was dark but the frequent lightning in the west showed enough of the path. She heard Tango before she saw him, a soft chuffing breath.

"Give me a minute," she said.

Jamie stood alone in the yard while Allison stepped into the stable; she fumbled with her good hand along the shelf just inside the main door until she found the flashlight that rested there. She clicked it on and aimed the beam at the ground, shielding it with her hand so that the light didn't blind the horse. He was looking at her from the darkness, his eyes a reflected glow, his breath faint steam.

"Hi, baby," she said. "I'm home."

He gave a soft snort and lifted his head and lowered it in trademark Tango fashion, always tilting it slightly to the side. She'd wondered if his vision was bad in one eye, because he always seemed to want to look at you from an angle, but the veterinarians had tested him and proclaimed his eyesight fine. He was just a horse who wanted a different perspective, apparently.

"Can you do it?" Allison asked. "You have a last ride in you, kid?"

That sounded bad, sounded awful, and she corrected herself, as if he might be offended. "*Another* ride," she said. "Another ride, baby, that's all I meant."

Snort, snort. He shifted as much as the tethers allowed, eager for her to come closer, to touch him. She walked to the stall and laid her undamaged palm on his snout.

"Please be strong," she said. She was looking at his leg. "Oh, please be strong again."

Out beyond the stable, Jamie Bennett was moving around in the dark. Allison glanced at her shadow and felt a chill, memories of the shadows that had appeared in her yard last night returning.

She removed the horse's mouth bit and then unfastened the tethers that held Tango in place and that had kept him from lowering himself for three months. He tossed his head as if relieved to be free of them. Then she moved to his leg, speaking softly, well aware that he might be uneasy when touched on his damaged foreleg whether it caused him pain or not. She removed the soft wrap that had replaced the cast, and then he was standing free and unprotected. He regarded her calmly, no trace of pain.

"Let's see you walk," she said. A simple thing, in theory. But it had been so long.

She replaced the protective bit with a standard version and then opened the stall door and led him out. He walked smoothly, without a limp, but his gait was tentative.

"You're doing fine," she said. "You're doing great."

"What's going on?" Jamie Bennett called from outside, and Allison felt an irrational annoyance at the disruption of her private moment with Tango.

"Fine," she said. "Just give me a minute."

She led Tango from one end of the stable to the other and watched his stride carefully. There was no trace of weakness. She'd been told that there wouldn't be any, she'd been promised that the bone had healed well, but still, it was wonderful to see.

Could he hold a rider, though? Let alone two? He wasn't supposed to have any weight-bearing work for several weeks still. The rehabilitation process moved slowly. If you rushed it, you risked the horse. And if the foreleg fractured again...

"I need you to try," Allison whispered. She rested her face against the horse's neck, feeling his heat, remembering the way he had warned her of the arrival of the Blackwell brothers in the night. What if he hadn't, what if she'd not had a chance to at least grab the bear spray? He'd saved her once already, she realized, and she was asking more of him. She was afraid it would be more than he could give.

"I'm hurting too," she told the horse. And Lord, but it was true. The pain had risen steadily since she'd left the hospital and now it was distracting in its power. Just standing filled her body with jagged aches, and she thought of the jarring that would be required on horseback and wasn't sure if she could bear it.

If he could, though...if Tango could bear it, she knew

that she could too. When your own well of strength was emptied, you had to draw from other sources.

"Let's try it," she said. "And, baby, if you can't do it, show me now. Please show me."

Her voice broke and she stepped away and found a saddle. He seemed pleased to have it on his back again, and it made it harder, somehow, to see how enthusiastic he was. She'd ridden Tango with a child behind her, so she knew he wouldn't necessarily object to a second rider—some horses did—but two adults might be different.

She walked him out of the stable and into the darkness where Jamie Bennett waited.

"I'm going to mount him first," Allison said. She tried to keep her voice steady. "Watch how I do it."

"All right."

Allison handed her the flashlight and then put her left foot in the stirrup. She paused, waiting to see if Tango would respond negatively. He had no reaction at all. She swung her right leg up and over him as a bell choir of pain sounded through her body, enough to make her gasp.

"Are you okay?" Jamie said. "If you can't make it, you need to—"

"I'm fine. We'll see if the horse can make it." She slid forward in the saddle, clearing some room, and said, "Are you ready?"

"I think so."

"You'll be fine," Allison said.

"I'm not afraid of him."

Allison had actually been speaking to Tango. When Jamie Bennett swung her weight onto the horse's back, Allison closed her eyes, certain she would hear the dry-wood crack of his foreleg snapping.

He made no sound. Shifted a bit, but less than Jamie, who was trying to arrange herself in a saddle that was designed for one and coming close to sliding right off the horse.

"How am I supposed to stay on?"

"You hold on to me."

Jamie reached with tentative hands and took a loose hold of Allison's waist, the touch of a shy boy at his first dance.

"I wasn't kidding when I said *hold on* to me. You're going to fall off otherwise."

"I feel like..."

"What?"

"Well, you've got a lot of bandages."

"I sure the hell do," Allison said. "And, no, it's not going to feel good. Any of this. But we need to move."

She gave Tango the faintest pressure with her heels, and he started forward at a walk. Even at that pace, Jamie was jostled and she finally realized that she was going to bounce off the horse if she didn't hang on. She slid closer to Allison, wrapped her arms tighter around her, and squeezed, and Allison felt the bell choir of pain return, playing with gusto this time. Allison let out a slow breath, trying not to show how much it hurt. She was watching Tango step in the darkness. So far he was moving solidly. Still, his only activity for months had been exercises to prevent muscle atrophy, and she wondered if he could carry them for long. She wasn't sure how long it would be. Wasn't even sure if there was a chance of this working. What if Ethan was wrong and the boy hadn't tried to use the escape route at all?

She nudged Tango to a faster pace, a trot that made her wince with each step, both from her own pain and from imagining his. As the horse sped up and lightning flashed in the west, Jamie Bennett clung to Allison tighter, and Allison could feel a hard object pressing into her spine.

"Are you wearing a gun?"

"Of course."

"Can you shoot it? I mean, can you shoot it *well?* Anybody can pull a trigger."

"I can shoot it well, Mrs. Serbin."

"You may need to. If we see them...they aren't the kind you run from. They're the kind you have to kill."

"It would be my pleasure," Jamie Bennett said. "You find them for me, and I'll kill them. You're right—running and hiding doesn't work. I'm done trying that approach."

The words sounded right, bold and brave, and maybe Jamie believed them. Allison wanted to as well, but she couldn't. If she saw them again, she knew she wouldn't be walking away. Not twice.

Survivor-mentality requirement: gratitude.

You had to find small things to be grateful for even in the worst of circumstances, because that large thing—the simple, obvious statement of *I am alive*—didn't always win the day; there were times when you did not *want* to be alive. As the three of them worked their way up the base of Republic Peak, Ethan made a point to be grateful to whoever had passed this way for the tracks they had left. The trail led up the slope like a divine path. It was not hard to follow, even in the night—when people hiked over a scree, they caused rock displacement with virtually every step, exposing the dark, damp undersides of stones; there were long gashes where feet had slipped, and the places of dirt between rocks trapped clear prints. One of the hikers was outfitted with poles, and those punched holes in the dirt here and there above the footprints.

Because it was convincing enough for the Blackwells, because they did not know Connor's boots, they were content to follow it. Ethan was able to move faster, killing time no longer a problem, because he was eating up plenty of it by chasing a false path.

The moon was entirely hidden now, and most of the stars. The famous Big Sky vanishing to blackness as the storm front swept ahead. They were two-thirds of the way up the slope when Ethan saw a strike near Amphitheater, the next peak west. White light like a flicking snake's tongue. Ahead of them there was a sound like hard rain, and he believed it was hailing just a bit higher up.

"I know pace is an issue to you," he said. "But we're going to be at high risk up there right now. *High* risk. Twenty minutes of pause should be enough. Let that lightning go over, and then we carry on. But if we keep climbing, then—"

"We'll keep moving," Jack Blackwell said. His breathing was heavy now, ragged even, and Ethan savored the sound, enjoying every rasp of pain.

"Here's the thing," he said. "They won't be moving. They'll do the sane thing and take shelter. I suspect they have already. We won't be losing time."

In truth, he was growing damned curious about who these two hikers were and where in the hell they *had* camped. He knew what the prints told him—two women, most likely, or one woman and one boy or a very small man, but not Connor Reynolds. He couldn't make sense of the route, couldn't see what the average backpacker might hope to achieve by taking it. If the goal was Republic Peak or Amphitheater, there were better ways in. It was a curious trail.

"What do you think the odds of Ethan's being struck by lightning are?" Jack Blackwell said.

"Slim. It's a possibility in our current environment, certainly, but still slim."

"And his odds of dying if he decides to delay us needlessly?"

"Oh, I'd say they are substantial. I'd also point out that the high pressure is moving away from those peaks. I suspect Ethan knows this, so the storm might be a bit of an excuse."

Ethan paused. It was a fascinating observation, for two reasons. First because Patrick had made it, and there weren't many men who could make such a proclamation about a high-pressure system while on the move through the wilderness, and second because he was wrong.

It was called Buys Ballot's law. In the Northern Hemisphere, if you stand with your back to the prevailing wind, the area of low pressure will be on your left and the area of high pressure on your right, because wind travels counterclockwise inward toward a center of low pressure. The directions are reversed in the Southern Hemisphere. Patrick had made the observation but drawn the wrong conclusion.

A mistake, Ethan wondered, *or are you not from this place?*

He thought then of their voices, that oh-so-careful speech. Flawless English, but too clean of accent. They seemed to come from nowhere.

Southern Hemisphere, he thought. *You are far from home, boys.*

Patrick's world was backward here. His observation about the storm might not cost him—or it might cost them all—but this was good to know. If Ethan was right, this was very good to know.

"My thoughts exactly," Jack was saying. "Do we take a vote, then, or do we leave it up to Ethan? I'm a firm believer in democratic process."

"This I know."

"But at some points, clear leadership must be taken. For the greater good. So perhaps—"

Ethan began to move before they reached a decision. Up ahead, the clattering on the rocks was louder, and he felt the first stinging lashes on his own skin. Definitely hail. He watched ice gather and melt in the beam of his flashlight.

The men followed him, and up on the rock scree, everyone was silent; gasping breaths filled the night amid the sounds of the hail on the rocks and the wind whistling and moaning around them and the oncoming thunder. The world was lit time and time again by brilliant flashes. At the top of the rock scree, on the plateau at the base of Republic Peak, the hail was gone and all that remained was the lightning and whatever chased after it.

Ethan's mind was no longer on the storm, though. It was on those hikers ahead of them. The false path, the decoys. Their behavior was making less and less sense to him the higher they climbed. The prints up here were fresh. Not just recent, not just left within the day, but left within maybe an hour.

The grass held depressions from where two people had removed packs and sat on the ground. Those depressions were dryer than the rest of the plateau. That meant that their bodies had acted as shelters from the hail. That meant they were not far ahead at all.

Who was willing to hike toward a mountain peak in the

dark and during a hailstorm? Who was willing to climb the ladder to meet lightning?

It's not him, Ethan insisted to himself. *I know that boy's boots, and these tracks do not belong to him.*

Survivor-mentality requirement: an open mind. Rigidity was the door to death.

Ethan looked at the depressions again as the plateau was illuminated in a series of four rapid-fire strobes of lightning, and he saw his mistake. He'd underestimated them.

He's wearing new shoes. He's wearing a pair of her shoes.

It was a wise precaution and a handsome trick, and if they'd been chased by anyone else, it would have worked, or at least bought them some time. A good tracker would have seen those prints and disregarded them, knowing they were not the same as the boy's.

The only problem was that Ethan and the boy were both trying to be clever. The boy was trying to protect himself by changing his trail, and Ethan was trying to protect him by chasing a trail he knew wasn't the boy's. Now he'd not only found the boy's trail for his killers but closed the gap between them.

35

IT WAS THE HUMMING that finally shook Hannah free from the fog, a loud electric buzz, like an alarm clock, that called her grudgingly into reality.

"What is that?" Connor shouted. "What's that sound?"

It fell around the mountains like a trapped ancient chant, something stumbled upon in a place where humans did not belong. They had hit some invisible trip wire and now the wilderness was being called to respond to the intruders, the high hum a siren announcing their presence on the peaks.

"The corona effect," Hannah said. She spoke slowly, and though she knew she should be in a rush, a panic even, that felt beyond her now. She was aware that the choices had already been made, and the avenues of escape already ignored.

"What is it? What does it mean?" Connor was almost screaming.

"It's electricity," she said. "There's a lot of it in the air."

But it meant more than that. It meant there was already

MICHAEL KORYTA

a ground charge. It meant one of those lightning bolts had met the mountain. They were connected now, earth to sky, and Hannah and Connor between. They were almost to the rim of the glacier that lay between the peaks. Far below them the crimson and scarlet ribbons of the fire still glowed, but that wasn't the light that concerned her anymore. There was suddenly a blue luminescence to the rocks all around them. The white of the glacier looked like glass over a Tahitian sea.

Saint Elmo's fire. The eerie light that had haunted sailors for centuries, scaling the masts of tall ships in empty oceans. Now, far inland, it crackled on the high rocks to their left, sparked upward in a cobalt cloud that climbed and then was snuffed out in blackness, overeager in its attempt to claim the sky.

And all around them, that possessed hum. Not a static sound but dynamic, the pitch rising and falling, though the air was flat and still. Lightning flashed and vanished and flashed again and the mountain quaked from thunder. She felt a tingle then, not the kind born of panic but the kind that should create it. When she looked at Connor, she could see that the hair on the back of his neck was standing straight up, the arched fur of a defensive cat.

"Run," she said.

But he couldn't run. They were too high and it was too steep and all he could do was take three unsteady steps before his feet caught and sent him stumbling to his knees. The blue world boomed with thunder and then bloomed with an aggressive flash of white before fading back to blue. Hannah hadn't moved, hadn't taken a single step, and below her, Connor was still trying, crawling on his hands and knees now, to get back down the mountain.

She thought of the boy who'd boiled in the river trying to reach her.

Connor tried to push himself up. Braced his weight on his hiking sticks, and she fixed on them: an aluminum pole in each hand. A lightning rod in each hand.

"Connor!" she shouted, and now she was moving, finally untethered from the fog, stumbling and slipping after him. "Drop the poles! Drop the poles!"

He turned back and looked at her and then registered the instruction and shook his hands free of the wrist straps. The poles bounced down the mountain. She took a step from one rock to the next, heading toward him.

Then she was on her back.

She stared at the night sky and realized her boots were in the way of the sky. Why was she looking at her boots? Why was she upside down? She was upside down on the mountain and somehow Connor was above her when before he'd been below. He was also down. The high hum was back—had it ever been gone?—and her body ached.

You got hit, she thought in wonder. *You got struck.*

She tried to move, expecting that she wouldn't be able to, but her body responded, and she saw that Connor was moving as well. They hadn't been hit. The mountain had been hit, again, and it had absorbed the strike for them, again. It might not continue to.

She crawled toward Connor and stretched out her hand. "Come on." When his hand met hers, the touch carried a static jolt. She tugged him toward her and they began descending the slope together, and then the crawling turned to falling and they slid down, jarring pains and jolts as they gave in to the gravity they'd fought the whole way up here. She knew that they didn't have long to fall—one of the drainages awaited, and she was braced for the impact when they hit it.

The landing was less painful than the trip down. They smashed into a crevice of rock, and Connor took most of the impact for her. They were wedged in the rocks now some forty feet below the peaks. Connor tried to struggle upright but she held him down.

"Stay low," she said. "Stop moving and stay low."

They huddled there in the rocks together and above them the world boomed and bloomed, boomed and bloomed.

No rain fell.

It wasn't a salvation storm. It was a flint-and-steel storm. Down below, the fire crews were watching it and waiting for rain, although they probably realized by now that it would not come. All that wind carried was dry lightning, the worst kind for a red-flag day. There would likely be new flare-ups now, with all these strikes around them. It was what could happen when you put your faith in a cloud.

She held on to Connor and pressed them both into the rocks and watched the electric storm pass and felt true hatred. She'd trusted in it and it had turned on her and become an enemy. She'd met enough enemies along the way. They chased behind and loomed ahead, and she did not need them to fall out of the sky above as well.

"We got hit," Connor said. He'd been silent for some time, watching. The worst of the storm was moving on, it seemed, though Hannah knew you couldn't count on that, not when the skies could throw something deadly at you that was an inch wide and five miles long.

"No, we didn't. The mountain got hit."

"But I felt it."

"I know. I did too. You okay?"

"I can move. You?"

"I can move."

She looked at him in the darkness and then looked at the scarlet snakes of fires below. There was a hotshot crew down there. They might have reached them before daylight if she'd just committed to it. Instead, she'd stayed high to avoid the fire and nearly killed them both.

"If we can both move," she said, "we should. It's time to get you out of here, Connor."

"We're going down here?"

"Yeah."

"The drainages are tough walking," he said, but he didn't continue arguing for once, even though it was true.

"I know they are. But we've done some tough walking to get here. I know you can make it. You do too, right?" When he didn't answer she said, "Connor?"

"I can keep going. We'll be walking straight down into the fire, though."

"Yes."

"To find the firefighters?"

"To find the firefighters. They'll get us out fast."

She pushed herself up on the heels of her hands and considered the long, winding drainage ahead of them. It was the worst kind of climbing, steep and filled with windfall. But it led straight down too. It was the sort of path you could follow even in the darkness.

"We'll have to get close to it."

"Yes."

"I can smell it so strong from here. Is it even safe? Is it safe to get that close?"

A crimson tree flowered in the darkness and then faded.

Spot fires flaring in the burned-out area, trailing the main blaze, as if they'd been separated from the herd and were starving fast because they could not share in the meals.

"There's a risk to everything," Hannah said. "I know something about what's in that direction. The men behind you, I don't know anything about."

"I do."

"There you go. And you think they'll kill us."

"They will kill me. I don't know about you."

"There's no you or me anymore, Connor. Not at this point. Just us. It would seem like the best chance for us is to walk toward that fire."

He might have nodded. In the darkness she wasn't sure. He didn't speak, though.

"We'll make it, Connor," she said. "Listen to me: I promise you, we're going to make it down there, and you're going to get out of this place and never see it again. Not unless you want to. You ready to get out of these mountains?"

"Yes."

"Me too."

They'd left the fire tower a few short hours earlier, walking with a plan. This time when they started out, they were crawling. As the storm faded and dawn came to replace it, they moved out of their old world and into a new one, as if the lightning had bridged the divide and taken them over to another land. It was all gray, this world, from both the light offered by a sun still trapped behind the mountains and the smoke rising to meet it. Once they made it out of the drainage, they found a flattened stretch of land, and it was Connor who realized its significance first.

"This is the trail," he said. "This is the Republic Pass trail."

So it was. Four miles to go. Roughly the same distance they'd covered since leaving the tower, and yet it would—or should—feel like a tenth of that. They'd be walking downhill on a trail now, not fighting over the peaks and into a storm.

"Almost home," Hannah said, "and nobody's behind us yet."

36

W HEN THE LIGHTNING BEGAN to strike the peaks,
even the Blackwell brothers knew it was time to
pull back.

"Just for a bit now," Jack said in a soothing singsong, as
if urging a sick child to rest. "Just a few minutes is all."

They knelt below a shelf of rock carved out by an ocean
some thousands of years before, and for the first time, they
were all within arm's reach of one another.

Survivor mentality: appreciate the opportunities the environment gives you.

But what were those grand opportunities? Ethan could
grapple with one brother in the dark and wait for the other
to kill him.

The mountain trembled with thunder, and the wilderness was illuminated again and again in a rolling strobe of
light. A few hundred yards away, one of the lightning bolts
connected with a jack pine; it went up in a glitter and then
part of it fell to the ground and continued a slow burn, half
of it standing, half of it down on the mountain. Wildfire

season. This was how most of them would begin. Dry, angry fronts like these. Isolated strikes in desolate lands.

"Seems to be passing," Patrick said.

"The worst of it is over, at least," his brother said. "A bit
more lies behind."

"Enough that we should waste the time?"

"At some point there's a measure of risk to be assumed.
You think we've reached that point?"

"We're close to him. It's still dark. I'd hate to waste those
things. Too much has been going on behind us since morning. When they come for him tomorrow, they'll come big."

"Let's finish it, then."

Ethan watched them slide out from under the rock shelf
and then separate, as was their way, and whatever chance
he might have had was gone. He didn't move right away.
He stayed crouched beneath the rocks and watched the
lightning and smelled the smoke and thought of how close
they were to the boy now.

"Ethan?" Jack Blackwell called, congenial. "I hate to
press you, but we're on a bit of a deadline here."

He slid out from under the rocks. Thunder cracked
again but it lacked its earlier bass menace as the storm
drifted eastward. The lightning flashes were still there, spo-
radic but still there, and not a single drop of rain had fallen.

"That's the peak you wanted," Patrick Blackwell said, indicating Republic as it lit up in another flash. "Correct?"

"Yeah. But there's no point going up there now."

"I thought you were certain that was their destination.
The trail seems to agree."

"They'd have gotten off the peaks when the lightning
started."

"If I might interrupt," Jack said, "I seem to recall Ethan's notion about the visibility afforded up there. The idea that we might be able to see anyone in the vicinity."

"He did have that notion, you're correct, Jack."

"Worth the climb, then, I'd imagine."

Ethan didn't know where Connor and the woman from the lookout were, but he was certain they would be within visible range of an observer at the top of Republic Peak. Would fall within the crosshairs of the scope on Patrick's rifle.

Ethan thought again of his father, and for the first time he had an answer to the man's question. *How will I know that it works? Connor Reynolds can tell them. When he walks out of these mountains alive, he can tell them that it works.*

"You climb first," he said to Patrick, nodding at the steep wall of rock that now lay in shadows, knowing what the response would be.

"No, no. We've entrusted you with leadership. You go on and climb. Don't worry, Ethan. We'll be right behind you."

Where Republic Peak turned from a steep walk into a true climb, Patrick Blackwell slung his rifle over his shoulder and stayed close to Ethan, and Jack fell back. They did it without discussion but Ethan understood it, and of course it was the right move, they never seemed to make anything but the right move. On the rocks a rifle shot would be awkward and difficult, while the pistol, requiring just one free hand, was much more functional.

Ethan watched it take place and saw it for what it was: his last chance extinguished. Any hope of killing them both, always minuscule, was now nonexistent. He could take one, though. When Ethan died, he wouldn't die lonely.

The brothers were silent for once, focused on the climb,

reaching for hand- and footholds in the shadows. Hand and foot, rock to rock, on toward the sky.

To the east there was a thin band of pink, and the black sky of the storm had lightened to a pale gray that allowed them to see just well enough; the rocks were still dark, but their shapes were clear. The forested hills fell away behind them and they climbed to meet that lead-colored sky, more than two vertical miles in the air now. It was a climb Ethan had made many times and always enjoyed and he wished that it would go slower, because it was his last climb and it seemed he should be allowed time to think. There were prayers and wishes and whispers required, but they were moving too fast and he couldn't sort them out, couldn't even land on an image of his wife; everything was simply another rock with his hand closing over it and the summit getting nearer and with it the end.

That was fine, then. It would end with a hand on a rock anyhow, so focus on that, he decided, think of nothing else: hand on rock, rock on skull—all he had left to achieve. He was hoping that his own rock was still on top of the summit pile, the last one he'd held, the one he'd been imagining for so long on this hike, when Patrick Blackwell swung away to the left and scrambled past him.

The sudden speed came without a word or a warning. All along Patrick had been content to remain just below, hovering near Ethan's feet, following his path, and then as the summit neared, he'd moved away and onto a more difficult path but he moved faster, and now he was in the lead and Ethan was between them both and Patrick was not looking back, but moving faster still, as if he were in a race over the face of the rocks, like so many of the boys Ethan had watched, each determined to be the first one to the summit.

No, Ethan thought, *no, damn you, I had to get there first, you were doing just what you should have been doing, you were staying just in the right place...*

He tried to match him then, tried to catch him and pass him, and below him, Jack Blackwell saw it and called, "Patrick." That was it, just his name.

Patrick Blackwell glanced back at Ethan and said, "What's your hurry?" as he pulled himself up onto a ledge below the summit and slung the rifle free.

Ethan stopped with the barrel a foot from his face, Patrick's hand casual on the trigger, his back braced against the rock, where he would have no trouble shooting. Below them, Jack had stopped moving.

"Everything all right, Ethan?" he called. "Seemed to become a race there for a moment. Why don't we let my brother take the summit first. He's always been the competitive sort. It would mean something to him."

Patrick Blackwell was smiling at Ethan. Understanding some of it, if not the specifics.

"Maybe you can relax a minute?" Patrick said. "You just relax." He slid sideways on the ledge a few feet, far enough to clear the rifle out of Ethan's reach, and then he turned and grabbed the rock above him and pulled himself up, one fast springing motion, dragging his rifle over the stone, and then he was at the summit and standing upright again, and at his back was the pile of loose stones on which Ethan had pinned his hopes.

"Come on the rest of the way now," he said.

Ethan looked at the rock in hand. A slab of stone, useful for holding on to the face of the mountain, useless as a weapon. His weapons were waiting above, and he was below, and he felt as if it had always been that way.

He climbed up and straightened and stood and there they were at the top of the dark world. Patrick Blackwell held the rifle on him until his brother had also reached the summit and then he moved several steps away and lowered his eye to the rifle scope and began to search the slopes. Jack had his handgun drawn and was looking at Ethan with curious amusement.

"You seem flustered," he said. "Have we troubled you?"

Ethan moved to the pile of stones, the pyramid that marked 10,487 feet in the air. He was facing Yellowstone now, his back to the Beartooths and his home. He looked at the rocks and told himself the job would have been impossible to accomplish even if he'd beaten them to the top, even if something, anything, had gone according to plan.

There will be another chance, he told himself. *Getting down, maybe, there will be another chance, another way, a better one.*

"Jace, Jace, my old friend," Patrick Blackwell said, staring through his scope. "So good to see you. So very good."

Jack turned from Ethan and looked at his brother, and the amusement left his face.

"You can see him?"

"Indeed. He's with a woman. His friend from the lookout tower, I imagine."

"You're sure it's him?" Jack asked.

"If there's another pair like them hiking toward a forest fire, I'd be rather surprised, but come have a look. It's the first time we've seen him live, after all. You're entitled, brother."

Jack moved away from Ethan and toward his brother. Patrick was kneeling with the rifle braced on the rocks, facing the northern slope.

Why did they go high, Ethan thought, *why in the hell did she take him high? I was supposed to be buying them time. I was supposed to be winning this.*

Jack walked over, knelt beside his brother, and accepted the rifle while passing Patrick the handgun, keeping them both armed. The right move. They never made the wrong move.

Except for their eyes. For the first time since the hospital, Jack Blackwell's eyes were not on Ethan. They were on the rifle scope, and Patrick's followed, both of them gazing north, away from Ethan. He looked down at the pile of stones and saw that his own was no longer on top. Someone had been here since and covered his with a bigger piece, a jagged slab. He reached down and picked it up. He did it slowly and gently, so as not to make a sound. Neither of the Blackwell brothers turned.

"It would seem to be him," Jack was saying. "An interesting route they've taken. Why go up to go down? But no matter."

"I can take them both."

"From this distance?"

"Yes."

They were still facing down the slope, and Ethan had advanced four steps almost soundlessly, though he didn't know if a sound would have mattered; they had stopped regarding him as a threat at this point and were focused on their quarry. They were close together, finally.

"I hate to see it end from here," Jack Blackwell said. "But I suppose it doesn't matter that the boy won't know. His mother will."

"Yes."

"A miss would be bad, if it gives them time to take cover. Prolong things and carry us farther in the wrong direction."

"I won't miss."

"Hate to see you do such fine work for free. I'll pay you a dollar for each."

"Deeply appreciated."

They would have to trade weapons again. It was clear that Jack deferred to his brother in regard to the long gun. There would be a moment of exchange, a moment when both of them held guns but were not prepared to fire them, and that was all Ethan sought. He was five feet away. The rock in his hand was heavy but not heavy enough to slow him down if he rushed at them. He could swing it, and he could swing it with force.

Get the handgun, he told himself, because the handgun could be fired quickly in the chaos. His breathing had slowed even as his heart rate quickened, and he focused on the back of Patrick Blackwell's skull, because that was where it would have to start, everything would begin and end from the spot where Ethan could place the rock against those bones.

"Earn your dollars, then," Jack said, and he sat up, both knees planted on the rocks, and passed the rifle to Patrick, who lowered the handgun to make the transfer, and there was the moment, both of them unprepared and vulnerable and finally, finally, close enough together for both to be at risk at the same time. When he began to move, Ethan felt astonished that such an opportunity had presented itself, because he'd never imagined that he could get more than one of them, and yet here they were, his for the taking.

He traded silence for speed over those last five feet, drawing the fist with the rock in it back and then slinging it forward, focused on that skull, ready for it to shatter.

The skull wasn't there by the time he reached it.

They were fast men. Lord, but they were fast.

He'd surprised them and still they knew what to do; their instinct, these two who made one united force, was always to part. Patrick rolled left and Jack rolled right and then there was distance between them and the guns somewhere in the middle, and Ethan's rock missed Patrick entirely and found air where he was supposed to be, Ethan falling with the force of the blow. A hand flashed out and found his neck in what was no doubt supposed to be a killing blow, or at least a crippling one, but here Ethan benefited from his own stumble and the hand chopped at the side of his neck instead of the center of his throat.

A choice to be made then, split-second, he had to look either left or right, because you couldn't do both simultaneously, and so he stayed with the target he'd come for and swung the rock again and this time found success, caught Patrick Blackwell full in the face and felt jawbone shatter beneath the rock, tore the flesh of his own hand on Patrick's broken teeth as he punched through his mouth. The rock fell free and then Patrick was silent and down in the darkness and somewhere behind them Ethan could hear Jack scrambling.

Guns, he thought stupidly, urgently, *there are guns and you need one.*

But he couldn't find one, and it was happening too fast and he knew Jack was quick and deadly and so he did the only thing he could think of and wrapped one arm around Patrick Blackwell and then rolled with him and heaved him upright, thinking that if he had one brother between himself and the other brother's bullets, he'd be fine. He could feel the metal barrel of the rifle under his arm, pinned against Patrick's limp body, and thought that if he got a

little space and little time, just a little, he could not only
equalize this situation but control it.

He was halfway to his feet when the first shot rang out
and something scalded his side and knocked him back to
the ground. Patrick dropped with him, onto him, and there
was a pause before the second shot, because Ethan had now
inadvertently achieved his goal—he was shielded, and Jack
saw two heads side by side in the darkness, and one of them
was his brother's and he would not take the kill shot until
he was sure which one he was aiming at. He'd seen Ethan's
body clear enough for one shot and had taken it, but now
he couldn't take another, not with Ethan lying there tangled
with his brother in the dark, and so that most precious thing,
time, had been offered to Ethan again—fleeting, but there.

Get up, Ethan demanded of himself as the blood spilled
hot down his side, *get up, and get back.*

Down to the other most basic instinct now, down to
flight. The fight had come and now it had gone; he knew
where the threat was and knew that he had to retreat from
it and knew that only if he kept Patrick with him did he
have a chance.

There was just one problem with that: Ethan had run out
of mountain.

It was only when he tried to drag himself upright the second time that he realized how close to the edge he was and
that to retreat was to fall, and fall a long way. He ducked his
head to keep it pressed against Patrick's. He had to dance
his way toward death, cheek to cheek; there was no other
way to keep the bullets at bay.

"Ethan."

Jack Blackwell's voice came out of the dark rocks, firm
and impossibly steady. Unfazed.

"Put him down, and we can go on about our business here. I make it very quick, or very slow. You're making the choice for me right now. You're choosing to go slow, and that's so foolish."

Ethan was struggling to keep his head pressed against Patrick's, and it limited his vision, but he could see Jack Blackwell's silhouette. He'd risen and stood tall against the shadows, a solitary interruption against that band of pink sunrise. He had the gun pointed at Ethan but was unhurried as he advanced, and that was fine for Jack, because he had no need to hurry, he had the gun and time and space, and Ethan had none of those things, he had only the fall waiting behind him.

So he took it, and took Patrick Blackwell with him.

Part Four

BURY THEM HIGH

37

TANGO WAS SLOWING BUT still steady when they
reached the burnout. Allison and Jamie had entered
the mountains and two sides of the world were lit with two
different deadly lights. Up above them, lightning was
working on the mountaintops. Below, to their right, the
forest fire glowed in the woods just south of Silver Gate.
The wind fed it and drove acrid smoke toward them. Allison could also see the lights of a large campsite—that
would be the firefighter base. There they'd have the ground
crews and pump trucks and all those who were prepared to
defend Silver Gate and Cooke City from a threat that had
arrived here because of the two women who now rode
silently into the hills like ghosts.

"There will be police down there," Allison said. "I think.
Maybe not. Maybe just the firefighters. But they still might
be able to help."

"No," Jamie Bennett said.

Allison pulled back on the reins and brought Tango in.

He seemed grateful for the stop. She eyed his foreleg and waited to see if he would try to shift away from it. He stayed balanced.

"I'm sorry," Jamie said. "But I told you why. I thought you understood—"

"I do."

Yes, she understood. You whispered the wrong word in the wrong ear—hell, maybe even the right ear—and two wolves arrived at your door in the night. Lives were lost, good men were burned on mountainsides, boys vanished. There were plenty of reasons that there was no trust left in Jamie Bennett's world. She was, after all, part of the system that was supposed to be able to keep people safe. And she hadn't been able to do it for her own son. Not against those two.

So how are we supposed to do it, Allison thought, *if the best she could do led to this?*

"You don't have to come," Jamie said, as if Allison had voiced her doubts aloud. "You can go down to them. All I'm asking is that you let me go on."

They were silent, Allison thinking and letting the horse rest and watching the fire below and the lightning above. She nudged Tango back into motion. He started slow.

"How fast can it burn?" Jamie Bennett asked. She was turned in the saddle, watching the flames. She didn't need to be told to hold tight anymore—once the fire had come into view, her grip on Allison became painful. Each of Tango's steps hurt Allison as well, jarring her. Allison tried to distract herself by watching that foreleg, studying it for any sign of weakness. His pace wasn't quick, but each step was firm and confident.

"I'm not sure," Allison said. "But it looks like it went through here pretty fast."

"So we're safe here. It won't come back, even if the wind shifts?"

"It doesn't have fuel here. Where we're going, it does." She pointed into the shadowed tree line of untouched timber above where the flames were burning now.

"Jace will be up there?"

"I have no idea, Jamie. The trail he was told to take out of these mountains in an emergency is up there. Whether he…" She caught herself before saying *Whether he made it* and instead said, "Whether he decided to take it, I don't know."

Jamie didn't say anything to that, and so they rode on in silence, and Allison tried to imagine where Ethan might be. If he'd started at Pilot Creek, then he'd be well into the mountains now, up at the elevation where the lightning was hunting for fools.

Her eyes left the peaks when Tango balked. It was the first disruption she'd felt in his stride, and she was sure it was his leg. When she looked down, though, she saw all four feet planted firmly on the ground. He was trying to back up. Her mind went to snakes then, wondering if he'd somehow seen a diamondback in the darkness, even though they were never up at this altitude, but then she saw the faint cloud that his hooves were raising.

Fire had passed this way, and not all that long ago. Recently enough that the ashes were still warm.

She coaxed him forward, watching to see if it was too hot, if it hurt him or frightened him. There was no sign of that, even though there were glimmers of crimson amid the gray.

"This is where it was yesterday," she said. "We'll get up on the rocks above and follow the ridgeline."

She winced when Tango moved off the trail and into the rocks. The footing here was much more treacherous.

319

He didn't break stride, though, just kept climbing. Below them, charred trees lined the slopes like fallen soldiers, and the wounded among them cried out in pops and snaps as smoldering flames found pockets to feed on. Each step raised ashes that were promptly swept back by the wind.

"What if Jace was here?" Jamie said. "When the fire passed through? Could he have been here?"

Maybe, Allison thought, *and if he was, then we'll ride over his bones and not much else,* but she said, "He couldn't have made it this far that fast. Not even if he just dropped the pack and ran. If he took this trail, he should be on his way down it now." She paused and then added, "You keep your hand close to your gun, all right?"

"You don't have to come with me," Jamie said. "You don't have to go any higher. I'll be fine with the horse."

"You don't have any idea where you're going."

"Tell me, then. Just tell me where to go. I'm not going to make you stay with me."

"I want to be there," Allison said, "when you see your son."

And, oh, how she did. How she wanted to bring about that reunion. As they went on up the mountain and through the smoke, Tango beginning to labor beneath them, Allison became certain that she was going to bring about *a* reunion, at least. Maybe it would be between Jamie and Jace, mother and child.

Maybe between herself and the brothers of blood and smoke.

Jace dropped to his hands and knees when he heard the gunshot. For an instant he waited on the impact, as if the bullet were taking its time reaching him, but there was none, and then he waited for the next shot.

"Connor," Hannah said. "Connor, it's all right."

"They're here! They're shooting!"

"It's the stumps," Hannah said. Her voice was gentle but confident. "Hon? It's just the stumps."

"What do you mean?"

"Listen," she said.

A few seconds passed and there was a muffled pop and a plume of smoke rose from one of the charred tree stumps that lined the slope below them.

"They trap the heat," she said. "The fire hides in them, long after most of the rest of the flames have moved on. Then it pops through. That's all you're hearing."

He didn't think she was right. What he'd heard sounded like a gunshot. But then another stump went off with a dull crack and he got slowly to his feet.

"You're sure?"

"It sounded like a gun to me too," she said. "But if somebody was shooting, why didn't he keep at it?"

He didn't have an answer for that. He turned and looked back the way they'd come, saw nothing but shadows and smoke in the pale dawn light. Republic Peak was silhouetted above them, but none of the shadows moved. If there was anyone else with them on the mountain, there was no sign.

"Let's hurry," he said. He had a bad feeling all of a sudden. He tried to remind himself that it had been only an unexpected noise, no different than the backfiring of an engine, and that he needed to keep his mind calm, but all the same, his heart was hammering. "Let's keep moving."

"We're going to. We're almost there." Hannah had

paused for a sip of water and her face was turned away from him as she looked down at the gulch where the fire was burning freely. Jace didn't like the way she was looking at the fire.

"How close are we?" he said.

"You can see it as well as I can."

"I mean how close to the firefighters?"

She took the loose end of her shirt and lifted it to her face and wiped the sweat away. Her stomach was visible for a moment, and he was surprised by how thin she was. Her pants were cinched by a belt, as if she hadn't always been that size.

"A half mile brings us to the outer edge," she said. "Then we skirt the burnout side and keep working down toward the creek. That's where they'll have camped. They'll be using the creek as a natural boundary and that's where they'll fight it. How far they go depends on what the wind does before we get there. I'd say we've got forty-five minutes to go. An hour, tops. We're almost out, buddy."

"Okay."

They began walking again, and Jace was aware of a strange smell. It reminded him of the summer some kids had dumped trash in the quarry and tried to burn it out but it had just smoldered, and eventually Jace's dad went down to deal with it. There'd been a stack of tires at the base that put out thick black smoke, and the flames hadn't wanted to quit. The smell trailed him now as he walked, and eventually he looked down and stopped again.

"Look at my shoes," he said.

Hannah turned. "What about them?"

"Get closer."

She knelt near his feet and this time she saw it—there were wisps of smoke rising from his shoes. The rubber soles were melting. She reached out with one palm and he said, "Careful!," afraid that it was going to sear her hand. She touched his feet one at a time with her palm and then stood and said, "They're melting, but not fast." She sounded far too casual about his feet being on fire.

"What do I do!"

"You can't feel it yet, can you?" she said.

"No. I just saw it. But…they're melting." Her boots, however, were fine. He wanted to trade for them, and the thought was so childish that it embarrassed him.

"I didn't do anything wrong," he said.

"Of course not. It's just what happens, but they aren't going to catch fire, they're—"

"No," he said. "That's not what I mean. I *didn't do anything wrong.*"

She stared at him. Not getting it. He tried to swallow and coughed and then tasted more smoke. He was thirsty and he was tired and his shoes were literally melting off his feet and this woman didn't understand.

"I was just…playing," he said. He wiped his eyes and coughed again, spit into the ashes. "I got home from school and went out to *play.* That's all it was. That's all I did. And now…" He looked away from the ashes and into her eyes and said, "They want to kill me."

Hannah reached out and took him by his shoulders. Her hands were stronger than he would have expected for someone so thin.

"Connor, we're almost out. No, damn it, don't look away. Look at me."

He looked back. Her eyes were wet and shining.

"Where do you want to be?" she said. "Go ahead and say it. Tell me."

"Home," he said, and he was about to cry and he didn't want that. He was supposed to be as strong as her. Then he remembered that she'd cried earlier, he'd seen her, even if she'd lied about it. "I want to see my dad," he said. "I want to see my mom. I want to be *home*."

He hadn't said it out loud before, not once.

"Okay," Hannah said. She gave him a squeeze, and it was the closest thing to a hug he'd had since his parents brought him to Montana, and he found himself hugging her back even though he didn't want to. He didn't want her to think he was weak.

"You've come so far," she said. Her voice was soft, her lips not far from his ear, her head resting on his. "You're almost there, I *promise* you, you are almost there. We're going to walk to that creek and we're going to get across it, and then...then you're going home."

"I'm sorry," he said. "I'm just so tired, and I don't know —"

"Connor? Stop apologizing."

"Jace," he said.

"What?"

"My name is Jace. I'm Jace Wilson. Connor Reynolds was my fake name."

"Jace." She said it slow, then smiled at him and shook her head. "Sorry, kid, but I think it's too late now. You're Connor to me. Let's get you back to where people know you as Jace."

He nodded. "Forty-five minutes?" he said.

"At most."

"Let's not stop again. I won't make us stop."

"Then we won't stop," she said. "It's been a long walk, but what's left is short. I promise. And don't worry about your shoes. It's good news."

"How is it good news?"

She turned back to the smoke and gestured at the fire below.

"Hotter it gets, the closer we are," she said.

38

Jack Blackwell found his brother halfway down the western side of Republic Peak. He was pinned against a boulder, and Ethan Serbin was no longer with him, but a clear track of loose dirt and scraped stone and streaks of blood indicated his path on down the mountain, rolling farther, rolling faster. Jack strained his eyes to find him but could not. The slope was very steep. It had been difficult to reach his brother, and it would be more difficult to pursue Serbin.

"Patrick. You hear me? Patrick."

Patrick Blackwell's eyes opened. Their gaze dull but alive.

"Bad," he said, and he tried to spit but succeeded only in bringing forth a bubble of blood. "Pretty bad, isn't it?"

Jack rocked back on his heels and studied him. Took his time. Patrick's face spoke for itself: broken jaw, shattered teeth, not much of a cheekbone remaining on the right side. The flesh was already distorted by swelling. There was clean white bone showing in his left hand too; at some point, trying to stop the fall, he'd bent his hand double, and the bones broke before his momentum did.

"*Pretty* is the wrong word," Jack said. "But maybe not so bad. Maybe not so bad."

Patrick coughed and more blood came, and that's what was truly bad. Jack braced himself on the slope and leaned close, set his pistol aside, and touched his brother gingerly. Rolled him just a fraction, and then closed his eyes when Patrick tried to scream and got nothing for his efforts but a strangled howl. Jack felt along his ribs and found the problem. There was plenty of trouble on the inside of his brother. The outside looked bad, but Patrick could endure it. Jack knew that he could. The edges of those sheared ribs, though, could have done a great deal of damage. He was not certain that even the likes of Patrick could endure what was wrong on the inside.

It wasn't until Jack moved his hand away and leaned back that he saw the lower leg. No bone visible here, but Patrick's left foot was bent to the side in a way that suggested he no longer had control over it, and the swelling was already pronounced and grotesque.

Jack sat down in the dust and looked into his brother's blue eyes and said, "Pretty bad."

Patrick nodded. "Foot's no good," he said. "And in the chest…" He stopped when a rivulet of blood dripped from his mouth and choked his speech. The jaw was giving him trouble but he was getting the words out, albeit with a lot of blood. He licked some of it away and neither of them spoke until he'd cleared his lungs best as he could. "In the chest is the real trouble. Am I right?"

"It would be hard going for us," Jack admitted.

"It wouldn't be going much at all."

"I can patch you up a bit. I can carry you. It'll hurt, and it'll be slow, but it'll still be going."

"Going where?" Patrick said, and this time he was able to spit some of the blood out. "Up that mountain? Down the others?"

Jack didn't answer.

"We are a long way from home," Patrick said.

"Yes."

"How many dead to get here, do you think? And for how much money?"

"I couldn't say."

"Say what you know, then. Tell me what I want to hear."

"What's that?"

"How many fights lost."

"None, Patty. None."

Patrick nodded. "Strange life," he said.

"Took what we could from it."

"Always. Came a time, didn't think anyone could take it back."

Jack looked away from his brother and scanned the rocks again, searching for Serbin.

"You see him?" Patrick asked, understanding.

"No. You fell down the wrong side of the mountain." Here on the western slope, the rising sun hadn't crested the peak, and around them was nothing but gloaming light and shadows. Another hour, maybe just thirty minutes, and all would be illuminated. For now, though, the darkness lingered.

"I'll go find him," Jack said. "Bring him back so you can see him yourself."

"No time for that." Patrick blew out another bloody breath and said, "You know how badly I want to see that boy dead now?"

"I've more of a mind to see Serbin dead, myself. And his wife."

"It started with the boy," Patrick said. "End it with the boy. Make him first, at least." He hung his head down and found a few more breaths after a lengthy search and then said, "Hell with that. Kill them all, Jack. Every one of them."

"I will."

"You know it's time for you to get moving."

"Past time."

Silence came then and held them, and still Jack Blackwell sat with his brother.

"The question is yours to answer," Jack said finally.

"Yes."

"So tell me, then."

"At your hand."

Jack looked away. His jaw worked but no words came.

"Not at theirs," Patrick said. "And not alone. The end would probably come for me before they did, but I'd be alone."

Jack still did not speak.

"Please," Patrick said. "Don't let me go alone. Not after all these years. This life."

Jack picked up his pistol and rose to his feet. He brushed the dust from his pants, turned to look at the forest fire they'd given birth to, its smoke beginning to show in the sunrise. He stood with the burned side of his face toward his brother and said, "I'll start with the boy, but I'll finish with them all. You know that. You believe it, yes?"

"I do."

"I've never enjoyed traveling alone, though. Not a bit."

"You never had to. But you'll be fine. You'll be just fine."

Jack nodded. "You as well."

"Of course."

"You're sure of this."

"I am."

"And so here the paths part. For a time."

"Love you, brother," Patrick Blackwell said.

"Love you too," Jack Blackwell said, and his voice was coarse. He coughed and spit into the shadowed stones and breathed a few times. The mountain was silent but for the wind. When he turned back, Patrick's eyes were closed, and they remained closed when Jack fired one bullet into the center of his forehead and then two more into his heart.

Jack removed the black Stetson he'd worn since arriving at Ethan Serbin's cabin and used it to cover his brother's face so that when the sun rose above the summit, it would not shine on the blood or his dead eyes. He spun open the cylinder of the revolver and removed the three casings, still warm, touched them to his lips one at a time, and put them in his breast pocket.

Then he reloaded with fresh bullets and began to pick his way through the rocks and toward the fire and the killings yet to come.

39

Ethan was one of the dying kind now, and he knew it. He had spent his life instructing others on how to avoid joining this group and yet here he lay, bleeding into the dark rocks.

Survivor mentality: blank.

Positive mental attitude: at least he'd killed one of them.

Or he hoped he had. Here in the broad shadow of the mountain, he could not see where Patrick Blackwell had landed. For a time he had tried to watch for motion but then darkness came and he folded beneath it and when he opened his eyes, he was not certain he was looking in the right direction even, let alone the right place.

Got him good, though, he thought. *Got him good.*

There was something to be proud of in that, wasn't there? All his mistakes aside, he'd swung when he needed to.

He wondered where the rifle had gone. That was the killing tool, that was what threatened the boy most, and if they got the boy, then all of this... He couldn't think about that. Not now. He'd just let the time pass and let the end come, knowing that he'd done the best he could and lost and that there was still honor in that.

He wished he would bleed out quicker. Every time he closed his eyes he didn't expect to open them again, but time and again he did, and then he was more aware of the pain and of his predicament and he wanted to be gone from all of that. He'd come far enough that he deserved the peace.

His eyes kept opening, though. He couldn't control those two bastards, one went with the other, and then he was awake and almost alert and watching the sun edge toward the summit of the mountain he'd fallen from, and finally it was bright enough for him to assess the damage.

A lot of blood. That much he saw early and found some hope in. A man couldn't bleed like that for too long before the end, so he was close; all that was required of him now was patience.

Other than the blood, it was not so bad. Bruises, yes. Breaks, probably. His left wrist had turned into a pincushion, and somewhere below it his hand remained, but he didn't have much interest in that, because he saw no need for the hand between now and the end. His right shoulder ached in a way that suggested something broken, but he didn't move enough to be sure because he saw no need for the shoulder either.

Damn that sun. Kept right on rising. It was hard on his eyes, even when he closed them. He'd blink back into consciousness and see the widening band of scarlet in the east and the peaks taking shape before it.

Good Lord, what a beautiful place it was.

He could smell the fir trees and pines and the rocks themselves and the cool crisp of the morning, could feel the breeze on his face, already warmer than the pocket of air he'd found himself in, promising another hot humid day, and he thought he could smell the glacier. Something colder than anything the modern age knew of, something that had weathered man for generations upon generations, but then man discovered fire and now the glacier surely could not weather many more, would melt until all that was left was rock and rumors of what covered it once. He was dying in a land carved by oceans he'd never seen and reborn by fires.

He shut his eyes again but the sun was higher and hotter and he gave up on a peaceful dark exit. That wasn't how it came for everyone, and he deserved no better than anyone else. Let the sun rise, then, let the smoke drift his way, let it clear those clean cool smells and tastes from him. He opened his eyes. He'd still die in his mountains, and that was fine.

Except for Allison, that was just fine.

He wished that he hadn't thought of her, squeezed his eyes shut and tried to will her away. He didn't need her with him now, not at the end, because he knew what he was leaving her to and it brought on a guilt and sorrow more powerful than he could bear. She'd survived. She'd made it through, and now here he was, ready to die and not displeased by the idea at all, at least not until she'd entered his mind.

He opened his eyes and for the first time looked at himself instead of the peaks and the rising sun. It was important to see, because this was how the searchers would find him. This was what they would tell her they'd seen; this was all she would have to take with her into the rest of her days.

He was upside down with his head against a downed

pine and his feet pointing up the slope and at the sky and he was bleeding from his left side and one of his wrists was broken and maybe a shoulder. That was what they would tell her. Because she would ask. Allison would certainly ask.

It bothered him. He blinked again and wet his lips and shifted against the tree and felt the pain from a hundred different places. It was enough to bring him to a stop. He took a few deep breaths and then said the hell with it. She'd know the full story in time, she'd know the way they found him, Luke Bowden or someone would tell her. Wait—Luke was dead. Good Lord, Luke was dead. Ethan had found the body; how had he forgotten that? Now others would find his, and then they would go tell the story. Hats off and heads bowed, they would explain the way he'd come to lie on the mountain, and Allison, woman that she was, strongest woman he'd ever known, she would ask questions. Even through tears, even through agony, she would ask some questions.

Was he dead when he hit the bottom?

No.

How long did it take him to die?

A good bit of time.

Did he suffer? Was he conscious?

Odds were, they'd tell her the truth. Ethan always had. And Allison, who had set herself on fire to survive these same men, would know exactly what sort of man Ethan had been.

The dying kind.

No; worse.

The quitting kind.

Survivors, Ethan had told this last group of boys while

his wife listened from the stable, *do not quit. Ever. They STOP. They sit, think, observe, and plan. That, boys, is a stop. Anything else is quitting, and quitting is dying. Are you the surviving kind, or the dying kind? We'll find out.*

Damn all.

Screw her, then. Screw her for staying alive through it all, for being better than he was, for being stronger, and for taking from him the only thing he wanted now, which was merely to die in peace and without shame.

But she deserved something. Pointless as it was, he wanted to give her something, so that when Luke Bowden and the others—no, not Luke, why couldn't he remember that, why couldn't he believe it?—came to her bedside, they could tell her that Ethan had died trying. Because unless he left some evidence behind, how would anyone know he'd done a damn thing other than fall off a mountain?

He had a QuikClot in the pocket of his hiking pants. Always carried one, because the thing he feared most out here with the boys was arterial bleeding. One fall, one slip of the knife, one surprised bear, all of those things led to the same place—blood loss—and so he walked prepared for it.

Give Allison that much, then. Give her the blood-clotting dressing, and then they could say, Well, Allison, he died trying. Didn't give up even when it was over.

It took him some time to find the right pocket, but he got it unzipped and fumbled out the plastic package that contained the bandage. He had two of them, he'd forgotten that, but he figured one was enough. Hell, just opening the package would say that he hadn't quit.

He used his right hand to bring the package to his mouth and then he tore it open with his teeth and fumbled out the bandage. It was a mesh packet filled with a coagulant; blood already had coagulants, but not enough to stop a traumatic bleed quickly. Ethan had used it a time or two, but never on himself. He rotated, wincing and hissing at the pain, got two buttons of his shirt undone, and then put the mesh packet down on the bullet wound at his side and pressed hard.

His eyes closed again, although this time it was involuntary. Still, he held the dressing tight, and after a while the world stabilized and he could look at the wound. A bad one, but that steady pulse of blood was already slowing.

Maybe one more, he thought, *not because it will make a difference, but because it will show her how hard I tried.*

He got the second package out and tore it open with his teeth and pressed it to the still-exposed part of the wound and then it occurred to him that he had a belt and he loosened that and freed it with an effort and then, moving slowly, because his left wrist and right shoulder would not cooperate, managed to get the belt wrapped around the bandages and cinched tight.

The pulse of blood had stopped.

For a moment, he was pleased as hell with himself. When they found him, they'd be able to tell her that he had not only survived the fall but been able to stop his own bleeding where he lay.

One problem remained, though: the idea of people finding him where he lay. His wife had moved when the end came for her, and kept moving, and moving had saved her. Ethan had no place to hide from death, but maybe he could try to move. Try to get upright.

At least stand up for her, he thought, and then he leaned against the tree and used the heels of his hands to push himself up.

And fell right back onto his ass.

Okay. Once more, and slower now, and use the legs, because the legs seemed more solid than the arms. The arms were not so good.

He made it up on the fourth try, and the sensation was remarkable. The simple act of getting to his feet was like something almost forgotten, an ancient skill.

He stood there and he breathed and then he looked at his side and saw that the QuikClot hadn't given up yet. The dressings were keeping the blood at bay. He looked at the pool of drying blood in the dust beside the fallen pine where he might have been found, and he was immensely pleased to have parted ways with it.

He took the first step, and then the second, and the motion was not a bad thing. It hurt, but the hurt was a sweet ache that reminded him his body still moved and that pain afflicted only the living.

He wasn't moving fast, but he was moving, and again he was aware of the land around him. Republic Peak loomed above and there was an eagle circling between him and the summit, and below it the mountains spread to forest and all around him the world lightened with pink hues. It was a beautiful day for a walk, he thought, even if it was your last walk. Maybe even better if it was the last walk. The smoke was in the air and that was a shame, but he knew that from the ravages, the land would be reborn and that these mountains had seen more fires than he had seen days on the earth and that they could bear them again.

He was happy just to be walking, then, happy that he had not quit, and he was so pleased with this that he almost missed the rifle.

It was above him, on the rocks, maybe thirty feet up, and

the climb seemed mighty and the reward unworthy, because who was there left to shoot?

All the same, it was there.

A man who was happy to die walking, he reasoned, ought to be happier still to die climbing. Getting upright had meant something, and those first steps another thing, but to climb? The story he wanted to leave out here was that of a climbing man. A fallen one, to be sure, that part was undeniable by now, but one who'd climbed as far as he could.

He paused long enough to fill his lungs and check the bandages. They were both a shade darker, but not dripping. Then he fixed his sights on the rifle and began, one unsteady step at a time, to climb toward it.

40

THE WIND SWUNG AROUND after sunrise, started blowing out of the northwest and regaining the
momentum it had sacrificed for the lightning storm.

The fire shifted with it, and Hannah knew then that it
was going to be far closer than she'd wanted to imagine.
In her mind, she'd always kept them half a mile from it, at
least, a wide swing over the top of the fire ground and down
to the creek, the two of them staying well away from the
dangerous heat of it and from the ghosts that waited for her
within the flames.

They weren't going to have half a mile. Maybe a quarter
of a mile. Maybe less, if that wind kept blowing.

Don't show it, she told herself. *Don't show him that you're
scared.*

They had taken too long getting down the mountain.
They were about half a mile from the creek and she
couldn't see the crew that should be there, and that was
more trouble, because it meant they'd camped farther north
than she'd realized, and this was even worse news, thanks

to the wind. It would push the fire up the gulch, which the team on the ground would regard as a fine thing, because that was exactly the direction they wanted the blaze to move, away from forest and fresh fuel and on toward the rock. Rock always did a better job of fighting fire than humans did. The mountains took care of themselves in the end; all you did was help.

This was turning into a beautiful morning for the fire crew, then, because the wind was helping them, and they'd stay north and appreciate their good fortune since there wasn't anything up the gulch worth fighting for. Maybe three acres of fir and a ridge of grass and then the rock.

And Hannah and Connor.

"It's high," Connor said.

She understood that he meant the fire itself. They were close enough to see the flames clearly now, see how they climbed the pines and still weren't satisfied, kept flapping higher, tasting the air to see if there was anything edible up above. She remembered being struck by the same thing in her first fire season, remembered swinging a Pulaski and trying to keep calm and pretend that flames so high above did not unnerve her.

The sound of it was powerful now too. As the wind provided reinforcement, the fire took on a sound like soft thunder, but steadier, the echo of distant trains.

"It's going to be a problem," she said.

"What is?"

"That fucking wind," she said, and then looked at him and said, "Sorry."

"Call it what you want," he said.

She nodded and wiped sweat from her face and saw

that her palm came away smeared with ash. Her eyes were stinging from the smoke and tearing constantly.

Hotter the fire, cooler the head; hotter the fire, cooler the head, she told herself, one of the mantras that Nick chanted at them as they worked, and it meant two things: Keep yourself hydrated and as cool as possible against the fire heat, and, more important, keep your thoughts clear. Keep your mind working, and keep calm.

"Here's what the fire wants to do," she told Connor. "Jump that creek and find the forest. Why? Because it's on a quest, just like us. We want to find help; it wants to stay fed. But here's what the wind is instructing it to do: push up the gulch. The problem for the fire is that it doesn't know what we know, and it won't realize that going up the gulch is a mistake. It will know that only when it finds the rock shelves."

He was staring at her. "Why are you talking like that? Like it has thoughts."

"Because it does." She ran her tongue over her teeth, trying to draw up some saliva, wishing for water. They were both out now. "It has needs, at least, and it knows how to meet them and what to do if something gets in its way. And right now...we are very close to doing just that, Connor."

"It's still pretty far off."

It seemed to be, anyway. Looked as if it were taking its time chewing through the timber, and they had elevation on it and some distance, and the creek loomed, shimmering in the sunrise.

"You said we just need to get across the creek. Right?"
"Right."
"The creek isn't that far. We can make it. We can run."

God bless him, he still thought he could run. How long had he been on his feet; how long had he been awake?

"Hannah?" he said. "We can make it if we run."

"There's one problem," she said. "It can run too, buddy. You haven't seen that yet, but trust me, it can run."

The temperature of the main fire was maybe twelve hundred degrees, maybe fifteen hundred, and it was finding plenty of fuel, and the wind was pushing oxygen in, so that temperature was rising. When it got hotter, it would get excited, and it would be ready to run.

Hotter the fire, cooler the head.

She had cost them both dearly by keeping them high, and it was fine to acknowledge that but imperative to know that continuing to climb would no longer be a mistake. The creek was tempting but she wasn't sure that they could make it, not even running, and if climbing again might save them, then they had to do it. The very idea of climbing made her feel defeated.

"We're going to backtrack a bit," she said. "I'm sorry. But it's the right thing. We need to go back up the drainage and get up on that ridgeline, you see it?"

He followed her pointing finger and nodded.

"We can walk along that. It's not too steep. And it gives us plenty of space if the fire makes a jailbreak and decides to run. It won't like the rock, and there will be plenty of rock between us and the last of the trees. Slower going, but safer. We'll just make our way along that ridgeline and then deal with the creek."

He didn't say anything, but his face told her that he didn't agree, and she knew the look well, had worn it herself on the day she convinced Nick that there was enough time to get down and save the family and make it back up.

"It may not get that high," she said, "but we've come too far to risk it. So it's just a little more time, and then..."

The rest of the explanation faded into silence and inconsequence when a horse with two riders appeared out of the smoke ahead of them.

The sun had risen above the fire in a war of red heat, but the light had shown them nothing and Allison was unwilling to push Tango any longer. It was too vertical here and they were too close to the fire, and if Jamie's son had made it down the back side of Republic Peak, they should have seen him by now. She had been prepared to announce all of this for the past fifteen minutes but hadn't managed to get the words out, because how did you tell a mother that it was time to give up the search for her son? So she rode just a bit longer, slowing Tango to a walk. He was uneasy with the fire, trying to pull them farther away from it, but farther away was steeper and more treacherous ground and so she made him hold the ridgeline. When he stopped entirely, her first instinct was to look at his leg again. Jamie's first instinct was to look forward, and so Allison had her head down when Jamie said, "Who is that?"

Allison looked up and saw them then, two figures, and because it was two and they were some distance away, her immediate reaction was a cold chill of fear—she had ridden right back into their arms.

But the heights were wrong. It was not the brothers—she would know them even in distant silhouettes, no question. The two figures were on the other side of a steep drainage lined with deadfall, and they weren't moving, just staring ahead.

"Who is that?" Jamie repeated. Her voice was measured,

as if she was fighting for calm, and so Allison tried to match it when she said, "Let's go find out."

She urged Tango forward—*Just a little more, please, buddy, just give us a little more*—and watched the silhouettes take clearer shapes. The fear was transforming into triumph, because it looked to be a woman and a boy.

"Is it him?" she said.

"I don't know. Get over there and see."

"I can't take the horse through that." The drainage fell off sharply, a drop of at least eight feet, and the deadfall offered a base filled with gaps and holes, leg-breakers in wait.

"Then let me down. Please stop and let me down."

Allison brought Tango to a stop and Jamie tried an awkward dismount and nearly fell off the horse's back. Allison caught her arm and said, "Easy," and then Jamie found the stirrup and swung down and nearly fell again trying to pull her gun from its holster before she even had her legs under her.

"Relax," Allison said. "It's not them. It's not the ones you need to be worried about."

"Then who is it?"

That was a fair question. One of them was a woman, Allison could see that from here, but who? Jamie kept the gun in her hand and started toward them on foot without waiting for Allison.

"Hang on," Allison called, but what was the point in slowing her? One of the two was Jamie's son, it had to be. She dismounted too, and she didn't think of tying Tango because Tango wouldn't run from her, never had. She put one grateful palm on his snout and it came away slick with sweat.

"Be right back, buddy," she said. "Then we're getting the

hell out of here." But already she was troubled by the logistics of that—she wasn't sure how much longer he could go with one rider, let alone two, and four would be simply impossible.

It wasn't the rescue Hannah had imagined. She'd marched them across the mountains and back down toward the fire with the expectation of reaching men and women with hoses and axes, pump trucks and ATVs, and maybe a helicopter.

Instead, she had two women on horseback.

"Do you know them?" she said. "Connor? Do you know who these people are?"

"I'm not sure." He hesitated and then took a few steps forward, closer to the drainage, and Hannah followed, feeling a powerful need to be between him and any strangers, even if they meant no harm.

"Hello!" Connor shouted. "Hello!"

The women had dismounted and were approaching, one bandaged up, the other well ahead, and Hannah realized there was a gun in that one's hand. She reached out and caught Connor by the arm, jerked him back.

"Stop. We don't know—"

"It's Allison!" he said.

"Who?"

"Ethan's wife! That's Ethan's wife!"

"Your instructor?"

"Yes, it's his wife." He waved an arm at them and shouted, "Allison! Allison! It's me."

"Who's with her?" Hannah asked.

"I have no idea," Connor said. "But at least she's got a gun."

* * *

Allison was struggling to catch up to Jamie Bennett—riding had been painful, but running was worse—when the boy began to shout at them. At first she couldn't make out the words, because the wind was carrying the sound of the fire up the gulch, but then she heard her own name.

It was him. It was Connor, Jamie's son. They'd actually found him.

"We've got him," she said to Jamie. "He's safe, he did just what he was supposed to do and took that escape route, even though it led into the fire." She didn't have any idea who he was with, but he didn't appear to feel threatened, he seemed healthy and unharmed, was calling out for her, and Allison was flushed with relief and triumph, saying, "We found your son," when the disconnect that should have been obvious finally hit her.

Allison! Allison!

He was calling to her. Why wasn't he calling to his mother?

"Doesn't he see you?" she said, but she already knew the answer to the question, and her mind was slowly catching up to what this meant when Jamie Bennett turned back to face her.

"He doesn't know who you are," Allison said. "Why didn't you tell me that? He doesn't know that you're his mother."

"I'd appreciate it if you'd go on ahead now. You'll need to be in front of me." The gun was in Jamie's hand, and it was pointed at Allison, who looked at it as if she weren't clear on its purpose.

"What are you doing?"

"Get in front of me. Please."

346

Allison looked from her to Jace and said, "That's not your son."

"I'm afraid not. Now, walk over there to him. He's come a long way, and he deserves to see you, don't you think? We'll all figure it out from there."

Allison stared at her, not moving. The boy and the woman were moving, though; they were approaching fast, were within pistol range. *I can shoot it well,* Jamie Bennett had said.

"What's happening?" Allison said. "What in the hell is really happening here?"

Jamie gave her a pained expression and a small shrug and said, "Not everything I told you was a lie. I truly came to get some people out of the mountains, Mrs. Serbin. Just not my son. I've come for my brothers."

4 1

For the first time since Ethan had woken him in the night, Jace was actually convinced that he was going to get out of the woods. Not just that it was possible. It was *happening*. Ethan had sent Allison for him, somehow, and she'd come with someone who'd protect him.

"We can take the horse," he was saying as he fought his way through a downed pine, feeling his ankle twist in the branches. It was a dry, dead tree, and when the fire made it up here, it was going to burn fast. But that didn't matter anymore, none of it did, because they'd be gone by the time the fire got here. The journey was done.

Behind him, Hannah said, "Connor, slow down."

He kept going, though; he didn't need to slow down, not anymore, because it was *over,* they were getting out of this place. Hannah hadn't lied—he was going to see his parents again. It was actually going to happen.

"Connor. Jace! *Jace!*"

When she finally used his real name, the first time she had, he turned to look at her. She was standing in the base of the drainage herself now and her expression didn't look right. The joy that should have been there wasn't. It was darkness. As if she saw something she didn't like.

"Come back down here," she said.

"What?" He was halfway up the slope, on his hands and knees, holding on to a tree root. All he had to do was pull himself up and he would be on the other side, standing with his rescuers.

"Come back down here," Hannah repeated, and right then Allison Serbin spoke as well. Didn't just speak, actually, but shouted.

"Jace, run. Get away from her!"

Get away from Hannah? Why didn't Allison trust Hannah? If Hannah had meant to harm him, she'd have done it by now. There was something Allison didn't understand, and Hannah didn't either, and Jace knew he could set them all straight—everyone was just confused. He pulled up on the tree root and got over the lip of the ditch and then stood up on the other side. The woman he didn't know was only a few feet away, and she was looking at him calmly. She was the only one besides him who wasn't showing any fear.

She was also pointing the gun at him. She knew how to hold it too, a two-handed shooter's grip. But why was it pointed *at* him?

"Who are you?" Jace asked.

She ignored him, taking two slow steps back, into a position where she could see Hannah and Allison clearly.

"Allison," she said, "do not tell him to run. That's not good advice. What Jace needs to do is sit down."

Jace looked back at Hannah. She was still standing at the bottom of the drainage, and she looked defeated. She didn't take her eyes away from the woman with the gun as she said, "Jace, sit down. Please. Do what she says."

He sat. The woman said, "Thank you. And if you ladies could join him, we'll all be able to relax a little bit." There was a pause, and then she said, "Understand that we don't have to relax. You get to pick how it goes."

Allison sat down. She was about ten feet away from Jace, and he could see now how badly hurt she was, with bandages all over and dark stitches around her lips. Behind her, the horse paced and watched them all. He seemed as confused as Jace felt, and he was facing the fire. Jace could see that he was afraid of it.

"Two out of three," the strange woman said. "Let's get everybody up here."

She was talking to Hannah, who slowly climbed out of the drainage the way Jace had. When she sat, she sat very close to him. The woman said, "Don't get in between us. That's very brave, but I think you understand that I need to see everyone clearly."

Hannah moved away, but not far. She said, "You're going to die too if you keep us here. You realize this is not someplace we can just sit and wait?"

The woman ignored her. She was looking right at Jace. "Where are they?" she asked.

"Who?"

"The men who came to kill you. Have you seen them?"

She was partners with them, he realized. Not here to help him at all; here to help *them*. He looked at Hannah, then at Allison Serbin, searching for an explanation, for something, but the woman snapped at him again. "Jace, you need to tell the truth about this, and do it now. Where are they?"

"Behind us," he said. "We lost them."

"I doubt that. Are they with Ethan?"

"I don't know."

Jamie's eyes shifted to Hannah, and she said, "What happened, lady? Who in the hell are you?"

Hannah didn't answer. She had turned away from the woman as if the gun didn't bother her at all. She was staring down at the fire when she said, "You don't have time to find them. Don't you realize that?"

Allison Serbin said, "They're your *brothers*? You sent the boy up here to be killed?"

"It wasn't anyone's first choice, Mrs. Serbin. The boy's parents are very distrustful. Even when they agreed with my plan, they wouldn't turn him over to me. Insisted on sending him to Montana themselves, and I'll give them credit, they did a fine job getting him out under cover. Could he have been taken at the airport in Billings? Certainly. But at such great risk. In the mountains, though? So much easier. Had your husband not decided to be such an overachiever, it would have ended for the boy with a bullet from a rifle no one ever saw. That was the idea. It might have been hard on you both, sure, but nobody else would have been harmed. What we have here, though, is a situation that got a little out of hand. Too many people tried too hard to help our friend Jace."

Her brothers. Jace stared at her and realized he could see it. Tall and lean and blond and with the same calm. But she wasn't shooting yet. They wouldn't have waited, he was pretty sure. That was the difference.

"You sent him out here so they could find him?" Allison was asking, and Jace hadn't heard that much anger in anyone's voice in a long time—he thought she might disregard the gun entirely and try to kill this woman with her hands. "You asked Ethan to keep him safe but all you wanted was to know where he was? You evil bitch. You actually sent him to—"

"To be fair, Mrs. Serbin, a good deal of this was your husband's fault. He tried too hard. It wasn't supposed to take so much work. I feel bad for the rest of you, because all of this didn't need to happen. Jace here was the only one who…who was required." She shifted and blinked a few times—she was the only one facing the smoke, and it was blowing hard now, and the fire was louder than before—and said, "Jace, would you like me to let these women go?"

He nodded. The tears were threatening. He didn't want to cry in front of this woman, though, in front of this evil bitch. Allison had called her exactly what she was. He didn't want to give her the satisfaction of crying his way to the end. It was what she expected from him.

"Please," he said. His voice was a whisper. "Yes, please, let them go."

Hannah reached for him then, trying to take him in her arms, and the woman fired her gun and Jace ducked back and lifted an arm as if he might protect himself from the bullet. She'd shot high, though, and it was gone, into the smoke.

"Next one won't be a warning," she said. "Now, Jace, these women can go. If you tell me the truth, and you work with me, they can go. That's your choice."

"Yes," he repeated.

"All right. How far away are they? Where was the last place you saw them? Or have you not seen them?"

"They're behind us," he said. "That's all I know." He

waved a hand up the mountain, and that was when he saw the man in black coming down toward them. Jace's face must have shown something, because the woman turned and saw him too and apparently recognized him, even at a distance. She seemed pleased.

"Well, would you look at that. We don't need to go anywhere, Jace. We can all just sit here and wait."

"You said they could go." His voice rose to a shout. *"You said they could go!"*

"I'm going to leave that decision up to other people. For now, we're all going to wait."

Hannah's voice was soft when she said, "Then we're all going to die. Not just the ones you want. You will too."

The woman turned and looked back down the slope to where the trees were burning and said, "I think we've got plenty of time."

Jace didn't even look at the fire. He was still staring at the man. It was a single man coming down off the mountain, on their trail. It was one of them, there was no doubt.

"I told you," he said to Hannah. "They don't quit."

Allison had been considering a rush at Jamie Bennett, so infuriated by the betrayal that she was hardly afraid of the gun, thought she could take the bullets and still kill this bitch, but now there was another one, and she knew how it would go from here.

"I hadn't expected to see you so soon," the man in black called to them as he approached, and Allison wasn't sure whom he was addressing until Jamie responded.

"I hadn't expected to be needed. It looks like things got away from you."

"It has not gone as planned."

He was close enough now to be heard without shouting. His eyes took them in one at a time and lingered on Allison.

"Mrs. Serbin, I have traveled with you in my mind for a full day and night now. You see what you've done to me?" He waved his free hand toward his face, which was a blistered mess. "And, no, you don't look well yourself, but at least you have received proper medical treatment. I've suffered. It has not put me in a good frame of mind."

He turned then to the boy and spoke with a softness in his voice that sounded almost sweet, the awe of a new father addressing his child.

"Jace, Jace, you beautiful lad. My, how you've troubled me. You've run far enough, don't you think? If it makes you feel any better, you've taken a toll on me, son. You have truly taken a toll."

Jamie Bennett said, "Where is Patrick?"

Allison had been wondering the same thing. One of them was horror enough, but there should have been two.

Jack Blackwell did not speak for a moment. He was facing away from Jamie, his eyes on Jace Wilson, when he said, "Our brother is dead."

Jamie didn't seem to believe him. Didn't answer, just gave a little shake of her head.

"Mrs. Serbin's husband," Jack said, "was not the aid I had hoped he would be." He looked back at Allison and said, "He is dead too, but you understand that is not a fair trade to me."

Ethan was dead. He had been in his mountains, and it hadn't seemed possible that he would die in them.

Jack Blackwell looked away from them now, stared down into the fire that feasted below. For a time he just stood there, as if he were alone in the world and no troubles weighed on his mind.

"Look at it go," he said, almost to himself. "That was Patty's, you know. That was his idea. And it may yet be effective, though he won't know it. There are bodies to hide and stories to silence and it might be his fire that will do the trick."

He swiveled his head abruptly, faced the woman who'd guided Jace Wilson this far, and said, "Who are you?"

She didn't answer.

"I know your *role,*" he said. "You're supposed to keep watch. You're supposed to keep something like that"—he indicated the fire—"from being allowed to spread. But I'd like to know your name. Would you share that much, please, before we proceed?"

She hesitated for a moment, and then said, "Hannah Faber."

Jack Blackwell nodded and mouthed the name once without speaking it aloud. A slow, thoughtful gesture, as if he were striving to commit her to eternal memory.

Then he lifted his pistol and shot her.

Allison had never before heard a sound like the one that came from Jace Wilson then. Something between a scream and a howl, and he scrambled toward the woman as she fell, and bright blood cascaded between her fingers while she held the wound, which was centered in her right knee. Jack Blackwell lowered the pistol and said, "Have a minute with her, Jace. Go on and take a minute. We're pressed for time, but I'll not rush this. Not after so long a journey."

"Hurry," Jamie Bennett said. "Hurry or we'll never get out of here."

"You'd like to finish it?"

"I can."

"No." He shook his head, watching Hannah Faber, whose feet were still moving on the rocks as if she intended to find a way to stand. "No, the work that remains is mine alone. And, Patty, he'll get them in the end. He lit the match, you know. I'll let them wait on his work now."

He tilted his head to study Hannah's face. He watched with great interest, and then he said, "Jace, please step aside."

Jace Wilson didn't move, and Jack Blackwell sighed and then lifted the pistol and fired again, and this time it was Allison who screamed.

He'd fired around the boy, just inches to the side of him, and put another bullet into Hannah Faber, this time in her left foot. Blood ran out of her boot and her head dropped back and her mouth opened but no scream came. She just writhed in silence.

"I believe she's good to wait on our brother's work now," Jack said. "I think that's a fine way to bring it all to a close."

"Hurry," Jamie Bennett said again. She was looking down at the oncoming fire and her face was wet with sweat. Jack Blackwell ignored her and turned to Allison and lifted the pistol, then lowered it and shook his head.

"For you and me, things should be a bit more intimate, don't you think?" he said, and then he flipped the gun in a smooth twirl so that he was holding it by the barrel, like a club, and advanced on her.

"I'm glad he killed your brother," Allison said. Her voice was shaking.

"Are you, though?" he said. "Is that pleasing to you?" The soft, musical tone was gone. "I'm going to—"

The rest of his words and most of his face left him then.

His head burst in a red cloud and he dropped sideways and didn't even roll when he hit the rocks.

For a few seconds, Ethan had no idea what had gone wrong. His skull was ringing and blood was pouring out of his face, soaking his cheeks and coating his lips in coppery warmth and dripping into the rocks where the rifle lay.

Was I pointing the son of a bitch backward? he thought, and then he lifted his right hand to his forehead and brought back a palmful of blood and thought, *You are one dumb bastard.*

He'd had his eye pressed to the scope. Right up against the metal ring of it, of a scope with high eye relief that allowed the shooter to keep his face away, because guess what, boy, there was some serious kick when you shot a bullet the size of your index finger a thousand yards.

But he'd shot it. And where had it gone?

The QuikClot bandages were dark with blood, and he knew how bad that was, but right then, right there, sitting on top of the world, Montana and Wyoming spreading out for miles in all directions around him, he couldn't bring himself to care. He just needed to know what his shot had done.

He sat against the rocks where it had all started, where the fall had begun, and he got his breath back as sweat ran salty into his open, gasping mouth, and then he turned and looked down to the place from which he'd come, and he started to laugh.

It was not so far. From up here, it did not look so far. A man with a strong arm would probably believe he could hit it with a baseball, and maybe he wouldn't be wrong.

But that man wouldn't have climbed from there to here,

bleeding and broken. You didn't know the distance until you'd done that.

He rolled onto his stomach and found the rifle where it had fallen, and he brought it up again. Put his eye to the scope—same dumb mistake, but he wasn't shooting this time—and realized he couldn't focus. He had to pull back and wipe at the blood in his eye; he was awash in it. When he looked again, all he saw was smoke and fire. The forest was burning hot now, the wind carrying the fire up toward him, but it would never reach him, not across all of that stone. Then he moved the scope a touch and he was looking at his wife again.

The first time he'd seen her through the scope, he hadn't believed it. He'd heard enough stories of the things men thought they saw when death was near, and this one fit, a mirage of his wife, but then the rest of them had taken shape, his wife and Connor Reynolds and Jamie Bennett and another woman, one he didn't know. The fire lookout, he supposed. All alive. All with Jack Blackwell.

He hadn't had time to wonder over it, the way they'd all met there, the paths they'd taken. Not when Jack Blackwell started shooting. Ethan had wanted to fire fast then but knew that he couldn't, because, just as Jack had warned his now-dead brother, a miss at this distance would be costly. This was no AR-15; he wasn't going to be able to fire a burst of shots and adjust along the way. Shoot once, and shoot true. He'd forced himself to aim and think, trying to remember the basics of shooting at a target that was so far downhill. He'd been taught these things once and all that stood out was something that seemed counterintuitive but was the reality: Whether you were shooting uphill or downhill, the bullets would always pull high. Slightly higher on a downhill shot, for the simple reason that gravity was less of an enemy to the bullet's path when it was already headed down.

He'd aimed at Jack Blackwell's waist first and then decided that wasn't low enough. It was a damned steep slope and the bullet would be climbing above his aiming point, and it would be better to hit him in the hip than not at all. He lowered his aiming point to the knees, moved his finger to the trigger, and let out a long, slow breath. Tried to let everything within him go loose and liquid. A tense shot was a missed shot. His father had taught him that. Tense muscles jerked on the trigger. Jerked triggers produced wild bullets.

Then Jack advanced toward Allison, and Ethan kept those black knees in the center of the crosshairs and let his index finger graze the trigger and pull it home and the world exploded on him.

Now, scope to his eye again, he had the world back, if in a bloody haze, and he could see his wife and the boy and...he could see Jack Blackwell.

Jack Blackwell was down.

Ethan started to laugh, and then he realized it sounded more like sobbing, and he tried to stop but couldn't.

Got him, got him, got him. Got them.

But beyond the survivors was a rising scarlet cloud. The fire was pushing hard and fast. They needed to move.

For a few seconds, no one made a sound. Then Jamie Bennett let out a low moan and fell to her knees and stretched her hands out to her brother as if she could put the pieces back together. She dropped her gun when she reached for him and Allison had the slow, stupid thought *Someone should get that,* but she didn't move. Jace was still sitting on the ground, and though he'd registered that Jack Blackwell was dead, he seemed catatonic. His focus on the woman Jack had shot was total. He was whispering to her, and Allison couldn't hear the words. The woman had her eyes closed and was breathing through her teeth.

"Who shot him?" Jamie Bennett said. "Who took that shot?"

There was no one in sight. The mountain was empty.

Jack Blackwell was gone, but the fire was not, and the sound of it was louder now, a roar beneath the black smoke that boiled out of the tree-lined ridge below them. The heat was intensifying every minute. Jamie Bennett got to her feet and looked at Allison and then the other woman.

"It wasn't supposed to go this way," she said. "This one was supposed to be easy."

Nobody answered. She began to walk away with a weaving, unsteady stride. She almost went down once, caught a tree, held herself up. Nobody moved or spoke or attempted to stop her. The kill shot from nowhere had stunned them all. Jamie steadied herself and continued walking toward Tango. The horse turned to meet her.

Allison finally moved, crawled over the ground for the two guns that lay there in the blood, got her hand around the pistol, and then looked back at Jamie when Tango let out a whinny. Jamie was trying to mount him. It took her three tries but she got into the saddle, and then she began to kick him. Trying to drive him downhill.

He was already uneasy from the fire; the only reason he was still there at all was Allison, and he did not want to carry another rider. Now he was trying to rid himself of Jamie Bennett; it was as if he understood what Allison had not been able to. Jamie stayed on the horse maybe fifty yards before he succeeded in throwing her. She landed in the rocks and her leg snapped beneath her and when she tried to rise, she let out a cry. The horse hesitated, as if he felt guilty despite himself—Tango was nothing if not a good horse—but then he began to gallop, into the trees and out of sight.

Jamie Bennett tried again to rise, and this time her scream was louder and she went down faster and then she was silent and they couldn't see her anymore and it was just the three of them left there as Jack Blackwell's blood poured down the slope and dripped toward the fire.

Allison looked at what remained of his skull and then up into the mountains and said, "Ethan is alive."

42

THERE WERE GHOSTS on the mountain now. Hannah could see her old crew, all of them, but it was better this time, better than it had been. There were no screams and no one was running, and even Brandon was on his feet again—he hadn't given up, was standing tall and strong.

And watching her.

They all were.

Nick came down close and looked at her patiently and said, "Hannah? Deploy or die."

He'd screamed it the last time she'd heard the command, but this morning he was calm. They all were. It reassured her. They were the best, after all. Hotshots. If they were not panicking, then she shouldn't. They were the best.

Nick said it again, his blue eyes earnest, imploring: "Hannah? Hannah?"

He left her then, and the spoken name remained, but the voice was different and the face was different. The boy. Hannah looked at him and thought, *Thank you, God, he made it across the creek. I didn't think that he would. I didn't think he had a chance.*

"Hannah?"

Wrong boy. Wrong mountain, wrong day. Hannah blinked and looked into a tear-streaked face and said, "Yeah." It came out as a croak and she wet her lips and tried again and this time it was easier. "Yes, Connor. I'm fine."

"Tell me what to do," he said. "I've got the first-aid kit, but it's so bad, and I don't know what to use, I don't know what to do, you've got to tell me what to—"

"Stop," Hannah said.

He stopped talking, waited on her. Hannah blinked and breathed and now she saw the woman behind him, and for an instant she was afraid, because the woman held a gun. Her eyes held no harm, though. The woman's face was wrapped in bandages and she looked down at Hannah and said, "We'll get it fixed. It's not going to kill you."

"Of course not," Hannah said. She didn't look where the other two were looking, though, at the places where it felt as if her legs were on fire. That was a trauma basic—let somebody else look. You didn't need to see it yourself.

So everything was good, then. Everything was fine.

No.

Nick's voice, maybe. Brandon's? She couldn't tell. It was so faint.

Look.

Who was talking? And whoever was talking was wrong, she wasn't supposed to look, it wasn't going to help a damn thing. She wished she could hear him better, the voice was too soft and the sound of the fire was a roar now, advancing through the timber, and—

Oh. That was it. Yes, that was it.

"I need to look at the fire," she said. "Help me."

"No," the woman said. "Lie still. Let me see what I can—"

"Let me see the fire."

They helped her while she turned. The pain turned with her—it wasn't about to let her sneak away. She got her first glimpse of her wounds without intending to, managed to keep her eyes away from her knee, where the pain was worst and the bleeding heaviest, but she saw her left foot, the beautiful White's fire boot now with a jagged hole in the black leather, blood bubbling through it. A surge of nausea rose but she looked away and fixed her eyes on the flames, and while the pain didn't step aside, the sickness did.

The fire was near the edge of the timberline now, and then it was open grass, and then it was them. The route Hannah had wanted to take originally, backtracking into the high rocks, was no longer an option. They'd been delayed long enough to allow the fire to find the drainages, and it was moving through them fast.

If you died in a fire, you died at two speeds, Nick had told Hannah more than once. One was measured with a clock, and the other with a stopwatch. Your death began in the poor decisions you'd made that led you to the place you did not belong, and your death ended in the poor decisions you made trying to escape it. They were on the stopwatch now, and she knew it was running fast.

Time, time is our friend, because for us, there is no end…

"Hannah?"

She was aware then that Connor had been saying her name over and over, and she blinked hard and refocused and said, "I'm fine. I'm just thinking."

"We go back, right?" Connor said. "Isn't that what you said we should do? I can carry you. We can carry—"

"We're not going to get high enough, fast enough."

"We'll run," he said.

"It will run faster."

The speed of fire increased going uphill, one of the great evil tricks of a forest fire. They were on a slope of about thirty-five, maybe forty degrees. At thirty degrees, the speed of the fire would double. It would also have more of the wind by then, because right now the trees it was burning through were shielding some of the wind. By the time it reached the dry grass, empty of trees and on the upslope, it would turn from a marathon runner into a sprinter, and they'd be trying to cross directly in front of it.

No chance.

Somewhere behind her, just out of sight but so close she could feel his breath on her ear, Nick said, "Hannah? Deploy or die."

"I had a fire shelter," Hannah said. She was losing focus, though, losing the place and time, was telling them about another day and another fire, and so she was annoyed when Connor began to open his pack, paying no attention to her. It took her a moment to realize that he was getting out the fire shelter. The one he'd brought down from the tower. The one she'd said she would never get inside.

"That works?" the woman named Allison said. She sounded beyond skeptical. Hannah got that. Everyone who'd ever looked at a fire shelter did.

"It works."

But not always. It was wrong to tell them lies; you should never lie at the end. Whether the fire shelter worked or not was a matter of heat and speed. If the fire passed over them quickly, the fire shelter might save them. If it lingered, though…then it was the worst kind of end. You'd be better off sitting and waiting like Brandon had.

Hannah pushed herself up on the heels of her hands and then closed her eyes when the pain came on. When she opened them again, her mind was clearer but the pain was sharper.

"Connor?" she said. "Listen to me now. Do what I say. You need to get that shelter up. Can you do that for me?"

He nodded. His hands were shaking, but he nodded.

She told him how to do it, and it took him only two tries, even with the shaking hands. He was good like that, but the fire shelters were also designed to be deployed by shaking hands. It was the only way they were ever put up.

Even as he deployed the shelter, she was doing the math and coming up short. You were supposed to have one shelter per person, and she had three people and one shelter. She'd heard of only one time, ever, when three people had survived in the same shelter. It was the Thirtymile fire. But back in South Canyon, where thirteen lives had been lost, attempts to share shelters had failed tragically.

In Hannah's mind, that still left an odd man out here in the slopes above Silver Gate.

"That's going to work?" Allison Serbin said. "You're serious?"

The flimsy, tube-shaped tent hardly looked inspiring. Particularly not against the awesome backdrop of scarlet terror behind them.

"It works. You're going to get inside of that," she said. "And you're going to stay there."

She was looking at both of them, and Allison Serbin

seemed to understand the problem, because she said, "Jace, listen to her and get in it," without suggesting anyone join him.

"You go with him," Hannah said.

"What?"

"It'll be tight. But it's worked before."

"What about you?"

"I'll be fine."

"You'll *be fine?*"

Hannah looked away from her. "Please get in," she said. "You don't understand how far we've come. I can't lose him here." Her voice broke on that and she gave up trying for any more words.

Allison stared at her for a moment, and then she said, "Okay. I'm getting in."

Hannah nodded. There were tears on her face but she didn't care. "Thank you," she said. "Connor...I mean Jace...please get in."

"What about you?"

What about her. She said, "You remember the promise I made to you? I said you were getting home. I promised you that. But what did you promise me?"

"That I wouldn't make you get in this."

"Be true to your word," she said.

"It's not fair," he said.

"Didn't say it was. But we made an agreement. Be true to your word."

"No. We'll carry you. I can carry you."

Hannah looked away from him and over to Allison and said, "Help. Please."

Allison took his arm and finally the boy listened; he dropped to all fours and crawled inside the shimmering silver fabric that rippled against the wind and the heat. Allison knelt to follow.

"You pull it shut, and you wait," Hannah told them. "Now, guys, it's going to be bad." She was crying freely. "It's going to be worse than you think, but it will work. You just promise me that you won't get out too early."

She was so dizzy that the words were very hard to organize now. She wasn't sure how many of them she was actually saying.

The fire threw a sparkling spiral onto the edge of the grass no more than a hundred feet from them, some limb or pinecone that exploded out of a tree like an advance scout, and the grass to the east of her, toward the creek, began to burn and then smoldered out. This was how it would begin, with the spot fires, and this was how they did their most devious work, jumping trench lines and gulches and even creeks. She looked at the spot fire as it sputtered out; that one was not quite hot enough, not quite strong enough, but it wouldn't be long now before one was.

"You did it again," she whispered. The boy was going to die—after all of this, he was going to die burning. A second chance had walked out of the wilderness and into her arms and she was going to kill this one too. The fire shelter would buy them a bit of time, but not enough. There was too much fuel around it. For them to have a chance in there, the fire would need to pass by fast, a desperate hunter in search of fuel. But she'd set their shelter up in grass that was knee-high and deadly dry. They'd melt inside of the shelter, and they'd go slow.

Words from the dead found her then, more memory than ghost, although it was hard to separate them now. The last thing Nick had said that wasn't a scream. The final thing he'd wanted—shouted—was for her to deploy her fire shelter. The second-to-last thing, though, the last thing he'd said calmly, was that he wished there were grass around them.

At the bottom of Shepherd Mountain, there had been none. It was all deadfall and jack pines and some fescue clumps, but no open stretches of grass, and he'd wished for some, and Hannah was the only person on the crew who'd understood why in the hell he had desired to be standing amid faster-burning fuel.

You need it to pass by in a hurry.

Up here, it wouldn't. Up here it would burn slowly and they would die inside that shelter.

They were still not running. What in the hell was the matter with them? Ethan had saved them, damn it, he'd come so far and fought so hard, and he'd won, he'd dropped the son of a bitch, and they wouldn't even give him the simple gift of running? The fire below was a constant roll of thunder now, he could feel its strength in the stone beneath him, and he thought with great sorrow that it had to be far worse down there, too powerful to imagine, and so killing Jack wasn't enough to help them, because he couldn't kill the fire. They had given up, and he could do no more for them now but watch.

He didn't want to watch. Couldn't. And so he brought them centered in the scope and he prepared to say good-bye because he refused to see it end like this, but instead of looking away then, he stared, entranced.

They had some sort of a strange silver tent out. It looked like the material on the emergency blankets he handed out to each group, and he realized then what it was: a fire shelter, the sort they dispatched to the crews on the fire line. Where they'd come up with it, he couldn't imagine—it didn't seem like it'd be standard issue in a fire tower—but there it was.

While he watched, Hannah and Connor argued, and then he crawled inside, and then his wife followed, joining the boy in the tent, and the other woman sat in her own blood beside a dead man and waited to join him.

You need to take the shot, Ethan thought. *It will be better for her. Faster.*

But he couldn't do that.

The blood clouded the scope again and washed the woman away from him and that was the last he saw.

43

I T WAS THE WRONG WAY to die. Jace knew that before he got into the shelter, and once he was inside and he couldn't see Hannah anymore, he was sure of it. It would have been better for all of them to sit there and wait, and then she would not be alone, none of them would be. Right now, it was just like the quarry, hiding and waiting, and if he was going to die like that, then he should have let it happen long ago.

"I'm getting out," he said.

"No, you're not." Allison Serbin had her arms tight around him, and he began to fight her, kicking and wriggling. She fought with him until they heard Hannah's voice.

"Connor! *Connor!* Get out here. *Fast.*"

"Listen to her!" he said. "Let me listen to her!"

Allison Serbin either gave up and released him or he finally fought free of her; he wasn't sure and it didn't matter. He was out of the awful shelter again, back into the world, and while it was a terrible world, filled with the smells of smoke and heat and blood, it was better than the tent. He'd come out facing what remained of Jack Blackwell's head; there was not much of it to speak of, and he felt a strange, savage happiness, although once such a thing would have made him ill.

At least he didn't get me. Neither of them did.

But it was his brother's fire. He'd said so himself.

Hannah said, "You told me you could build a fire. You told me you were good at it."

He had no idea what she was talking about. He just turned to her and nodded.

"Were you telling the truth?" Her voice was urgent, her eyes clear for the first time since the bullets had found her legs. *"Do not lie to me now.* Can you build a fire and do it fast?"

"Yes."

"You're going to need to do it."

"What?"

"You have one chance," she said. "You can save yourself and save her. But, buddy, you've got to be able to do it, and do it fast."

He nodded again. He felt light-headed, glad he was on his hands and knees, anchored to the ground.

"Listen to me," she said. "You're the one who doesn't make mistakes, right? You can't make one now. You've got to listen and do exactly what I say. If you do that, you're going home. I promise."

"I'm listening."

"Okay. You see the grass down there? That little plateau?"

He followed her pointing finger. She was indicating the last thing between them and fire in the trees. A circle of grass that died out at the rocks where they sat now. It was maybe a hundred yards away from them, and just fifty in front of the fire.

"Yes."

"You're going to make a fire there," she said. "And you're going to let it spread."

He looked back at her. Was she in shock? Was this what happened when you went into shock?

"It will work," she said. "Here's why: You're stealing what the fire needs. Do you understand that? It's going to need —"

"Fuel and oxygen," he said, thinking of the brace piece, the way you'd give it that lift to provide fresh air, keep the flame from drowning. The way the fire was smothered by larger pieces of wood. But this was no campfire. This was a monster.

"Yes. You're robbing it of the fuel."

"It won't work. Not on that. It's too big! It will never burn out."

"No," she said. She wiped her face with her hand and left a streak of blood across her forehead. "It won't burn out. The fire will move faster. That's what we need. It has to go over that shelter *fast,* do you see?"

He wasn't sure, but before he could answer, she said, "Go down there and start a fire, Connor. Can you do that?"

"I can do that," he said. He didn't think his legs would hold him when he stood, but they did. The fire steel was in his pocket. He removed it and held it in a sweating, shaking hand and said, "I'll go make a fire."

Allison tried to go with him. Tried to *stop* him, actually, but when Hannah Faber yelled at her, she paused, turned back, looked in her eyes, and saw the truth in them.

"It's your only chance," Hannah said. Very soft. "If he can do it, you bring the shelter down and set it up in the ashes."

"Won't it melt?"

"Not down there. Not at that heat. Just set it up the way you have it, and make sure it's as close to the center as you can. Once the fire gets there, it's going to race. It will have no choice."

Allison looked away from her and back down to where the boy walked alone. He seemed smaller than ever before, his silhouette framed against the orange sky.

"You believe this," she said.

"It's the only chance. And, listen—when you get back in there with him, you hold him tight, understand? You'd better hold him tight."

Allison looked at Hannah's blood-soaked right leg and the devastated left foot, then back into her intense eyes, and nodded. "I won't let it be for nothing."

Jace picked up a brace piece as he walked, a perfect length of deadfall, and he was thinking that he didn't have time to get kindling, there was no way he had enough time, but then he remembered that it didn't matter. All he needed to do was make the grass catch. He wasn't trying to build a campfire. Just burn the grass.

Every step was hotter, and louder. His mouth was so dry, his tongue felt fat and swollen against his lips.

I can save them.

He walked on, closer, closer, and only when he was in the middle of the ring of grass did he stop. He knelt then and dropped the brace piece—he didn't need it, just the spark—and he tore handfuls of dry grass out and set them in a loose pile at his feet. He held the fire steel and prepared to strike it, knowing that he could do it, that he could get that shower of sparks.

He dropped the tool on the first strike. His hands were shaking too badly.

You're going to kill them.

He grabbed it again, and that was when he heard the scream. It was loud, but it didn't last long. It came from the woman who'd been thrown off the horse.

The fire had found her.

That's what's going to happen. That's what it will feel like, Jace, that's how you're going to die.

Stop being Jace. Be what Hannah still called him. Connor Reynolds could start this fire; he had before.

He gripped the fire steel in his left hand and the striker in his right and this time he didn't drop it when he made contact. Sparks fell in a shower into the grass.

Died immediately.

He was starting to panic, but then he remembered the first day, Ethan telling him to slow down, slow down, and he tried again, and then again, and on the fourth time, some of the grass caught.

He lowered his face to the ground and blew on it and it smoked white and then he blew some more and watched it glow red and then he added more grass, trying to move slow, trying not to smother it.

The fire was already spreading, though. Already pulling away from him, the sun-scorched grass going up fast, spreading out in an expanding ring. He stood and looked up into the rocks and saw Hannah Faber lifting a hand, one thumb up. He ran then, out of his own fire and back up the rocks to her.

"Told you I could," he said when he reached her. He was out of breath, gasping.

"Never doubted you, buddy. But you just saved some lives. Now you two go down there and put the shelter up right where you started that."

"It won't make it up here," he said. "There's nothing to burn now. It's just like you said."

"Right," she told him. "But it's protocol, Connor. We go ahead and deploy, just in case."

"Then why are we moving the—"

"Because it's the right choice," she said. "I'm fine. Look at this! There's nothing for it to burn. It's just rock. I can sit here all day. It might get a little warm, but I'll be fine."

"Okay. Then we can all stay."

Hannah said, "Connor? I need you to help her. I *need* you to."

He looked at Allison, then Hannah, then back at his fire. It had caught the full force of the wind and found its slope and gathered speed, then sprinted to meet the rocks and foundered there. Behind it, the main blaze was very close.

"Finish the job," Hannah said. "You can't quit halfway through. Now help her get the shelter up."

He didn't say anything. Couldn't come up with words, let alone get them out. He knew she was lying to him. At least about some of it.

"Get back in," she said. "Connor, get back in, and this time, you *stay there*. I'm fine. Know that I'm fine, I'm not going anywhere. And thank you. You saved people. You don't understand it yet, but I promise you that you did."

"Then we don't need to go down to—"

"You're why I'm here, do you get that?" she said. "I'm here to make sure you get in that shelter and *stay* in it. Both of you. Now listen to me. You do *not* leave that shelter until you hear the sound of my voice. You've got to promise me that. It will seem like the fire's gone, like everything is done, but you won't know that for sure, not inside there. You won't know what to trust. So you wait on the crew boss to release you, all right? And right now, buddy, I'm the crew boss. You wait on my voice."

44

THEY HAD THE SHELTER up in the ashes before the fire broke the timberline. Hannah watched it come on and she knew that it was up to the wind now.

She'd spoken with Nick only once about the possibility of dying in a fire. It had been the day he confessed that he would never deploy a fire shelter, that he didn't like the idea. She'd argued with him then, told him how stupid it was, told him that attempting to run away from a forest fire was like running from the very hand of God—you knew you had no chance, so why would you try? All he would become, she had said, was another cross on a mountain. And his answer, with the sly smile that defused the debate before it could become a fight, was that he just wanted to make sure his was the highest cross.

I want to be winning the race at some point, at least, he'd said. *Bury me high.* Because he'd stayed to get her in the shelter, though, his had been the lowest cross at Shepherd Mountain in the end.

She couldn't have run now if she'd wanted to, but she didn't want to. She needed to watch. She owed them that.

God, it was gorgeous. A thirty-foot-high wall of orange and red dancers. She wondered vaguely if any of them at Shepherd Mountain had appreciated its beauty at the end. Thought that Nick would have, maybe. That seemed possible.

She knew it would pick up pace once it broke the tree line, but she had forgotten just how fast it could go. The astonishing thing was the way it raced uphill. Gravity owned much of the world, but it did not own fire. The flames broke the timberline in a rush and found what should have been a field of grass.

All that remained was ash.

It seemed to anger the fire.

A quarter of the way up the slope, the fire doubled its speed, advancing as if zipping along a fuse cord, rushing toward its detonation point. It reached the fire shelter at that speed and then she couldn't see the shelter any longer. She could feel the wind, though, and the wind was good, it was gusting, it was what they needed, a fast-and-holding wind. There was nothing back there for the fire to eat, and so it wouldn't stay. The smoke was thick but she could see the silver shimmer of the shelter, and she knew that the boy was alive inside.

"He's going to make it," she said. "He's going to make it home."

No one argued. The ghosts circled behind her in silent, respectful fashion and watched the flames move on, faster than would have been possible if the grass had remained, racing past the fire shelter, riding that beautiful wind up the mountain and on to meet her.

Nick came and sat beside her, close enough so that they were just barely touching, that graze of contact that gave her butterflies the first time and never stopped. She leaned against him and felt his warmth, and neither of them said a word. They didn't need to. They could watch in peace now.

The job was done and the boy was safe.

45

H E INSISTED THAT HE'D heard her voice. His story never changed. At first nobody had seen the point in trying to change his mind—what did it matter? Later, Allison wondered if it was possible. If she could actually have called to him in the end.

All that Allison had heard was the fire. It had thundered over them and sounded and felt like nothing else she'd experienced in her life. It was like lying on the tracks as a long freight train scorched above you and somehow none of the wheels ever made contact.

Jace had tried to get out of the shelter and she had fought him. It wasn't easy to hold so tight; it hurt terribly, but she had told Hannah that she would hold him tight and so she did and eventually he stopped fighting and held her too as the fire thundered on and on and the shelter began to feel like a burning coffin.

The sound faded but did not go away, and Allison was sobbing and terrified that they were running out of air; there didn't seem to be enough oxygen.

"Air," she said. "Air. We've got to get this thing open."

He fought her again then, but it was different, he was holding her in, not the other way around. Allison wanted to claw her way out, even if the flames still waited, anything for a breath.

"Not until we hear her voice," he kept shouting, "not until we hear her voice."

She wanted to scream back that they were never going to hear her voice, because Hannah was dead and they would be too if he didn't let her open the shelter. He kept fighting her, and then, just when she was certain she could bear no more, he said, "That's her. That's Hannah. Go on and open it."

Allison had heard nothing but the fire and the wind, but she wasn't going to argue the point, she *had* to escape that shelter, and so she fumbled it apart gratefully and they fell out into a world of smoke.

The fire was gone. The charred landscape showed where it had run on past them, and orange flames burned in the drainages on either side of them, but there on the hillside, all that was left was smoldering embers.

They were alive.

It was there that firefighters found them an hour later, after they'd been spotted by a helicopter. Two of the three survivors on the mountain, they told her.

"Three?"

"Two of you and a man on top. He signaled the helicopter, otherwise we might have been a long time finding you in all this smoke."

"Ethan," she said.

"I don't know his name."

But she did.

"You're lucky," he said. "You're damn lucky. Three survivors, but we've got four bodies too."

"No," Jace said. "No, there are four survivors. If Ethan is
up high, then there are four of us."

The firefighter didn't want to answer that, and Jace began to shout at him then, saying there were four, he knew
that there were four because he'd heard her, because she'd
called to him to tell him that it was safe, and then Allison
held him again, and she did not let go until they were off
the mountain.

The bodies told the stories that witnesses never could have,
even though they had come to the mountains to eliminate
witnesses. In the hospital, in a haze of pain and blood loss
and medication, Ethan told anyone who would listen that
the brothers were not American, and he knew this because
one of them read the winds wrong. Nobody paid much attention. Ethan was saying a lot of things at that point.

Their DNA connected the brothers to names long unknown and long discarded even by them. Thomas and
Michael Burgess.

They were Australian. They knew different skies, it was
true, though it had been a long time since they'd operated
beneath the ones under which they were born.

Thomas was Jack, the elder brother, a figure in the Syd-
ney crime world until he traveled to America at the turn
of the twenty-first century to kill a man and liked the place
enough to stay once the man was dead. His brother, who
had washed out of the Australian army for dishonorable
conduct, joined him, first in Boston, then New York, then
Chicago. They wore many names during those years but
settled on Blackwell for reasons unknown. Jack and Pat-

rick were names they'd given each other in childhood while passing through various foster homes after their father was murdered. He was shot through the windshield of his car with a semiautomatic rifle when Jack was nine and Patrick six. They'd watched it happen from the steps of their front porch.

Their sister had joined them in the country ten years earlier. She'd tried—unsuccessfully—to become a U.S. marshal, a position they saw great value in her having, given their line of work. They'd had a contact in the U.S. Marshals, a man named Temple, but now he was gone and they needed a replacement for him. It didn't work out, but she moved into the world of executive protection as a private consultant, a job that took her to some interesting places and once to Montana to be taught survival by Ethan Serbin while she silently protected a witness who later disappeared, a rumored high-dollar hit.

In Chicago, the brothers had met a police sergeant named Ian O'Neil, who also needed some witnesses to disappear. Ian O'Neil was currently on the board as an unsolved homicide victim himself.

The Burgess brothers died on the slopes below Republic Peak as the Blackwell brothers, Jack and Patrick, and the task of connecting their DNA with the crime scenes of unsolved homicides began slowly and then bore steady fruit, starting that summer and going on into the autumn and the winter and the year beyond.

The Ritz was not finished yet, though it could have been. Ethan and Allison lived in the bunkhouse while they completed the main house. Originally, Ethan feared that it would be home to nothing but horrifying memories, and he wondered if they should go somewhere else entirely. Allison talked him out of that.

Their bodies had healed by summer's end, and in the fall, as the tourists left and the first snows teased the slopes and padlocks were placed on the doors of the fire towers, they worked together, measuring and cutting boards and driving framing nails. There were new aches and new weaknesses for both of them, and the work was harder now than it had been but, on some days, maybe a little sweeter too. They got as far as they could before winter shut them down, and then in spring they resumed, and by then they understood better what they hadn't been able to give voice to at first. The house had to be rebuilt, and they had to do it, because to do so was to heal, and it was either that or run. The two of them were rebuilding everything. Doctor visits were constant—burn specialists and plastic surgeons for Allison; physical therapists for Ethan—and even in their words, their touches, it was not a matter of reclaiming but rebuilding. Things were broken now, but not irreparable. And so they went about repairing, and the house became a part of it, and then it became the central part of it as the doctor visits fell away and the words between them came easier and with less weight and the touches were familiar and not desperate again.

It was, Ethan realized, what he'd never understood about survival in all these years of studying it and teaching it.

Survival didn't end when you were found. The arrival of the search-and-rescue teams wasn't a conclusion. Rescue, rejoice, rebuild.

He'd never known the last step.

It was summer again and the sun was hot and Ethan was shirtless as he worked laying shingles on the roof, Allison sanding drywall tape along the ceiling below him, on the day when Jace Wilson arrived with his parents.

The boy was taller, in that startling way that children between certain years could achieve. Voice huskier. He looked good, but he looked guarded, and Ethan knew why. It was the rebuilding season for him too.

His father was named Chuck. His mother, Abby, worked for a bank in Chicago, where last year she'd been approached by a professional bodyguard, a woman with kind blue eyes who'd said she'd heard about Abby's son's situation from her police contacts and thought she could help with the problem. Jace's parents had divorced when he was young, but this summer day, they all made the trip together, and whatever tensions there might have been were well below the surface, where they belonged. They all had a good afternoon and a good quiet evening and after the sun went down behind the mountain, and Jace went to sleep in the bunkhouse, the adults had glasses of red wine on the porch of the unfinished house and there Allison asked Jace's parents if they wanted to know what had come of the identification of the corpses of those who had pursued their son so relentlessly. And so they listened and learned of the exploits of the Burgess brothers and their sister. As far as Ethan could tell, the only questions that had been answered were which men had been paid how many dollars to kill which other men. But it mattered to Jace's parents, it was part of their rebuilding season, and so Ethan listened as Allison told what she could of the story, even though Ethan knew, and was certain that she knew, that they had all parted ways with the story on Republic Peak on a hot June day when the western wind breathed fire across the mountains.

The next morning they rode back to the place where Jace and Allison had survived the fire. They borrowed extra horses from a friend, but Allison rode Tango. The burned riding the burned. She told Ethan that she was curious to see if the horse would remember the spot. Ethan didn't ask her how she would know, but he believed that she would.

They rode out just after sunrise to the ravaged slopes below Republic Peak, and all around them was the grim gray of the burnout. Ethan was worried about the visual effect, was trying to come up with a way to balance the sorrow, when Jace said, "Her grass is already coming back."

He was right. In the land of burned timber, there was a circle of green, an acre of grass. It had fallen victim to the flames faster than the trees, but it had come back faster too. Jace looked at it for a long time, and then his mother asked, gently, if this was where he wanted to put the cross. It was the first time anyone had mentioned it, though he had been carrying it with him the whole ride.

"Nobody died here," he said. "She was higher than that."

And so they went higher, up past the withered and blackened remains of trees, over a ridge of rock, and onto a short plateau. They dismounted there and Ethan knew that the boy had studied the maps that had been released during the inquiry into the fire, because he knew exactly where she had fallen. Ethan was sure of it too because he'd made a trip here himself in the fall, a long slow walk, and then he had sat alone among the black rocks and spoke aloud when he thanked Hannah Faber for his wife.

That was just before the first snow.

Now Jace Wilson cleared a spot in the earth and took a hammer and began to pound the cross into the ground. It was rough soil and he had some trouble, but when his father and Ethan offered to help, he said that he would do it himself. In time he did, but then he decided it wasn't straight enough, and they waited in silence until he got it aligned in a way that pleased him. He ran his hands along the surface of the wood and then turned back and looked down the slope and said, "She made a good run at it. She made a really good run."

They all acknowledged that yes, she surely had.

For a long time he sat there and looked at the burned mountain below and did not speak. Finally he got to his feet and got back onto the horse.

"It's a good place for her cross," he said. "You can see the grass from this spot. You can see where we were. I know that she did. She was high enough to see us." He looked at Allison then and said, "Did you really not hear her voice?"

Allison never took her eyes off him as she said, "Did you really hear it?"

Jace nodded.

"That's all that matters," Allison said.

They rode down from the cross then, and over that circle of healthy green grass, and even beneath the blackness, you could see the rebirth beginning, if you looked hard enough. The land would hold the scars for a long time, but it was already working on healing them and it would patiently continue to do so.

That was the way of it.

ACKNOWLEDGMENTS

This book wouldn't have been written if not for Michael and Rita Hefron, who introduced me to the mountains, first in stories and pictures when I was a child, and later in welcoming me to Montana and the wonderful communities of Cooke City and Silver Gate. Their friendship and support have helped me in many ways over many years, and I'm forever grateful. To the group who made the first Bounce over the Beartooths—Mike Hefron, Ryan Easton, and Bob Bley—I'd like to offer a special thanks.

For all things related to wilderness survival, I send my deepest gratitude to Reggie Bennett and his wife, Dina Bennett, who endured and indulged far too many dumb questions. If it makes you feel any better, Reggie, I can still start a fire in the rain! Many thanks.

It was an enormous privilege to work with two incredible editors on this book, Michael Pietsch and Joshua Kendall. Thanks to you both for marvelous work.

A nowhere-near-exhaustive list of the people who actually made the book happen once I did the easy part: Reagan

ACKNOWLEDGMENTS

Arthur, Heather Fain, Marlena Bittner, Sabrina Callahan, Miriam Parker, Wes Miller, Nicole Dewey, Tracy Williams, Nancy Wiese, Tracy Roe, Pamela Marshall, and all the others at Little, Brown and Company are the best in the business, and it is a pleasure to work with them.

Richard Pine, David Hale Smith, and the rest of the InkWell Management team deserve their standard accolades, as does Angela Cheng Caplan.

Finally, the lion's share of the gratitude belongs to my wife, Christine. She tolerated various off-the-grid research trips, participated in others (in retrospect, maybe we shouldn't have done both the waist-deep wading and the mountaintop lightning on her first day out), and read more pages than any editor.

This book was inspired and informed by countless nonfiction works, and a list of the best of them is available on my website, michaelkoryta.com.

ABOUT THE AUTHOR

Michael Koryta is the *New York Times*–bestselling author of nine previous novels. His books have won or been nominated for many awards, including the *Los Angeles Times* Book Prize, the Edgar Award, the Shamus Award, the Barry Award, the Quill Award, the International Thriller Writers Award, the Great Lakes Book Award, and the Golden Dagger. His work has been translated into more than twenty languages. A former private investigator and newspaper reporter, Koryta lives in Bloomington, Indiana, and St. Petersburg, Florida. For more about Michael visit michaelkoryta.com.